0015.

A Permanent Home

Greta Marlow

To Deb —
I hope you enjoy the
new adventure!
Greta Marlow

EMZ-Piney Publishing
Hagarville, AR

A Permanent Home
Copyright 2014 by Greta Marlow

This is a work of fiction. Names, characters, places, and incidents
are either the product of the author's imagination or,
if real, are used fictionally.

Published in the United States by EMZ-Piney Publishing
Hagarville, AR 72839 USA

ISBN: 978-0-9899597-2-8

To my parents,
Noel and Charlotte Rowbotham
All those days shut up in my bedroom writing
finally led to something

May the words of my mouth and the meditations of my heart
be pleasing in your sight,
O Lord, my Rock and my Redeemer.
Psalm 19:14

Also by Greta Marlow

His Promise True

WHEREAS, it being the anxious desire of the Government of the United States to secure to the Cherokee nation of Indians, as well those now living within the limits of the Territory of Arkansas, as those of their friends and brothers who reside in States East of the Mississippi, and who may wish to join their brothers of the West, a permanent home, and which shall, under the most solemn guarantee of the United States, be, and remain, theirs forever—

TREATY WITH THE WESTERN CHEROKEE,
May 6, 1828

Chapter 1

Pa had tried all my life to make a praying man of me, but it never took hold until the morning I woke up flat broke and homeless on a pallet of ragged quilts at the Dwight Presbyterian Mission to the Cherokee in Arkansas Territory. Even then, I don't think Pa would have approved of my prayer. There was no kneeling or bowed head, and my eyes were open and resting on Maggie. There weren't even any words, just overwhelming gratefulness that ran through my whole body, filling me with peace after months of struggling.

Pale streaks of light squeezed through cracks in the wall of the log cabin where we'd bedded down last night. They fell across Maggie's face as she still slept, and the prayer inside me swelled with knowing we were together for good now and I'd never sleep without her again.

I touched her soft hair, not yet grown back over her ears, and then I ran my finger along the curve of her face. Her cheeks were sun-browned from standing out on the deck of the keelboat all those slow miles up the Arkansas River. We'd managed to pass her off as just another boy in the crew, though I couldn't see how. Even with her hair cut like a man's and dressed in britches, she'd still looked mighty pretty, I thought, and womanly. How had the other keelers missed seeing it every night as she served us supper?

Even in sleep, her arm tightened around me in response to the touch, and she tucked her head closer against my chest. For a few drowsy moments, I let the rise and fall of her breathing tempt me back toward sleep. But the sunlight was growing brighter, and the day was wasting, the first day I had to find us a home in Arkansas Territory.

"Maggie," I said, lifting her arm away from my side. "Wake up."

She opened her eyes the littlest bit and shook her head. "Not yet."

"Yes, wake up." I sat up and reached for my britches. "I want to talk to Reverend Washburn first thing about where we can find land around here."

She sat up and wrapped her arms around me, laying her chin over my shoulder. "Can't it wait? We ain't had any time alone together to speak of since we left Arkansas Post." Her skin was warm and soft against mine, and for just a minute, I wavered. But first things first.

"Patience, woman!" I paused in buttoning my britches to put a kiss on her forehead. "Let me find a place around here where we can settle down for good, and then, I promise, you can have all the time together alone with me you want."

⋇ ⋇ ⋇

Talking to the Reverends Cephas Washburn and Albert Finney put my feet back flat on the ground. They had been in the Territory for nearly four years with the mission, so they knew all the rules of the country.

"There's no land for white settlement here," Reverend Washburn told me. "By treaty, the land north of the river belongs to the Cherokees, and everything south of the river belongs to the Choctaws."

"I saw whites in the settlements along the river heading to Fort Smith," I said.

"They were probably conducting business with the Indians," Reverend Finney said. "They have contracts with the government that allow them here to trade. They aren't permanent settlers."

"So there's nothing?"

Reverend Washburn shook his head. "Nothing. It's against the law for whites to be on this land."

"If whites try to squat on Indian land, the soldiers have orders from the government under the Intrusion Act of 1807 to evict them," Reverend Finney said. "There's also a fine to be paid, a hundred dollars, I believe."

I stared into my cup of tea. I knew about the Intrusion Act from the short time I'd spent as a student in my uncle's law practice back in Nashville. Eviction was the least of the penalties.

Maggie was quiet beside me, but her shoulders seemed to sag a little. I tried again.

"Where can white folks go in Arkansas Territory, then?"

"The eastern part of the territory is open for settlement," Reverend Washburn said. "There's land to be bought around Arkansas Post and to the northeast, along the Southwest Trail across the Mississippi River from the Chickasaw Bluffs."

I thought of the swamps of brackish, ankle-deep water we had trudged through on our way to Arkansas Post. Why would anyone pay good money for that land? Corn wouldn't grow in such muck.

Reverend Finney glanced at Reverend Washburn. "There are rumors of a new treaty with the Choctaws," he said. "That would open land south of the river for settlement."

"That's only a rumor," Reverend Washburn said. "Even if there is a new treaty, it would be some time before the land was surveyed and made ready for sale. It won't be available for settlement for at least another year or two, even if the rumors are true."

"So we can't stay in this part of the country," I said, and they both nodded.

"Your best choice is to go to Dardanelle and wait for a boat to take you back to the eastern part of the Territory," Reverend Washburn said. "You can buy land there."

Maggie followed me back to the cabin where our goods were stored. For a while we didn't speak. I rested my hand on the bag of seed corn. I'd brought that corn all the way from Tennessee, taking care to keep it dry and never dipping into it, even when we could have used something to eat. It was good seed, from Pa's last harvest. I'd never known seed from Pa's fields to fail, but April was nearly over and soon it would be too late to plant corn, even Pa's good corn. I didn't have time to wait in Dardanelle for a boat to take me back east, where I'd have to wait to find land and then wait more while I cleared it before I could plant anything.

"I guess we should have gone back east with Captain Russell on the keelboat, after all," Maggie said.

The words hit me like a fist.

"No," I said, trying to keep my voice low and calm. "We're staying where we are."

She whirled around to face me. "You heard what the reverends said! There's no place for white folk in this part of the Territory."

3

"And you know we don't have money to buy land in the eastern part."

"Whose fault is that?" she started, but then she clamped her mouth tight. I knew what she had been about to say, though. My keelboat wages were gone, squandered on a drinking binge in Fort Smith, when I'd been sure everything—even Maggie—was lost to me.

"It's not just the money," I told her. "We've got to get the corn in the ground. If we have to wait around in Dardanelle for a boat to go east, we'll have no crop this year."

"If we don't go east, we'll not have a crop this year for sure," she said. "At least there we could maybe put in a late crop. But there's no place at all around here to plant corn."

"There's plenty of places around here to plant corn."

Her eyes narrowed as she looked at me.

"What are you saying? You want us to squat on Indian land?" She grabbed my arm. "John David! It's against the law! They'll send soldiers after us! You'll get a fine, and we ain't got money to pay it."

"That's only if they find us. And I'll make sure they don't find us." I put my hand over hers. "We've got to raise a crop this summer. If we don't, we won't have anything for next season. We'll never get ahead."

"We won't get ahead squatting."

"We have to start somewhere."

She looked up at me for a while without speaking, her hand still resting on my arm. A little worry wrinkle folded between her eyebrows, and I tried to smooth it away with my fingertip.

"We have to do it, Maggie. Say we don't plant corn this year and I find some kind of work instead. It would probably take most of the money I could make just to pay for a place to live. We couldn't put aside enough to buy land outright, and the government won't sell land on credit. If we squat, the place to live is free, and everything from the crop can go toward a section of land."

"We don't have to squat," she insisted. "You can ask your folks for money."

Every muscle in my body went stiff. "No."

"It's time to ask, John David. Before we left home, Zeke said your pa would help if you asked. Remember?"

What I remembered was Ma saying I'd be like the prodigal son, coming home to throw himself on the mercy of his family after squandering the money he had.

"No," I repeated. "I don't want—"

"I don't care what you want or don't want!" she snapped. "This ain't the time to be proud. We're desperate for help, and Zeke said your folks will help."

"I'm not so sure of that." She turned her back on me with an aggravated huff of breath, so I tried a different path. "Even if Pa agreed, I'd lose months going back home to get the money. Months, Maggie, months I could use to raise corn and get money on my own. You'd have to stay here in Arkansas Territory by yourself while I was gone to get it."

I knew that last would convince her. She turned back and looked at me a minute, her fists on her hips.

"All right," she said. "Maybe there's a middle ground. One crop in new ground probably won't bring in enough to buy a parcel of land. It won't, and you know it!" Her voice rose to cut off my protest. "But knowing your pa, he'd probably be more likely to give you the money we need if you were coming up with part of it on your own."

I gave a sour little laugh. "That's true."

She looked at me a minute longer, and then she sighed. "I reckon we'll be squatting. But promise me something—it's only for this one season. You'll raise your crop this summer, then you'll go back home to get the money we need to buy land and be legal."

"Pa won't go for it," I said.

"At least write to them and ask for some help to buy a place." She took both my hands in hers. "I want us to get started right, John David, honest and legal. If you say we have to squat for now to raise a crop, then that's what we'll do, but I don't want that to be what our life becomes. Promise me you won't do like my pa, always tricking folks and taking advantage."

Tears were rising in the corners of her eyes, and I didn't want to make her cry.

"I'll write to my folks," I promised.

※ ※ ※

She looked through our packs until she found some paper, and then I went to Reverend Finney and asked for the use of an inkpot and quill. Maggie sat across from me at a table in the dining hall while I slowly dipped the quill in the ink and pondered my first words. I'd not had any contact with my family since we'd left Campbell County. That was only six months ago, but it seemed like it had been a different lifetime. I'd been a man of age when we left Tennessee, but if the truth was told, I'd been more of a boy back then, the youngest son indulged and babied by them all, though they'd chided me time and again for my feckless ways. How could I convince them I was different now? Especially since I had to confess to them I'd failed in my plans to get to Texas, just as they had hinted I would. Maggie said it wasn't the time to be proud, but I was proud—too proud to go crawling back with my tail between my legs, defeated and cringing as I admitted they'd been right about me all along.

"Just get started," Maggie said. "Maybe the words will come easier then."

I glanced at her. She couldn't read; she wouldn't be able to tell what I was writing. I made my choice; this letter would go to Zeke, not Pa.

April 23, 1824

Dear Zeke,

I'm writing to set your mind at ease concerning us. For the moment, Maggie and I are at the Dwight Presbyterian Mission to the Cherokees in the heart of Arkansas Territory. We no longer plan to go to Texas. Instead, we will settle here in the Arkansas Territory. The land is fine. It is much like home, mostly covered in timber with plenty of clear, fast-flowing streams. The bottom lands along the creeks should make good cornfields. The weather, too, seems like home. We've been in the Territory a little more than a month and have seen only pleasant spring days, with passing showers of rain.

Time doesn't allow me to tell you all that has happened since we left you. We spent part of the winter with Uncle Abner in Nashville. I worked in his law office for a time, though I should tell you we parted on unfriendly terms. Maggie and I found passage in February with a group of folks headed to Texas, but the party disbanded in the town called Arkansas Post after the unfortunate death of one of our men. I found employment then on a keelboat headed to the midst of the Territory. Maggie fell ill on the trip, but it was good fortune we were near this mission where she could be cared for. Don't worry, she had no disease, she miscarried a child. Though both our hearts are still tender from that loss, she seems to have recovered her strength and is as eager as I am to leave the mission and find a place to settle.

I will leave this letter with the Reverend Washburn to be taken down the river with the next boat. I don't know when I will have opportunity to write again, so I will close by saying our hopes are high and we believe ourselves to be in God's hands. I hope this letter finds you and Sarah and the girls in good health. Please tell Pa of our circumstances, as I believe he might be interested in knowing them.

Most respectfully yours,
John David McKellar

"There," Maggie said as I folded the letter, "I know you don't want to depend on your pa, but it will be for the best."

"I suppose."

She'll never know, I told myself, so it's not really a lie. Once I've raised a good crop and we're settled on our own land, she'll forget she ever wanted to ask Pa for help.

Chapter 2

The rest of the day, no matter what my body was doing, my mind was working out how we could manage to squat on Indian land without being caught.

"I reckon it would be best to find a place south of the river," I told Maggie once we were settled back on the pallet in the timber house that night. "If those rumors about a treaty coming are true, we might not be squatting long before we'd get the chance to buy the land."

"How will we cross the river?" she asked.

"We'll have to get someone to ferry us across." I sat up and reached for our bag of coins, weighed it in my hand. "We should have enough to pay for a ferry and buy some food to get us by until the crop comes in. But food's likely to be dear in this part of the territory."

"Probably so." She took the money bag and tucked it under the pillow. "How will we get our household goods to the river? Ask Reverend Washburn for the use of a mule?"

I laughed. "No. The less the reverends know about our plans, the better. If we ask for their help, they'll get us settled in some place in Dardanelle to wait for the next boat down river. I don't want them to catch on that we're not going back east. I'd rather pack every piece of our goods on my own back than have one of them along."

"You can't do that," she scoffed. "The bag of seed corn alone would make more of a load than you could carry any distance." She moved over to the packs leaning against the wall. "I guess we'll have to leave some of it behind. Let's go through these bundles and pick out the things we can't do without."

I watched as she sorted the first one. There was little enough to start a household with—a few dishes, a few clothes, my rifle and lead. Sometimes she made up her mind quickly about whatever she pulled out. Sometimes, though, she would pause and look over at me, showing me some item.

"What about these books?" she asked once. "We don't strictly need them, and they would be awful heavy to carry. But still—it's nice to have some books in a house, and you probably can't get one out here."

I didn't answer, and she looked back at the book in her hands, pondering. I smiled, a little smile she wasn't meant to see. Watching her—it felt almost as good as holding her in my arms. How many times in those weeks coming up the river had I watched her just this way, having to be satisfied with only the sight of the way the back of her neck curved gently and disappeared inside her collar? But no more.

"Don't worry about it tonight," I said, reaching out to tug the hem of her shimmy. "I'll come back for them sometime. Come on to bed and let's get some sleep."

She swatted at my hand in exasperation. "Sleep ain't what you're wanting."

"Not just yet," I admitted, grabbing her hand. "But you can't fault me, Maggie. How's a man supposed to keep his mind on business when he's got a wife as beautiful as you this close?" Her face softened a little, and I scooted myself closer. "I can't think about anything but you, not even about getting land."

"You devil!" Her laugh was soft. "You can always talk me into anything you want, you know that?"

"I mean it, though."

She smiled, the little half-smile she gave to only me. She put the book on the pile of things to stay behind, and then she moved down to the pallet beside me, laying a soft kiss against my mouth.

"I know," she whispered.

❧ ❧ ❧

I tried out several ideas the next day before I managed to rig a sling that made it possible for me to carry the bag of seed corn on my back. Maggie finished sorting our goods and tied together bundles we could carry in our hands. Our bedding and spare clothes were in a roll on her back, and though she insisted she could carry more, I wouldn't allow it.

The sun was nothing but an orange glow above the horizon as we shouldered our packs after a quick breakfast on what was going to be another fine April day. The reverends and Mrs. Washburn came to see us off.

"We will give you loan of a mule," Reverend Finney said. "We trust you would bring it back."

I shook my head as I helped Maggie straighten the straps holding the bedding on her back. "I don't know how long it might be, though, before I could return it, and you might have need of it before I could. If you'll just store our other goods until I'm able to come for them, I'll be back as soon as I can find a place in Dardanelle. That should be only a few days, I hope."

Reverend Finney assured me our goods would be unmolested. Reverend Washburn kept quiet, with his mouth set in a straight line and his brows low over his eyes that seemed to be digging into my very soul. Lying to him was as bad as lying to Pa had ever been, and I turned away from him to look down the creek. The woods were quiet, but they beckoned to me with promise, and I was eager to walk into them and find it. I looked down at Maggie.

"Is everything set right for you?" I asked. She nodded.

"Then let's go. It was nice to have met you, Reverends, Mrs. Washburn." I shook their hands solemnly. "I can't thank you enough for caring for Maggie. It was lucky for us you were here during her time of need."

"It was God's will," Reverend Washburn said. "May He guide you on your travels back east."

"Amen," I answered, but I stepped away quickly, away from those sharp eyes, toward the welcoming arms of the woods.

❧ ❧ ❧

We walked without speaking until the trees had hidden the clearing and fields of the mission. I glanced at Maggie.

"Are you making it?" I asked. "Will you be able to carry that load?"

"I'm fine. How about you? That sack of corn is bound to be heavy."

"It is. But I don't mind. I just think about dropping these kernels into my own piece of ground, and that makes the load seem easy."

"You may not think so when you've carried it a few days."

I laughed off her prediction, but truth be told, by the time we came up on the burned-out ruins of Walter Webber's store only an hour later, I felt like I was carrying the whole of Pa's corn crop. I paused beside a big dead log and shifted the straps of the sling to a different spot on my shoulders. A small group of dark-haired men were clearing away the rubble. Cherokees, no doubt. The fellows from the keelboat crew had said Walter Webber was a chief of some kind in the Cherokee nation, even though he was a half-blood.

"Look at this log," Maggie said. "It looks like someone was trying to burn it out. Reckon that's how the fire started?"

I looked down at the huge log. Sure enough, someone had burned and chipped a wide trench about half the distance of the trunk. Suddenly my load lightened again.

"It's a dugout canoe," I said. "That's just what we need. With a canoe, we can get across the river without paying for a ferry." I slipped the sling off my shoulder, then lifted Maggie's bundle from her back and laid my arm around her shoulders. "Let's see if Walter Webber would part with his canoe. Have a seat while I talk to him."

The Cherokee men looked up as I came toward them, but they kept working.

"Is one of you Walter Webber?" I asked. "I was hoping to do some business with Webber."

A stocky man stepped forward. "I'm Webber. But as you can see, I'm not open for business."

"Yes, sir," I said. "I'm sorry about your store. But I was hoping I could buy a horse from you. I need one for my wife, see. We were on a boat headed to Fort Smith when she took ill, and the captain put us off the boat. She's well enough to travel now, but I'm afraid if she has to walk and carry a pack, she'll have another bout of that sickness." I pulled the limp money bag from my pocket. "I can pay you as much as thirty American dollars."

All the men laughed. Walter Webber shook his head.

"I wouldn't sell you a half-lame jackass for thirty American dollars."

I turned to look back at Maggie. She was sitting with her head resting in her hands, just as I'd hoped she would.

11

"Look at her," I said. "She's barely over that sickness. She can't walk all the way to Fort Smith. How am I going to get her there?"

"I'm sorry for you," Webber said, "but I can't sell a horse for thirty dollars. I already lost thousands of dollars in this fire."

I let my shoulders droop and turned to walk away. One step—two—one more ought to be about right—

"What about that half-finished canoe?" I turned back to him. "Could I buy that from you?"

Webber glanced at the other men. "I don't know—there's a lot of work in that canoe."

"There's a lot of work left to do on it," I said. "Looks to me like you've got plenty of work ahead of you cleaning up and rebuilding your store." He was looking at me, his face unmoving, but I could see I'd made a point. "I'll pay you five dollars for the canoe."

"Five dollars?" He laughed and spit on the ground. "You were going to pay thirty for a horse."

"A horse is ready to go. That canoe's not."

He was quiet for a couple of minutes.

"I'll sell you the canoe for twenty dollars."

"Twenty?" I sputtered. "That's robbery!"

Walter Webber smiled, a nasty sort of smile. "It will get your sick wife to Fort Smith."

"Would you take fifteen?"

"Twenty."

He had me. I rubbed my hand over my hair, but I knew the bargaining was done.

"Twenty, then. But you'll throw in a couple of paddles. And your men will saw off the chunk that's not finished."

The men took turns working a crosscut saw to slice off the trunk a few inches past the end of the trench. I paid Walter Webber the twenty dollars, a sizeable portion of what money we had. It's worth it, though, I told myself. We'll have an easier trip, riding up the river instead of walking, and I can plant corn sooner, before it's too late for planting.

Maggie and I put our bundles in the canoe, but when I bent to lift it and drag it toward the creek, it barely moved. I pulled again, harder, but a tug in my groin told me to be careful. I straightened and turned back to the Cherokee men.

"Can you give me a hand getting this to the creek?"

"We're busy," Webber said as he walked away. "It's your canoe now."

The other men laughed as they went back to their work sifting through the charred mess. They didn't even look my way. Something small and cold fluttered in my stomach, and I had to swallow hard to press it down.

"Damn Indians," I muttered.

"Maybe it will help if we take out the packs," Maggie said.

We unloaded our goods, and then with Maggie pushing and me pulling, we got the canoe across the clearing and down the bank into the creek. It handled well enough in the water. I was satisfied to see how fast the trees on the bank were passing compared to when we'd been walking, and it seemed no time before we were edging into the wide spread of the Arkansas River. Maggie gripped the sides of the canoe, her back straight and rigid in front of me. She hated being on a boat, that was sure. I dipped the paddle deep into the water, trying to move us across the river as quickly as I could so she wouldn't have to suffer it long.

We hadn't gone far when she gasped aloud.

"It's all right," I called to her. "It won't be long now."

She glanced at me over her shoulder. "There's water in the boat!"

My blood seemed to go cold. "What?"

"Up here in front of my knees—my skirt's getting wet. I think there's a crack." She bent forward for a bit, then looked at me again, her eyes wide. "Sure enough."

Since she was listening, I didn't say the words that crowded onto my tongue, but inside I cussed Walter Webber straight to hell.

"How fast does it seem to be coming in?" I asked.

"It's made a little puddle."

I did cuss aloud then. "Move the corn back. Keep it dry, if you can."

I steered the bulky canoe back toward the bank and together we pulled it far enough onto dry land that I could look for the problem. It was easy enough to find, a place where the grain of the wood had split when the tree was cut. How had I missed that before I'd paid Walter Webber the better part of our money? I threw my hat on the ground and ran my hand over my head.

"What can we do?" Maggie asked in a small voice.

"I'll have to fix it somehow. We don't have enough money left to buy the supplies we'll need for the summer and to get someone to ferry us across the river." I turned to look into the woods. "I guess we'd better find a camping spot."

We chose a small clearing near the river so we wouldn't have to carry our packs too far. I left Maggie to set up the camp while I searched the woods for a pine tree with an ooze of resin. I brought back all the dried knobs I could find, then I set about making pitch over the small fire Maggie had built. By the time I'd worked as much pitch into the crack as it could hold, it was late afternoon, too late to start out again on the water.

We sat side by side on the river's edge that evening and watched the sky over the water grow dark.

"We'll have to stay on the north bank," I said. "I can't risk having the patch give out halfway across the river with you and all our goods in the canoe. You know what that means."

She sighed. "We'll have to squat on Cherokee land."

I nodded, and for a minute we sat in silence, looking across to the south bank, where a treaty might soon open land for settlement. It was no more than a quarter-mile away, yet it might as well have been separated from us by the great, fixed gulf in the parable of Lazarus.

Maggie suddenly patted my knee.

"Well, as Ma used to say, might as well hang for a horse as for a hen," she said. "Squatting's illegal, no matter which side of the river we're on. We'll just have to chance it until we can get money. You did give that letter to Reverend Washburn to mail?"

"I did." Before she could say any more about it, I changed the subject. "I'll take the canoe across tomorrow and get what supplies we need."

"What if the patch gives out with you halfway across the river?"

"Don't worry—that patch will hold to get me across and back," I told her. "It won't sit as deep in the water with only me in the canoe. I'll take some more pitch, too, and plaster it over again before I start back. And if it does fail—" I laughed. "You can't swim, but I can."

"All right." Her voice was quiet.

"Don't worry." I wrapped my arm around her. "I'll make it fine.

I'll get the supplies, then we'll go far enough into these woods no one will find us. We'll finally settle down somewhere."

Her only answer was to lay her head against my shoulder. I pressed my lips against her hair. We sat in silence for a while, but then she turned her face up to me.

"I reckon it's like you said, that day you came back, remember?" she said. "We don't have to know how everything's going to work out. We just have to believe the Lord's going to make it all right. Our hard times will be our good times."

"I reckon."

She sighed and settled back against me. The sky was nearly black now, and everything around us was quiet in the growing night. But inside, I was anything but quiet.

I know what I said, Lord, I thought. But I'd sure be obliged if you'd give us a string of good times and not so many hard times on the road ahead.

⁂ ⁂ ⁂

I crossed the river the next morning to get to Dardanelle, where I stocked up on corn meal, salt, and salted pork. The next day, I went back to the mission for the rest of our goods, cutting through the woods to avoid the clearing where Walter Webber and the others were working on the burned-out store. The day after that, we dragged the dugout canoe into the shallow water at the river's edge, and Maggie handed our bundles to me as I knelt in the canoe and placed packs so no space was wasted.

"We'll stay close to the bank," I told her. "Now that the canoe's loaded, it sits deeper in the water. I'm not sure I really trust pine pitch to keep the water out."

"It didn't fail when you crossed to Dardanelle. If you put on a new coat every night at camp, it ought to hold."

"That's what I'm hoping. Is that everything?" She nodded, and I held out my hand to help her make the long step from the bank to the canoe.

"This is sure easier in britches than it would have been in a dress," she said. "But I still don't see why it matters whether I'm dressed like a woman."

"No one's going to look twice at two men going upriver in a canoe," I explained, again. "But you put a woman in that canoe, everybody's going to notice and wonder what she's doing here. Having a woman along is a sure sign a feller's looking to stay." I set my hat over her short curls. "We don't want anybody looking at us too close, Brother Matt."

❧ ❧ ❧

I'd been over this stretch of the river before, working on the keelboat, so I knew the place we were most likely to see people was a few days upstream, near the old government trading post at Spadra Bluff. I thought I remembered a good-sized creek that flowed into the river from the north before we would get to Spadra, though, and sure enough, within a couple of days, we found it. As we worked our way north, we did see some Indian settlements along the edges of the creek. If I hadn't known this was Indian land, I would have thought the settlements were filled with white folk, for the clusters of small log houses looked just like any I would've seen along a creek bank back home. We kept paddling until the houses thinned out and finally disappeared altogether. The creek became too shallow then for floating the canoe, so I tied a rope to the prow and we dragged the canoe along until we would hit another deep spot we could ride across.

After more than a week of moving up the creek, the deep spots were farther and farther apart, and we were having to drag the canoe most of the day. One afternoon, we were crossing another of the deep pools, and I saw ahead of us another run of shallow water broken up by rocks. That meant more cordelling. The afternoon was hot, and I was tired.

"Let's take a rest," I called to Maggie.

We pulled the canoe into the ankle-deep water along the gravel-covered bank, then walked up a little rise into the shade of the woods. I dropped down onto the ground and lay flat on my back. Maggie sat by me.

"Reckon it's always this hot here at the beginning of May?" she asked.

I opened my eyes and looked at her. Her face was flushed pink with the heat, but her lips were pale, and greenish-gray shadowed the skin beneath her eyes. She didn't look right, I thought, and with a jolt

I remembered it had been only a few weeks since she'd lost a baby. Something in my gut suddenly felt cold despite the heat of the sun. Had I been pushing her too hard these last few days? The canoe was too heavy for me to manage alone, so she had been pulling it with me, across every shallow spot in the creek and onto the bank every time we stopped. She'd not said a word of complaint, it was true, and I knew she wouldn't. But what if she wasn't healed yet? What if I was using up all the strength she had? I'd seen women like that, like Nick McCutchen's wife, who was so sickly she could barely creep around their cabin to cook for him. I couldn't let that happen to my wife.

"Let's stop for the day and set up camp here," I said. Maggie stopped fanning herself with my hat to stare at me.

"It's still hours till sundown. We ought to push on for a while yet."

"We've got to end this trip sometime. I'd just as soon it be before we had to drag the canoe over that stretch of rocks ahead of us."

Her eyes widened. "You mean we're stopping for good? But what about the Cherokees?"

"I believe we're past them all. There's been no sign of folks for a couple of days. I'd say if any of the Cherokees had a place this far up the creek, we would've seen something, some trees down or something." I stood and took her hand to lift her to her feet. "Let's look over the land. If it's not what we like, we'll push on farther upstream. But this might be the spot, Maggie."

For the rest of the afternoon, we walked over the land on both sides of the creek. The east bank rose sharply, covered with good hardwood and pine, but the west bank sloped gently upward away from the creek for so far that we grew tired of following it and turned back before we hit another big hill. The woods were thick right down to where the creek bank dropped off and gravel led to the water's edge. But every now and then, through a gap in the branches, I caught a glimpse of dark blue mountains against the pale blue of the sky, and longing for the mountains of home flowed through me as heavy as it ever had when I was working in my uncle's office in Nashville.

We ended up back where we'd started, near the creek. I squatted and scraped away the thick layer of dead leaves on the ground with a stick, and then I dug deep into the dirt. It was dark brown and mealy all the way to the bottom of the hole.

"Look at that." I scooped up a handful and held it out to Maggie. "The dirt looks good. It should grow fine corn."

"It's good dirt and the land's mostly level," she agreed. "It would make nice fields about like what your pa had along Stinking Creek. But it would be some work to clear all the trees."

"That's for sure." I looked at the tall oaks and sycamores around us, and my hands itched to grab the ax handle and get started. But first things first. "We'll spend the night here, at least."

We set up camp on a sandy patch among the gravel beside the water. We ate hoecakes and fried salt pork, and then Maggie wiped the dishes while I brought in a little more wood. The night was warm, though, and we let the fire burn itself out as the sun dropped behind the trees and twilight filled the woods. The creek murmured as it slid over the rocks, only a little louder than the crickets in the woods around us. It was getting dark, and we should have been laying out the blankets to sleep, but we sat in the quiet, watching the orange flickering of the coals.

Maggie laid her head on my shoulder, and I rested my cheek against the softness of her hair.

"What do you think?" I asked. "Is this where we should settle?"

"I don't know."

"I like the lay of the land. The dirt is good, there's plenty of trees, we'd have a source of water—"

"It's good," she interrupted. "But I'd feel better if we were a few more days farther away from the Cherokees and their farms."

"We're far enough," I argued. "There's no sign any man's foot other than mine has ever been on this ground. We haven't seen so much as a hatchet mark on a tree for miles." She didn't answer, so I tried again. "You're not changing your mind, are you? You agreed we'd have to squat on Cherokee land."

She moved away from me. "I know what I said. I just want to be sure we're not going to be found out."

"I've kept us moving up the creek longer than we probably needed to, just so we'd be sure to be past all the places the Indians are claiming. It's clear as anything—nobody's claiming this land. What's the use of letting such a good spot waste when we need it so bad? Who's it hurting?"

The last of the firelight fell across her face, pinched with reproach. "It ain't honest."

I bit back the sharp answer I wanted to give—getting mad wouldn't go far with her.

"Why not? Nobody's claimed it. It's not stealing if it nobody wants it." I reached out for her hand. "Don't worry about the Cherokees," I said softly. "We haven't seen a soul for days. Here's a good spot nobody else wants, a spot we can build our cabin and come to a rest."

She frowned and pulled her hand away. "Build a cabin? I thought you were going to raise just one crop."

"The Cherokees aren't going to come this far away from the river. They'll want to stay close by their own kind. If somebody wanted this land, they'd already have claimed it." She didn't answer, just stared into the coals, and I knew I could win this battle. "I'm tired of roaming around looking for a place," I added. "Seems like we've been on the move someplace the whole time we've been married."

I reached for her hand, and she came back to me, burying her face in my shoulder. She was trembling a little as I wrapped my arms around her, and I touched my lips to her ear.

"This can be our place," I whispered. "It's just sitting here waiting for us. Nobody else wants it—nobody's going to take it away. Let's stay here. I'm ready to have a home of our own where I can settle down with you. That's what I really want." She turned her face up to me.

"I want that, too. But the Cherokees—and what Reverend Washburn said about the army—" I hushed her with a kiss.

"I swear, we're done with traveling around. This will be our spot, Maggie. This is our home."

Chapter 3

Before the sun climbed over the horizon the next morning, I was awake, building up a fire and putting a good, sharp edge on the blade of the hoe I'd bought in Dardanelle. Maggie laughed at me.

"Are you even going to wait for me to cook your breakfast, or do you just want a handful of meal?" she asked.

"Call me when it's ready." I shouldered the bag of seed corn, tucked the hoe and ax under my arm, and started up the bank. She grabbed my arm.

"Wait! We're going to set up a better camp first thing, ain't we?"

"You find a place. I'll help you set it up a little later." And then I took off, headed for the spot where I planned to make my first corn field.

It sure didn't look like a corn field. The land was covered with brush and trees of all sizes, but it was level and mostly free of rocks, and that was good enough for me. I didn't bother with trying to clear the bigger trees. I hacked down the smaller ones and the brush, piling them together to be burned later at what would be the edge of the field, when I wasn't in such a hurry. I worked my way from one big tree to the next, scraping away the layers of dead leaves between the small stumps to show the bare soil. Then I could finally make a shallow hole and drop in a kernel of the seed corn. I had planted barely a handful when Maggie brought breakfast.

"Corn won't grow under trees," she reminded me. "That's one reason Pa never had much of a crop. He wouldn't clear out the woods around his patch and it got too much shade."

I wiped the sweat off my forehead and took a hoecake. "I know that. When the corn's in the ground, I'll come back and girdle the trees.

They'll die out over the summer, and then the sun can get through to the corn. Once the corn is out of the way this fall, I'll come back and cut the trees for our cabin. It's not how Pa would do it, but I reckon I'm in different circumstances than he ever was."

"You still think you'll build a cabin here?" she asked.

I nodded. "I'm telling you, we're so far out, by the time anyone knows we're here, other white folk will have pushed the Indians on to the west, just like that soldier in Fort Smith said."

"Or we'll have money from your pa to get you out of jail." She handed me a dipper of water. "Be that as it may. It don't have to be a cabin, but I'd sure like to have a roof of some kind over our heads before we get any more rain."

"Let me get the corn in the ground," I said. "Then I'll put up a shelter."

We had more than a week of sleeping in the open, though, before I was ready to start building a half-face shelter. It would have been longer even than that if Maggie hadn't helped with planting the corn. I chopped through the saplings, briar roots, and thick tufts of grass while she cleared away the brush and put out the seed. At the end of every day, I was so worn out I hardly noticed whether I was sleeping on the ground or a feather tick. I would like to have had a day to rest once the last of the corn was in the ground, but Maggie started dragging brush from the edge of the field to the campsite before I'd hardly had a chance for my breakfast to settle in my belly.

"Slow down!" I called to her. "What's your hurry?"

"I think it's going to rain before the day's out," she puffed, dropping another load of cedar branches. She lifted her skirt-tail to wipe her face. "You ever recall a day this muggy that didn't end with a rain shower?"

It was damn muggy, and we were both dripping with sweat in no time. I cut saplings to length and lashed them together with green grapevines we pulled from trees in the cornfield. As I secured the last knot holding the frame together, I glanced at her as she dragged in another load of brush for a roof, and I was shocked to see her face was nearly gray in the midday sun. I stepped over quickly and took her elbow.

"Maggie?" She swayed a little, and I tightened my grip on her arm. "You're not about to swoon on me, are you?"

"I'm all right," she said, but I helped her over to one of the rocks I'd brought from the creek for us to sit on. "I'm all right," she insisted. "It's just so hot."

I fetched a noggin of water for her. "Don't drink it too fast," I warned, so she took little sips, sitting with her eyes closed. As I watched her, worry writhed in my belly again. She probably shouldn't be doing such work just yet, not in this heat, for sure. But if I said anything about it, she'd just deny she was tired and work harder. That was her way. I looked away from her, into the woods between us and the creek. I couldn't see the water, but I heard it gurgling over the rocks in the shallows. Suddenly I knew what she needed.

"Come with me," I said, pulling her to her feet.

She stared at me like I was a crazy man when I paused at the edge of the creek and stepped out of my britches.

"What are you doing—John David!"

I grinned at the shock in her voice as I draped the britches over a nearby branch and pulled my sweat-soaked shirt over my head.

"Nothing's better than a dip in a creek to cool off a body on a muggy day." I waded out knee-deep in the water and turned back to look at her. "Come on in—you'll feel better right off."

"John David!" she hissed. "Be decent!"

I laughed and slapped a handful of water her direction.

"Decent? For who? Far as I can tell, you're the only other soul around—and I believe you're already familiar with what I've got to show." Her face reddened, and I laughed again and waded back to the bank. "We've been here nearly two weeks and we haven't seen any sign of other people," I reminded her. "There's nobody to see anything. Heck, Maggie, we could be Adam and Eve wandering around in the garden of Eden with no one watching us but God Himself, and you know what He said about it— 'And they were both naked, the man and his wife, and were not ashamed.'"

"You are a wicked man," she said, though she didn't do anything to keep me from loosening her skirt. "Wicked, wicked."

But she balked as I led her into the water. "I can't swim," she murmured. "You know I can't swim."

"You can stay in the shallow water," I promised. "I'll be right over here in that deeper spot, close at hand."

"This ain't getting the shelter built," she said as I plunged head-first into the cool green water. As I came back to the surface, she was making her way stiff-legged into knee-deep water, still grumbling.

"I don't want to spend another night sleeping outside if it's going to rain—" Her voice suddenly rose into a squeal as she tumbled backward, landing on her backside with a splash. I made my way back to her quick as I dared over the slippery rocks, certain the fall would sour her mood. But she was sitting on the creek bottom with her legs stretched out, letting the water flow over her as she dipped her head back far enough to get her hair wet.

She grinned up at me. "You won't be uppity if I say you're right, will you? This does feel mighty fine."

I laughed and lowered myself to sit beside her.

"Not a bit."

Though the sun was hot on my shoulders, the water was cool as it rippled across my chest and under my arms. Maggie kicked her feet under the water, making soundless little ripples. Somewhere in the woods, a mockingbird rattled off song after song in the quiet. As I looked down the creek and into the trees stretching over us, that contented prayer swelled inside me again. I moved closer to Maggie and wrapped my hand around hers, small and roughened by pulling on brush.

"Our own Eden," I said softly. "Like the Bible says, 'God saw every thing that he had made, and behold, it was very good.'"

She smiled. "Very good."

※ ※ ※

The day after the shelter was finished, I started on the job of hauling big rocks we could use in a foundation for the cabin from the edge of the creek up to our camp. But the day was another warm one, with a light, southerly breeze that ruffled through my sweaty hair and brought the smell of warm earth and young, green leaves tickling up my nose. As the afternoon stretched longer, I spent more time staring down the creek at the blue mountaintops peeking through the trees than I did picking up rocks. That evening, I picked up a dry rag to wipe the dishes as Maggie finished washing them.

"The corn's coming up," I said. "I saw shoots poking through the dirt this afternoon."

"That's good."

"I'll let it grow for a week or so before I try to hoe it, let it get some size. That gives me plenty of time to finish hauling rocks. I've got a pretty good pile started, don't you think?"

She didn't answer, just nodded and handed me another wet plate.

"I was wondering," I said, keeping my eyes on the tin plate as I scrubbed it dry. "How's the meal holding out?"

"All right, I reckon. If I ain't wasteful, we ought to have plenty to last till the corn comes in."

"What about the salt pork?"

"About the same." She looked at me. "Why do you want to know?"

I shrugged as I wiped harder. "Just wondering. I thought you might be getting tired of eating nothing but salt pork. I thought you might have a hankering for some fresh meat."

"I wouldn't mind having some. Maybe you could catch some fish in that swimming hole. They keep nibbling at my elbows every time we go swimming."

"There are some good fish in that hole," I agreed. "But I thought I might take a day while I've got the time and do some hunting for real game."

"I'd like that. We ain't had any real meat in a long time. There's plenty of squirrels around. It's too hot to want squirrel stew, but I could roast the meat—"

I was going to scrub a hole through the tin plate if I kept on. I laid it down and looked her in the eye. "I'd rather save the easy pickings for a time when I'm too busy to get away. I thought maybe I'd go to the north of us, on up in those mountains, and see what I can find."

She was watching me with that half-smile, and I knew she saw right through my excuses.

"All right," she said finally. "I reckon that's a fine idea. The rocks will be here for hauling later."

She was up before sunrise the next morning, making a couple of extra hoecakes that she wrapped in a rag for me. As I tied the bundle to my belt, she held on to my hand.

"You'll sure be back by dark?"

"Of course." I tweaked her nose. "I'd like to be home in time for a swim about sunset." She didn't smile, so I wrapped my arm around her. "Don't worry. You'll be all right here alone for a day."

24

"I know—I ain't worried about that. I know how to handle the hatchet. But don't you get lost out in those big, empty woods—"

I laughed. "I never get lost, Maggie."

I kissed her quickly and then started toward the north, keeping close to the creek for my guide. The morning was a fine one, with streaks of bright sunlight streaming through the trees and all kinds of little birds twittering in the leaves above me. I began to whistle along with them, under my breath so as not to scare any game, though I had no intention of shooting anything this early. I was exploring, not hunting yet—I'd shoot a couple of squirrels on my way back, after I'd looked over the mountains.

Except for the tangle of briars and brush growing along the creek, the walking was easy. These mountains were some different from what I'd known in Campbell County. Back home, the mountains rose at a steep angle; here, it was a longer, flatter rise. But otherwise the land was so familiar, with its rocky gullies and bluffs, that I might have been climbing one of the mountains around Pa's farm. I didn't hit anything I would consider rough ground until midmorning, when my path along the creek was suddenly blocked by a bluff. I had to climb to the top, coming out on a flat ledge above the treeline. Below me, the valley stretched out as far as I could see, miles of green tree tops without a sign of any other man. In the distance, more mountains wrapped the horizon with shades of blue.

"Look at this land!" I shouted into the stillness. "Eden itself couldn't be any prettier!"

The creek narrowed as I followed it into the higher country. After a time, it forked, and I stood for a while pondering before staying to the left, mainly because I didn't want to get wet crossing, but also because the left fork seemed to stay on a more northerly path. I kept on until it was well past midday and my belly was rumbling, and then I sat in a flattened area beneath a grove of big beech trees and ate the food Maggie had packed.

The day was warm and the woods were quiet. A crow cawed in a harsh voice somewhere in the beeches, but after a while he gave up and all I heard was the soft gurgle of the water as it pushed past the rocks sticking out of its bed. I scooped water from the creek with my hat and drank my fill, then sat back against a beech so big I couldn't reach around it. From the patterns of light and dark the sun made on the dead leaves on the forest floor, I could tell it was mid-afternoon. I'd start back home soon, I decided, but first I'd take a few minutes to just sit and soak in the peace of my woods.

I laughed at myself. "They're not my woods," I said aloud. "They're on Cherokee land."

But that made no difference. I didn't care a bit that the government said this land belonged to the Cherokees. It was just what I'd always dreamed of having, fertile bottom land near enough to mountain country that a man could walk to it in a morning's time. Now God had brought me to it, through all these months of trials worthy of hell that I'd been through, trying to get us to Texas. The grasslands in Texas couldn't make a better home than these mountains, though, not for me, anyhow.

"I reckon it's like it says in Proverbs," I muttered. "A man's heart deviseth his way, but the Lord directeth his steps. And I'm glad He directed my steps here."

Contentment flowed over me again, just like the creek water over those rocks, and I leaned back against the smooth, gray bark of the beech tree and closed my eyes, for a proper prayer this time.

I jerked awake when I heard a snort nearby. A pair of young bucks with velvety antler spikes stood not thirty feet away, staring at me, tails lifted just a little, unsure and cautious. I stared back at them, and the dreamy taste of a juicy venison steak seemed real in my mouth, after all these months of tough, salty pork. My rifle was across my lap, loaded and primed, but it would be some kind of trick to raise it and get off a shot without spooking them. I eased my hand around the rifle to cock the hammer, but one of the bucks suddenly threw his tail up straight and whirled around. The other followed as they raced out of the beech grove into the thicker woods. I whipped the rifle to my shoulder and fired, but they were already out of range. Quickly I reloaded and took off after them.

The going was rougher, uphill, with big, jagged pieces of gray rock sticking out of the ground at odd angles and tumbled together. I dodged through the boulders for a good while, but finally I had to admit I'd lost a good chance at some fresh meat. Trying to catch my breath, I glanced around at the countryside. I'd come to the edge of a ravine lined with a hodgepodge of rocks. On the other side was a tall bluff with thin layers of rock stacked as neatly as ever I'd seen the ledger books stacked in my uncle's law office back in Nashville. Below the bottom layer was a hollowed-out spot with a smooth, sandy floor, high enough that I could have stood under it without stooping. At the back was a dark lump that might have been a shadow—or was it a bear, sleeping through the warm afternoon hours?

The thought of a bear roast was even better than a dream of venison. It had been a long, long time since I'd had any meat except salt pork, and I suddenly craved a taste of rich, greasy bear meat. If this was a bear, it was a small one, and Pa always said the best meat came from young bears in the spring.

Quietly I cocked the rifle's hammer. I crossed the ravine, keeping one eye on the black lump and using the other to find the best spot to put my foot down. I was halfway across, then stepping up onto the smooth ledge, and still the figure hadn't moved. As always, I checked for my knife hanging on my belt, just in case the rifle failed. Then I raised the rifle butt to my chest and sidled under the overhang, holding my breath. My eyes adjusted to the dimmer light, and I could see a clear outline—

"Damn," I grumbled. "A rock. It's just a hunk of mossy rock."

Releasing the hammer, I glanced up at the sun—and then I cursed again. Between the nap and following the bucks, I'd let the afternoon get away from me. The sun was already below the tree tops, and even though the season was coming on to summer, I doubted I'd be able to get back home before dark. Maggie would be in a frenzy or a huff, or maybe both at once.

I turned on my heel and started back across the ravine. If I could get through the roughest of the territory while I still had light, it wouldn't matter so much if I had to walk the last bit in the dark. I'd be following the creek those last miles, anyhow, and except for the briars, that had been easy going—

I still can't say for sure what happened. Best I recall, I was stepping from a rock to the edge of the ravine when the rock shifted under me and slid away with a clatter. I dropped my rifle as I fell forward onto the edge of the ravine, banging my shoulder on another rock. But that pain was nothing compared to the knife-like pain in my foot and leg, spreading in a tight ripple from somewhere deep inside. I dug into the dead leaves with my elbows to pull myself over the edge of the ravine, fighting the urge to puke.

That urge kept growing as I raised my knee and carefully pulled up my pants leg. My ankle was already so swollen I could hardly see the knobby little bone normally on the side.

"My God," I groaned. "I bet it's broken."

The bile refused to stay down any longer. I emptied my belly and then lay back on the ground with my arm over my eyes. My heart was racing and I was shaking all over. I'd heard stories back home of men who never came home from a hunt. Sometimes folks found a body, but here no one was around to look. The solitude I'd relished all day seemed to be mocking me now, with no sounds around but the little birds in the trees, twittering away with no concern at all for the pain shooting through my leg, all the way to the hip. I couldn't get home. I'd die here on the edge of this ravine, a slow death by starving, and the buzzards would pick my carcass clean while Maggie waited, all alone, at camp. How long would she wait? Would she come looking for me? But even if she did, how could she ever find me in these miles and miles of trees? All she knew is that I'd headed north—

The leaves rustled softly nearby, and I turned my head toward the sound, half fearful but half hoping it really would be a bear this time to finish me off quick. But it was just a little bird, searching through the leaves for something. I watched her hopping lightly over the leaves, and something of my sense came back to me. I sat up to look at my ankle again.

It was nearly as thick around as my calf now, and though the light was starting to fade, I could tell dark splotches were settling above my foot. Gritting my teeth against the pain, I tried to move my foot. It hurt like the devil, but I could force it to wiggle up and down and then side to side. I dropped back on the leaves again, swallowing another round of bile.

"No blood," I told myself. "No bones sticking out. And it moves. Maybe it's not broken."

I sat up and leaned into the ravine to fetch my rifle. Using it as a sort of crutch, I managed to get to my feet, or at least to standing on one foot. Every time I shifted weight to my bad foot, a wave of pain nearly overwhelmed me. But I forced myself to take a few shuffling steps, and I didn't swoon.

"All right," I said, wiping the cold sweat off my brow. "I can make it home if I take it slow."

Slow is not hardly the right word to describe the pace as I made my way back toward the creek. I hobbled down the way I'd come, placing every footstep with care and scooting across the big boulders on the seat of my pants. It was twilight by the time I'd finally made it back to the beech grove. Every muscle in my body was trembling, and my head was throbbing almost as bad as my ankle. I lowered myself to sit with my bare foot in the cool creek water.

I had to face it—I couldn't get home tonight. Even with no weight on it and resting in the creek, my ankle hurt so bad my gut muscles were tensed against the pain. If I tried to walk over this rough territory in the dark, I was likely to fall and maybe get hurt bad enough I wouldn't make it back at all.

The thin strip of sky above the creek was a dark grey, with a couple of pale stars showing. I knew the moon was a fingernail sliver hanging low in the west somewhere behind me; Maggie had said just last night how pretty it was. I pictured her tonight, standing outside the half-face shelter, looking toward the creek and wondering when I'd be coming along. The thought grieved me with a pain almost as sharp as the one in my foot. But there was nothing for it—the smart thing now was to wait for daylight, even if it meant she would be alone and worried all night.

A soft splash hit the creek a little upstream, probably a frog but maybe a snake, so I pulled my foot out of the water and scooted to sit under a big beech tree nearby. I closed my eyes and tried to will myself to sleep. I had a long way to go tomorrow, and it wouldn't be an easy trip, even once I got into the lower country. But now that I wasn't putting all my mind on walking, the pain in my foot seemed worse, and before long a new pain plagued me—I was caving-in hungry. Maggie probably had supper started by now, even if she was waiting for me to bring in fresh meat. How long would she wait for me before she finally gave up and ate alone? How long would she stay awake, listening for my footfall coming through the dark woods?

I shook my head hard to clear those thoughts. I couldn't think about Maggie, or I'd do some damn-fool thing like try to start home.

"Think about the land," I said, out loud. "What all does a man need from a stretch of land?"

I ticked off in my head all the things land had to give a man for him to live well, and this land passed every test. The soil seemed good and rich enough for crops. There was plenty of clear water. Miles of trees, hardwood and pine, stretched around me, and there was game, even though I'd let it get away from me today. Besides that, it was pretty, as pretty as any I'd ever seen. Sure, it was rough in spots, and because of that, I was sitting here in the mountains instead of sleeping in our half-face camp along the creek. But that was my own fault for not taking enough care.

Ma never understood how I felt about the land. She always insisted at least one of her sons must be something besides a farmer, "to make something of himself," as she said. Just to please her, I'd tried making something of myself. I'd tried being a lawyer and living in town. But I'd never felt right with it. Even with a swollen, purple ankle, miles from a hot meal and a cozy bed with my wife in it, I felt right in Arkansas Territory, against the smooth gray bark of this beech tree, on the edge of this creek, surrounded by miles of trees.

Pa did understand it, I reckon. Nobody demanded hard work like Pa did, yet I'd seen him pause to pick up a handful of dirt when he was plowing in the spring, sniff it, sift it through his fingers. Many a winter evening as we walked from the barn to the cabin after chores, he'd stop and stand staring at the stars in the clear, cold sky. He'd passed on to me that love of the land. But I knew that was all I'd get as an inheritance from him. Pa still went by the ways of the old country, and all his land would go to Paul as the oldest son's portion. He'd advised me once to find some type of life other than farming, but I don't think he was near as mad as Ma was that I'd squandered my chance to be a lawyer. He understood. Maybe Maggie was right; maybe I should ask Pa for some money to buy land. He would listen to all the advantages of the spot I'd chosen along this creek, and he'd say I seemed wise in my choice—except that, by law, it was Indian land. Breaking the law—that's something Pa would never understand, no matter how pretty and good the land was, no matter how much I loved it.

❧ ❧ ❧

I must have slept some, because I was jolted awake by the scream of a screech owl. The sky was still dark, but a pale fringe glowed through the trees to the east. I raised my foot carefully to feel my ankle. It seemed even bigger than it had last night, and the pain was still bad, making the emptiness in my belly roil with every movement. But I'd just have to bear up under it. I was getting down this mountain to home and Maggie if I had to crawl. As soon as there was light enough to see, I used my knife to cut a sapling I thought could bear my weight, with a fork placed so it would fit under my armpit. I took a last long drink from the creek, then picked up my rifle and started the slow trip south.

By mid-morning, I had a new pain to take my mind off the pains in my ankle and my belly—my underarm was raw from rubbing against the sapling. I wadded up my shirt and stuck it in the sapling's fork, and having the extra padding helped ease the discomfort some. By late afternoon, I was finally back to the flatter ground, but the going wasn't as easy as I had thought it would be. I couldn't push through the brush so well with a crutch in one hand and my rifle in the other, and low branches or briars kept whipping against my chest and face, leaving little bloody spots that stung when sweat ran into them. I kept following the creek, looking for something—anything—I could name as a landmark. It was just about sundown when I saw the dying trees of my cornfield, and I have to admit a few tears mingled with the dirt and blood on my cheeks.

"Maggie!" I called, but my voice was scratchy and I doubt it carried more than a couple of feet. Taking a deep breath, I forced myself to move faster, through the rows I'd tried to lay out under the trees. Worn out as I was, I still noticed the corn was taller than it had been yesterday when I left.

I was finally in sight of the shelter, and Maggie was coming up from the creek with a bucket of water, her face turned toward the mountains with an expression of searching. She saw me before I had to try to call to her again, and when her eyes met with mine, I felt the strength I'd been holding on to these last miles draining out of me. She set the bucket down, carefully—Maggie was never one to waste anything—and ran to me. Her arms went around me and I dropped the sapling crutch and leaned against her.

31

"I hurt my ankle," I explained, but my voice sounded garbled. I tried again. "My ankle—I don't think it's broken, but it hurts like hell—"

"Come on," she said, fitting her shoulder against my side and shuffling with me toward the shelter. "I've got you."

Her small hands felt good against my sore body as she helped me stretch out on the bed.

"I knew something had happened. I prayed all night that you were all right." Her mouth was tight and her eyes were more brown than green, worried eyes, like a creek after a heavy rainstorm. "I was afraid you went off a bluff, or got snakebit—"

"I turned it crossing a ravine. I figured I shouldn't try to walk on it last night."

"It's a good thing." Her lips were quivering. I took one of her hands in mine, and she paused a minute, looking into my eyes. A tear was hanging on her eyelashes.

"I knew you'd be worried," I said. "I'm sorry for causing you to worry."

The tear dripped onto her cheek, but she smiled, and then her hands were moving again, pulling my pillow under my head, putting her own pillow under my foot.

"I don't know where to start," she said. "Do you want me to tend your foot first, or would you rather have something to eat? You ain't had anything except those hoe cakes since yesterday."

"What I really want is some water from that bucket you were bringing from the creek. I've not had anything to drink since I started out this morning—I was afraid I wouldn't be able to get back up if I squatted to drink."

"Oh, John David!" She looked again like she might cry.

"It's over now," I said quickly. "I'm back, and there's no need to fret."

"I know. I'll get your water." She turned to crawl out of the shelter, and I watched as she got to her feet and started back to where she'd left the bucket. I settled my head into the pillow, smiling. I'd never been so weary in my life, and now that I'd stopped moving, my ankle hurt worse than ever. But the peace I felt in this half-face shelter of cedar branches was deeper than any weariness or pain. I was where I was meant to be.

Chapter 4

It was several weeks before my ankle was right again. Maggie found pokeweed growing along the edge of the woods near the creek. She made a poultice from the roots and bound it tightly to the sole of my foot as a painkiller. I don't know, though, that the poultice helped nearly as much as the poke greens she cooked up to break the monotony of salt pork and corn pone.

The main problem was, I couldn't do much of anything in the way of work. I'd never realized before how much a man relied on being able to stand on his two feet to do what had to be done around a place. Swinging an ax was out of the question, for clearing the cornfield or cutting firewood. Even working a hoe was more than I could manage with the sapling crutch under my arm. There was really only one way I could hold my foot that didn't hurt, and Maggie laughed at my awkward gait.

"You look like one of your ma's geese, with your toes all spraddled out like that," she told me.

"You'd best watch out, then," I said, grinning. "I'll chase you around camp just like they used to chase you around the yard, nipping at your skirt."

She laughed. "They'd come closer to catching me than you would. You can't even waddle down to the creek to wash yourself without that stick to lean on."

She was a patient and good-natured nurse—at least at first. She wrapped my ankle morning and night with strips of linen, and she kept that stinking poultice on it until the swelling was gone. She did all the work around the camp that I couldn't do, like keeping enough firewood to cook our pone or knocking down the weeds in the corn patch. She even fetched water for me to drink so I wouldn't have to be on my ankle. During all that time, I never heard a grumble pass her lips. But as the summer came on, with long, stifling hot days, I noticed a little tightness about her mouth as she bent over my foot and quiet sighs as she gathered the dishes after supper. One evening after she'd loosened the bindings, I flexed my ankle and twisted it gently between my hands.

"That doesn't hurt as bad tonight as it has," I told her. "We could probably go without wrapping it."

"Are you sure?" Something in her voice told me she'd be glad to be relieved of that chore. I nodded.

"Let's try it a couple of days without. I bet it will be fine." She folded the strips neatly, and I laid my hand on her shoulder. "I'm sorry for all the trouble I am to you."

She shook her head. "It's not that. Folks can't help some of the things that happen to them."

I put my arm around her and pulled her close enough I could lean my head against hers. Her hair was soft against my cheek. It had grown enough during the past months that she could pin it up again. I felt her shoulder rise against my chest in a deep sigh.

"It's just—I'm tired of sleeping in a half-face shelter with crickets—or worse—crawling over us all night. I reckon you were right about the Cherokees, since we've been here for weeks and ain't seen anybody. I guess I was wishing we could start a cabin." She sighed again. "But with your foot like this, there's no telling how long it will be before we can start."

Her soft mouth was turned down in a pretty little pout. I pulled the pins from her hair, and it tumbled down to frame her face. I have to admit, at that moment, a cabin was the last thing on my mind. Or my foot, or Cherokees, or crickets, either.

"I'm nearly good as new," I said. "We'll be starting that cabin any day now." Her face tilted up toward me, and my heart thudded heavy in my chest.

"Any day now?"

But I'd had enough of talking.

"Tomorrow," I promised, and then I surrounded that pretty mouth in a kiss before she could say anything else.

🦎 🦎 🦎

I forgot about that quick-made promise, but Maggie didn't. Next morning while she stirred up the corn mush, it was all she talked about.

"You're sure you're fit to do this kind of work?" she asked as she handed me a bowl. "I thought it hurt you to try to use the ax."

"Well, there's plenty of work to be done before I chop down any trees." Her face fell, and I quickly added, "We've got to find a place to set this cabin first."

So after we'd tidied up the breakfast dishes, we took out walking. I left the crutch back at camp, more to make Maggie think my ankle was ready than because it actually felt ready. We went west of the creek for a while, beyond the dead leaves in the brush that marked the flood line, onto a little rise in the land. As we walked along, Maggie's chatter reminded me of Hannah, Zeke's oldest girl. It was a pleasant sound, and I let her chatter on.

"We need to be close enough to the creek that it ain't much trouble to get water." She looked up at me quickly. "I know you aim to dig us a well, but I figure that'll be a while."

"Likely to be," I agreed.

"And it ought to be handy to your cornfields. You thought about where all you're going to put corn? I figure you'll want more than the one field."

I admitted I hadn't thought on it, so we spent the better part of the morning scouting out the best spots for corn. We ate our dinner in a shady spot between a big oak and a hackberry. By mid-afternoon, we had it all laid out—the cornfields, a garden spot, and a site for a barn, and we'd circled back to end at the oak and the hackberry. Maggie stood between them, hands on her hips.

"It's pretty near the middle of everything, ain't it?" she said. "We'd have a clear path to the creek, but we'd be on enough of a rise we'd stay plenty dry. We could keep these two big trees in the yard—they'd make nice shade. And back here—" She took a few steps to the west. "There's nothing back here but little stuff, easy to clear. We could put the cabin here."

"Sounds fine." I leaned against the hackberry and looked through the trees to where the faraway blue of the mountains met the blue of the sky. My ankle was aching, and I shifted to find a way to take some weight off it without her noticing. "There'll be a nice view of the mountains through here, too."

"Where?" She came to take my elbow, stretching on her toes to see. "I don't see it."

"I'll have to clear some trees before you can get a good view. But it ought to be real pretty."

She was well-satisfied with that. She went back to the cabin spot.

"Say we put one corner here. How big are you planning to make the cabin?"

I managed to help her step off a rough outline for a two-room cabin, but by the time we got back to camp, my ankle was throbbing again. I dropped to the ground and stretched it out carefully while Maggie went about starting our supper, still chattering cheerfully. She suddenly came over and bent to kiss me on the cheek.

"What was that for?" I asked.

She smiled. "I know I wore you out today."

I laughed. "It's nothing—nothing some warm food won't take care of." She smiled again and gave me another kiss. Her eyes were shining, more green than brown, like a creek running deep and peaceful.

"I'd best get to that, then."

≈ ≈ ≈

She didn't stay happy with me for long. My ankle was swollen big again the next morning, and it was several more days before I was able to take the ax to the cabin site and hack down the smaller brush. After sitting around the camp for so much of the summer, I got tired quickly. There were a couple of times Maggie came to the site and found me sitting down, and I could see by the way her lips pressed together that she was annoyed. To make things worse, the summer was deep into July and it was hotter than any summer I could remember back home, and so humid my clothes were always damp and clinging to my body. Between the heat and my tender ankle, finding and hauling rocks up from the creek was slow work. With Maggie helping, though, by the middle of August I had piled up enough rocks that I was able to start laying out a foundation. Once I'd actually started, Maggie seemed to become even more impatient.

"That's good enough!" she snapped at me one afternoon when I lifted a rock off a corner column. "Every one of them don't have to be perfect! And I don't see why you think you have to make so many pillars!"

"You want a level cabin, don't you?" I growled, wiping the sweat from my forehead with my arm. "I'm going to do this right so it won't sag out from under us in a few years. I don't want it to end up like your pa's cabin."

That shut her up for a while, but then I had to lay off working on the cabin for a couple of days to harvest the corn. It wasn't as good a crop as I'd hoped for, but I reckon it was as good as could be expected, growing up between dying trees without having the dirt plowed proper. I figured we'd have enough to eat over the winter and to sow another patch next spring, although I did worry some about where we'd get money for things like salt and some pork. I didn't say anything about my worries to Maggie, though, partly because I didn't want to admit she'd been right about a crop in new ground, but mainly because her temper was mighty short these days.

The second morning of the harvest, just before I left camp to start the day's work, I found out why. Maggie left off stirring the mush to duck into the woods at the edge of camp, and I heard her puking.

"Are you all right?" I asked as she stepped back into the clearing, wiping her mouth with her skirt tail. "Reckon that fish we had last night was bad? I thought maybe it had kind of a funny taste."

"It ain't the meat." Her face was grim as she looked up at me. "John David—I reckon I'm with child again."

It was like my heart plummeted straight to my feet. I stared at her. "That's awful soon."

"Well, that's what comes of having a man laying around a half-face camp all summer! Your ankle may be lame, but your fleshy urges are hale and hearty!" She buried her face in her hands. "That's bound to be what's wrong with me—I ain't had a monthly yet, and now I've been sick these last couple of mornings—"

I fought back the jitters that were gathering in my own belly. "It might be something else—"

"It's the same sickness as before. It can't be anything else."

"Well, then, if you're sure." I ran my hand over my hair. "How long—when do you reckon it'd be born?"

"Early next spring, March or April." She looked up, and her face was streaked with tears. "About time to plant corn again."

I insisted that she rest on the pallet in the shelter while I worked in the corn, and I brought her a damp cloth for her face and a noggin of fresh water for sipping. But once I was standing in the far end of the field, I left fly a string of words I wouldn't ever have wanted Maggie to hear. I pulled my knife from my belt and threw it, hard. It stuck, quivering, into a dead ash. I sank onto a stump at the edge of the field and covered my own face with my hands.

A baby! That meant instead of two mouths to feed, there would be three. Even though the child would be nursing, if a woman was anything like a cow or a mare, Maggie would need more food so she could make plenty of milk—and better food than corn pone and salt pork. She said the baby would be born in early spring. That meant I had to get a cabin built soon. A man might be able to winter over in a half-face camp, but a woman carrying a child would need a warm place out of the weather and something to sleep on besides a pallet on the ground.

I cursed again and looked up across the cornfield. A baby. I'd figured we'd have babies someday—most married folk did—but having a baby was the last kind of trouble that would've crossed my mind right now. I sure wasn't ready for it just yet. How could it happen so quick after she'd lost the first baby? Looks like a woman's body would lie fallow for a while, to give her a chance to rest and regain strength. It hadn't been six months, even—it just wasn't reasonable for her to have conceived again already. Of course, as Maggie had pointed out, it was my own fault. I'd been awfully eager all summer to make up for what I'd missed while we were traveling down the Mississippi River and up the Arkansas. I could nearly hear Pa's voice in my ears— 'Uncontrolled desires of the flesh lead to naught but sorrow, son.'

I sighed and went to fetch my knife from the ash tree. Reasonable or not, ready or not, Maggie was carrying another baby. My baby. Slowly I bent to cut off the first cornstalk near the ground. She sure seemed to be taking it hard. No wonder, though—she never said anything about it, but I knew she was still grieving the loss of the first baby. Or could it be more than that? My hands stilled as I remembered the hateful things we'd said to each other when I'd found out about the child before. She'd kept it from me, she'd said, because she was afraid I'd be mad about having an added burden. True to her promise, she had told me about the baby this time, but maybe she was so troubled over the news because she was still afraid of what I'd say. I hadn't exactly been a comfort to her the first time—no, I'd left her alone and grieving at Dwight Mission. I could say it was because we needed my keelboat wages so badly, or I could blame it on her and say she'd told me to go, but I knew the truth—part of me had wanted to go, to escape the responsibility. I knew the truth, and it shamed me.

How often did a man get a second chance to right what he'd done wrong? This time, I'd do things right, so Maggie would have no cause to worry. This time, I'd act just like Zeke had when Sarah was carrying their girls, like I was plumb thrilled at the idea of becoming a pa.

"A baby's a blessing from God," I said, repeating what I'd heard Zeke say many a time. I suddenly laughed and threw a look up toward the cloudless summer sky. "But I sure would've been obliged if You'd waited a few more months before dropping this blessing on us, Lord."

❦ ❦ ❦

She brought me dinner, and then she stayed to help because she said she felt better and there was nothing to do at the camp. We didn't talk much, and not at all about the baby, just worked steady all afternoon. About the time the sun was starting to turn toward the little hill to our west, we had pulled all the ears and carried them back to camp, and we'd cut all the stalks and piled them along the edge of the field. Maggie was dirty, her face streaked where sweat had carved through the dust on the sides of her face. With sweat dripping from the ends of my hair, I figured I looked every bit as bad.

"Let's go to the creek," I said, taking her hand. "We can cool off and wash ourselves at the same time."

We left our clothes hanging over a low branch and waded into the warm water. The creek was low since we hadn't had much rain lately, and we had to go nearly all the way across to the other bank before the water was more than knee-deep. We'd been in the creek often enough by now that Maggie didn't fear the water so much anymore, and she sat idly splashing the water up onto her shoulders and neck as she watched me swimming in the deeper water. I took one last dive under, then crawled on my hands through the shallower water to sit beside her.

"Feeling better?" I asked. She smiled in answer. I lifted my hand under the water and laid it across her belly. "So you say we've got a baby in here."

"Probably so."

"It don't feel any different," I teased, but she just smiled.

"It will."

I leaned my elbow against the creek bottom so I could rest my head on her shoulder without taking my hand off her belly.

"I've never been around babies much," I told her, "or women with child, either. Just Sarah, and that wasn't too often."

"I've been around them a bunch. But it's different to think about being the one who's got the big belly—and the one who's got to bring that baby into the world."

A sudden fear stabbed through my gut, and I sat up. "I'll find somebody to help you—" But she was laughing at me.

"Who? We're Adam and Eve, remember? And anyhow, you can't bring anybody here without letting folks know we're on Cherokee land." I stared at her, horrified as the truth of what she was saying sank in, and she laughed again. "That's a long time off, John David. No call to worry about birthing the baby just yet. I've got to carry it a while first. Or try to, at least."

Her voice had gone low, and her face was serious. I leaned back against her. "Are you scared?"

She didn't answer right away, just stroked the back of my hand over her belly. "A little," she finally said, softly. She shifted so she could look into my face. "What if—what if something's wrong with me? What if I ain't able to carry a baby? I've heard of women who lose every baby they conceive. John David, I can't stand to think about losing another one—"

"You won't lose this one. I'll take better care of you this time."

She settled back and laid her hand over mine. "Are you mad?"

"No!" I said quickly. "No, I'm not mad. I'm happy. Real happy. A baby's a blessing from God."

We sat quietly until my arm was going to sleep and I had to get off of it. The sun was slanting with thick, golden beams through the trees along the bank, making the pale skin of her shoulders seem to glow against the water. She was so beautiful, like one of those water nymphs in the Greek stories I used to read in my uncle's parlor back in Nashville. I moved so my arms were around her, pinning her in place, and I leaned in to kiss her. But she laughed and pushed me away.

"None of that!" she said. "It's such as that that got us in this fix!"

"Since you're already in a fix, it won't matter what I do," I said, leaning toward her again. She twisted away and ducked me under the water, laughing as she scrambled to her feet and started away from me. I came up sputtering and started to crawl after her when I noticed she had suddenly gone still, and then she quickly squatted back in the shallow water, her arms crossed over her breasts. I followed her gaze to the bank and what I saw made my arms and legs go weak. Two men on horseback watched us without a sound.

Though they were dressed like white men and their horses had regular tack, I somehow knew right away they were Cherokees. One was an older man, stout across the middle and with a straight, hard line of a mouth. The other was younger, not even my own age, smiling slightly as he stared with no shame at Maggie. Something hot and bitter swirled in my belly, and I was about to run at him and knock that blasted smile off his face. But as I moved to stand, I felt the push of the water against my bare legs, and I stayed on my knees. I glanced at my britches hanging over the branch, and quick as a snake's strike, the older man followed my eyes. He leaned out from the saddle and pulled our clothes off the branch, wadding them into a ball before him on his saddle. Although the water was cool, I felt an uncomfortable heat flooding my whole body.

"Who are you?" I demanded. "What are you doing here?"

The older man frowned and looked at me without blinking. "This is Cherokee land."

"There weren't any Cherokees on it." I tried to hold his gaze. It was hard to keep my voice level and calm. Both the men were looking at me now. I wished I had my britches.

"You belong south of the Arkansas River, squatter," the older man said. "Your government says so. You have to go. I'll give you a little time to leave here on your own and go to the south."

My knees were starting to ache from kneeling on the creek's rocky bottom. "What if I won't go?" The boy glanced at the man, who didn't take his eyes off me.

"You will go." He suddenly raised his reins, and the two horses turned, almost like they were one horse, and started away from us, toward our camp.

"Hey!" I yelled after them, making an awful splash as I tried to get to my feet and slipped on the slimy bottom. I fell face first into the water, and Maggie grabbed my arm to pull me up. Her eyes were huge in her pale face, and her hand on my arm was trembling.

"They took our clothes," she whispered. I jerked my arm free of her grip and stood, trying to see over the slope of the creek bank where the horses had gone. There was no sign of them.

"I've got to see what they're doing at camp," I called over my shoulder as I sloshed toward the bank. "You can wait here if you want. I'll bring something back for you. If there's anything left to bring, dammit!"

"Don't leave me here alone!" she wailed. "They might come back." I stopped and waited for her as she carefully made her way across the water. It took an awful long time because she was trying to cover her nakedness and she kept jumping and looking off into the woods at every little sound. Finally, I stepped back to take her elbow and help her along, so we could maybe get to camp before everything was gone—the corn, my rifle, what little money we had. Of course, I thought bitterly, I can't do much to stop them, naked as a baby bird and facing into a rifle. As we hurried along the path from the creek to camp, I broke a good-sized branch off a dead tree that had been felled by a beaver. By God, I wouldn't be completely naked when I faced them again.

But there was no sign of them at the camp, and nothing seemed to be missing. Maggie gasped and let go of me, running to the wad of our clothes that was lying in the dust in front of the shelter. She jerked on her shimmy without even bothering to shake it out.

"Here," she said, handing me my britches. "Make yourself decent."

I slowly stepped into the britches as I looked around the camp. Nothing was even scattered or out of place. It looked like no one had been here at all. If it hadn't been for the pile of clothes, I might have thought I'd dreamed the whole thing. Without bothering to put on my shirt, I hurried to the cabin site. Everything was just as I'd left it. I turned to see Maggie coming up the path, fully dressed, with my shirt over her arm.

"They didn't bother a thing," I told her, still feeling a little dazed. She tapped my arm and I bent my head so she could pull my shirt over it. "Not a thing."

"It's a good thing we finished the corn harvest today," she said, still in a near-whisper, like the woods were full of ears. "We can start south tomorrow."

I shoved my arms into the sleeves. "No." I said it loud. "We're staying right here."

"But they said—"

"I don't care what they said."

"But we've raised our crop, John David," she argued. "That's why we were squatting, to raise one crop. We duped ourselves into thinking we wouldn't be found out. This is Cherokee land. We can't stay here. You can sell the corn in Dardanelle to get the money to go back to the eastern part of the Territory. Your pa is sure to have your letter by now. You can go get money from him and buy land over the winter, then we'll have a legal place to plant corn and build a cabin come spring."

I looked around at the clearing and at the woods wrapped around us and at the patch of sky above, streaked orange and pink with the setting sun. The oak and the hackberry stood like friendly guardians by the path Maggie and I had made coming from the camp. Lately, I'd spent more time here at the cabin site than at camp. Though all I had finished were a few rock pillars, in my mind I'd already warmed my hands in front of the hearth in this cabin, already sat on the porch looking at the mountains in the distance past my cornfields. Something in my chest tightened.

"We're not going anywhere," I said.

She frowned and stuck her hands to her hips. "You promised! One crop and then we wouldn't squat anymore!"

"I didn't promise anything." I pulled my ax out of the stump where I'd left it. "We're not going anywhere."

Chapter 5

I lay awake most of that night, and as soon as the sky began to brighten, I got up and went to the cabin site. I walked between the rock pillars for the foundation. They were mighty fine pillars, sturdy and level. I'd taken the time to put two extra pillars along each of the long sides of the cabin and two where the center beam would run, instead of just putting one at each corner of the house, like a lot of folk would do. The floor of my cabin wouldn't sag.

I sat down on one of those solid center pillars and looked at the outline of the cabin. Everything was ready for me to start on the floor. I already had the oaks picked out that I wanted to use for the sills, good, straight white oaks that would never rot; I just had to fell them and hew them out square. That could take as much as a week, since I didn't have a broad ax, just the pole ax. Then there would be floor joists to hew out, and the puncheons to make and smooth for the floor…I wanted those boards to be so smooth our baby could scoot across the floor without getting a splinter in its tender skin. I ran my hand through my hair. At least a month's work lay ahead of me before I could ever get to raising walls.

A week ago, I'd been looking forward to that work. There was something satisfying about watching a finished joist come out of a rough log. But yesterday had changed everything. With a baby on the way, I had to get Maggie in better shelter, especially since I didn't know what winter was like in Arkansas Territory. More than that, though, I had to get a firm footprint on this land to mark it as mine. Now that the Cherokees had found us, my only hope was to look like I meant to stay, to make it more trouble than it was worth for those fellows to root us out.

Not that I believed for one second that it would work. 'I'll give you time to leave here on your own,' the older one had said, no more, but I knew enough from my work on *fieri facias* cases for my uncle's law office to understand the threat behind the words. If I didn't leave on my own, he'd see to it that I left anyway, against my will. And he had the full backing of the United States government to do it.

Maggie was calling, so I went back to the camp, where she was fixing breakfast. Her manner was stiff, and I knew she was still mad at me.

"Where have you been? To the cabin site?" she said, and I nodded. She frowned. "I don't suppose you've changed your mind about leaving?"

"I've changed my mind, but not about leaving. I'm starting the barn today."

"The barn? Why?" She suddenly turned and stepped into the bushes to puke. I waited for her to finish, and then handed her a dipper of water to rinse her mouth.

"That's why," I told her. "Carrying a baby, you need better shelter. You need a roof over your head, and you need a bed up off the ground. We don't know when the weather will turn cold in Arkansas Territory, but it's coming on to September, so it won't be much longer, if it's like home. I want to build the cabin right, which will take some time. But I can throw up a barn pretty quick. Plus we need a place in the dry to store the corn."

"I don't know why you'll go to the trouble," she said wearily. "You'll do all that hard work, wear yourself down, and that Cherokee man will still make us leave. I can't see why you want to stay. Why be so stubborn?"

I stared into the east, where mist rising from the creek glowed bright in the sunlight between the long, dark shadows of the trees. How could I put into words how I felt about that sight? How could I explain to her the pleasure that filled me as I walked through my cornfield, rough though it was? Or the peace I'd felt every night lying in the bosom of the land—at least until last night, after that Cherokee man and his boy appeared.

"I can't explain it," I said softly. "It's just like when I knew I wanted you for my wife. It made no sense, but I wanted it anyway."

She stared at me a while, her arms crossed and her eyes narrowed a little. Then she went to the pot of mush bubbling in the ashes and scooped out a bowl.

"Here," she said. "Eat up. You'll need a full belly if you're going to build a barn."

I took the bowl and sat down to eat it, but she stayed there by me, and next thing I knew, she was stroking my hair. I looked up, surprised, and she smiled.

"It won't be the first time we've slept in a barn," she said. "At least there won't be livestock in there with us, stinking up the place."

"I'll make it tight," I promised. "There won't be any crickets crawling on you."

She laughed. "Only a mouse or two, if we're sharing the room with a load of corn. But I doubt I'll mind the company too much so long as I'm warm and dry once the first snow comes."

※ ※ ※

I cleared a spot for the cabin down to the ground that day, and the next day I felled a big oak and split it in half to make sills. Within another week, I had walls up nearly chest-high. I was glad Pa wasn't around to see what a sloppy job I was making of the saddle notches. He would have taken the strap to me when I was a boy if I'd done such work on even a hog pen. But the need to finish quickly pushed me on, and I eased my guilt by promising myself that the workmanship on our real cabin would be perfect.

As the walls grew higher, the work got harder, especially since I was working alone.

"I can help you," Maggie kept saying, but I turned her away each time.

"You're in no condition to help," I told her. "I'll manage."

I decided to add only a couple of logs higher than my head on each side, just enough that I wouldn't be banging my head on the ceiling joists every time I walked through the barn. I cut smaller logs, but they were still heavy. The first time I tried to add one to the wall, one end of the log slid off the corner as I was lifting the other into place. It knocked me off balance, I staggered backward a little, and quick as that, pain shot through my bad ankle. I might have been able to shake it off and keep going, but it happened as Maggie was bringing me water, and she saw the whole thing.

"Just sit still!" she commanded when I protested there was no need for her to look at it. She pushed up my pants leg, and sure enough, the ankle was starting to swell.

"Dammit," I muttered. "Is this going to happen every time I step down on it wrong?"

"Maybe if you rest it for a couple of days, it won't take so long to heal this time," she said. "Come back to camp and I'll wrap it for you."

She was right, and even I had to admit the time spent away from working on the barn wasn't wasted. We'd used the last of the salt pork some time back, so I made a couple of snares and caught a rabbit that Maggie made into a good, thick stew seasoned with dandelion greens. When my foot wasn't quite as tender, I crossed the creek and sat all day near a briar thicket waiting on the deer to pass. Luckily, one shot dropped a buck in his tracks, and the hardest work I had to do was toting the carcass back to camp. I built a rack of green locust sticks, and for the next couple of days, Maggie and I worked together to slice the venison and dry it over a small, smoky fire.

The break also gave me time to figure out a new strategy for working on the cabin, a way to get some help without putting the baby at risk. When my ankle felt fit to work again, I took Maggie and a rope to the cabin site with me. She watched as I knotted the rope around one end of a log.

"You'll sit astride the short wall with the rope," I told her. "As I lift the log, take up the slack in the rope, then hold the log steady while I lift the other end. You shouldn't have to strain yourself at all. You'll just be making sure it doesn't fall. If it does start to fall, just let it fall." I looked up at her. "That won't be too hard on you, do you think?"

She laughed. "No."

"Pa would break out in hives if he knew I was using a woman with child to help build a cabin."

But Pa didn't know, and Maggie was a great help to me. We finished the walls in two day's time. Since the plan worked so well and since she didn't seem to suffer any ill effects, she helped me as well with getting the roof supports in place. All that was left was to place the rafters and laths, then to cover the roof with something. The day we set the ridgepole, she practically skipped beside me as we went back to camp.

"It won't be long now," she said. "A few more days and we'll be in a cabin, our own cabin, even if it is a barn. Just in time, too—it's been a little cold these past nights. But it's no wonder—it's—" She paused to look up at me. "What month?"

"The middle of October."

"The middle of October." She took my hand. "I think you were right—those Cherokees must have forgotten us. We haven't seen or heard anything all this time."

"Nope."

Of course, I hadn't seen or heard them the first time, either. That night, lying on our pallet in the half-face shelter with her head on my shoulder, her hand resting on my chest and her breath rising and falling softly against me, my muscles felt tensed, ready to spring into action. She didn't know I would be awake for hours, listening for something, maybe the crack of a twig, maybe the brush of a moccasin against a dry leaf. I was waiting for something I knew would come.

❧ ❧ ❧

It finally came late on a blustery day a couple of weeks later. Maggie had gone back to camp to check on the venison she'd left roasting in the coals, and I was on the roof of the cabin, astraddle a wall and wrestling to pull a rafter up from the ground with the rope. I had it nearly clear of the walls when I heard the unmistakable jingle of a bridle and I looked up to see six or eight uniformed men on horseback coming out of the woods. My heart seemed to drop into my gut.

The men fanned out to make a half-circle around the cabin. One of them bent down from his saddle and picked up my rifle from where it rested on a stump. He laid it across his lap and looked up at me, just as they all were doing. Another man came out of the woods then and pulled his horse up just shy of the line of soldiers. It was the older Cherokee man, with his thin lips curved a little in a tight smile. I sat frozen, the rafter still dangling from the rope.

The man in the center of the half circle straightened his shoulders.

I figured him to be the commander, with his high-collared uniform and the sash across his chest.

"I am Colonel Matthew Arbuckle, commander of the 7th U.S. Infantry Regiment stationed in Cantonment Gibson," he said. "I am here to inform you that you are trespassing on land designated by the United States government for use by the Cherokee nation, and that you are herewith ordered to desist your activities, relinquish your claim on this land, and remove to the southern border of the Arkansas River."

I nearly laughed, because I recognized that tone of voice—hell, I'd used it myself, trying to intimidate the debtors my uncle sent me to turn out of their homes in Nashville.

"Possession is nine points of the law," I called down to him. He didn't blink.

"Not here. This land is a portion of that allotted by treaty to the Cherokee nation. I am under orders to remove all white persons from that portion."

"No Cherokees were using this portion," I said. "I don't see what difference it makes to them if I use it."

Colonel Arbuckle sat even taller. "Come down from that roof." I didn't move, and he jerked his chin toward some of the soldiers. A couple of them dismounted and started toward the cabin.

"Stand back!" I called, and they stopped. One of them looked back toward Colonel Arbuckle.

There was no point being stubborn, I knew it. I was one man, unarmed, against a detachment of soldiers who were armed, and well. I could fight, just as I'd seen debtors in Nashville fight, but I knew eventually I'd be dragged off the land, just as those debtors had been dragged out of their houses. All I'd get for my effort would be a knot on the head or a bloody nose, and I wasn't too interested in pain that served no good purpose. I let the rope slip from my fingers, and the rafter fell with a smack to the ground. Carefully, I worked my way across the top of the wall to the corner of the cabin, and there I stood for a minute, looking over them all.

That's when I saw Maggie come running out of the woods, her head held high straining to see what was going on. She stopped dead in her tracks as one of them lowered his rifle to block her path, and her hands flew to cover her mouth as she stared up at me. The look on her face struck me like a bullet in my chest. I suddenly understood why those scrawny, debt-ridden men had fought me so hard as I was pulling them out of their houses. What kind of man could let another man order him out of his home without a fight, especially with his woman looking on? How could he ever look her in the eye again if he didn't at least try to resist? How could he ever expect her to look at him the same way, or to feel the same when he reached for her?

"God help me," I mumbled under my breath, and I started to climb down the criss-crossed ends of the logs, trying to decide how to do it. They wouldn't really hurt me, I was pretty sure of that, not with her standing there with her body thickened just enough from the baby that a clever person might guess her condition. The worst they would do, probably, would be to rough me up a little, try to put a scare in me. My hands were trembling as my foot touched the ground. I had to do something, now—

With a roar, I threw myself at the nearest soldier, knocking him off his feet so we both landed with a thud on the ground. I threw my leg astride his chest and managed to get in one good punch to his jaw before something collided with my head and sent little sparks of light flickering before my eyes. The soldier beneath me pushed me off him, and from where I sat on the ground I saw two Maggies quivering behind a blur of rifle barrels.

Colonel Arbuckle had dismounted and was standing over me.

"It's useless to fight," he said. I squinted up at him, trying to make his face stay in one place. He leaned down so he was closer to me, and his voice didn't have the clipped, harsh tone of authority now. "You can't win, boy, and you'll just distress your wife needlessly. We don't want to harm you. Just go south of the river and start over." He straightened and waved his arm. The soldier who was keeping Maggie back raised his rifle to let her through. She knelt beside me, and her fingers were shaking as they scrabbled through my hair to find the lump that was rising on the side of my head.

"Don't, don't fight them," she murmured, close to my ear. "Let's just go, let the Indians have it. We'll find another place."

I closed my eyes against the throbbing in my head. Colonel Arbuckle spoke again.

"We can escort you to Dardanelle or to Fort Smith, whichever you'd rather."

"Not Fort Smith," I said quickly.

Colonel Arbuckle actually chuckled. "Dardanelle, then."

"My wife's with child," I told him, in case he hadn't noticed. "We don't have any place to stay in Dardanelle, and she'll need a place."

Maggie broke in. "Can you take us to Dwight Mission? We know Reverend Washburn. He would probably let us stay at the mission a while."

I frowned. The last place I wanted to go – besides Fort Smith – was the mission where that strict Presbyterian minister could give me the lecture Pa wasn't around to give. But Colonel Arbuckle was nodding.

"We'll do that. You got a pack animal, son?"

"Hell, no," I growled. "I'm the only jackass we've got on the place." He ignored my grumping.

"Where's your camp, ma'am? We'll help you get your goods together."

※ ※ ※

With Colonel Arbuckle's men helping, it didn't take long to bundle together our household goods. They tore down our half-face shelter and piled it together to burn, and then Arbuckle sent men back to the barn site with orders to do the same there. I stood watching them go with a sinking feeling in my gut, and Maggie came to me and slipped her arm around my back. But I didn't say a word, not to her and surely not to the soldiers. My head still ached from that lump, and I didn't fancy getting another one to match it. But when I saw Arbuckle and a couple of his men standing in front of my pile of corn, I hurried over fast as the throbbing in my head would let me.

"You won't burn my corn!" I snapped. "I'll pack every ear of it on my back to Dwight Mission if I have to—"

"We don't burn a man's crop, McKellar," Colonel Arbuckle said. "Foodstuffs too hard to come by in this territory. We were talking about how to pack it."

"We could fashion a sled of sorts from some saplings, sir," said a young, pimple-faced soldier. "I noticed a couple of skins under their

51

bedding that we could lash to the saplings. We could drag it along behind."

"The ground's too rough," I said. "Those skins would be torn to shreds before we got to the river."

"True enough," Arbuckle said.

"What about this dugout canoe, sir?" Another soldier kicked at the canoe. We'd been using it all summer as a place to sit.

"It leaks," I warned them.

Colonel Arbuckle gave me an annoyed frown. "How did you get it here?"

"Pine pitch will work, sir," the soldier said. "I found a wad of it in the shelter earlier." Colonel Arbuckle turned away from me.

"Fetch it, Nelson. Take McCall and set to making the canoe tight. We'll take the rest of their goods, and you can bring the corn separately." Without another word, they all moved away, leaving me standing alone.

There was nothing to do but watch as the soldiers took care of everything with the skill of men who'd done such as this many a time. They loaded our household goods onto one of their horses, then Colonel Arbuckle came for Maggie. He settled her onto a horse behind a strapping soldier with the kind of good looks women always seemed to favor. The soldier turned to say something to her and smiled as she answered, then turned and lifted the reins to start into the woods. With a jolt, I started after them, noticing from the corner of my eye that two of the soldiers were striking flints to start a fire at the jumbled pile of brush that had been our home for these past months. Smoke, thick and black, was already rising from the cabin site. I looked around at it all, and nothing seemed real. I might have been in a nightmare, spinning and falling into a pit with nothing solid to grab on to. But this was no nightmare. It was all too real—the flames licking at the dry brush that had been our roof, Colonel Arbuckle sitting his horse with a grim face as he watched the soldiers go about their job—

I realized then one thing was missing. I hadn't seen the Cherokee man since I'd started down from the roof. A hot, sour taste filled my mouth, and I spat on the ground to clear it. But it stayed.

"Damn him!" I muttered. "Damn him to hell!" I looked around at the trees clinging to the last of summer's leaves, our well-worn path to the creek, the dark blue mountains showing clearly through the bare branches. "I'll come back," I promised. "He won't keep me off this land. Not him, not the whole damn Cherokee nation. I'll come back."

Chapter 6

On the long march to Dwight Mission, I managed to come up with a story to tell Reverend Washburn that I hoped wouldn't make me look like such a fool.

"I was worried about Maggie," I told him with a straight face, though an uncomfortable heat prickled around my ears. "With the baby coming on this spring, and it being her first to deliver, I thought it would be better to bring her in where she could have other women around."

Colonel Arbuckle didn't say anything to contradict my story, but I'm sure Reverend Washburn knew the 7th U.S. Army Infantry Regiment wasn't in the business of helping folks carry their goods from one place to another just from kindness. The soldiers unloaded our goods and the corn into the half-finished cabin where Reverend Washburn said we could stay, and then they rode away into the deepening twilight. Maggie called after them with thanks for an easy trip. I said nothing.

The day after we got to the mission was a Sunday, so we sat on the split-log benches along with all the wiggly Indian children and a few of their parents and listened to Reverend Washburn preach. It didn't take long for me to figure out Reverend Washburn must have stayed up late preparing this special sermon for one member of the congregation.

"The Lord God expressly warned his people in the Ten Commandments about the sin of coveting what rightly belongs to another," he started. "Exodus, chapter 20, verse 17: 'Thou shalt not covet thy neighbor's house, thou shalt not covet thy neighbor's wife, nor his manservant, nor his maidservant, nor his ox, nor his ass, nor anything that is thy neighbor's.' The warning extended also to greed that causes men to covet land belonging to others. In Deuteronomy the Lord promises a curse on the man who removes a neighbor's landmark, and that same promise of a curse is repeated later, in Hosea, chapter 5, verse 10—'The princes of Judah were like them that remove the bound, therefore I will pour out my wrath upon them like water.'"

I kept my eyes on the peeling bark of the bench in the row before us as he thundered on.

"The text tells us the Lord's anger rests on the man who desires what is not his own, the man who would cheat others to have what is rightfully theirs. It is sin such as this that causes the Lord to proclaim in Isaiah, 'When ye spread forth your hands, I will hide mine eyes from you, yea, when ye make many prayers, I will not hear; your hands are full of blood. Wash you, make you clean, put away the evil of your doings from before mine eyes.' Hear the word of the Lord!"

Just as my pa had always done, Reverend Washburn insisted we all spend the Lord's Day sitting quietly, doing nothing that could be considered work. First thing the next morning, though, he came to sit with me and Maggie as we ate breakfast in the dining hall. I wondered if he might be about to continue the sermon, but he simply offered a handshake.

"You are welcome to stay at the mission as long as you need to, Mr. McKellar."

"I'm obliged." I forced myself to look at him eye to eye. "I can't pay for our keep, though."

"Don't worry about that. If you're willing, you can earn your keep by working for us, say, by finishing out that cabin."

Maggie took in a hopeful little breath beside me.

"What needs finishing?" I asked.

"The roof needs shingles, mainly. Actually, most of our cabins could use shingles. It's such a slow job and our carpenter, Jacob Hitchcock, has so many other duties. Do you know how to make shingles?" I nodded, and he smiled. "Perhaps you could teach the skill to the Indian boys."

I said nothing.

That's how I got by during those days, by saying as little as possible. I spent my days splitting blocks of red cedar into thin sections and then thinner sections, or trying to explain the process to the Cherokee boys, who weren't all that eager to learn.

"No, look!" I'd say, a dozen times a day. "Don't whack it so hard! You can't break the whole shingle off with one blow. Hit the froe a little tap, see, like this, just enough to get it started a crack, then work your way down a little at a time."

I'd get it started right, thin and pretty, and then the boy would give another hard whack right away and break off my work halfway down, making another piece of scrap wood for the fireplace while the others giggled. More than once I considered giving some of them a tap on the head with the mallet, just to see if it would make a difference in their ability to understand.

After several weeks working with those boys, I hardly even looked up when they came to the carpenter's shed after dinner. One cold day early in January, I heard them laughing as they came across the yard for their carpentry lesson. Sighing, I laid down the drawing knife and went to set out the cedar blocks for the day. Hitchcock laid his calloused hand on my shoulder.

"It's not all that bad, McKellar," he said. "I think a couple of them are starting to catch on."

"I think most of them are playing like they can't figure it out so I'll split out all their shingles for them," I said, and he laughed.

"That might be."

The boys crowded into the shed, shutting the door against the bitter wind. I held out the mallet and froe to the first boy on my left.

"All right, have a go at it. Remember, not too heavy—just a little crack." He didn't take the tools, and I gave them a little shake. "Come on!" I snapped. "I'll drop it on your foot if you don't take it."

"I'll take them," the boy said, "but I don't know how to use them. I'm new to your class."

I actually looked at him then, and I just about dropped the mallet on my own foot. It was the younger of the Cherokee men who'd watched us from the creek bank at our camp north of the river, back in August. He was smiling at me, or smirking, more like. My face flushed hot.

"What the hell are you doing here?" I demanded.

"It's a school for Cherokees," he said. "I'm here to learn to read

56

and write in your language. And other useful skills, McKellar. That's your name, right?"

I didn't answer, just thrust the tools at another of the boys. "Here. Show him how it's done."

The shed was soon filled with the thud of the mallet against the froe and the loud crack of the wood splitting apart. The boys didn't play around as much as they usually did, and several of them kept throwing glances my way as they smoothed yesterday's shingles. I pretended not to notice as I walked around through them, stopping every now and then to undo the mess a boy had made of his work. But through it all, I watched the new boy from the corner of my eye. Little El, they all called him. He was older than the rest of them, 17 or 18, I guessed. It was hard to tell, with him being scrawny and not very tall. He didn't have any sign of a beard, either, though I'd noticed Cherokee men's faces were nearly as smooth as a woman's. He had all those features I'd come to recognize as pure Indian—the coppery skin, the shiny black hair, the thin nose and black eyes. Some of the younguns at the mission clearly had white blood mixed with the Cherokee; I'd even seen some with blue eyes. But not on this one. He was as Indian as could be.

We'd been working for a while when the shed door swung open and Maggie came in, red-cheeked and breathless from the wind. Sour as I'd been since we'd come to the mission, I had to admit she'd been thriving here. The baby was definitely showing on her belly now, and there was a bright look in her eyes. She dropped her cloak over a stack of drying lumber and held up a pitcher.

"Mrs. Washburn thought ya'll might have a hankering for something warm to drink," she said. "She sent over some coffee."

"That's a welcome sight," Hitchcock said, laying aside his hammer and coming to take a steaming cup from Maggie. I moved over beside her to wait as she poured another cup for me.

"You're a welcome sight," I murmured, and she smiled up at me. For a minute, the tightness that had my innards all bound up eased. I wrapped my hand around hers as she handed me the noggin of coffee.

"I'd like a cup, too, if there's some to share," Little El said, coming toward us. Maggie glanced at him, and then her hand jerked so some of the hot coffee splashed out of the cup and onto my fingers. She looked up at me and then back at him.

"That's Little El," I said, wrapping my scalded fingers in the tail of my shirt. "He's just started here, I reckon. Says he wants to learn to read and write."

"In English as well as in Cherokee," Little El added. "The white man's language from the missionaries, and the language of my people from Sequoyah."

"Sequoyah?" I asked.

"George Guess," Hitchcock said. "Lives not too far from here. He's come up with some kind of alphabet for the Cherokees to use."

Little El was standing next to Maggie now, was talking right to her. "My pa says I can be a benefit to my people if I know both languages. He said I can help to read the white men's papers and make sure we are not being cheated."

"How's he so sure you're going to be cheated?" I grumped. Little El's eyes flicked toward me, and he smiled.

"There is a great greed for land in the white man's heart. We saw it back in the east. White men will stop at nothing to get what they want. Empty promises, outright lies, stealing and squatting—"

"Pour his coffee, Maggie," I interrupted. With a frightened glance at me, she did it, then she mumbled something about getting back to Mrs. Washburn and snatched up her cloak. I stood for a minute in the cold of the doorway, watching her hurry back through the gray afternoon. With a sigh, I shut the door and picked up the froe to split out more boards.

"So your young doe will drop a fawn in the spring, McKellar," Little El said, close to my shoulder. "She's certainly rounded out nicely since I first saw her."

Something inside me cracked just like a bad shingle breaking off a bolt. I whirled around and pressed the froe tight against his throat.

"She's my wife," I growled. "Don't you say such things about my wife."

"McKellar!" Hitchcock bellowed, charging from across the shed. I lowered the froe and gave Little El a push.

"Lesson's over," I said. "Get out of here."

It didn't take the boys long to all hurry out the door. I turned back to the bolt, but my hands were shaking and I couldn't seem to position the froe in the right place to section off another shingle. It didn't help any that Hitchcock stood with his arms folded watching me. Finally, I gave up, and with a curse, tossed the mallet to the floor.

"I shouldn't have done it, I know," I said. Hitchcock took the froe from me and tested its edge with his thumb.

"You're an angry man, McKellar." I waited for him to go on, but he took his time, taking the froe to the whetstone and grinding it a few rounds. "You let that anger sit inside you too long, it'll eat you away like a big oak with heart rot." He looked up at me. "So what is it that's eating on you?"

He stood still, waiting for an answer, and finally I ran my hand over my hair and sat on a hunk of cedar.

"You ever make a promise you can't seem to keep?" I said. "I promised Maggie when we got married back in Tennessee that I'd give her a cabin and cornfields. But here we are living off the charity of missionaries. We've been in Arkansas Territory damn near a year, Hitchcock, and we're still living off charity. And now there'll be a baby, too, come spring."

He took the mallet from me, laid the froe to another bolt, and struck off a perfect slice for shingles before he answered.

"Just because you haven't kept that promise yet don't mean you never will."

I bent forward to rest my head in my hands, listening to the thud of the mallet against the froe and the sharp crack of the cedar as it broke away from the bolt. There was something steady and calm about the rhythm of Hitchcock's work. He was never hurried, never got fussed if a board split wrong or a peg broke off. He would just toss aside the bad piece for some other use and go for a new piece without complaining or cursing. I listened with a rising sense of despair that I would never be a man like that, content with my work and my place in the world.

"You know Reverend Washburn will hear about this," he said. I looked up. "Elwin is a hero to the younger boys, and they'll be talking about what happened. I won't go to Reverend Washburn with the story, but if he asks me about it, I'll tell him the truth."

I nodded. "I wouldn't expect any different."

The story spread fast. That evening after supper, Reverend Finney came by the woodshed where I was splitting kindling and asked for a few words with me. I followed him to Reverend Washburn's cabin. Reverend Washburn was sitting in front of the fireplace, and he motioned for me to sit in the empty chair opposite him. Reverend Finney leaned against the wall with his arms crossed. My heart started beating faster, but I said nothing.

"The boys are telling a story that you attacked Elwin Root with one of the tools in the carpentry shop this afternoon," Reverend Washburn began. "Is this true, Mr. McKellar?"

There was no point trying to avoid the truth.

"It is."

"Why would you do something like that?"

I pondered possible answers for a minute, finally settling for the simplest choice. "I lost my temper."

The Reverend pursed his lips. "The boys said it seemed you and Elwin are already acquainted."

"I've seen him before."

"Where?" Reverend Washburn's eyes were steady on me.

"I'd rather not say." He watched me for another moment, then he sighed.

"As you will. But know that Elwin Root and his family have only recently come to Arkansas Territory. They still have connections to powerful men among the eastern Cherokees. It would not be helpful to the government's cause to have word get back to those men that Cherokees are being attacked by men with violent tempers in Arkansas Territory." His eyes narrowed as he leaned toward me. "Can you promise me no such thing will happen again?"

I thought of the brazen way Little El had stared at Maggie in the creek last summer, and of the smug, overly-familiar sound of his voice this afternoon in Hitchcock's shop as he talked about the changes in her body.

"I can't promise it," I said quietly. Reverend Washburn sighed again as he sat back.

"Then I'll have to ask you to leave the mission, Mr. McKellar. Not immediately, of course—I wouldn't turn you out with Mrs. McKellar in her condition. But you need to begin looking for other arrangements. And you need to stay away from Elwin Root. I would consider it a personal boon."

I stood outside in the cold twilight for a few minutes, trying to think of what to tell Maggie. She was bound to be disappointed, upset even. And who could blame her? Every time she got comfortable in a spot, I uprooted her and dragged her off someplace else.

She was already in her shimmy, ready for bed, and tending the fire when I came into the cabin, and she stumbled a little as she got to her feet.

"You oughtn't to be doing that," I said, hurrying over to take her elbow.

She smiled. "I'm all right. I just didn't have my feet under me good. Where have you been?"

"Talking to the Reverends." I wrapped my arm around her shoulders. "Maggie—I told them we won't be at the mission much longer." Her smile faded, and I could see in her eyes she was remembering another night I had uprooted her and led her off into the cold.

"We won't go right away," I said quickly. "I'll find some work and a place to stay first."

Her face relaxed a little, but the worry line was still there between her brows.

"Where will we go?" she asked, moving away from me to push a log closer to the flames. She stayed by the fire, apart from me.

"Dardanelle, I reckon. I can probably find work there."

She looked up at me. "It's because of him, ain't it?" Her voice was hushed, like she thought someone was listening at the cabin door. "That Cherokee boy, Little El. He's going to tell them we were squatting on Indian land, and the law will come after you to put you in jail—"

"They won't do that—all they wanted was us off the land, and Colonel Arbuckle and his men accomplished that job already. If they were going to take me to jail, they would have done it then. I just think I ought to be making some kind of progress toward getting us a new piece of land to start on. We can't do that here. I need to be making money." She didn't say anything, and I stepped forward to touch her shoulder. "I know you're comfortable here, and I'm sorry to take you away. But I've got to provide a real living for my family, not depend on the charity of missionaries. You can understand that, can't you?"

She stood staring into the fire without speaking a moment longer. Then she looked up and smiled again. "Speaking of your family—the baby's been moving a lot today, just squirming all over."

I laughed. "He's getting ready to help me hoe corn. I'd better hurry on finding some land."

She laughed too and I watched as she moved away from me to turn down the bed. Little El was right—her body had changed. It was not just the bulge of the baby; there were pleasing curves now in places where before she'd always been skinny. The slender twig of a girl she'd been when I first saw her at Charlie Huckett's was blooming into a woman, the kind of woman a man might look at with unholy thoughts—

"John David?" She was already under the covers. "Is something wrong? Ain't you going to come to bed?"

"I'm coming," I said, jerking my shirt over my head and letting it drop to the floor as I headed to her. I would go to Dardanelle first thing in the morning, I promised myself. I'd find work—any kind of work—and a place to stay. I'd take Maggie away from this mission for good and we'd be happy in Dardanelle, far away from Reverend Washburn's stern face and the Cherokee boys' giggling and most of all, far from the sharp gaze of Little El's bright, black eyes.

⁂ ⁂ ⁂

Finding work in Dardanelle was no easy task in mid-winter. All I could get were small jobs with small pay—cutting and splitting firewood, cleaning muck out of barns, patching holes on a roof or two. Still, in a little over a week I had saved up enough to rent a small cabin from the owner of the only store in town, David Brearley. It was a cabin he'd put up when he first came to the area, thrown together quickly and without even as much care as I'd taken in building my barn north of the river.

The next few days, then, I didn't hire myself out, but spent time getting the cabin ready for living. I stuffed every crack in the chinking with a mix of new mud and dead grass, and I scraped the floor down to the fresh dirt. I made a bed with saplings and rope, and I bartered a half-day's labor mucking out Brearley's barn for clean hay that Maggie could use to fill a mattress. Three boards sitting atop a stump became our table, and I fashioned three others into shelves where Maggie could store the dishes. One fellow paid me with a chair for cutting and splitting a stack of firewood, and I was well-pleased until it collapsed the first time I sat on it. One leg had broken along a crack that ran all the way to the seat. I spent my evenings then by a fire in the cabin whittling a new leg. Although the chair would stand on the leg I made, it always sat a little crooked, probably because I was in such a hurry to finish. Three weeks to the day after my brush with Little El, I was back at the mission, ready to bring Maggie home.

It was a raw morning, with a fine mist in the air. Hitchcock had offered to drive us and our goods as far as the ferry, an offer I was glad to accept, in no small part because I didn't want Maggie to walk so far. In the time I'd been gone, her belly had grown noticeably bigger. It scared me a little, for I thought she looked almost as big as Mrs. Hitchcock, who was due to deliver a child at any time. But Maggie seemed content enough as Mrs. Washburn and Mrs. Finney fussed over her, bringing an extra quilt to tuck around her once she was in the wagon. She was nestled snug between me and Hitchcock on the wagon seat, holding to my hand under the quilts as he chirruped to the horses and we left the mission.

We hadn't gone too far before a rider appeared in the road coming toward us.

"That looks like Elwin Root's horse," Hitchcock said. "Junior, I mean. Little El."

I groaned. "Couldn't we get away without having to see him?"

Hitchcock grinned, but his voice was sober. "Mind your tongue, now, McKellar. You don't want trouble."

Little El reined his horse even with the wagon seat and touched the brim of his hat in greeting. But surprise flickered across his face as he noticed Maggie sitting on the seat with us.

"We're leaving the mission," I said, saving him the trouble of asking.

"We're sorry to see him go," Hitchcock said, quickly, like he would head off any trouble that might be brewing. "McKellar's a good hand in the shop. But I reckon we didn't expect him to stay long. A man wants his own place."

"Where are you going?" Little El asked. I snorted.

"It's none of your affair, I reckon, so long as we're south of the river."

His black eyes stared at me intently. "You're always unfriendly, McKellar. Why? Is it because you fear me?"

"Fear you?" I sputtered, and Hitchcock raised the reins.

"We'd best be going if we want to get to the ferry before midday," he said. But Little El had turned his horse and was keeping pace with the wagon.

"The days of violence, when the Cherokees warred against the white man, are over," he said. "We live as you do, in cabins, and we farm just as you do—instead of our women working the fields, as in the old times, our men do it, just as your men do. We wear your clothes and pray to your God. My people learned to live with yours, but your people refuse to live with us. They push us out of our homes in the eastern mountains, with the promise we can live here in the West unmolested. But wherever we turn, there is another white man."

"There will be more," I said. Hitchcock flipped the reins to urge the horses to a faster pace, but Little El stopped and let us pass on.

"Stay on your side of the river, McKellar!" he called after us. I didn't turn back, but Maggie peered over my shoulder.

"He's watching us," she said.

"Don't worry about him, Mrs. McKellar," Hitchcock said. "Elwin Root comes from good folk. He knows better than to stir up trouble." He pulled back on the reins, and the horses dropped back to a walk. "I'll slow down now, Mrs. McKellar, so you're not jostled so much. I just wanted to get out of that situation before any trouble could start."

"Hey, now!" I said. "If Little El knows better than to stir up trouble, who were you thinking was going to start trouble back there?"

Maggie and I laughed as Hitchcock's face went red. "I didn't mean—"

"I know," I said. "You're probably right, anyhow. But that's done now. We'll be settled in Dardanelle by nightfall, with nothing more to do with Cherokees."

※ ※ ※

Hitchcock dropped us at the ferry on the banks of the Arkansas. Once we were over the river, I used a couple of my remaining coins to hire a pushcart from the ferryman, and we walked the short distance on into Dardanelle and to our rented cabin. As I pushed open the door and stepped aside to let Maggie in, my gut seemed to tighten like a knot. This cabin was definitely a step down from the fresh new cabin we'd stayed in at the mission. The room was dark and cold, and a draft I hadn't noticed before was coming from somewhere. My efforts to put together furniture suddenly seemed pitiful. A stump table and a broken chair? What had I been thinking?

Maggie stood silently peering into the room. She suddenly gasped and rushed across the room to the chair. She turned back to me, a wide smile across her face.

"A chair? John David! We ain't ever had a chair!" She sat down, and it tipped sideways, and for a minute I was sure she was going to land on the floor. I jumped across the room to steady her.

"It was broken," I confessed. "I tried fixing it, but I couldn't seem to get that leg quite right. I'll keep working on it to make it better."

She laughed and tipped the chair back and forth onto its short leg. "You made me a rocking chair! A ma needs a rocking chair!"

I was glad then for the darkness of the room, so she couldn't see the tears gathering in my eyes. "You like it, then?"

She looked up at me, and I reckon the room wasn't quite dark enough, for she smiled and gently pulled me toward her. I knelt on the floor by her, and she wrapped her arms around my neck and kissed me.

"It's a fine place," she said.

"Not as fine as what we could've had," I started, but she put her finger over my mouth.

"There's no use thinking about what we could've had. Remember what you told me when you were trying to convince me we should stay in Arkansas Territory?" I looked at her, confused, and she laughed. "About making hard times our good times?"

"Oh—that."

Her smile looked more like a smirk. "It sounded good enough to you when you were trying to get your way, eh? Anyhow, we can make it true. We're south of the river now, not on Cherokee land, so we don't have to worry about that Indian or the law catching us as squatters. We're settled in a place where you can find work and earn some money. And someone will be around to help when it comes time for birthing this baby. I reckon this is the best place for us right now. Like you said, maybe God's hand has been at work in all this."

"Looks like if God's hand had been at work, you'd have better," I said sourly. "This is what you get when my hand's been at work."

She smiled. "You've done a fine job, John David."

"I'll do better," I promised.

She drew me close and kissed me again, a tender, lingering kiss. Then, using me for support, she pushed herself up from the chair.

"It's sure cold, ain't it? That mist soaked right through my cloak on the walk here. If you'll build a fire, I'll start bringing in the goods to get this place set up like a home."

Chapter 7

Shortly after the army had escorted us to the mission, Reverend Washburn told us a letter for me had come to the mission during the early part of the fall. Since he'd thought we were headed back to the eastern part of the territory, though, and he never expected to see us again, he'd burned it. I told him I'd probably have done the same, and I forgot about it. But Maggie didn't forget. Once we were settled in the little cabin in Dardanelle, she started in on me about writing to my folks again.

"That letter was probably from your pa," she would say. "I bet he was saying he'll help with the land. If you don't write back, he'll think we don't need help anymore."

She kept after me until I was so weary of hearing it I gave in one night.

"But I'm writing to Zeke," I told her. "Since we don't know for sure what Pa said."

She agreed that was a good plan, and she busied herself with clearing the dishes from the table so I'd have a place to write. I carefully whittled the end of the quill as I pondered what to say, and when Maggie started to give me impatient looks, I sighed and put ink to the piece of paper she'd saved from a package of tea at the mission.

Dear Zeke,

I hope this letter finds you all well. If you wrote to me this summer past, I did not receive the letter, as the postmaster thought we had left the area and so destroyed it. We are staying at the settlement called Dardanelle for the winter, for Maggie is expecting a child in early spring and I thought it for the best to stay close to where women can help with her lying-in.

I brushed the feathery end of the quill across my chin. What else could I tell him? I couldn't tell the truth—that I was working odd jobs, barely bringing in enough money to keep us in this cabin, that I had no seed corn for planting, for I'd taken the corn from my crop to be ground into meal so we'd have something to eat this winter. Part of me longed to spill all my troubles to him, just as I'd done so many times as a boy in Campbell County. But I was a man now, and soon to be a father. A man shouldn't depend on his big brother for help.

Once the baby is born, we will find some land. From talk around here, the land south of the Arkansas River is soon to be ready to sell, and I will get acreage here. Before long, I'll be clearing fields for crops.

At least that part of the letter was true. Within a week of sending the letter, I finally found steady work helping clear a tract of land where some rich man from back East was planning to plant cotton. Word was, he was bringing in slaves come late spring, and he was willing to pay well to have the soil ready to drop the seed when they got here. His partner in the venture was a thin fop who reminded me too much of my uncle Abner. But come every Saturday, he paid us in coins. Most of the men on the crew spent their money in one of the taverns almost as soon as they got it.

"Have a drink with us, McKellar," one of them said as we walked back toward Dardanelle late on a clear, mild Saturday afternoon.

"Naw," I said. "I better get home. My wife will be looking for me."

"She must have your bollocks in a mighty tight grip," another one said, and he dug his elbow into my side as he added, "Maybe she's made a capon of him, fellers! Is that it, McKellar? You're afraid to come have a drink with us? Afraid the wife will find out?"

I didn't answer back to their clucking and crowing, and after a while they lost interest and walked on ahead, laughing as they glanced back at me. Thomas Mallory, the oldest man on the crew, fell in step with me.

"They're hard on you, McKellar."

I shrugged. "It don't bother me."

"It don't? It would bother me for them to jest about my manhood. Hell, it bothers me for them to jest about your manhood." He shook his head. "Young fools like that, they don't know what it is to really be a man and take up the burden of responsibilities. I've been watching you fellers on the crew. You work hard, McKellar, and you take your money home every week. You may be young, but I'd say you're more a man than any of them." I stared at him, not sure how to answer, and he slapped my back. "I know you turned them down, but come have a drink with me. Look at it as a chance for the men in the crew to get acquainted."

"I don't drink anymore—it costs too much."

A smile cracked across his face. "Just one, McKellar."

We passed by the first place we came to, knowing the other fellers from the crew would be there, and instead stopped in at Brearleys' store. I sat for a while staring at the glass of whiskey between my hands.

"It's been nearly a year since I had any whiskey," I said. Mallory raised his glass.

"To breaking your fast!"

I raised my glass to meet his, then took a sip. It was harsh whiskey, burning all the way down my gullet.

"So you've got a wife," Mallory said. "Any young'uns?"

"We're waiting on one—a few more weeks, she says."

He smiled and leaned back in his chair. "That first baby, now that's something. Once you got five, like I got, you don't notice every little thing they do. Where do you folks come from?"

"Tennessee. Campbell County, out in the east."

"I thought maybe you sounded like a Kentuckian, same as me. How long you been in the Territory?"

"Nearly a year."

He grinned. "About the same time you laid off the whiskey, eh? Is that just coincidence?"

I laughed. "No, I'd say there's a direct cause and effect. We've been hand to mouth since we got here. If I somehow get an extra pence, there's a hand waiting to pinch it out of my pocket. I can't even manage to set aside enough to buy one acre of land for myself, let alone eighty."

"Amen to that!" Mallory slapped his hand against the table. "Every day I wish I was working my own piece of land instead of hiring out to clear land for someone else. Nearly kills me to think I could be getting my own ground ready to plant corn."

He'd put into words what I'd been trying to keep in the back of my mind every day as I hacked at the sumac and tree roots on the rich man's property. The closer we got to warmer weather, the heavier the empty bags that had once held my corn crop weighed on me. I took a good-sized swig of the whiskey.

"I had a crop last year," I said, "not much of one, but not a bad one for being in new soil. If I hadn't been driven off the land, I reckon I could've had a good crop this year."

Mallory leaned forward. His eyes were bright. "Drove off? Were you on Indian land?"

I nodded. "North of the river. That all belongs to the Cherokees. The U.S. Army was kind enough to escort us back to the south."

Mallory seemed nearly beside himself. "Same damn thing happened to us! Only we hadn't had time to raise a crop. We got here in September, came up from Little Rock on a keelboat. I looked at property around Cadron, but it's too pricey for a farmer from Kentucky. I reckon you got to be a rich cotton grower's son from Carolina to have any advantage in buying property around Cadron. Anyhow, a man's got to have someplace to keep his family. We found a right nice spot, but like you, we was north of the river. We hadn't been there two months when the Army come and rooted us out. Like to broke my woman's heart."

"We had a cabin started," I murmured, "nearly had the roof on, and they burned it."

"It's a damn shame," he growled. "Driving off decent, hard-working white folk so them Indian savages can have it. What are Indians going to do with it? They don't farm, not the way white folks do, anyway."

"I reckon that's no matter. The government says the land belongs to them."

"That just sticks in my craw." He downed his whiskey and motioned to Brearley for another. "It's our own government doing it. The Army's supposed to protect citizens, ain't it? Soldiers shouldn't be driving folks off good American soil! Hey, Brearley! Have the folks in Washington City decided yet who's going to be president?"

"Still no word," Brearley said as he refilled Mallory's glass. "I saw in last week's *Gazette* it may be another two or three weeks before we know." He tipped the bottle toward me, but I waved him off.

Mallory was shaking his head. "I sure as hell hope it ain't that stuffy Yankee Adams. Clay's my man, but I'd rather see a good Indian fighter like Jackson in office than that lily-livered frump. I reckon you're a Jackson man, being from Tennessee."

I'd never paid much attention to the discussions of politics around the law office back in Nashville. I'd been too young to vote, and I'd never considered that who was president made any difference to me. The government seemed far away and removed from day-to-day life.

"My uncle was a big supporter," I said.

"Clay or Jackson, that's who we want, a man from the West who knows what we're up against. Then soldiers won't be running white folks off the land. It'll be the red devils who are running."

"Here's to that day coming soon." I raised my glass, and Mallory clicked his against it with a grim smile.

"Amen."

※ ※ ※

The job clearing land was over within another week, but as the spring rains fell, traffic on the river picked up and I found work unloading boats at the Dardanelle wharf. It wasn't regular work; one day I might work an hour, and two days later it might be midnight before we were finished. One of those long days, I got home after sunset and found Maggie standing stone still, gripping the back of the chair, her shoulders hunched. My heart seemed to stop.

"What's wrong?" I asked, but she didn't answer. I took her arm. "Maggie?"

She suddenly relaxed and looked up at me with a little smile. "It's time."

I don't think any two words ever set me into more of a panic than those.

"You're sure of it?" I asked, and she nodded.

"The pains started this afternoon. They're coming more often now, harder too. I reckon we're going to have a baby tonight, John David."

"I'll get someone for you," I said, whirling back toward the door, but she grabbed my arm to stop me.

"Not yet."

"Why not? If the pains have been going all afternoon—"

She hesitated a minute, like she wasn't sure she should say anything.

"I don't want to have to pay a midwife to sit around waiting," she said finally. "Judging from how it went for Ma, it's likely to be a while yet. I'm fine for now. Sit down and have supper."

She went about making pone and frying pork like it was any regular night, stopping a couple of times to brace herself against the fireplace or the table's edge while she waited for her pains to pass. I couldn't take more than a couple of bites of what she set before me, though, for my stomach was tossing like maple leaves during a windstorm.

"You ought to sit and rest," I told her as she washed the dishes. "You'll wear yourself out, walking around so much."

She shook her head. "Ma always walked. She said it made for an easier time of it."

"Then let's walk," I said, jumping to my feet and putting my arm around her. "Let's make it as easy as we can."

We went round and round the cabin, stopping when her pains came.

"You're trembling," she said. "Are you scared?"

"Are you?"

"A little," she admitted. "I know these pains will be a lot worse before the night's over." I tightened my arm around her as she stiffened against another one. It seemed to last forever, and little beads of sweat glittered on her forehead in the firelight.

"Let me go get someone for you," I pleaded when that one was over, and this time she nodded. I walked with her toward the door. "I won't be long. You'll be all right till I get back?"

She nodded again and started back to walking. I went through the door calm and steady, but as soon as the door closed behind me, I took off running like my britches were on fire.

Brearley's tavern was the closest place, and I whipped through the door, knocking into a feller who was leaving. I set him up again, then rushed over to the counter.

"I need a woman!" I panted, which set the whole room to laughing. I shook my head impatiently. "No, not like that! I need a woman to be with Maggie. The baby's coming!"

That changed their tune real quick, and Brearley sent his son Joseph to fetch a woman he said was the best around for tending at births. He offered me a drink while I waited, but I couldn't settle down long enough to take it. Just when I thought I couldn't stand waiting anymore, Joseph came in with a dried-up little scrap of an old woman and a black-haired girl who couldn't have been more than 10 or 12.

"Who's the girl?" I asked.

"I'm Lona Joseph," she said. "Grandmother don't speak English, so I come along to help."

"Wait a minute!" I said, looking at Brearley. "She doesn't speak English? What kind of deal—"

"She's Cherokee," Brearley said.

"Is there no white woman around?" I asked. The old woman looked like one of the dried-apple dolls Sarah used to make for her girls.

"They say she's the best around," Brearley said. "But if you'd rather have a white woman, I can send Joseph out for Miz Hankes, and see if she can leave her younguns for the night—"

How long would it take to rouse Mrs. Hankes and get her here? I wondered. I'd been here a long time already—how many pains had Maggie suffered through in that time, with no one there for her? I shook my head.

"No, no, I've already left Maggie alone too long." I looked at the girl Lona. "Come on, I reckon."

I'd taken only a step toward the door when the old woman laid her hand on my arm and spoke in a low, grunting voice.

"Whiskey."

I looked at Brearley and then Lona. "I thought she didn't speak English."

"She knows a few words," Lona said. I shrugged and flipped a coin to Brearley, who handed me a bottle. Then we finally started back to the cabin at a pace so slow I figured the baby would be born and weaned before we got there.

Maggie was just coming out of one of the pains when we came in the cabin. She was pale, and I knew it must have been a bad one. She clung to me like she hardly had strength to stand.

"I'm glad you're back," she whispered. I couldn't have said anything if there had been a gun at my back. I brushed the sweaty hair back from her face and tried to swallow the lump in my throat.

"Whiskey," the old woman said again. I pulled away from Maggie to splash some of the whiskey into a cup, maybe enough to at least take the edge off her pain. But the old woman took it from me and downed it in one gulp. She said something in that grunting voice, jerking her head toward the door.

"She says for you to leave," Lona said. "Men don't belong here."

So I sat on the ground outside the cabin in the dark, listening to the women's voices through the walls, the low murmur of the old woman's voice and Lona's high, young voice. Sometimes I heard Maggie too, groaning. The sound cut through me like the sharpest blade. I remembered how her slender hands had gripped my arms before the old woman had banished me, and I looked at my own hands in the light coming through the crack around the cabin door. They were big hands—I was a big man, and she was a small woman. What if the baby took after me and was too big for a small woman like Maggie to birth? I recalled eavesdropping from the attic when I was a boy, listening to Ma and Trisha talk about some woman across Stinking Creek who had suffered terribly for three days trying to birth a big baby. She'd finally died, though they'd brought in a doctor from Jacksborough with his forceps. I put my hands over my face, trying to shut out the picture of Maggie suffering in such pain for three days. And the thought that she could die—I jumped to my feet and walked around the cabin a couple of times, willing the pounding of my heart to slow down. She couldn't die.

I should pray, I reminded myself, but my words seemed to struggle to rise into the black sky. 'I will not hear'—wasn't that the quote Reverend Washburn had pulled from Isaiah just for me? 'Though you make many prayers, I will not hear—I will hide mine eyes from you—'

I shook my head, hard.

"She won't die," I whispered aloud. "She won't die."

The day had been hot for so early in April, and I wasn't surprised to see lightning flashing in the west as the night dragged on. I watched it come closer, until the rumble of thunder drowned out the sounds inside the cabin. When a bright streak of lightning lit up the night like moonlight, I stood and stuck my head inside the cabin door. Maggie was stripped down to her shimmy, squatting on a pallet by the bed. The old woman stood over her, chanting something that got lost in the loud clap of thunder. The girl Lona was hovering nearby.

"Lona!" I called. "It's fixing to storm. Can't I come in? There's nowhere else to get out of the rain."

She put my request into Cherokee for the old woman, who nodded and even motioned for me to come to her. She said something that sounded important, waving her hands, and I looked at Lona, my heart pounding in my ears.

"She says for you to kneel here behind her, to support her. The baby is close." I quickly knelt and put my arms around Maggie. If she noticed I was there, she gave no sign of it. Her skin was ghostly pale in the candlelight, and her head was bowed. Her breath came in short, shallow bursts. My insides melted in despair. She was dying, and the old woman had enough kindness to let me say goodbye.

"Is she all right?" I managed to choke out. Maggie suddenly grew tense against me.

"I need to push," she said, in her regular voice. But the old woman was laying her hands on the top and side of Maggie's belly, shaking her head and babbling something.

"For God's sake, let her push!" I cried, but they all ignored me.

"Let it build," Lona said. "She says to wait—"

"*Ga-sa-do-yo-s-di!*" the old woman cried. "*Ga-sa-do-yo-s-di!*"

"Push!" Lona urged.

Maggie strained against me so hard it took a surprising amount of strength to keep her from knocking me over. She let out a sharp cry that pierced me through, and then she eased up on the pushing. She was panting and trembling, but the old woman seemed pleased, jabbering and patting Maggie's cheek.

"She says you are doing well, a very brave girl," Lona said, speaking over her. "A few more pushes like that, and it will be over."

I don't know if the storm or the baby came first. All I can say is that the rain hit with a force that made the cabin shudder about the same time the old Cherokee woman whooped in delight. Maggie slumped back against me, trembling all over, and I wrapped my arms tight around her. I hardly noticed the baby's piercing squalls. It was over, and Maggie was still alive.

"A girl!" Lona cried. "And she's on her back! Grandmother says that means good fortune."

From that point on, the night seemed unreal, like a dream that I couldn't wake up from. The women went on about finishing the business of the birth, with no more need for me. I stood in a corner by the fireplace and watched as the old woman washed the baby and Lona helped Maggie into a fresh shimmy. Maggie was soon settled into the bed with the baby beside her, and the old woman sat at the table with another cup of whiskey while Lona straightened up the cabin. She brought me a bowl covered with a cloth. I was too tired to even ask what it was.

"Grandmother says for you to bury this," Lona explained.

"Bury it?" I repeated stupidly. The old woman jabbered something.

"It's the afterbirth. She says you should take it far away to bury it. The number of ridges you cross before you bury it tells how many years it will be before there is another baby."

"That's rubbish!" I scoffed. "Indian rubbish. I don't believe such as that."

Lona turned to the old woman and repeated my message in Cherokee. The old woman shrugged and laughed as she looked at me. She jabbered something else.

"Maybe you don't, she says," Lona said. "But just throw it out, and there will be another baby at any time. Grandmother is wise. She's seen many babies, many more than this one of yours."

I gave them a bag of our meal and the bottle of whiskey for their trouble in tending to Maggie, then took them to their home near the Indian agency. I walked back to our cabin through the last light rain that lingered after the storm, as fast as I could push myself against the tiredness that was starting to overwhelm me.

Maggie stirred when I came in, and I went to stretch out beside her on the bed. The baby was awake, too, her dark eyes catching the faint shimmer of candlelight.

"She's all right?" I asked. "Like a baby ought to be?"

"She's healthy," Maggie said. "I got her to nurse a little while you was gone."

"That's good, I reckon."

"It's good. Want to hold her? You ain't had the chance yet to hold her."

I sat up and she laid the baby in my arms. She was such a tiny thing, squinting up at me from a wrinkled little face.

"Who would've thought it, back in Campbell County," I said. "That rascal John David McKellar's got a little daughter." I touched her hand. It was hardly bigger than the end of my finger. "She's a fine-looking one, too."

"Ain't she sweet?" Maggie murmured. "Our own young'un. Reckon what we ought to name her? A lot of times folks name a baby for family. I don't want to give her my ma's name, but if you want to name her for your ma—"

"I don't." I laughed. "Why lay that burden on the child?" She laughed too, and she pulled the wrap back a little from around the baby's chin.

"Well, I thought we could name her Penelope, you know, like the wife in that story about the Greek feller. If that ain't too foolish a notion, I mean."

"Penelope." I tried it out. "Penelope McKellar. There's a nice sound to it."

"We could call her Penny."

I grinned at her. "You've been figuring on this, I can tell."

Her smile was a little sheepish, like I'd caught her at something foolish. "Just while you was gone. All I had picked before was boy names, and I saw the book over there on the shelf, and I figured it was as good a name as any—"

"I like it fine," I said, and then I laughed. "You know what this means, don't you?" She looked at me, puzzled, and I grinned. "No matter how low we get, no matter how broke, I'll always have a Penny to my name."

She laughed too, but her face sobered quickly.

"John David…you ain't disappointed? I know a man needs a son to help him work a farm—"

"Hush! Of course I'm not disappointed! A woman needs help, too. Anyhow, I don't have any farm to work right now. The next one can be a boy."

"I reckon so." She sighed and settled back into the pillow. I laid the baby beside her and brushed my fingers over the dark shadows under her eyes. She looked like she'd taken the worst of a rough fight.

"You had a hard time of it," I said.

"It was hard," she admitted. "I'm mighty tired now, and sore, in places I wouldn't have thought about hurting. I'm glad to have it done with." She grinned up at me. "I hope you're in no hurry to get that son."

I suddenly swung my legs off the bed and stood.

"Where are you going?" she asked, as I took the covered bowl from the table.

"I won't be gone long," I told her. "I just nearly forgot to do something the old woman said to do. You get some rest, and I'll be back to make breakfast."

Lightning still flashed to the east, but in the west, pale stars were showing against the black of the sky. The air was cool against my face as I set off toward the big, loaf-shaped mountain near Dardanelle, with the bowl in the crook of one arm and my hoe in the other. Indian rubbish or not, I wasn't taking any chances.

Chapter 8

Maggie liked to say it was coming into the world during a thunderstorm that made Penny such a loud and intense child. Whatever the reason, our little daughter cried more than any baby I'd ever heard tell of. Maggie said it was normal for Penny to cry the way she did, and the child surely didn't look sickly. Within a week of her birth, she was rounded out and pink, and when she was asleep, I thought Maggie and me had procreated a mighty handsome child. It was no wonder, though, that she was so fat and pretty—she always seemed to be hungry, either suckling at Maggie's breast or crying for it, even during the night. I thought Maggie started to look a little thin and bony, like a cow whose calf was taking all her nourishment.

Fortunately, it was the warm season, and work was plentiful in Dardanelle. The river was getting low, so I lost my job unloading boats, but within an hour I had hired on to help build cabins at better pay. While I should have been holding more of it back, I thought it was worth spending some on luxuries that might help fatten Maggie. I might bring home a bag of dry beans and a chunk of ham, or I might lay a measure of wheat flour and a fat ball of fresh butter on the table and tell her I had a hankering for flour biscuits. Once, in a fit of extravagance, I bought a small crock of honey for her. I bought her a pair of hens and a little shoat hog that we kept in a pen behind the cabin, and I swapped out my labor plowing a garden spot for Brearley for the use of his plow to make our own garden. By mid-June, we had our own beans and a little patch of corn knee-high.

Maggie was pleased as could be with it all.

"Even if we ain't settled on our own land, at least we have something of a farm," she said. "And we're going to church, like decent folk do."

Joseph Brearley had come to the cabin one Saturday evening to tell us about the preaching in Dardanelle. One of the missionaries would come over from Dwight to have a service once a month for the folks living south of the river. She liked it, but I went only because it pleased her. Listening to the preacher talk about human sin, judgment, and predestination for salvation or eternal damnation made me feel hard inside as an underdeveloped hickory nut. I always bowed my head for the prayers, but what ran through my mind wasn't anything close to what the preacher was saying. God wasn't listening to me, anyway, of that I was sure—it was clear as day I wasn't one of His elect. Why keep wasting my breath?

One Sunday in July, we were at another of those services, and as usual, I was letting my eyes and my mind wander around the stuffy room. It was the usual collection of folks, the few women in the town, and all the men I'd been working with yesterday who had no doubt spent all their wages last night on whiskey and who probably weren't appreciating Reverend Finney's booming voice any more than I was. But then I saw something that made my blood turn cold. A shiny black head, coppery skin—sure enough, it was Little El, sitting on the side of the room with his face a mask of piety. I shifted in my seat, and it took all my will to keep the rancor in my heart from spewing out my mouth, church service or no. Lucky for me, Penny took to fussing right then.

"I'll take her out," I whispered to Maggie, plucking Penny out of her arms and standing before she even had time to respond.

I stopped in the shade of a big oak in the yard, jostling Penny hard enough her little head was nodding some.

"What the hell is he doing here?" I growled. She smiled and buzzed her lips, which made me laugh. I jostled her more gently. "You were tired of the preaching too, eh, my girl? Let's just stay outside." She fingered the top button of my shirt and pulled it toward her mouth as I walked around the circle of shade. But my mind had gone back to Little El. "Why would he be here?" I wondered aloud. "They have plenty of preaching for the Indians at the mission."

I couldn't come up with any answer before the service was over and people were spilling out of the building. I stayed in the shade, watching for Maggie, and I waved to her when I saw her come through the door. She started toward me, but before she had taken two steps, Little El had come over to her and said something.

"Dammit!" I said, loud enough that an older woman passing gave me a startled look. I stalked toward where Maggie stood, with her arms crossed tight, but still listening.

"Hello, McKellar," Little El said. "So there's your baby. She's a fine-looking child."

"What are you doing here?" I didn't care that Reverend Finney was only a few steps away to hear the malice in my voice. Little El gave that smug smile.

"Worshipping, just as you are. Reverend Finney needed someone to help today, so I volunteered. Don't be so suspicious—I'm not here to see you."

"Looks like you came to see my wife," I snapped. "You sure singled her out pretty quick."

"I'm being polite." He smirked. "Which is more than you seem to be capable of." He bowed his head slightly toward Maggie. "Good day, Mrs. McKellar."

I watched him walk away. "What did he say to you?"

She reached up to take Penny. "Nothing much. Asking after our health, such as that. Just what regular folks would say. Nothing that would cause us trouble. Come on." She pulled on my elbow. "Let's head home."

We didn't say any more about him. After dinner, when I should have been keeping the Sabbath, I walked out into the tiny corn patch. It was growing well, but I felt empty as I walked through the rows, brushing my hands against the dark green leaves. What difference did it make whether the crop was a good one? Because it was planted on Brearley's land, I hadn't been able to put out enough to do more than just give us cornmeal for the year. All the work I did was for some other man's benefit or to keep our bellies filled—it was not very often I had extra coins to set aside for buying land. At this rate, I wouldn't be planting corn in my own fields for years to come.

I was still lying awake in the muggy darkness when Penny started bawling for her middle-of-the-night meal. I watched as Maggie nursed her, sitting in that rickety chair with only the moonlight filtering through the crack around the door for light because we couldn't afford to waste a candle. As Maggie got back into bed, I sighed. She turned over to face me.

"You're awake?" she asked, and I figured there was no use denying it. "I'm sorry. It ain't that much longer till I'll wean her off the night nursing and we'll be able to sleep the night through."

"That's all right," I said, rolling over so my back was to her. "That comes with having a young'un, I reckon."

She was silent for a minute, but I could tell she wasn't bedding down to sleep. Sure enough, she laid her hand on my side.

"What's wrong, then? I can tell you ain't happy. You hardly ever smile, or laugh, and you only halfway listen to me of an evening. What's bothering you?" I didn't answer, and her hand slid across my chest as she moved closer. "Are you fretting over that Little El? Don't let him worry you. He didn't say nothing today about putting you in jail. Since we left the land, they're satisfied, I reckon."

I still didn't answer, and after a bit her fingers began to rub softly, right over the spot where the ache inside me was deepest. I turned my face toward her.

"Remember the half-face camp?" I murmured. "Remember that hole in the creek where we'd go swimming? Remember the spot where we were going to put the cabin?"

"I remember."

"If I'd had a chance to clear out some of that brush, we would've had a clear view of the mountains. It was handy to the creek, too, remember? And that hackberry tree was sure a nice one. Remember what good shade it threw in the hot part of the afternoon?"

"John David," she said quietly, 'you can't keep hanging on to it this way. You'll make yourself sick inside."

I flopped onto my back. "I'm already sick inside, Maggie! I know it's wrong to think about it this way. Pa would call it covetousness. But I can't seem to let it go—I can't explain why. There was just something right about it. I knew it that day I went up in the mountains, the day I hurt my ankle. All that night when I was sitting up there in the dark hurting so bad, it still felt right, like I was cradled in a mother's arms—I can't explain it." I threw my hands over my face, and for a minute I was sure I was going to break out squalling, just like Penny.

Penny saved me by letting out a wail right then. Maggie raised her head but didn't let go of me.

"She can't be hungry again," she said. "It ain't been 10 minutes since she finished. She's probably needing to burp."

"Let me get her, then," I said, throwing back the sheet and leaning over Maggie to scoop up Penny. Her little body was tense as I lifted her to my shoulder and got out of bed.

"Got a bad belly, do you?" I crooned to her, gently slapping her back. "Mama eat something that don't agree with you? I bet it was the turnip greens."

"They looked too good to pass up," Maggie said. "Watch out—"

Penny let loose a burp before the words were even out of Maggie's mouth, and a little wad of puke flew onto my bare shoulder. I flinched and yelped, which set Penny off on a whole new round of wailing. Maggie laughed and got out of bed to wipe my shoulder with a rag from the table. She watched as I swayed Penny side to side, humming some song I remembered from long ago. After a while, Penny quit her crying and I felt her go limp. Still humming, I laid her back in the bed.

"Look at her," Maggie said, laying her hand on Penny's head. "Ain't she just the most perfect thing?"

"She is."

She slipped her arm around my back. "After I lost our first baby, I thought I'd never feel right again," she said softly. "I'd thought about him and dreamed about him all the way up the river, and even though I'd never even felt him move, he was as real to me as you are. I thought I'd never be able to love another child the way I loved him. But I reckon I couldn't love anything more than this little girl here." I didn't say anything, and she wrapped her other arm around me. "You can come to love another place, John David."

She laid her head against my chest, and her hair was soft, just like Penny's had been on my shoulder. Maggie and Penny—that was the heart of my life, and they deserved more than a man turned bitter and hard with disappointment. I bent to kiss the top of Maggie's head.

"I can try, anyhow," I promised her, and I meant to keep it.

❧ ❧ ❧

When next I went to pay the rent on the cabin, Pearson Brearley asked if I'd be willing to take on a job digging a pair of graves. It was late July by then, hot but so humid sweat wouldn't dry, and the building business was slow, so I agreed. I was a little surprised to see Thomas Mallory show up at the grave site; I hadn't seen him since we'd finished clearing the land in the spring, and I'd figured he'd moved on.

"McKellar!" he called. "So both our men lost and that Yankee rascal Adams bartered his way into the White House!"

"I reckon your man Clay benefited from it, though," I said, and he laughed.

"He did, at that."

Besides the two of us, Brearley had hired Nathan Shaver for the job, so we could spell each other and take turns resting in the shade. It was slow work, for the ground was hard and dry. Even though we started digging at first light, we'd all shed our shirts before the sun was very high into the sky.

"Ought to be a rule," I grunted as I stabbed at the ground, "nobody can die in summer. Folks can only die when the ground is soft and the weather is fine."

"Who we digging for, anyhow?" asked Shaver, a young feller with a pocked-up face.

"A feller named Eastman and one of his young'uns, was what I heard," Mallory said. "I heard they died of the intermittent fever."

"What's that?" I asked. Shaver stopped digging to stare at me.

"You ain't heard of intermittent fever? Settler's fever? How long you been in Arkansas Territory? Seems like everybody around here gets it."

"It's fever and ague that comes and goes," Mallory said. "They say it's caused by bad air, like from the rot in swampy places. We never had such as that back in Kentucky, and I'd wager you didn't have it in your Tennessee mountains, either."

"Doesn't sound like anything I ever heard of," I said. "You say everybody here gets it?"

"Sooner or later," Shaver said. "Some suffer with it for a while and then go back to normal. But some die. Plenty die. Like these ones."

"I heard he left a widow and some more young'uns, and they're sick with it, too," Mallory said.

We were all quiet for a moment, pondering the fate of this unknown family, wondering if there would be a job to dig more graves before long. The hair on my arms raised, even in the heat, and I felt a cold fear creeping toward my heart—

"Damn mosquitoes!" I said loudly, slapping at the high-pitched whine near my ear. "I don't see how they think they've got any place left to bite on me."

"They'll just go to putting bites on top of bites if you run out of fresh skin," Shaver said. "God, I hate them pests."

"You can't hate them as much as my wife does." I laughed. "If Maggie hears one of them in the cabin, she'll run around with a dishrag, trying to swat it out of the air."

"Lot of good that does," Mallory said. "You kill one, three more come back in its place."

I grinned at him. "I tell her that, but she's a stubborn little mule. She wears herself out chasing after them. She nagged me into making a cradle so she can throw a dishrag over it and keep them off the baby. I told her she's likely to suffocate the child, but she won't listen. I reckon I don't care, though, as long as one don't bite Penny and set her to crying again."

They laughed. Mallory laid back on the crispy grass, shading his eyes with one arm.

"That's another thing didn't worry us back in Kentucky, moskitters. It's all this swampy land. Lordy, I wish I could get myself back to some higher ground, away from this nasty river."

"The high ground is north of the river," I said, more bitterly than I meant to. "The Indians get it, while white folk are stuck with the swamps."

"The high ground ain't all for the Indians," Shaver said. "There's some of the land ain't been decided about yet. West of here—Lovely's Purchase."

Mallory sat up, and I quit digging. We both stared at Shaver. His face, already red from the heat, flushed even darker.

"I ain't lying!" he said. "I heard folks talking about it when I was on the boat coming from Little Rock. The government ain't never surveyed the Cherokee land, so nobody's real sure what the western border is. There's this section of land called Lovely's Purchase that some say goes to the Indians and some say is outside of what they was promised. Won't nobody know until the government does its survey."

"Still, if there's any chance at all it's Indian land, they'll get the Army to throw white folk off," I said. Mallory shook his head.

"Maybe not, McKellar. The Yankee government may want to coddle the Indians, but I bet our territorial government sees it all different. They got the interest of the white folks at heart—after all, we're the ones who vote for 'em, not the Indians. Could be they might be willing to give some hefty consideration to the desires of the citizens of the territory."

"I heard some white folks was already moving into Lovely's Purchase," Shaver said. Mallory hopped to his knees.

"Of course! That's how we do it! We take it! If there's enough white folks living on that land, the government ain't going to give it to the Indians. They wouldn't want to risk making their citizens mad. That's what folks got to do—go claim it before it's for sure given to the Indians!"

"Settle down, Mallory," I said. "You'll bust something in your head in this heat."

Mallory swiped one of our shirts over his sweaty forehead. "By God, I'm going to do it! Soon as I can get some means together, I'm going to take the family and we'll stake a claim in Lovely's Purchase! Why let the filthy savages have all the best of the country? Why let them waste the land? I'll put down a good farm and show the government what a real citizen can do with the Territory!" He suddenly leaned toward me. "How about you, McKellar? Bring your wife and baby and come with us! You said you want some place north of the river, in the high ground—this is your chance! The more white folks we get on the land, the harder it will be to give it to the Indians."

"I don't know," I said. "I've hauled Maggie around so many places already in the little time we've been married. I don't know how I'd tell her I'm rooting her up to go someplace else, especially if there's any chance of us getting tossed off again, when she's so contented here."

Mallory snorted. "Contented? What's it matter if a woman's contented?"

"If his woman ain't contented, a feller may find he ain't all that content, especially come nighttime," Shaver said with a grin. Mallory smirked.

"I still say, what's it matter? She's his wife, ain't she? A man takes what he wants." His eyes were hot and bright. "Your wife will get over her discontent if you say for her to. You just have to take a firm stand with her. You got the backbone to do that and get what you want, McKellar? Or is it like them other fellers said about you, back in the winter?"

Shaver suddenly slapped my bare back with a sharp smack. He held up his palm to show me a bloody spot the size of a thumbnail with a dead mosquito in the center.

"Got that one!" he said. "That's one less you have to worry about, McKellar!"

"I appreciate it, Shaver." I pushed the handle of the shovel toward Mallory. "Take a turn. I need some water."

"Think about it," he said, jumping into the grave as I hoisted myself out. "It's our best chance to get that land we want. Just promise me you'll think about it."

I glanced down at him. "All right. I'll think about it."

"We'll talk about it!" he called after me as I started toward the river. "Soon!"

❦ ❦ ❦

A week later I came home from helping split out fence rails feeling chilled, even though the evening air was still hot. By bedtime, Maggie said she was sure I had fever. All that night I went back and forth between shaking with chills and beading up with sweat. In the morning, though, the fever seemed to be gone, and I went on to work, though I felt nearly too weak to even lift an ax. In another three days, the fever was back, and I huddled by the fire wrapped in a quilt, despite the hot sunshine outside. Maggie rolled up her sleeves and fanned herself to stir some breeze in the close air of the cabin.

"Reckon you went back to work too soon?" she asked. "Maybe you needed more time to rest after that other bout of fever."

"That's not it," I said as best I could through my chattering teeth. "I bet I've got the intermittent fever." She frowned, and I could see she'd never heard of it. "Settler's fever. They say most folks who settle here get it."

"How long till it's over with?" she asked.

"I don't know." She pulled the quilt higher around my shoulders.

"Well, it can't be that long. Ma used to use snakeroot for fever. I'll see if I can find some and brew a tea for you, and you'll be over it before—" I grabbed her hand.

"Maggie—some folks don't get over it."

"What do you mean, they don't get over it?" Her eyes widened. "They—die?"

I nodded and dropped her hand. "That grave-digging job I had a while back—that was for a couple of folks who died from intermittent fever." She stared at me. "I'm not trying to scare you, but you ought to know what we might be up against."

She didn't say anything or move, and it wasn't until Penny made a sudden squall from under the dishrag on the cradle that Maggie seemed to shake back to herself. She didn't go to Penny, though. She pulled me out of the chair and back to the bed. I lay back, easing my aching head into the softness of my Ma's limp feather pillow, brought all this way from Campbell County. Maggie laid the quilt over me, and then she sat on the edge of the bed a minute, stroking my hair. Much as I normally liked for her to do that, even the softest of her touches seemed to make my brain rattle inside my skull.

"You'll get better," she whispered. "I won't let you get worse."

I closed my eyes. "Tend to Penny, will you? That squalling is making my head hurt."

She took Penny and went looking for snakeroot. Whether the tisane helped or not, the fever left me the next day. But within three more days, it was back, and worse. I didn't even try to get out of bed. Time seemed to be locked in a haze of chills that shook the bed beneath me and hot spells when I wished I could lie naked in the cool water of the creek back at our half-face camp. Sometimes I was aware of Maggie's face above me, with that worry mark between her brows, but sometimes it was Ma who leaned over me. Sometimes I thought I saw Thomas Mallory and Nathan Shaver, waving their arms and shovels at a cloud of mosquitos. Once I opened my eyes to see a shadowy form with the likeness of Little El standing by the fireplace with flames leaping around him.

"It's the devil," I muttered. "He's tormenting me—"

A face appeared, close, with a thick beard and a flattened nose. "He's talking crazy," its mouth said. "He's deranged. We need to draw off this fever quick as we can."

There was a rush of cold as the quilts were thrown back, and then a searing heat in the bend of my arm. I bellowed like a wounded bull and thrashed, trying to get away from it, but strong hands, a man's hands and Maggie's small hands, held my arm pinned to the bed while tiny, sharp teeth stabbed into it. I twisted my head to look up into Maggie's face. Her eyes were swimming with tears and she was biting her lip. She tried to smile at me but did a mighty lousy job of it.

"I brought a doctor," she said softly. "He's bleeding you to bring down the fever. Just lay still now."

I felt too weak to move once the hands let me go, and Maggie held a cloth against the hurt on my arm, bending to kiss me and leaving the splash of a tear on my chin. She pulled the covers over me and moved away, and then men's voices—or was it only the one?—mumbled again. Penny was squalling again. The cabin door scraped open on the floor—I'd been meaning to shave a little off of it so it would swing free—and then the only sound left was Penny's crying. Maggie came back to check on me. I was just able to snatch her skirt with my hand as she turned to leave.

"Don't let him do that no more," I begged her. "Please. Don't let him do that."

She made a choked kind of sound before she took my hand from her skirt and pushed it back under the quilts. I saw her go to the cradle for Penny and then sit in the crooked chair to nurse her, rocking it awkwardly back and forth. Every now and then I thought I heard a sob mingled with Penny's eager smacking.

"Don't let him come back," I begged again, but far as I could tell, she paid me no mind.

❧ ❧ ❧

Like clockwork, I was laid up with fever and ague every third day. The doctor came back twice more with his little sharp-toothed wheel, but though he drained nearly a noggin of my blood each time, I was no better. Finally, he came on a day when I was well enough myself to pay his fee and tell him his services weren't needed.

"Why did you do that?" Maggie fumed once the doctor left. "He said bleeding is proved to draw off the bad humors in the body and set you right. There's no other doctor around to do it."

"Thank God." I tucked the money bag, now limp, back under the hay mattress. "All I can tell is being set right by that bleeding is his pocket. Both me and the money bag would be completely flat if he kept coming."

"You'd rather be sick—or die, even—than spend money?"

My laugh was thin. "I'm Pa's son, I reckon. If it cost a shilling for a ride across the Jordan into heaven, he'd swim." She didn't smile.

"I don't know remedies for something like this. What will I do?"

I laid back on the bed, slowly. "I don't know. But my head's starting to hurt, so I'm guessing another spell's on its way. Just mix another tisane of some kind."

Once the fever had hold of me, I didn't know what she was doing. I heard her voice, praying, shushing Penny, talking and being answered by a man. Had she gone against my wishes and called the doctor back? I opened my hot eyes and saw a man in the doorway, but the daylight was too bright and I couldn't tell who he was, only that he was too thin to be the fat-bellied doctor. With a sigh of relief, I closed my eyes again and sank back into what passed for sleep.

Some time later, Maggie was gently shaking my shoulder. The cabin was dark.

"Drink this." She helped me raise my shoulders and held a cup to my lips. The liquid was lukewarm and bitter. I turned my head, but she moved the cup back to my mouth. "It's a tisane, like you asked for, from dogwood bark. Here, drink it all, that's a good fellow."

Dogwood bark? How had she come up with that idea? But I was weary of being sick all the time, and ashamed that she had to tend me like a child. Bitter it might be, and useless, but I drank it all.

Chapter 9

Maggie seemed as surprised as I was when my fever came down within hours of that first cup of the dogwood tisane, days sooner than it usually did. I felt enough better to sit up and play a little with Penny to keep her happy while Maggie did the washing and brewed another batch of the tisane. She gave me a dose every few hours until the fever had gone completely. Even better, the third day after passed without fever, and then another three days, and we figured I'd survived this bout with the settler's fever.

"You look good, but you look awful," Maggie said one morning when I'd been without fever for more than a week. "I never saw anybody so thin and hollow-eyed, about like a scarecrow."

"How do you like that, eh, Penny?" I joked. "Your ma married a scarecrow, with hay for brains. Look, my skin's even a little yellow, like straw." I set her down and stretched my stiff shoulders. "This scarecrow better get out to the corn patch. If it's September already, the corn's probably ready to harvest."

It took me two days to pull the corn from our small patch, a job I should have finished in a morning. I tired quickly, and each time I had to stop to rest, it seemed to take me longer to gain strength to go back out to the work.

"That's normal," Maggie said as I fretted about it. "You were sick a long while. Of course you'll need some time to rest before you can be back to yourself again."

"I don't have time. The rent's due in a few more days. Paying that doctor took all we had saved."

"I can help. Let me take in washing to do. There's plenty of single men in this territory that could use someone to do their washing."

"You can't do that." I put up my hand to shush her protests. "You've got Penny to tend to, and that's plenty. Besides, I don't want you doing it. It's a man's place to provide for his family. " I sighed. "I reckon I'll go into Dardanelle tomorrow and see what work I can find."

What work was there, though, that a man could do when his arms had no more strength than willow twigs and his breath grew short just from the walk into town? I ended up back at Brearley's store before the morning was out, dreading the words I'd have to say to him. Lucky for me, all the other men around were off working, and I could say my words in private.

"I can't pay the rent this month." I forced myself to look him in the face. "It may be some time before I can pay you. I'm sorry to do this, but I'm asking if you can extend us credit till I have the money."

The only consolation I had was that Brearley didn't agree right off, like I was so pitiful he couldn't turn me away. He studied me for a minute, and then went back to sorting envelopes.

"Credit's bad business, you know," he said.

"I know."

"I never see any money back in my hand again most times when I extend credit." I didn't say anything, and he kept sorting those envelopes. I waited a moment, but only a moment. I wouldn't beg him. As I turned away from the counter, he put down the letters and looked at me.

"My corn needs to be pulled. The big field, down closer to the river. I would take your labor of harvesting it as your rent this month and the next."

I knew what he was doing, and a big lump gathered in my throat.

"I might be slow getting it done," I said.

He laughed. "You've got two months. As long as it's dry in my barn by the end of October, I don't care when you pull it."

"All right, I'll do it." I held out my hand. He shook it, and I tried hard to have a firm grip. "I thank you, Brearley."

He grunted and went back to his letters. As I reached the door, though, he called out to me.

"Here's a letter for you, McKellar."

❦ ❦ ❦

I knew I probably should take the letter home to open it and read it for the first time with Maggie, but instead, I stopped under the shade of an elm between the store and our cabin and broke open the seal. It was from Zeke, and seeing his heavy, dark scrawl made me homesick for the first time since we'd left Campbell County.

Dear John David,

We are all well and hope this letter will find you and Maggie the same. We pray that all went well with the birth of your child, and that you will write soon to assure us it is a healthy child, and as Hannah says, to tell whether she has a girl cousin or a boy cousin.

I suppose you are well into raising a crop, as we read in the papers that the government reached an agreement with the Choctaw tribe concerning the lands south of the Arkansas River. The story we saw in the paper, though, was only a short item, so I would be interested in hearing more about this agreement and about the land and especially about the plot you are settled on. There is little news about Arkansas Territory here, and it seems sometimes you have gone to a place as foreign and far away as any on the earth.

As for our news here, Sarah and I are also parents of a new child, another girl, which makes Hannah all the more eager that your baby should be a boy, even though she will probably never see this cousin. The baby is named Abigail, for the wise and beautiful wife of King David, and she was born November last.

I sent this next news in my first letter, but if it was lost, you wouldn't have heard. Matthew married Bess Clardy about a year ago and they have a child, yet another McKellar girl. Bessie, they call her, and she has her mother's red hair as well as her name. Three babies to talk about in one letter—I think we McKellars are obeying well the Lord's command to "be fruitful and multiply." Everyone thought it was funny that you and Maggie hadn't been gone for a week before Bess turned serious about letting Matt court her. Trisha says it's because Bess didn't want to let her last chance at marrying a McKellar get away. But they are truly happy together and prospering. Pa gave them a strip of land on the section that borders the Clardys' place, so they farm on both sides of the boundary.

I passed your letters around the family and everyone is pleased to hear you are well and getting settled in Arkansas Territory. We all send our love. Sarah prays for you with our girls every night. Please send us word when your child comes so Hannah will know if she got her boy cousin. Take care of yourselves.

Respectfully, your brother,

Zeke McKellar

I sat against the tree on the dusty ground and stared without seeing down the path toward our rented cabin, the one I would be paying for by harvesting another man's corn. Matt was living with Bess on Pa's land that bordered the Clardy farm, a strip of land Pa had given him as a wedding gift. I knew the place. It was a fine piece of land, edging Stinking Creek, with wide, flat fields—not such big fields, but plenty big enough. I could see him, walking across those tame bottomland fields I had helped clear some time ago. His corn crop would be in the crib of a new barn by now. No doubt he had traded work with Pa and Paul at harvest time, and now they would spend the afternoons at one another's barns, stripping away the husks and shelling the kernels. A hot worm of jealousy tunneled through my chest as I pictured Matt's life, days of hard but satisfying work that was prospering, followed by evenings when Bess laid out supper with smoked ham and roasted sweet potatoes—

I shook my head, hard. What did I care what Matthew had? At least I was making my own way, in my own country, not depending on Pa for the ground under my feet or for even an extra pair of hands to shell my corn. It was better that way, better by far. And Matt was stuck now with Bess and her pretty little mouth that went from smiling to pouting within the space of a blink.

I heard Maggie singing as I came into the yard of the cabin, and I found her around back, spreading ashes over the bare patch of ground that had been our garden. She stopped and turned toward me when I called to her.

"The rent's covered," I told her. "I'm going to harvest Brearley's corn crop."

"Good," she said, wiping her forehead with the back of her hand. I showed her the letter.

"It's from Zeke."

Her eyes brightened. "Did he say anything about whether your Pa would help--"

"No."

She was quiet a minute, looking down at the bucket of ashes in her hand. She was disappointed. That bitter worm tunneled a little deeper into me. My folks would accept Bess Clardy as one of their own. They'd give her a section of Pa's farm to build a cabin and raise her babies. But during the whole time Maggie had been under their roof, she never got anything from them but hard looks and hateful words. They never saw anything in her but a coarse backwoods girl, not fit for a McKellar—not like pretty, well-bred Bess.

She turned back to the garden and started again to slowly sift the ashes from the bucket onto the ground.

"What's the other news?" she asked.

I took the bucket from her and set it off to the side before I took her into my arms. With a shuddering sigh, she leaned her face into my chest.

"We'll manage without them," I said. "Who needs them? We'll manage fine."

⚹ ⚹ ⚹

My strength came back slowly but steadily. Within a fortnight, I was able to work a full day in Brearley's corn patch, and I could see the end of the job was possible quickly. But he'd given me till the end of the month to finish, and we needed cash to buy supplies for the coming winter, and there was good work to be had elsewhere in Dardanelle. The fall rains raised the river, which brought back the boats, so I hired myself out to help load and unload boats again, pulling Brearley's corn on the days when there was a lull in the river traffic.

On one of my days at the wharf, I looked up to see Thomas Mallory walking along the road with a couple of men I didn't know. I raised a hand to wave, just to be friendly, but as I was hoisting another bale of hides to my shoulder for carrying to the boat, they stopped me.

"McKellar!" Mallory said. "It's been a long time since I've seen you. Word was, you were down with settler's fever. I didn't know whether you had made it through."

"I didn't know it myself for a while there."

"They say if a feller lives two months, he's off death's doorstep. But you've got to make it two years, they say, before you're really in the

95

clear. I'm glad to see you're able to be back working." He put a hand on my shoulder. "I know it's not the work, though, that you'd like to be doing."

I shrugged. "It's the work I have."

Mallory grinned. "We may be able to change that. It was good luck we saw you here this morning. Meet Aaron Fuller and Levi Webster."

I shook their hands, wondering what they had to do with good luck.

"We're getting together a group of folks to go to Lovely's Purchase," Mallory said.

"You're still thinking about that?" I asked. Mallory frowned.

"It ain't just thinking this time, McKellar. We're putting together a party and planning to leave in another week or two. The way we see it, if there's a solid front of white folks on the land, building cabins and raising crops, it's harder for the government to give the land to the damn Indians."

"We figure the government's going to see the right soon enough and open the area to legal settlement," Webster added. "There's already been some talk about it in the Gazette."

"It's nearly November," I said. "That seems late in the year for starting out someplace new with no cabin ready for winter."

"There's the best thing!" Mallory said. "We're taking a group of men, not just individual settlers. We're going to work together to put up a cabin for every family quick as we can. Then each man can spend the winter months clearing his own fields so he's ready to put in a crop come spring."

"That's a smart plan," I admitted.

"Come with us." Mallory was gripping my shoulder tight. "We need as many men as we can get to put our foothold on the area, and I know you to be a good, hard-working man."

"We could use every man we can get to come with us," Fuller said.

"I don't know—"

"What's the holdup, McKellar?" Mallory said impatiently. "You still worried about what your wife will say about another move? That's the stupidest damn excuse I ever heard. What's holding you here? You ain't got your own place. Every time I see you, you're working a different job for whatever wages you can get just to put food in your mouth. I'm beginning to wonder if you really have what it takes to claim a stake of land in this country, or if you're all talk. Do you have what it takes to get what you want, or are you looking for an easy path to lay out in front of you?" He smirked. "What are you made of, McKellar?"

I shook his hand off my shoulder. "I've got to get back to work, or I'll lose this job and won't have anything to put in my mouth tonight."

He called after me as I turned back to the boat.

"Think about it! We're planning to leave in another two weeks. If you decide you're man enough for it, you can find me on the east side of Dardanelle. Think about it, McKellar."

"All right, I'll think about it!" I waved him away. "Goodbye, Mallory!"

❧ ❧ ❧

That job didn't last more than a half-day, and as he handed me the few coins that were my wages, the wharf man told me these coins would be some of the last I'd see from him.

"Winter's around the corner," he said. "There won't be enough traffic for me to need more men once the fall season is over. I can handle winter traffic with just my boys. I wanted you to know so you could find something else."

My head was hanging low as I trudged down the path toward home. Winter's around the corner. Another winter in Arkansas Territory, in someone else's cabin and rent to pay. Winter, with only scattered odd jobs to pay that rent and keep food in the stew pot. Two winters in Arkansas Territory, and still no progress toward buying land of my own.

Maggie was laughing inside the cabin as I came close, and I wondered what Penny was doing now to amuse her ma. It cheered me a little, thinking of Penny's round, pink face and her little smile that Maggie swore was a copy in miniature of my own. I pushed the door open and stepped inside, squinting to try to see better in the dim light of the cabin. A man was sitting on the chair, holding a giggling Penny in the air above him—a man with shiny hair black as hell—

"Put her down!" I bellowed, and they all stared at me—Penny, Maggie, and Little El. For a minute, everything was still, like we were all frozen, and then it was like everything happened at once. Penny started squalling, Little El stood to lay her on the bed, I rushed toward him saying I don't even know what, Maggie was grabbing at my arm. I shook her off, harder than ever I would have done if I'd been in my right mind, and she stumbled and hit against the wall. I didn't even look at her. My whole being was taken over by a fever worse than anything I'd had in the past months, and I raised an arm to strike Little El's black head from his shoulders.

He grabbed my arm, though, and quickly twisted it behind me, snatching the other one too and pinning them both against my back.

"You'll have to be faster than that if you are going to attack a Cherokee warrior," he taunted.

"Some warrior!" I said, struggling to free myself. "More like a Cherokee snake, wiggling your way into a man's garden so you can sneak an apple off his tree!" I gave a mighty jerk, but his grip on my arms tightened.

"I came to see if you were still sick, you fool." He suddenly let go of me, and I stumbled a little without the support. "Maggie says you're over your fever."

"Don't talk about her like she's your friend," I growled. "She's my wife."

"And you treat her like she's your dog."

I glanced at her, standing against the wall with her arms wrapped tight around herself, her eyes wide and her lips pressed together tightly. I felt I might choke on the lump that was suddenly in my throat. Instead, I turned back to glare at Little El.

"Why are you coming around, huh? We don't have anything to do with you, no reason for you to be here. You got the damn land. Can't you be happy with that? Why do you have to keep showing up around us? You think you'll get something else?" I stepped around him and picked up Penny from the bed and held her close to my shoulder, rocking her a little to soothe her squalling. It didn't help.

"Leave," I told him, "and don't come back. Just leave us alone."

He gave a quick glance to Maggie but left without a word. Except for Penny's squalling, the silence in the cabin seemed like the heaviness in the air before a bad thunderstorm. I couldn't look at Maggie as she came and took Penny from me.

"I didn't aim to hurt you," I said.

"Why did you have to do that?" Her voice was low and angry, like the first rumbles of a storm's thunder. "Why did you have to act like such a jackass?" I did look at her then, and she looked straight back at me with her jaw squared in a way I hadn't seen since she told off her pa when we first married. She wanted a fight, did she?

"What was he doing here, inside our home?" I spat back at her. "What were you thinking, letting that dirty Indian touch our daughter?" She made a huffing sound, which just made me madder. "Sure was a cozy little domestic scene until your husband walked in."

Her hand rose like she meant to slap me. But she clenched it into a trembling fist instead and lowered it back to her side.

"He was doing what any white man, any neighbor, would do! He came to see whether you were well yet! But you treat him that way after he was so much help to me—a blessing from God, really—all the time you were sick."

My blood suddenly felt cold. "What are you talking about? He's been here before?"

"Good Lord, John David!" Her voice rose over Penny's bawling. "Does it really matter? When you first got sick and said you had that intermittent fever, I took Penny to go ask Mr. Brearley about getting a doctor for you. Elwin was in the store, and he volunteered to fetch the doctor so I wouldn't have to carry Penny all that way. Then you told the doctor not to come back, and I didn't know what I was going to do—"

"Brearley would've helped you—any of the white men around would've helped. You didn't have to go looking for that Indian—"

"I didn't go looking for him! He came here!"

"And you let him in?"

She didn't answer right away. Penny's crying had calmed into broken sobs, and Maggie hugged her close, whispering something into her hair until Penny was quiet again. Maggie moved away to set her in the cradle with a soft pat, and then came back to me, standing close. She kept her voice quiet.

"You have to understand how scared I was. You weren't getting any better. You made it so I couldn't call the doctor back. I didn't know what to do except pray. So I did. Within the hour, Elwin was here, and I figured that was God's answer to my prayers."

I rolled my eyes, and she grabbed my arm, tight.

"Elwin's the one who told me about the dogwood tisane his people use for fever. He went and got the dried bark, and he showed me how to brew the tisane. The reason you're standing here on your feet today is because of Elwin's help. But all you can think is that he wanted to bed your wife." She paused, and when I looked down, her eyes had a mournful look. "And that I'd be willing to let him."

"I didn't say that," I mumbled, sinking down to sit on the bed.

"But you thought it. I saw it in your face." She laid both her hands on my shoulders, and her eyes looked into mine. "You don't ever need to worry about that, John David. I'll never be unfaithful to you. I could never have the kind of feelings I have for you for any other man. You're my husband. You're Penny's father. That's something no other man will ever be. I love you—only you."

"I know," I said, and I kissed her back when she leaned in, but I wondered if she could really be so sure of it. A man who couldn't give her the home he'd promised her—a man who was barely bringing in enough income to keep food on the table—how long before a woman would be discontented? How long before she would look up some day and find a different set of eyes held more promise? He might be Indian, but Little El was clever, and it sounded like he'd been mighty sympathetic while I was burning with the fever. He'd brought relief of her worries and taught her something new to ward off future worries. It was clear enough that she thought of him in a friendly way. She might never intend it, but who could say she would never come to feel more than friendly toward him? If he gave her the opportunity by visiting, who could say she wouldn't prefer the sympathetic stranger, even if he was an Indian, to her failure of a husband?

She had gone over to stir our dinner over the fire.

"Maggie," I called, "I've been meaning to tell you. I've been talking to Thomas Mallory lately. We're all going to move to Lovely's Purchase and take up a claim."

Chapter 10

I went looking for Thomas Mallory the next morning. He and Fuller were cutting firewood in a small patch of trees on the east side of Dardanelle, and they seemed happy enough to take a break to talk to me about Lovely's Purchase.

"I've decided Maggie and I will go with you," I told him as he mopped his forehead with a rag. "When do we leave?"

He laughed. "When you decide something, you're all for doing it quick, eh, McKellar? Well, just slow down. We're sending a party of men ahead first to get things ready for our families. No use making the women and children camp during the winter. We'll build cabins this winter and come back for our families in the spring before planting time."

It made sense, but I was none too happy about the thought of leaving Maggie behind here in Dardanelle, with Little El sauntering around, coming and going as he pleased. All day, as I lifted boxes and bales at the wharf, I pondered what I should do. As I trudged home in the setting sun, I figured I had come up with the best solution, though I didn't like it much.

Maggie didn't speak when I came through the door. Her whole body looked stiff as she went about laying out supper for me. She didn't put anything out for herself, and a swift pang stabbed into my heart. Usually, she waited to eat her own supper with me, and we would sit together to talk. Tonight, she kept her back to me as she washed dishes in silence.

"This tastes good," I said. She threw a look at me over her shoulder. "It's only cornpone."

I tried again. "Guess what we were loading onto the boats today?"

She didn't answer, just banged the lid of the dutch oven down into the basin. I gave it up as a bad effort.

"I saw Thomas Mallory this morning," I told her. "We're sending a crew of men ahead in a couple of weeks to build cabins and get things ready for everyone to remove to Lovely's Purchase come spring. I reckon I'll be going with them to do the building." She did turn around then, with her forehead creased and her lips trembling, the very picture of misery. I went on. "To keep you from being here alone, I'm going to take you back to Dwight Mission for the winter. They'll let you and Penny stay."

"I don't want to go to the mission." Her voice was thick with tears.

"You can't take care of yourself, especially not with a baby."

"I can—"

"You can't! Cutting firewood? Getting meat for the table? That's a man's work, Maggie."

"Colonel Brearley would keep me in firewood—"

"He won't be around. He's the agent for the Creek Indians now."

"His son, then—what's his name? Joseph?"

I snorted. "Joseph Brearley won't remember to keep your firewood stocked. He's a boy."

"He's about the same age as you! He's as responsible as you are! More, maybe!"

"Listen," I said, pushing my bowl away hard enough that a little stew slopped on the table. "I can't pay rent to keep you here while I'm gone. You're going to the mission, and that's the end of it."

She stood with her hands on her hips, looking at me with her chin quivering a little. I could hardly bear the weight of her eyes on me, but I made myself look right back at her.

"Why are you doing this, John David? Why upset everything in our life just because you're jealous, and for no good reason—"

"We're not going through this again," I warned her, and I heard something of my pa's voice in my own. "I'm the head of this household."

She stared at me for a minute longer.

"Well, that's the way of marriage, I reckon," she said, her voice bitter and hard. "If the man wants it, the woman has to do it, even if it don't make any sense at all. A woman's pretty much stuck with whatever her man decides, even if he's a durn fool."

I didn't answer back to that, and after a minute, she turned away and I could hear her sniffling as she washed up the dishes. She'll get over it, I told myself as I finished the stew, though I had no appetite for it. She'll come to see it's for the best.

❧ ❧ ❧

She wasn't over it by the time I took her and Penny to the mission. I was glad it was Reverend Finney who came out to meet us; I had dreaded seeing the look on Reverend Washburn's face as I asked yet another favor of them. Reverend Finney agreed Maggie could stay and that she could help in the kitchen as she had done before. She would have to share a cabin this time, though, with another woman and her children. Maggie took the news without a word, but I noticed a tightening of her jaw that said plenty.

We unloaded our goods into the cabin with the help of the woman and her oldest son, who looked to be around eight. I hadn't thought anyone in the Territory could be poorer than me and Maggie, but this woman eyed our dishes with pleasure, and she was trying out our crooked chair as Maggie followed me to the door to say goodbye.

I took Penny in my arms and tweaked her little nose between my fingertips.

"You be good for your ma." She smiled and grabbed for my nose. I laughed as I peeled her hand away. "You're Pa's girl. Don't forget that while I'm gone."

"How long do you reckon that will be?" Maggie asked.

"I'll be back by spring, and then we'll leave for our own place. Keep that in your mind while I'm gone—when I come back, we'll have our own cabin on our own farm." I put my free arm around her, but she held herself stiff against me. I was getting used to that, though, and I didn't want to part on bad terms. I lowered my voice, for her ears only. "You know what time this is, don't you?" She looked up at me, and I smiled, even though she didn't. "It was two years ago this month I brought you off Pine Mountain as my wife. Remember?"

"Of course."

"I know it's not been an easy two years, but things are finally taking a better turn. We'll finally be settled in a home."

103

"It's still Indian land. We can't finally be settled in a home on Indian land."

She was a damn stubborn woman. But I pushed down the urge to snap back and instead handed Penny to her.

"I'll see you come March." I pulled her body close to mine and bent to kiss her frowning mouth. "Don't forget you're my girl, too."

She pulled away from me with an angry little huff. "I won't!"

"I didn't mean it that way, I just—" Suddenly I was tired of trying. "Never mind. I'll see you come spring."

⁂ ⁂ ⁂

We had already turned the cabin back to Brearley, so I spent the night camped by the river with several of the other men who were going to Lovely's Purchase. The evening air had the first chill of the fall to come, and I sat near the fire, watching the orange and yellow of the flames as they curled around the logs. On the other side of the fire, three men were playing cards and drinking whiskey, cursing or hooting for joy, depending on the hand a player laid on the ground. Already I missed the quiet sounds of an evening at home—Maggie's voice, barely louder than the crackle of the fire, singing some old lullaby to Penny, set to the soft, steady thump of the chair's short leg hitting the floor. I closed my eyes as a wave nearly like a physical pain rose from my chest.

"About to go to sleep, McKellar?" One of the men from the card game nudged my thigh with his foot. "It's early yet. Want Dickson to deal you into the game?"

"No," I said. "I always lose at cards."

"All the more reason we want you in the game," he said, and I joined all of them in a hearty laugh.

"I've got a letter to write," I told him. "I need to get it done tonight so I can post it before we leave Dardanelle."

"Yep," he agreed, "there's no post office where we're going."

I walked back into town to Brearley's store and after I'd bought a quill and a sheet of paper, Joseph gave me the use of the ink pot for free. I sat at the end of the bar counter to write.

Dear Zeke,

It is good to hear that you are all well and prospering. Maggie was pleased with the news about your new daughter. Hannah will have to get her boy cousin another time, for our child was also a girl, Penelope. We call her Penny, and she is as fine a child as ever I saw. She is beginning to raise on her hands and knees, and Maggie says she soon will be crawling. I suppose I will miss that—

I paused to dip the quill into the ink pot as that homesick feeling swelled in my throat again.

"Can I get a shot?" I called to Joseph, and he brought me a half-glass.

"Must be a bad letter if you want whiskey to help finish it," he said, in a voice that said he was fishing for news.

"You're reading me wrong, Joseph!" I said, with a laugh. "I'm telling my folks the good news about Lovely's Purchase. The whiskey?" I beckoned with my finger, and he leaned closer. "This is the taste of freedom. I can have a shot, or two even, and I don't have to listen to my wife nag about the smell on my breath tonight." I laughed again, and he laughed too, though he looked a little surprised. He moved away down the bar, and I turned back to my letter.

I will be gone for the next few months to set up a claim for us in a parcel of land known as Lovely's Purchase. It is in the western portion of the Territory, beyond the lands allotted to the Cherokees, although they claim the Purchase is part of that allotment. There has been no survey to determine their western border, however, so I am part of a group of men going to establish a white foothold in the area. Our thought is that the government will have a harder time giving the land to the Indians if enough voting citizens are already living there.

I pondered for a minute as I sipped the whiskey.

I am proud to be part of the movement to open new country to settlement for the citizens of the United States. I'll be raising corn in land that has never been farmed before. Come spring, Maggie and Penny will join me there, and we'll be a part of bringing civilized life to a new part of the Territory. If you ask me, that's worth the sacrifice of a few months away from my family.

I could think of nothing more to add. I ended with the usual hopes for good health for them all, and then left the letter and a coin for postage with Joseph before heading back to the camp by the river.

The card game was still going, but I took my bedroll and stretched out on the ground a few paces away.

I wasn't sleepy, though, so I lay on my back looking into the great blackness of the sky. My eyes were drawn toward the bright comet that had appeared in the sky late in August. Maggie and I had watched together every night as it grew brighter, with a longer tail—until, of course, I told her we were going to Lovely's Purchase. Maggie didn't like it.

"It's an omen," she had insisted. "Something bad's about to happen."

I'd laughed at her back then, but staring up at the unnatural sight on this night, lying on the ground alone instead of in bed with her, made my arms pimple with gooseflesh. Or was it only the chill October air? I turned on my side, away from the comet, and pulled my blanket tighter. I closed my eyes, but I saw the comet still, bright against the darkness in my mind.

"Omens can be for the good, too," I muttered.

☙ ☙ ☙

The next morning, we rose early to load mules with the building tools, gunpowder, and cornmeal we would need in Lovely's Purchase. Mallory got to our camp when most of the loading was already done, riding a bay stallion and leading a mare.

"Are we all here?" he called. "Are we all loaded?"

"Everyone's here but Webster," Fuller said. "I saw him last night and he said he's backing out."

A surprised murmur rustled through the crowd of men.

"I thought he was solid," Mallory said. Fuller shook his head.

"Said it's too big a risk. Said we're fools for thinking the government will let us stay."

"Well, to hell with him, then!" Mallory spit on the ground. "We can do this without him. Everything's loaded, you say?"

While Mallory greeted the other men and checked the loads, I looked over his horses. Since I was the only man in the party without a horse, Mallory had agreed to loan me the use of his mare. She was short, but she had bright, smart eyes, and I knew she would be fine transportation to Lovely's Purchase. The stallion, though—he was prime. There weren't probably a dozen other horses in the Territory that would be a match for him. As I ran my hand over his hip, Mallory tapped me on the back of the head with his rifle barrel.

"Don't be getting fancy ideas, McKellar," he said, trying to soften the warning in his voice with a chuckle. "That hand is all you're ever putting on this horse."

"A man can admire, can't he?" I gave the horse a pat. "I had a good stallion back in Tennessee, but I had to sell him to get us here."

"I'd part with one of my young'uns before I'd leave this stud behind. A man can always make more young'uns, but a stud like this is once in a lifetime." I stared at him, and he laughed, like he'd meant it as a joke. "I'm fooling with you. Ready to go?"

"I am. I thank you for the loan of the mare."

He shrugged. "Having you ride her beats leaving her in Dardanelle. But mark my words—she'll be hard-pressed to keep the pace this stud will set."

⋇ ⋇ ⋇

By the end of a day's riding on the rough trail west, it wasn't the little mare I was worried about. It had been months, lots of months, since I'd been on a horse, much less riding all day, and my legs and rump were so sore I had a hard time getting around to help gather firewood come evening. I'm sure the other fellows noticed my bow-legged gait, but they didn't say anything. After a week spent in the saddle, though, I was hardened again to riding and to sleeping on the ground, and I thought less about the old home in Dardanelle and more about the home to come in Lovely's Purchase.

While we were in Fort Smith, Aaron Fuller talked a storekeeper into giving him a couple of old issues of the *Arkansas Gazette* so we could catch up on the news since we'd left Dardanelle. That afternoon around the fire, he read aloud the text of a memorial the Territorial legislature had sent to President John Quincy Adams, asking him to give permission for white families to settle in Lovely's Purchase.

"'The salubrity of the climate'—what's that mean?" he asked.

They all looked at me. I shrugged. "Healthiness, I reckon."

"Here," he said, thrusting the paper at me. "You read it."

I skimmed the article until I found the spot where he had started. "'The salubrity of the climate and fertility of the soil which distinguishes this beautiful, extensive, and interesting section of our

107

country open such advantages and offer such strong inducements to emigrants, that, should your excellency authorize the survey and permit the settlement of this tract of our Territory, which your memorialists respectfully solicit and earnestly request, they anticipate, with the firmest assurance, that, in a very few years, this Territory will rapidly advance from a state of pupilage and increase in population and wealth in a ratio unparalleled in any former period.'"

"That Nicks, now he's a sensible man," Mallory said. "He knows we've got to have the way clear for folks to come in before the Territory can become a state. Opening Lovely's Purchase is a good first step."

"That's his argument," I said. "He goes on to say, 'Its number very soon will have more than doubled; that the gloomy and now useless forests on our western limits will be rapidly changed into cultivated fields, covered with a dense and respectable population of civilized inhabitants; and that this part of our Territory will then teem with life and vegetation, where the brain of industry and the spirit of enterprise will be roused and called into active and useful exertion.'"

"That's us," said a fellow named Lincoln, with a laugh. "We are that 'respectable population of civilized inhabitants.'"

"Damn right!" Mallory said.

"It's not open yet, though," another fellow said. "Here's an item in the paper from last month. It's a proclamation from the governor. 'I, George Izard, governor of the Territory of Arkansas and Superintendent of Indian Affairs, in order to prevent the difficulties which are daily arising by the Indians and whites trespassing on the lands of each other, and to maintain peace between them, do order each party to confine themselves within their own boundaries, under the penalties prescribed by law.'"

"It's true," Fuller said. "I heard talk in town that the army is still under orders to remove whites from Lovely's Purchase. I met a man who had been escorted out just three weeks ago."

"Three weeks ago?" I asked, folding the paper and handing it back to Fuller. "All the better—they probably won't be making another sweep any time soon."

"That's the spirit, McKellar!" Mallory slapped me on the back. "Let's quit wasting our time in Fort Smith and put the 'brain of industry and spirit of enterprise' to work building cabins in Lovely's Purchase!"

We paid a ferry man well to take us across the Arkansas River and to keep his mouth shut about it, and then we followed the river west for another couple of days before striking off to the north, straight into what Mallory told us was the heart of Lovely's Purchase. To tell the truth, I was a little disappointed in the country. There were no mountains to speak of, only low, rolling hills. Even the trees seemed shorter than what I was used to. The grass was tall with tough stems, and I could see it would be a hard job to make a cornfield of this land. But I wasn't afraid of hard work, especially since the work would be on land that was mine. I was helping to open the country for whites, and, best of all, it was far from Dardanelle and Little El.

We found a spreading valley along a shallow creek where we decided to set up our claims. We paced off what seemed to be quarter-section tracts, one for each man, and then we drew lots to see which man got which piece—all except Mallory.

"It was my idea to come here," he said, "so I reckon that gives me the right to first pick of the land. Everyone agreed to that?"

I glanced around the faces circling the fire, and I could see there were others, same as me, who didn't think the arrangement was quite fair. But no one said so.

"I reckon we'd all agree you should have some consideration for being the leader of the party," Anderson said.

"I'll claim the spot with the ford of the creek," Mallory said.

As expected, he'd chosen the best of the tracts. The rest of us drew lots and took what chance gave us, and my lot fell at the end of the row, on a section that had more woods than clear land. The job of making corn fields would be even harder now.

We drew lots next to see whose cabin we would build first, a lot no one really wanted to win, for the plan was for the whole group of us to winter over in the first two cabins built. My luck was better this time, as my lot came near the end of the draw again. I might not have much in the way of corn fields this first year, but at least I'd have a fresh, clean cabin for Maggie when we brought our families to Lovely's Purchase next spring.

The morning following the draw each man went to his own section, to size it up and figure a layout for his farm. I wandered around my tract for the better part of the day, exploring every corner of the woods, counting the number of trees and marking the kind of tree and the size. I was walking through the thick, stringy grass in one of the few clear spots when I stepped into a puddle of water.

"At least there's a spring," I mumbled to myself, pulling off my moccasin to dump out the water. That's when I noticed the white, flaky crust around the edge of the pool of briny water. I dipped my finger in the crust and touched it to my tongue, and it tasted just as I had hoped.

"I'll be damned!" I hooted. "It's a salt spring!" And there was another no more than three feet away, and another beyond that—

The future seemed to open up before me. Folks prospered from making salt—no, more than that—folks grew rich. I could see myself giving Maggie everything I'd promised to her, the cabin with glass windows, a silk gown, a real rocking chair. With a lightness to my step I'd not felt in ages, I turned and started back toward the camp. Mallory would be pleased as anything to hear his gamble on Lovely's Purchase had paid off so handsomely.

Suddenly, I stopped.

"I believe I'll not say anything about it," I said aloud. "Not just yet. There's all the cabins to build, and fields to break and plant—we need to do that work first."

The woods around me were silent.

"Mallory wouldn't say anything, if it was on his place, or Fuller, or Presley," I said, like the trees had argued against my decision. "It's been clear all along that each man controls his own land from the draw. Once the cabins are up, it's each man for himself. Who's to say this is the only spring around, anyhow?"

And so I kept my mouth shut around the fire that evening. While the other fellows joked over their cards, I figured on what it would take to set up a salt-making operation. The most pressing need was a big iron pot for boiling the brine, and I'd need money to get that pot. Maybe I could raise enough corn this first year to sell some and buy the pot next fall. That would give me time to build a shed to work in and to cut a good stack of firewood—

"You're awful quiet, McKellar, even for you," Presley joked. "What you got up your sleeve?"

"Nothing," I said quickly. "I'm just—" They were all looking at me. "I was just missing Maggie."

They all laughed, but I saw a couple of faces that were sober, too. Mallory clamped his had around my shoulder.

"Hang on, McKellar," he said. "You'll have her back in your bed quick as we can get these cabins up, and we'll start that job tomorrow."

So the winter passed, slowly, with all but the coldest and wettest of days filled with swinging an ax and raising cabin walls. Once the men found I had skill with making shingles, they set me to doing it full-time, so even on the cold and wet days I sat in the little shed by Williamson's cabin, turning bolts of red cedar into a pile of shingles. By mid-February, all the cabins had walls and rafters, and most of them were roofed. One by one, the other fellows moved in to their own cabins, but I stayed with Williamson while I made up enough shingles to cover the last of the cabins. Every morning, I watched Williamson head out to turn the ground that would be his cornfields while I was chained, so it felt, to the froe and mallet.

Mallory called us all together on an evening early in March and announced it was time to take a group back to Dardanelle to buy seed corn and fetch our families.

"There's still a couple of roofs to finish, so you'll stay here, McKellar," he said. "We need a few men to stay behind and keep an eye on everything, anyway, to see there's no trouble."

I didn't say anything, but I suppose my face said plenty, for Richard Bean, my nearest neighbor, caught up with me as I was walking back to my pallet at Williamson's cabin.

"Sorry about that, McKellar," he said. "That's what comes of being so handy with a froe."

I cursed aloud the day I ever learned to strike a shingle from red cedar, and Richard laughed.

"That was a lucky day for us," he said. "Your work is good. How many do you have left to make?"

"I have half of Lincoln's roof to go, then there's mine, and of course yours." I cursed again. "Everyone's corn will be shoulder-high before I even have a chance to break ground."

We walked in silence for a while, but then Richard stretched out his hand to stop me.

"Your cabin is next to be finished after Lincoln's, right?" he asked, and I nodded. "What would you say to a trade? You'll finish my shingles next in line, and I'll ready a cornfield for you. That way, you can plant as soon as we bring back the seed, and I'll have a finished cabin for my wife."

He started in the next morning on the plot I'd picked out, as far from the salt springs as it could get. Before they left for Dardanelle at the end of the week, at least the one field was plowed and ready for seed corn. Mallory and the others decided to leave behind the unmarried sons of a couple of the older men to help me finish the last of the cabins. The weather held fair, and the boys helped me all day, every day until every cabin was roofed and ready.

Then came the waiting. I tried to work out in my mind how long the wait might be. The men had been gone two weeks, and with the river running high from spring rain, they were bound to have reached Dardanelle. It might take a week or more to gather seed corn and supplies and to make arrangements to bring everything up the river. Then there would be the slow trip back, this time against the river current, and all the miles to travel on land from Fort Smith—it would be late in April, most likely, before I would see my girls again.

I passed the time by making ready inside the cabin. First I built a sturdy bed frame, high enough off the floor that the trundle bed I built for Penny could slide underneath. I made a real table and bench of leftover planks and a cupboard like the one I remembered from Zeke's house, with shelves above and doors mounted on leather hinges below. One fine spring afternoon, I was turning a garden spot with a spade when the young fellows walked up with cane poles over their shoulders.

"Come on, McKellar," Presley's son urged. "There's a good fishing hole down the creek a mile or so. Lay off the work and come fishing with us."

"You go ahead," I said, wiping the sweat from my forehead. "I want to finish this job today."

"What's your hurry?" Lincoln's son kicked at a clod of dirt. "You act like somebody's holding a brand to your buttocks. Ain't anybody here to boss us—who are you trying to please?"

"He's got a wife he's trying to please," Presley said. "There's no enjoying life once you got a wife—everything goes to please her."

We all laughed. "There might be something to that," I said.

Presley slapped my shoulder. "Well, it's your loss. While you're sweating in the sun, we'll be sitting by a shady fishing hole catching more fish than the three of us can eat. I sure hope your wife appreciates that garden spot."

"Me, too," I muttered as I watched them head toward the creek. "Me, too."

⁂

Another week passed. Then one afternoon, Justus Wright rode into my yard, and my heart made a big jump and started to beat faster. They were back.

"I rode ahead to let you know," he told me. "We're all meeting at Mallory's to sort everyone's goods and divide up the seed corn. They should be there in another hour."

I dropped what I was doing right then to go wash myself and shave off my scruffy beard. My heart kept pounding hard the whole time, until I thought it would burst in my chest once the first sight of them came through the woods across the creek from Mallory's cabin. I stretched myself as much as I could without seeming to, searching for Maggie in the crowd. She was near the back, riding a black mule I'd never seen, with a bundle in front of her that I figured was Penny. My heart nearly choked me then, it was so good to see her face and the outline of her shoulders.

Still, I wasn't sure what to say to her when I stepped up to help her off the mule. Did her eyes light when she first saw my face? Or maybe I had imagined it, for her face was still and cool as she handed Penny down to me.

"Penny!" I threw all my nervousness into a warm hug, which set the child to squalling.

"Don't crush her," Maggie said. She shifted to dismount, and I lifted a hand to steady her.

She was on the ground then, and we were standing face to face for the first time in months, and I didn't know what to say to her. All around us, families were reuniting with hugs and laughter, but we stood still, simply looking at each other. Damn, she was a stubborn woman.

"Here you are, in Lovely's Purchase," I said, and she nodded. I put out my empty arm to hug her, and she didn't pull away. After a

113

moment, she even slipped her arms around me, and I knew things would be all right. Maybe not today, but someday before long.

"I'm glad you're here," I whispered into her hair, and she nodded again.

Mallory whistled, and we all turned toward him.

"God blessed us with a safe trip," he said. "So here we are, ready to get to the business of settling Lovely's Purchase. We kept every family's goods together as much as we could. It shouldn't be hard to separate it all so you can get on to your homes."

I followed Maggie around as she collected our bundles.

"There's more than I expected," I told her. "It's good to see we've prospered a little. I'll have to make two trips, at least, to get it all back to our place."

"You don't have to carry them." She pointed to the mule she had been riding. "Mr. Mallory said he's yours."

I didn't want her to think I doubted her word when she finally seemed to be warming toward me a little, so I waited until she was fussing with Penny to make my way over to Mallory.

"Maggie says you told her that black mule is mine," I said. "I figure she's misunderstood somehow."

He smiled like he had played a great joke on someone. "No, she's right," he said. "The fellers and me thought you deserved something extra for making all those shingles. We all chipped in to buy him for you."

"I didn't do any more than the rest of you," I started, but he cut me off with a wave of his hand.

"There were always several of us working at once to build the walls. You made every last shingle on your own. Nobody feels cheated." He grinned again. "Now, if we wake up during a rainstorm with water dripping on our faces, we might feel different toward you."

"There won't be any leaks."

He laughed. "I know. Go load up your mule and head home."

My throat felt strangely scratchy. "I thank you," I managed to say. He just winked and dug his elbow into my side.

"Get on home, McKellar. I reckon you have plenty of catching up to do with your wife."

※ ※ ※

Except for Penny's happy jabbering, we walked in silence along the path by the creek that led to our place. As we rounded a bend, I caught sight of the cabin, sitting on a little rise behind a sweet gum tree. It looks like a home, I thought, and I glanced down at Maggie. For the first time in a long time, there seemed to be something soft in her look, like a bud just beginning to swell after spring rains.

She didn't say anything as I showed her the cabin. The logs were still bright and yellow where I'd peeled off the bark, and the pine odor was just strong enough to give the place a fresh, new smell. She ran her finger over the table top, made from memory to be just the right height for her. I gave her another minute to consider the cupboard, and then I took her hand.

"I have something else to show you. Come outside with me."

I led her through the woods to the salt springs. She walked around them, still without speaking, but I could see her mind was leaning into the future, just as mine had.

"In another couple of years, I'll be able to give you all I promised," I said. "Glass windows and all. We'll be rich, Maggie."

We ended up on the northerly side of the cabin, where I'd built a bench from a half-log pushed up against the cabin wall. It would always be shaded, a place she could sit and look up into the woods while she did her work. But what I wanted most for her to see was the clump of violets I had dug out from the woods and planted beside the bench. They had finally decided to live in this spot, and one had even stuck out a spindly stem with a tiny purple blossom.

"What do you think?" I asked, unable to wait any longer. She sat on the bench and her eyes were first off to the woods, then back to the violets, and finally to me.

"It'll do," was all she said. But that was enough.

Chapter 11

It'll do. I found myself thinking that time upon time over the next months. I told myself I had everything a man needed to be happy. After a few days in the new home, Maggie was through pouting and back to her regular self. Penny was a healthy, good-natured child. Richard Bean and his family made good neighbors. The salt springs promised a good living in the future, and the sandy soil promised a good crop for this year.

The corn sprouted well. Every evening, I walked between the stalks as they grew to my knees, then my hips, then over my head. Penny learned to walk, and most evenings I took her to the field with me to give Maggie a few minutes of relief from having to keep a constant eye on her. She waddled ahead of me on her fat, bare feet, sometimes stopping beside a plant to stroke the soft, pale silks. I always made sure to catch up with her quick then, to rescue my crop from her curious fingers.

"That's the silk," I said, squatting beside her. "It's what makes the kernels of corn. It's like the corn's flower. No—no—don't pull on them now. You wait until they turn dry and brown, like hair. Then you can pull them off and Ma will make a cornshuck dolly for you."

She stretched to reach for another ear, and I pulled her away, sweeping her up in my arms as I stood. I set her on my shoulders for the rest of the tour through the patch, and she laughed and kicked her legs against my shoulders and wriggled her fingers in my hair. Maggie was pouring the evening's wash water on her flowers, the Black-Eyed Susies and butterfly weed I'd dug up for her from along the creek and the hollyhocks she'd planted from the seeds Justus Wright's wife gave her. She picked one of the flowers and met us as we came toward the cabin.

"Want a flower, Penny? You smell it, see?" She held the flower to her own nose before handing it up to Penny. "Not in your mouth—against your nose. Smell it, don't eat it."

Penny babbled and cooed about the flower as I took Maggie's hand and we walked back to sit on the porch.

"The corn looks good," I said. "We should have a decent crop."

"God willing." She smiled. "You'll finally get what you've been wanting so bad."

"I reckon so."

We sat for a few minutes watching the sun set over the woods that separated our place from the Bean place. Penny was nearly asleep in my arms, still clutching the wilted flower, when Maggie stirred and stood.

"I hate to wake her, but her feet are filthy." She took Penny from me. "Come, baby, let's clean your feet so your bed won't get dirty."

"I'll be there in a bit," I called as they went inside.

The heat of the day had gone with the sun, though the evening air was warm and still. Across the yard, lightning bugs flickered among the stalks of corn. It was good corn, and yet, it didn't stir in me the same satisfaction I'd felt looking at the corn growing between the dying trees on the plot north of the Arkansas River. I closed my eyes and I could still hear the gurgle of the creek over the stones, could still see the blue of the mountains through the tree branches, the memory still as clear and bright as the real thing had been the day the Army forced us away—

I shook my head, hard, and looked out again at my corn patch. It was straight and tall, every stalk with two ears.

"It'll do," I murmured. "It'll do."

❧ ❧ ❧

It was easy to forget, sometimes, that we were living in a contested area. Every once in a while we would get some kind of reminder. A small group of Indians with their black hair and coppery faces might ride through the yard, going right past the cabin like it wasn't even there. One of the other men might ride over with word of mischief, that someone's fence rails had been scattered or a couple of chickens had been stolen from a flock. Folks always blamed the Cherokees, and

117

we complained to each other about it mightily, but mostly, life was quiet and we went on about the business of raising our crops. If the U.S. Army knew we were in Lovely's Purchase, they turned their eyes the other way.

Late in July, Lincoln and his son went to Ft. Smith and brought back news. Mallory rode with them as they shared the word with the rest of us that Lovely's Purchase was to be surveyed and sold.

"It says so here," Mallory said, handing me a tattered copy of the *Arkansas Gazette*. "The wheels are turning now."

Maggie had come from the cabin, wiping her hands on her apron, and I read aloud for her the short article in the paper.

"'We congratulate our fellow-citizens of Crawford County, on the pleasing and highly important information contained in the following letter from the Honorable Henry W. Conway'—he's the Territory's representative to Congress," I broke in to explain. She nodded, and I read on. "'The object which they have so long anxiously sought for is at length attained—Lovely's Purchase, instead of being surrendered to the Indians, is to be surveyed and brought into market.' Looks like you were right, Mallory."

"Damn sure!" he crowed. "Read on, McKellar."

"This is the text of the letter itself," I told Maggie. "'It will be gratifying to the people of Arkansas to know that I have prevailed on the Commissioner of the General Land Office to give instructions to the Surveyor General to have twenty townships of land surveyed this year, in Lovely's Purchase.'"

"Is that a lot?" Maggie asked. "Twenty townships?"

Mallory laughed at her. "It's a hell of a lot! Leave it to a woman!"

Maggie's eyes narrowed and she turned to me. "How much is it?"

"A lot. There's 640 acres in a section, 36 sections in a township, 20 townships—The government allows a man to buy no more than 80 acres—" I stooped to scratch the numbers in the dirt. "That's nearly six thousand plots of land that will be opened."

"Enough for everyone," Lincoln said. "Read what it says about folks moving in."

I looked back through the article. "'The knowledge that this fine tract of country will be brought into market in the course of the next year cannot fail to give us a very great increase of population.'"

"We've got a leg up," Mallory said. "It was a bit of a gamble to move out here, but it's going to pay off."

"I reckon so," I said. "Since the Army never bothered us—if they don't find us now that the news is out."

"They won't," Lincoln said. "I had word from a feller in Ft. Smith whose brother is a soldier with the 7th Infantry that Colonel Arbuckle is going to ask the government to suspend the orders to remove folks like us. Word is, he ain't too pleased with that job. Plus, they've got him assigned to build a road from Cantonment Gibson to Little Rock."

"They're building a road!" Mallory hooted. "It's happening! You'll see—the Indians will have no choice but to leave."

"Like it says here," I said, turning back to the newspaper. "'Now we may consider it ours, and look with certainty for those happy consequences which we have always expected would flow from its occupancy by our citizens.' You're a smart man, Mallory."

"Damn right," he said.

⁂

A week or so later, I found several ears in an outside row of corn that had been nearly ripped from the stalk. The husks had been jerked down and about half the plump kernels were gnawed and mangled. I took the ears back to the cabin where Maggie was nursing Penny and plunked them down on the table.

"Something's made mischief in the corn patch," I told Maggie. She leaned across Penny to look.

"Could be raccoons," she said.

"I thought so, too, but there were no tracks."

"The ground was probably too hard to leave tracks," she said. "We ain't had rain for a while." I shook my head. I didn't like the explanation that was forming in my mind.

"There would be some sign, scat or something. Everything was clean—too clean."

Her face was troubled as she looked up at me. "What are you thinking, then?"

"Could be someone wants me to think it was coons. We've not been touched yet, you know. Several folks around have lost something this summer. This is not enough to ruin the crop—it's just enough to bother us."

119

"Why would anybody do that? Especially now that the government says we can be here?"

"We can't be here just yet. The land has to be surveyed and we have to buy it before we can be here legally." I picked up an ear and turned it over and over in my hands. "Maybe someone didn't like the news. Maybe someone's trying to drive us out, make us think it's not worth it. Trying to warn us, maybe, that there's more to come."

Penny started scrabbling around and fussing because Maggie had let her slip a little. Maggie pulled her back up, a little impatiently, and I laid a hand on her shoulder.

"Don't start worrying," I said. "The corn's same as ready. I can start harvesting it today and let it dry in the crib instead of on the stalk. We won't lose any more. If it was Indians that did it—"

"We don't know it was," she interrupted. "It was probably coons."

"Well, I can't say. All I can say is, raccoons or Cherokees, they won't get any more of my corn."

I pulled as much corn as I could that day and stored it in the crib I'd built over the summer. Then I sat up all night with my rifle, leaning against the corn crib until I felt sleepy, getting up to wake myself by walking through the fields. But nothing disturbed either the field or the crib, which convinced me even more that the damage was the work of human hands. No raccoon would pass up an easy meal, once he'd found it.

I was slumped over a bowl of mush next morning, eating before I went back out to pull more corn, when we heard a horse come into the yard.

"McKellar!" called Mallory. "You up yet?"

I tucked my shirt into my britches as I went out to the porch. Mallory seemed agitated, yanking on the reins so the little mare was making stuttering steps in the dust of the yard. He didn't wait for any greeting.

"I don't reckon you've seen my stud horse," he said.

I shook my head. "Is he missing?"

"Sure enough! I noticed him gone when I first went out this morning. He was over in a fenced-in area to keep him separate from the mare, and the fence was broke down on the side fartherest from the house."

"Reckon he broke it down trying to get to the mare?" Maggie said. I hadn't noticed her coming outside.

Mallory snorted. "Women don't know nothing! If he was trying to get in with the mare, he'd have been in with her."

"I think I hear Penny waking," I lied. "Maybe you ought to check on her." With a sharp look at me and a little huff of breath, Maggie turned on her heel and went back inside. I leaned on one of the porch posts. "What do you reckon happened to him?"

"You know, well as I do, McKellar. The damn Indians stole him!"

"You sure of that?" I asked. "They've not done anything but cause a little mischief so far. Nothing too serious. Horse thieving is pretty serious, even for Indians."

"Damn right it is! And I reckon we're going to show them how serious it is! I'm getting some fellers together tonight and we're going to teach them stinking Indians to keep their dirty hands off a white man's property!"

"Now, Mallory," I started, "we don't want to stir up trouble—" He leaned toward me from his saddle.

"What's the matter, McKellar? You turning Indian lover on us all of a sudden?"

"Hell, no!" I snapped. "You ought to see what they did to my corn crop night before last. But the Army's looked the other way about us being here, so far. They could still throw us out—we're not legal, Mallory. I don't want to do anything to force them to look our direction. Especially if a ruttish horse just stepped over the fence for a little courting somewhere. Have you already looked around for him at all the other folks' places?"

"Not everyone's," Mallory admitted. "I reckon I should do that. But if he don't turn up before dark, I'm going to believe he's been took, and I won't let that pass without doing something. An eye for an eye, the Bible says. Can I count on you to help if I don't find him?"

I sighed and rubbed at the burning in my eyes with the heels of my hands. "Sure, Mallory. If he's not back by dark, come by here. I'll ride out with you."

All day as I was pulling corn and hauling it to the crib, I hoped I would look up and see Mallory riding past with his stallion on a lead rope. Even as I sat at supper, wearily lifting a slab of cornpone from my plate, I hoped he would come through the yard on his way home with news that he'd finally found the horse and there would be no need for riding tonight. Just at dusk, though, the sound of horses' hooves clattered into the yard, and I hoisted myself out of the chair.

"Don't go with them," Maggie said, leaving her dishwashing to block my path to the door. "Let Thomas Mallory worry about his own business."

"I said I would," I told her, taking her into my arms and wishing more than anything I could just stretch out on the bed beside her and feel her small, calloused hands soothing the aches out of my back. "A man has to keep his word."

She leaned against me. "I don't like him. I don't like you being around him."

"You don't like him because he won't let you get away with sass like I do." Her face jerked up toward me, and I laughed. "I won't be gone too long, I hope, but don't wait up."

"Ain't you going to take your rifle?" she asked as I let her go with a pat to her backside.

"Nope," I said, reaching for my hat on the peg by the door. "I reckon all we're going to do is knock down some fences and such. I don't need a rifle for such as that."

But I was surprised to see the moonlight glinting on several rifle barrels as I stepped out into the yard. I didn't say anything about it, though, just went to the barn to saddle up the mule. The men were gathered around the corn crib when I rode out to join them, and Aaron Fuller thrust a jug toward me.

"Have a taste, McKellar."

The whiskey was awful, obviously distilled by someone who didn't know much of anything about making whiskey. I took a second swig, though, before handing it back, as Mallory raised his hand and waved us out of the yard.

We crossed the creek and rode to the south, where Mallory said he'd heard some Cherokees had settled. The moon was just past full, so bright that I could see the buttons on the shirt of the man next to me. The whole ride made me remember times back in Campbell County, riding out for some kind of boyish mischief with Jed Evans and my brother Matt. We laughed loudly, without any worry about the noise, pausing every now and then to pass the jug. After the third pass, I didn't mind the soured taste quite so much, and I could tell by the way my whole body felt light that I was dangerously close to being drunk. Maggie would be mad as hell if I came home drunk, I told myself, and the next time the jug came around, I passed it on without taking a swig.

The whiskey was long gone by the time we came to the first Cherokee farm. To me, it looked like any other farm, with a cabin and barn surrounded by neat cornfields, but Robert Presley swore he'd heard this area was where several of the Indians had put down claims. We tied the horses at the edge of the woods and slipped silently—well, as quietly as a group of nearly drunk men could manage—down into the corn patch.

"Here you go, McKellar!" Mallory said in a hoarse whisper. "Get your revenge for what they did to your patch."

I stared at them for a minute, and then I squinted my eyes to look out over the corn. It was pretty corn, taller than my own, and not quite ready for harvest. I stretched out my hand, felt the dry silks against my fingertips and then the hard body of the ear against my palm. It was a damn shame to mess with such nice corn, to waste the effort of the man who had planted it back in the spring and nurtured it all summer. He was a Cherokee man, though. Someone of his kind had done the same to the corn in my patch, with no regard to my effort. I twisted the tops of the husks between my fingers and yanked them down, exposing the perfect kernels underneath to the night air. I grabbed another, and then another, and the men urged me on below their breath as I tore my way through several stalks. Ezra Pierce finally couldn't hold himself back, and he jumped over a few rows to thrash at the corn, leaving the stalks bent and crooked. That started them all, and by the time Mallory gave a low whistle to get our attention, I reckon nearly a third of that field was ruined.

"That'll teach them devils to mess with our crops," Mallory said, and he spit a wad of tobacco directly on the kernels of one ruined ear. "Let's mount up and ride some more."

It was like a game, trying to sneak up as quiet as we could and do what damage we could before anyone in the silent cabins roused. We tore up at least two more cornfields and broke down some fences, knocked apples off a tree and wrung the necks of a couple of chickens. The closest we came to getting caught was when Pierce shrieked like a woman when he lost his balance while taking a piss into somebody's cistern and nearly fell in. The rest of us broke out laughing, and we had to run off pretty fast when someone threw open the door of the cabin.

I had expected to be worn out from two days of corn harvest and my night of watching for raccoons, but as the hours wore on, I felt more and more awake. This was easy. Coming in under the cover of darkness, we could do whatever we wanted and no one would know exactly who had done the damage. Even if someone caught us, what could they say? The Cherokees had done the same to us these past months. The US Army wouldn't take their side over ours. They wouldn't favor the Indians over good citizens of the Territory.

The moon was turned toward the western horizon when we came upon another farm lying quiet. Mallory pulled up and turned to face us.

"Everybody had a chance to pay back what's been done to you?" He smiled as we all nodded our agreement. "I reckon, then, it's my turn. That stud was worth more than a few ears of corn or a couple of chickens. Let's burn this barn in payment for my horse."

"Burn a barn?" I said. No one else said anything for a minute, then Aaron Fuller spoke.

"Mallory's the one who put together this chance for us to get back at those red devils. If he thinks burning a barn is fair trade for his horse, I reckon I'm with him." Others murmured their agreement, and I knew it was no use to argue. We dismounted and tied the horses in a grove of trees about a quarter-mile from the barn, then began to steal toward the farm.

"I'll lead out the stock," I said, but Mallory laughed.

"Oh, no, you won't! Whatever pitiful stock that savage has in that barn ain't worth one hindquarter of that stallion. Brought him all the way from Kentucky—best horseflesh anybody out here will ever see. Just leave them be. If that feller wants them, he can come get them out himself."

I watched from the back of the group as Mallory and Fuller piled handfuls of dry grass around a corner of the barn and then struck their flints against it until the sparks caught. The grass burned quickly, and Mallory had us throw bits of twigs and leaves on the fire until it caught the bark on the log wall. The barn must have been fairly new, for the logs were slow to catch, but Mallory chipped out the chinking between the logs near a corner of the barn where the fellow had stored some hay. Once the hay caught, the barn was burning inside and out. I could hear animals thrashing around, and a horse screamed, a terrible cry.

We didn't notice at first that the Indian had come out, not until he yelled something and knocked Lincoln flat on the ground. Mallory was on the man in a second, pulling his arms together and jerking him to his feet. The Indian was small and wiry, and though he struggled hard against Mallory's grip, he couldn't break free.

"Somebody get a rope!" Mallory yelled, and there was a confused tangle of men as several tried at once to go in different directions. Finally, someone had a rope, and Mallory tied the Indian's hands together and jerked him around to face the barn, which was now fully in flames.

"See this?" Mallory yelled at him above the screams of the horse. "This is what you get when you steal from white folk! You tell your thieving friends this is only the start—we'll burn every damn Indian farm in Lovely's Purchase if you don't leave!"

The Indian man spit into Mallory's face. By the light of the fire, I could tell Mallory's face darkened. He grabbed a second rope that someone had brought and quickly looped it around the man's neck.

"Spit in my face, will you, nasty scum? I'll teach you respect for your betters—"

He dragged the struggling man through the dirt of the barnyard toward a low tree in the fence row.

"Wait!" I called. "Don't—the Army won't overlook a hanging—"

"Shut up, McKellar!" Richard Bean said, close at my side. "It'll be you hanging from that tree if you cross Mallory now."

Before I could answer, a woman came running out of the cabin, screaming at us. She ran to Mallory and began beating on his back with both fists. With one swing of his arm, he knocked her to the ground. As she fell, her shimmy stretched around her body, and I saw her belly was rounded the same way Maggie's had been while she was carrying Penny, back when I'd first been able to know for sure there was a child inside. Mallory kicked the woman, hard, in the shoulder.

"Stop!" I said, grabbing his arm. "She's with child!"

"Even better," he said, aiming a blow at the bulge in her middle. I stepped between them so the blow hit my shins, and I stumbled a little from the force of it.

"Come on, Mallory! We've burned the barn and their stock. That's enough! It's just a damn horse!"

"A horse worth more than three Indian bastards!" he screamed at me. "Get out of my—"

I knew I was going to do it, but I was still surprised when my fist flew up and hit him square in the face. There was a crunch and a sudden spurting of blood that was warm between my fingers before Mallory fell to the ground. I stared at him as the Cherokee woman scrambled to her feet and grabbed the rope, loosening it from the man's throat. Justus Wright was pulling me away by the elbow.

"Come on, McKellar," he said. "You don't need to be here when he comes to. Get on your mule and get home, quick."

"What about them?" I looked for the man and woman, but there was no sign of them. The other men stood around us, their hands limp at their sides.

"I reckon the party's over," Justus said. "Get on home, McKellar."

The whiskey made it hard for me to remember exactly how to get home. I had to keep the mule at a nothing faster than a trot while I made my way back through the reminders of our high-jinks—the fence line we'd pulled down, the carcasses of the chickens, the eerie, broken stalks of corn. Bile stirred in my belly that had nothing to do with the bad whiskey. I kicked the mule into a faster trot, leaving each sight behind me—until I came up on the next one.

Finally, I saw the reflection of what was left of the moonlight on the creek near our cabin. I slid off the mule and knelt by the cool water to wash Mallory's blood from my hands. The blood had dried, and I had to scrub to get it out from between my fingers. I scrubbed hard, and harder, and suddenly I threw my hands over my face and drew in a few deep breaths. I wanted to be home and yet I dreaded going through the door. I hoped, wished Maggie would be sleeping. I hoped I wouldn't have to look into her eyes just yet, to run the risk that she would see what I had been part of this night. How would I explain it to her? There was nothing to say that could make it sound like anything but what it was.

The bile rose from my belly to my throat, and I crawled away from the creek a few steps before it forced its way out. I threw myself back on the edge of the creek and splashed the water against my hot face. Then I rolled onto my back and stared at the pale stars.

"God forgive me," I whispered.

I don't know how long I lay there, but finally I got to my feet and led the mule across the creek and into the barn. Creeping as quietly as I could across the porch, I pushed the door open slowly, an inch at a time—

Maggie sat up in bed. "Is that you?"

"It's me." I sat on the edge of the bed, my back to her, and pulled my shirt over my head. She picked it up where I laid it on the bed.

"This smells like smoke," she said. "And you got a stain—" Her voice broke off, and I turned to see her staring at me with a look worse than I had imagined it would be. "What have you done?" she whispered.

I took the shirt from her. The front was spattered with blood, sticky and unmistakable in the last pale light of the moon coming through the greased paper covering the windows.

"I broke Thomas Mallory's nose," I told her, and then I got up and went outside to sit on the edge of the porch. I could hear the soft brush of her feet on the wood floor as she followed me. I was thankful she didn't say anything, just sat by me, not touching me.

"Maggie," I said, without looking at her, "I know I've dragged you all over creation ever since we married. I know this is the nicest place we've ever lived, a real home for our family, a place to settle down and raise our Penny." I stared into the darkness for a minute, trying to master the tears I felt choking my throat. "But this is not our home. This is not our land. It never was. It never can be. We're leaving tomorrow. I can't stay here."

I had expected her to protest or maybe even cry, but she touched my cheek and then pulled my head to rest against her bosom. Her heart was beating against my cheek, louder than her voice.

"I know."

❧ ❧ ❧

I was on Richard Bean's porch first thing the next morning. He came out to meet me and we walked away from the house, toward his corn patch.

"How's Mallory?" I asked.

"His face was swollen great big by the time we got him home. I imagine he's hurting some today. I wouldn't be surprised if he's laid up for two or three days."

"I expect he'll be coming to see me then." Richard nodded, and I sighed. "I didn't aim to hurt him. But dammit, I didn't expect to be dealing out Lynch Law last night."

"None of us thought it would come to that. I think I speak for us all when I say I'm glad you stood up to Mallory last night."

"Well, I reckon he'll make me pay dear for it," I said, with a bitter laugh. "An eye for an eye, you know. He'd probably make me stand still while he breaks my damn nose."

Richard grinned. "He'll cool off, whether he wants to or not. Mallory ain't the type to ride out on his own, and I tell you, there's not another man in this valley who would come with him against you."

"I appreciate that. But there's no need. That's why I came to see you." I stopped and turned to face him. "I'm leaving Lovely's Purchase." He started to protest, but I went on, quickly. "Save your breath—you won't talk me out of it. I'm here to see if you'll trade your wagon and a mule for the rest of my corn crop and the land, everything on the land or in the cabin we don't take. I need a wagon to carry Maggie and Penny." He was shaking his head, but I plowed on. "There's more, Richard. I hadn't said anything to you fellows about it, but there's a salt spring on the land." His eyes took on a different look, and I pressed the advantage. "It's worth more than a mule and a wagon, but that's all I'm asking, just a mule and a wagon—a way to get Maggie and Penny out of here."

His face was sober. "You don't have to do this, McKellar," he said. "Mallory's no threat to you."

I looked away from him, across the low, rolling hills and short trees.

"It's not about Mallory," I said quietly. "I could bust his nose again." I looked him straight in the eye. "Will you sell your wagon, or not?"

❦ ❦ ❦

By late that afternoon, we had our household goods in the wagon along with as much as would fit of the corn I'd already harvested. The rest I left in the crib for Richard. We ate a cold supper and slept on the floor, and the next morning, I hitched up the mules while Maggie nursed and dressed Penny. I expected her to be grieved as we pulled out of the yard, maybe to cry a few tears, but she didn't even turn back for a final look at the cabin or her flowers. I laid my hand on her leg.

"I'm sorry," I said, wishing I had better words to say, something that would ease the leaving and the loss, not just of this cabin, but of the rich life we could have had.

She didn't answer, just laid her hand over mine and gave a little squeeze. Then she straightened her back and raised her chin a little, looking toward the east where we were heading, back to Dardanelle.

Chapter 12

If I'd thought we'd just be able to pick right up in Dardanelle like Lovely's Purchase never happened, I was fooling myself.

I sold the wagon and mules in Fort Smith for cash money, enough to pay our fares on a boat headed to Dardanelle and for a month's rent on Brearley's cabin. It would cost too much to haul the corn crop with us, so I traded it to a miller for bags of meal, not as much as I could have had from the crop in Lovely's Purchase, but enough to get us by once I found work in Dardanelle.

But when we got to Dardanelle, Brearley's cabin was already filled with another family. We had to camp for nearly a week before I could find another place at the price I could pay. I was none too pleased with what I found. It was out away from town, which meant I'd have farther to go every day to work, once I had work. It was a small cabin, too, rude and dirty after the fresh, new cabin we'd had in Lovely's Purchase.

"It'll do," Maggie said, as she looked it over.

"It'll have to do," I said sourly. "Winter's coming on."

Dardanelle was different, in a lot of ways. More people were coming into the Territory, which meant there were more men competing with me for the few jobs in town. Many a day I'd walk to town before sunrise, only to find no one needed another pair of hands. I'd take my rifle out to hunt then, but more men were competing for the game, too. Most times, I'd walk back home empty-handed, knowing we'd have to depend on our short supply of cornmeal for another supper.

Maggie tried to stretch it, making corn mush for breakfast that was as thin as pap for a baby and hoe cakes no bigger than a hen's egg for supper. Still, the level of meal in the bag grew lower with a speed that scared us both, though we didn't say so. One night as we took nibbles off the tiny pones, trying to make them last longer, Maggie suddenly reached inside the neck of her bodice and pulled out her gold locket.

"I want you to take it," she said, pulling it over her head and laying it on the table by my plate. "See if Colonel Brearley will buy it from you."

She might just as well have smacked me with her iron skillet.

"No."

"John David, I want to help—"

"I can provide for us without you having to give up that locket, damn it. Don't you believe I can?"

She didn't say anything else. She just looked at me a minute with that worry mark in her forehead, and then she slipped the locket back over her head and went back to nibbling.

A few days later I came home to find the fire burned low and my girls nowhere in sight. I went back to the doorway and peered into the twilight. Nothing. Only the quiet of the woods around our yard.

"Maggie!" I called. My heart pounded as I tried to think what might have happened to them. "Maggie!"

"I'm here!" Her voice was faint, coming from the woods, and I rushed toward it. I found them a few paces into the trees. Maggie was struggling to carry Penny, who was asleep, in one arm and a basket covered with a cloth in the other.

"What's this?" I asked, taking it from her. But as I started to lift the cover, she stretched out her hand like she meant to stop me. "What is it?"

"Don't be mad," she said as I pulled back the cloth to show the basket full of acorns. Maggie tried to smile. "I thought I could stretch the meal a little further."

Something dark and ugly swelled inside me, and I wanted to throw the basket of acorns far into the woods, back where they could be found by the varmints who ought to be eating them. But she was right, and I knew it. My throat tightened as I laid the cover back over the basket.

"Good thinking," I managed to say. I took Penny from her, and she slipped her hand inside mine as we walked back to the cabin, slowly.

"I found a persimmon tree, too," she told me. "I had my hands full keeping Penny from eating enough to make herself sick. I bet possums or raccoons come to that tree. It might be a good chance to get some meat."

Possum—just a greasy, overgrown rat, Ma always used to say. She wouldn't serve it at her table. But Ma's table was never bare like mine. I swallowed hard.

"Could be," I said. "I could wait out here some night and see."

I spread the acorns to dry on the hearth while Maggie mixed up corn pone, once again without any bacon fat to flavor it.

"You're mighty quiet," she said.

"Just tired, I reckon."

I was tired, all right. Tired of dry, tasteless corn pone. Tired of wondering what we'd eat once the last of the meal was gone. Tired of the embarrassed, pitying look that came over Joseph Brearley's face every time he had to tell me he didn't know of any work I could do. Tired of knowing my brothers in Campbell County had bread enough on the table and to spare, while I would be filling my belly with the same mast wild hogs ate. Tired of me and Maggie putting on for each other like everything was going fine. Tired of Maggie pretending she thought I was a bountiful plenty.

She was by me then, her hand on my shoulder and her kiss on my forehead.

"You'll find something," she said. "You always have."

I said nothing.

❧ ❧ ❧

One morning late in December, all our pretending came to a quick end. I was sitting by the hearth with Penny on my knee while Maggie fixed breakfast. Penny was fussing, for Maggie was starting to wean her. She wrestled against my arms, crying and stretching out toward Maggie. I tried to coax her to take a cup with a little dab of the cow's milk that I'd bought the day before with the money from my last job. Penny screeched and knocked the cup out of my hand, right onto my lap. Quick as anything, I flopped her over my knee and swatted her bottom. And in the next breath, Maggie was snatching her away from me.

"Don't you smack her!" she snapped, glaring at me.

"She needed it!" I snapped right back. "Wasting good milk, dear as it is."

"She don't know it's so dear. She ain't happy because of the weaning, that's all."

"Don't wean her yet, then. She's barely old enough, anyhow."

She rolled her eyes. "Men don't know nothing about weaning babies!"

"I know enough to know it won't hurt to let her go on a while longer."

"It does hurt! She bites me every time she nurses."

"Don't let her bite," I said. Maggie scoffed.

"Just how am I supposed to stop her?"

"Give her a little swat—" Her eyes narrowed.

"No!

"She's spoiled—"

"She's hungry! I reckon my milk's drying up." She suddenly stopped short and turned toward the fireplace. "She's just trying to get more."

"So all that about it being good for a young'un to drink some cow's milk was a lie, eh?" She didn't say anything, just kept herself busy at the fire. "Well, be that as it may, you don't have to put up with her biting. A little smack—"

She suddenly whirled around and pushed a finger toward my face. "I ain't smacking her, and you ain't either." Her voice was mean and hard. "My Penny ain't going to have to put up with a pa like mine that smacks her for every little thing. And I ain't going to put up with you either if you're gonna be like my pa!"

My belly suddenly felt full of swirling bile. I stood up, so I could look down on Maggie instead of having her face to face.

"I'm not like your pa," I said, coldly. "And a little swat on the rump won't hurt a young'un. She'll wind up a spoiled little brat without it." I snatched my hat off the bed post.

"Where are you going?" she nagged as I opened the door.

"I'm going to work—if I can find anything, looking like I pissed all over myself."

"But you ain't had breakfast—"

"You eat my portion. Maybe it will keep your milk flowing one more day."

My britches were dried by the time I stopped at Brearley's store, first, as I always did. Another man was talking to Brearley, and as I came closer, I saw he was Levi Webster, the fellow who had backed out of going to Lovely's Purchase. He didn't seem to have prospered any more than I had—both of us were here to beg Brearley for work, any work.

"You want work today, McKellar?" Brearley asked. "I've got some hogs to be butchered."

It was work, and I took it, though it wasn't work I liked. Back home, Matt always teased me about being squeamish about killing and dressing out an animal. But Brearly was paying cash money, and I hoped I'd be able to talk him into giving me some of the fresh meat as part of my pay.

Webster slid a sideways glance at me as we walked to the lot where Brearley kept the hogs.

"So you didn't stay in Lovely's Purchase," he said. "Did you get drove off?"

"No." I didn't want to talk about Lovely's Purchase. But Webster did.

"I might have been wrong to pull out of Mallory's party," he said. "But how's a man to know what's the right thing to do in a situation like that? They say the government's going to survey the land and put it on the market—I reckon folks like Mallory who can stick it out until then will have an advantage over the rest of us. Squatters' rights, you know." I didn't answer, and he shrugged. "Well, here's the hogs. I'll get a fire going and make the water ready—you kill a couple and bleed them out good."

I felt more than half-sick that afternoon when Webster and I stopped at Brearley's store to collect our pay. Our britches were stiff with dirt and blood, so we waited outside for him to bring the money. To take my mind off my queasy belly, I idly scanned the handbills tacked to the wall, and I leaned closer to read one that caught my eye.

"LAND!" it screamed in a bold, black headline. Then in smaller letters, "Newly surveyed and ready for sale."

I read the details of the sale, even though I knew there was no use.

I shoved my hands in my pockets – empty pockets, without even a coin to buy myself a toddy to warm up after a cold day of killing and taking apart hogs. I was suddenly tired again—no, weary, so weary I leaned my forehead against the log wall. It was December, nearing the turn of another year. We'd been in Arkansas Territory two and a half years, and I had nothing to show for it, and no prospects for anything. All I had was a wife and a daughter, and with Maggie trying to wean Penny now, there would probably be another baby before long. Then I'd have four mouths to feed, and laying aside anything to buy land was going to get even harder. A bitter grin stretched my mouth. Maybe I was like Maggie's pa, after all.

"What's so funny?" Webster said. "What's it say?"

"Nothing."

He gave me a shove. "Come on, what's it say?"

"Fine." I read it to him, every word of it, in my best imitation of a lawyer-style voice that would have done me proud in any courtroom in Nashville. He stared at me, but I suddenly had the strangest feeling he wasn't the only one. I peered over my shoulder and blinked. Standing in the street was a sight I hadn't seen since I'd been in Nashville, certainly something I hadn't seen in Arkansas Territory—a man in a formal, dark suit, complete with a neat cravat, overcoat, and beaver top hat. He was watching me, and as I turned toward him, he tipped his hat.

"Pardon my staring," he said. "I heard you reading. It's not something one hears every day on the streets of Dardanelle." I shrugged, and he stepped onto the porch of the store. "Where did you learn to read like that?"

"I wasn't always a butcher," I said, and Webster laughed loudly. The man in the suit smiled and held out his hand.

"I'm Major Edward DuVal, U.S. agent to the Cherokee Indians."

I didn't bother to wipe my hand before shaking with him. There was no clean spot on my clothes to wipe it on, anyway. "John David McKellar."

"My question was a serious one," Major DuVal said. "Where did you learn to read like that? Do you have training in the law?"

"I spent some time in a law office in Nashville."

He smiled broadly. His teeth were a match for his clothing, clean and even.

"I guessed correctly, then. Mr. McKellar, might I interest you in a job opportunity?" I shook my head.

"I didn't stick with law studies. I don't want to be a lawyer."

"But I assume you don't want to be a butcher, either." There was something sharp in his voice, though he spoke pleasantly. "Anyway, I don't need a lawyer. I need a transcriptionist, a secretary to help with my correspondence. I'm also assuming if you can read so fluently, you can write as well."

"Well enough," I answered. Brearley had come outside and paid Webster, who wandered inside the store for a drink. I took the coins Brearley gave me and shoved them deep in my pocket. He paused as he turned to go back inside.

"I've got three more hogs I need butchered, if you want more work tomorrow," he said.

I had intended to ask him for some meat I could take home to Maggie, but I seemed to feel the steady gaze of Major DuVal between my shoulder blades.

"All right," I said. "I'll be here around dawn." I stepped off the porch and started against the cold wind toward home. Major DuVal fell into step with me.

"You aren't going to join your accomplice for whiskey?"

"I've got a family to get home to," I said, "not that it's your business."

"You have a family—all the more reason you should consider my offer. The government will pay for your efforts." I stopped and looked down at him.

"I'm telling you," I said sharply. "I'm not interested in lawyering or anything like it. If I wanted to be a lawyer, I'd have stayed in Nashville. And I sure as hell am not interested in working for the Cherokees."

"I see," he said slowly, but he didn't leave. We stood for a long minute in the street. I gritted my teeth against the cold wind cutting through my jacket like it wasn't even there.

"Mr. McKellar," he said suddenly, "pardon my saying so, but you are far too thin for a man of your size. If you bend your elbow one more time, I believe you'll split the sleeve of that jacket. You say you have a family—I don't know how large it is, but young as you are, it's most likely made up of small children. I'm guessing your wages for butchering hogs don't bring in enough to fill a stewpot more than one night in a week, and I'm guessing your wife and children are as thin and hollow-eyed as you are."

"It's not your business," I started, but he interrupted in the same matter-of-fact voice.

"It's not. My business is to find a man who can write well enough and read well enough that I can keep accurate records of agency business to report to the government. Now, you may not be the only man in Dardanelle who meets those qualifications, but I believe you need the work as bad as any man in town, and you are the man I want for the job. Surely you can set aside your compunctions about the Cherokees if it means you can feed your children."

I didn't answer. Truth be told, if I had tried to say a word at that moment, I would have bawled like a baby right there in the street. I was always grateful to Major DuVal later that he made a point of not noticing the way my chin was trembling.

"I tell you what," he said. "Come to my office and we shall have a test of your writing skills. You'll be able to see what I expect of you, and I'll be able to see whether my assumptions about your writing are correct."

I followed him to the agency office, and he settled me at a table that obviously served as his desk. I slowly dipped the quill in the bottle of ink. I hadn't touched a quill since my last letter to Zeke, before I'd left for Lovely's Purchase, more than a year ago. My fingers felt stiff and clumsy, hardened by cold weather and rough work. I couldn't seem to find a position where the quill rested naturally against my finger.

"Let's see how you do with transcription," Major DuVal said. "Did you ever take dictation?"

"I did."

"Very well. Address a letter to General William Clark, Superintendent of Indian Affairs in St. Louis, Missouri. Let's begin. Sir, the unsettled and long existing differences between the Cherokees and Osages, the unexpected obstacles which have, from time to time, been thrown in the way to an amicable—" He paused. "Amicable—do you—"

I nodded, trying not to lose the part of the sentence leading up to 'amicable.' He waited until I looked up.

"—amicable adjustment of them, and the great anxiety I feel to fulfill the wishes of the government in relation to them, induce me to send Captain Rogers, the interpreter, as a special messenger to you."

The letter was a long one, detailing the fuss over the murder of a Cherokee man by the Osages. I had to ask Major DuVal to repeat himself several times, since I wrote slowly to avoid leaving ink blots. He seemed patient, though, and when I finished, he held up the letter and read through it while I stretched my cramped, aching fingers.

"Here's a place where there should have been a new paragraph," he said.

My heart seemed to drop. "I'll recopy the letter." But he shook his head.

"No need for that—there are no other errors. I'll just add a note here at the bottom." He took the quill and bent over the desk, scribbling a line in a narrow, crabbed writing that made me understand why he wanted a transcriptionist. He laid the blotting sheet over the letter, then turned back to me.

"I'm sorry for the mistake," I said, but he waved his hand like it was no matter.

"I think you did quite well, Mr. McKellar, and I'm satisfied enough to leave the offer open to you. Would you like a cup of coffee to brace you before you head out into this cold for home?"

He pointed me toward a padded chair sitting near a fireplace, but when I protested that I was too dirty to sit, he laughed and said I could take the hearth instead. He called for a slave, who bustled about pouring the coffee. Major DuVal sat in the chair and cocked one ankle over the other knee.

"So you're not a butcher, and you're not a lawyer. What is your life's calling, Mr. McKellar?

I wasn't sure if he was mocking me, but his face seemed sincere enough. "I'm a farmer," I said. "Or would be, if I could get hold of a piece of land. I've not had much luck with that so far."

"I'm sure that is difficult, given the price of land," he said. "Many people turn to squatting on land illegally." He said it casually, like it was an interesting but faraway theory of the law, but it was clear as anything he was fishing for facts. I grinned at him.

"I tried squatting," I said. "I didn't have much luck with that, either."

The slave handed me a cup of steaming black coffee, real coffee, and I took in a deep breath of the good, bitter smell. Major DuVal stirred a spoonful of sugar – real white sugar – into his cup before offering the sugar bowl to me. I couldn't remember how much sugar went into coffee, so I followed his lead and took only a scant spoonful.

He studied me over the lip of the cup as he took a few careful sips. Then he set the cup down and discreetly wiped his mustache.

"What do you have against the Cherokees, Mr. McKellar?" The question caught me completely off my guard, and I sloshed a bit of the hot coffee down the front of my shirt. Major DuVal leaned forward to offer his clean hanky. "Is it their race? Many people around here, I know, believe the red man is more like the black man—little more than an animal, without the sensibilities you and I, as white men, have."

I thought of the faces that still haunted my dreams some nights—the terror in the Cherokee woman's eyes and the snarl on Thomas Malory's lips as he drew back his foot to aim a kick at the child growing in her belly.

"No," I said slowly. "That's not it."

A smile formed in Major DuVal's eyes, though his mouth stayed straight. "What, then?"

I took another careful sip of the coffee, and then set the cup on the hearth beside me. I looked straight into his face.

"It's the land. I was driven off a fine piece of land north of the river so a Cherokee man and his son could have it. I don't see why the government favors the Indians over its own citizens. It don't set well with me."

"I see." He pondered for a minute. "North of the river?" I nodded, waiting for him to tell me it hadn't been my land by rights, anyhow. But he never said it. Instead, he leaned toward me.

"A minor obstacle," he said. "There are ways to reconcile your wishes with the rights of the Cherokees. I should think a man like yourself would want to be part of creating that solution."

I shook my head. "I don't want to be part of helping Indians."

"Not even if it helps you as well?" He stood, and I knew the visit was over, so I stood too. Major DuVal offered another handshake. "Be that as it may, my offer stands, Mr. McKellar, and I make it even more eagerly than before. Talk to your wife about it tonight and think it over tomorrow while you are butchering Mr. Brearley's hogs. Then we can talk again."

Don't count on it, I thought, but I said nothing.

❧ ❧ ❧

The cold gray of a winter evening was wrapped around our lonely cabin when I finally got home. Inside, though, Maggie had a good fire going and the smell of hot corn pone made me remember how hungry I was. Penny ran to me, babbling "Pa! Pa! Pa!" I scooped her up, and she giggled as I pretended to toss her into the rafters. Maggie was quiet, her eyes searching across my face for any signs of the morning's anger still lingering. I tucked Penny, still laughing, under my arm and crossed the room to Maggie.

"I'm so dirty because I butchered hogs for Brearley," I told her, and then I paused. "I'm sorry," I said, letting the words hang in the air long enough she would know what I was sorry for. "He's got more for me to do tomorrow. I'll see about getting some fresh meat for us as part of my pay."

She smiled up at me, and I'm pretty sure the shine in her eyes wasn't just because of the prospect of getting fresh meat. "That'd be mighty good."

I was surprised when she sat down to nurse Penny after we'd had supper.

"I thought you were going to wean her." She shrugged as she stroked Penny's hair.

"You're right, I reckon. She's still young for weaning."

"But if your milk's low—" She cut me off.

"It ain't so bad."

Once Penny had her fill, Maggie handed her to me, and I rocked her in the chair with the bad leg while Maggie washed out my clothes. I sang to her and she waggled her little fingers in my beard until her eyes were rolling back in her head. When they finally rolled shut for good, I held her in my arms a little longer, feeling her hot, soft breath against my chest, until Maggie hung my wet britches over the edge of the table to dry during the night. Then I settled my daughter in her bed and took her ma in my arms instead.

140

Without the cover of her shimmy, there was no denying how skinny Maggie was. It grieved me to feel how little flesh covered her hip bones and ribs. A woman ought to have some soft flesh on her body, especially a woman nursing a young'un. But it would take more than corn pone to put it there. I stroked her bony back, and she snuggled her head into the hollow between my shoulder and my throat and sighed, contented-like, like she was resting on a fine feather bed with a belly full of roasted sweet potatoes and flour biscuits. That was Maggie—always acting like she thought I was a bountiful plenty.

Now I had a chance to be that for her. A blessing from God, she would say. Helping the damn Cherokees. If I did it, no doubt Little El would show up at some point. I'd rather gut a dozen hogs than see that self-satisfied smirk of his one more time. Myself, I'd tighten my belt a little more and keep looking for something better. But my pride had already cost Maggie plenty of suffering. How could I refuse this chance to give her what she so badly needed?

I tightened my arm around her.

"I didn't tell you," I said. "I've got some steady work lined out." She lifted her head to look at me. "With the government agent for the Cherokees, here in Dardanelle, writing letters for him and such."

"Really?"

"I went to his office this afternoon and wrote a letter for him." I kissed her forehead. "Things are going to turn around for us," I murmured. "We'll be all right now."

Chapter 13

I went straight to the Cherokee agency on my way to Brearley's hog lot the next morning, so I would be clean when I spoke to Major DuVal and accepted his offer. He was still abed, though, so I left word with the slave who had made our coffee. I heard nothing more for a couple of weeks, long enough that I thought the slave must have forgotten to deliver my message. For a while, I pondered whether I ought to go by the agency again, but I decided against it—I didn't want to seem desperate, though I was. Finally, I marked it down as a lost opportunity and, trying not to feel bitter, turned my mind to trying to find something else steady enough to fill our bellies.

Then one afternoon, Maggie came half-running to the spot where I was cutting firewood, with Penny wrapped in a blanket against the cold.

"There's a Negro man at the house," she panted. "He says the major wants you up at the agency."

I hadn't shaved in a week or more, but the slave—his name was Josiah—said there was no time.

"We got to hurry back," he said. "Colonel Brearley said you lived far out, but I didn't know it would be this far. Master DuVal's in a real state, yessir. Ain't seen him so riled in a long time. He says the governor ain't getting away with his tricks this time."

Major DuVal hardly let me get settled at the table with a quill before he was starting to dictate his letter.

"Address it to Secretary of War James Barbour," he spat, "from the Cherokee Agency, Crawford County, Arkansas Territory. Ready?" I nodded, and he began to dictate the letter. "Sir, the attitude assumed towards to me by Governor Izard, just before he left this Territory for

Washington, makes it expedient to lay before you a copy of his last letter to me and of my reply to it." He paced back and forth across the room as I carefully scratched the words on the paper. "Of the nature of the charges which he contemplated exhibiting and which he may have exhibited against me I have been and still am kept in profound ignorance. I will not now complain of this. In any scrutiny that may take place touching my conduct as a public officer, I will not deign to seek a favor, but I ask for the common privilege of every citizen of our country–the right of being heard in my defence."

The first letter itself wasn't so long, but once I had taken it down, Major DuVal set before me two other letters to copy. He didn't say a word until I was finished, just paced around the room, reading through each page as I finished it. Once I'd blotted the last sheet, he gathered them together, then paced through the doorway.

"Josiah!" he called. "Bring two plates of food and tell Mrs. DuVal I'll be eating dinner with Mr. McKellar here in the office." He turned back to me, and the temper that had hung so heavy in the air when I first entered the room was gone.

"Excellent work, Mr. McKellar," he said, pulling up a chair to sit across from me. He picked up the quill and put his signature at the bottom of each letter, then leaned back to look at me with a satisfied smile. "I hadn't intended that your first assignment with me would be of such a controversial nature."

"I haven't paid much attention to politics in the Territory," I said. "I don't know anything about Governor Izard."

He grimaced. "You're better off, if you ask me. The man doesn't understand the way business is handled in the Territory. He's trying to come in and interrupt the way we've done things for years, in an effort to magnify his own position." He tapped the letter. "I guess you could tell. It's a matter of sovereignty, so to speak. He thinks everything I do should go through him, as Superintendent for Indian Affairs for the Territory. But with the Choctaw in the region, and the Osage, and the Quapaw, he's not shown himself reliable in seeing that the concerns of the Cherokees are addressed. The Cherokees have a different situation than the other nations—Izard doesn't seem to know that or to care. It's my responsibility to see that the interests of the Cherokees get the best representation possible, and I can best do that by working directly with Thomas McKenney and Secretary Barbour." He suddenly leaned forward and struck his fist against the table. "I don't need that meddling Izard watering down my requests on the Cherokees' behalf!"

"I reckon not," I said, glancing toward my jacket hanging by the door. Major DuVal noticed. Sitting back, he smiled again.

"But I forgot. You're not that concerned with the rights of the Cherokees yourself."

Right then, Josiah brought in plates with a thick slab of beef roast, a pile of potatoes, and a chunk of real bread, made with wheat. Major DuVal spread a wad of butter over his bread as Josiah poured each of us a cup of coffee.

"Thank you, Josiah, that's all," he said. He offered me the butter, and I tried to be sure the wad I took off was no bigger than the one he'd taken, though it had been a year or more since I'd tasted good, fatty butter.

"You said before that your opinion of the Indians is based on competition for the land," he was saying. "That's what brought the Cherokees into Arkansas Territory, Mr. McKellar. People in Georgia want Cherokee land there. Our government made promises to the Indians about trading land in Arkansas Territory for what they give up in Georgia. If Americans now want the land in this territory, what are we to do with the Indians?"

I shrugged as I cut through the beef. It was so tender I didn't need a knife. "Send them somewhere else, I reckon."

Major DuVal wasn't eating. He leaned back in his chair, staring toward the window. "That's the answer everyone gives. Mr. McKenney has given me orders to see if the Cherokees would be amenable to trading their land north of the river for land in the western parts of Arkansas Territory. They aren't interested, of course. But it will happen, Mr. McKellar. The United States is too big and too powerful for the Cherokees to resist. It's hardly fair. That's why I'm needed—to guarantee the Cherokees are treated fairly." His eyes turned back to me. "And then you and your family may have that land you so desire. But enough of that. How did you come to be in the Territory?"

I answered his questions as quick as I could between bites of the beef. It was the best thing I'd ever eaten, juicy and rich. Though I was telling Major DuVal about Maggie and Penny, my fingers never left the fork, and suddenly, he was smiling like I'd said something amusing.

"So there's only the three of you. Very nice. More beef, Mr. McKellar?"

He did the talking then, telling me the names of the government officials who dealt with the Indian agency and how the offices all fit together to get work done. He gave more detail about the work I'd be expected to do for him and the records he kept. I listened and ate until my belly was full. I finally sat back with a sigh and only then did I realize what a big lot of food I had eaten.

"Join me for a glass of port?" Major DuVal asked.

"I should be getting home," I said, standing and reaching for my jacket. "Maggie's probably waiting to fix supper till I'm back, so it can be warm. Mush don't hold over so well."

"Wait!" Major DuVal held up a hand. "Josiah!" The slave appeared in the door. "Package up what's left of that beef and potatoes to send with Mr. McKellar."

"Oh, no, I didn't mean—" I started, but he just laughed.

"Consider it part of your payment for services today—for the previous letter, as well." He pulled a gold coin, more than anyone else in Dardanelle had ever paid for my labor, from a small iron box on the desk. "And here's the rest."

※ ※ ※

Maggie and I began to prosper after that. Major DuVal paid a good enough wage that I didn't have to scrounge around every day for whatever kind of work I could find, even on the days when he didn't need me. I could buy meat once a week at least, and I was pleased to see some pink showing again in Maggie's pale cheeks. Once winter gave way to spring, I bought enough seed corn to put in a decent-sized patch, and Maggie put in a garden patch with potatoes and beans and squash. The garden patch and corn weren't on our own land, something I could never forget, but I didn't dwell on the thought, and I reckon we were having the best times we'd had since coming to Arkansas Territory.

I began to be interested in the politics of the Territory. Major DuVal had me writing correspondence to most of the important men in the region, and sometimes I would be at the agency when one of those men would stop by. The first time I met Colonel Arbuckle of the U.S. Army at Cantonment Gibson, I was stiff with a mixture of resentment and embarrassment until I realized he didn't remember me at all. I might have been able to stir his memory of tossing us off the land, but I decided to let it lie, and he was real friendly to me, calling me "Mr. Secretary" and teasing me because I wouldn't take a cigar when he and Major DuVal sat to smoke and talk business.

I might be willing to forgive Colonel Arbuckle for his part in taking away my land, but I still bristled up inside when I saw Little El or his pa. A few times I looked up from my work to see one or both of them riding past the window, though they never came in the agency for business. It was probably a good thing they didn't, for I was fast losing patience with most of the Cherokees we dealt with. Too many of them reminded me of Maggie's pa, trying to use whatever small wrong had been done to them to gain an advantage. The biggest part of Major DuVal's business was dealing with complaints about stolen horses or some debt owed to the Indians by the U.S. government. Of course, it fell to me to keep records of all these matters, and as I collected information, more and more it seemed to me the Cherokees were playing on the generosity and good nature of our government. At the end of one week with several claims I thought were questionable, I said as much to Major DuVal. That was the only time he ever got sharp with me.

"It's not your job, Mr. McKellar, to pass judgment on the motives of the Cherokees!" he snapped, stepping toward me so that, without thinking, I drew back, even though I was the bigger man. "It's your job to faithfully record the facts and to pass those on to people with more experience dealing with the Indian nations—and with less prejudice against them!"

I pouted some over his words, and when I got home, I told Maggie all about it. If I thought she'd soothe my pride, I should've known better. She shook her head while she pulled on the tail of Penny's dress to keep her from climbing on the butt ends of the fence rails.

"Don't you be making Major DuVal mad," she said. "Just keep quiet about what you think about the Cherokees. Having that steady money is too good."

I couldn't argue with that. Not only were we having plenty to eat now, but we were putting back a portion of my wages every time I was paid. The talk around Dardanelle was that the government was getting ready to open more land for sale, and we wanted to have plenty of money when it happened.

"All right," I grumbled. "I'll knuckle under. But I thought that's what we were trying to get away from when we left Campbell County, and Nashville, too."

"Things are different now," she said. She lunged to grab Penny from pulling up a bean plant. Penny thrashed her arms and legs as Maggie held her tight and gave me an exasperated look. "We didn't have this one then."

So I kept my opinions on the Indians to myself, though there was plenty to have opinions about. The government decided to add the Quapaw tribe, or what was left of them, to the Cherokee nation, which added to the agency's responsibilities. We also had to deal with the nagging hatred between the Cherokees and the Osages. Years ago, Thomas Graves, a white man who had married into the Cherokees, had killed an Osage woman and child. He'd been set free because the federal court claimed it didn't have jurisdiction, but the trial hadn't been the end of the matter. The fuss had gone on for years, with several attempts by both sides to get revenge, and for whatever reason, the Cherokees were hot over it again. I wrote out a good bit of correspondence for Major DuVal that spring, to the agent for the Osages and to the Secretary of War in Washington City, trying to keep things smoothed over.

One muggy evening in July I was sitting on the porch, using the last of the sunlight to mend my moccasins, when I saw someone running down the path leading from town—Josiah, Major DuVal's slave. I stepped off the porch to meet him, and he doubled over, sucking in air like he'd run all the way from Dardanelle.

"What's wrong?" I asked. He took a deep breath and straightened to look at me.

"Master DuVal said for you to come quick—the Cherokees sent a war party to the Osages, and he wants you to help stop them!"

Josiah waited on the porch while I put a few things together for the trip. Maggie stood against the wall, her arms crossed over her bosom.

"Can't this business wait till tomorrow?" she asked quietly, so Penny wouldn't wake.

"I guess not. He wouldn't call me out at night unless it was important." I took my rifle down from its pegs over the door. She drew in a sharp little breath.

"What kind of business is this, anyhow?"

I looked up from checking the supply of bullets. In the candlelight, I saw the familiar worry mark creasing her forehead between her brows. I took her in my arms, and her heart beat fast and hard against my chest. My own heart was racing, too, more from excitement, though, than from fear.

"We're going to stop some fellows from doing something stupid," I told her. "The rifle is for show—I won't need it for shooting." I patted her back. "Don't worry. I bet I'll be crawling in bed with you before the night's out."

I could tell she didn't believe me, but she acted like she did, stepping back and laughing a little. A quick kiss, and I was out the door, trotting toward town with Josiah in the deepening twilight.

Several horses were tied in front of the agency, and I figured I must be the last man to get there. Major DuVal greeted me soberly. Scanning the faces of the other men he'd selected for this task, I saw I had a passing acquaintance with most of them—and then my gaze froze. Little El was standing in a corner of the room, tightening the straps on a bedroll. My heart started pounded furiously again, and I bent closer to Major DuVal, trying to bend my mind to what he was saying.

"I say, you don't have a horse, do you, Mr. McKellar? I'll have Josiah saddle one for you, then." He waved to Josiah, and as we waited for the slave to make his way to us, I saw that Little El had recognized me, as well. His jaw hardened, and he turned away, picking up a rifle and inspecting the firing mechanism. My head felt strangely hot as Major DuVal gave his orders to Josiah. As the slave left for the barn, I cleared my throat.

"How big was the war party?" I asked. "Do you need this many men?" Major DuVal looked closely at me.

"Rumor is, they took more than a dozen warriors. I've called together seven of you. That still puts you all at a numerical disadvantage."

"Still," I started, but he raised his hand to silence me.

"I understand, Mr. McKellar. You're right, this is not in the regular duties one would expect of a corresponding secretary. But I have my reasons for asking this of you." He smiled. "You must admit, your appearance is not that of a regular corresponding secretary. Between your size and that scar on your cheek, you have a rather rough look, and that's certainly of benefit on this excursion."

"What about him?" I jerked my head toward Little El, who was now checking his supply of powder. "Why is he here?"

Major DuVal looked surprised. "Elwin Root's son? I needed an interpreter."

"Why not Rogers?"

"He's too old to ride as fast and hard as this party will need to go. He's the one who suggested Mr. Root's son." He studied me for a minute. "Do you have problems with this party, Mr. McKellar? I've selected only men I know I can trust."

I pondered my answer. If I told him I wouldn't ride with Little El, I could avoid the confrontation for tonight. But it might cost me in the long run, in less work with the agency, just when Maggie was looking so much better. I ran my hand over my hair.

"There's no problem."

🐾 🐾 🐾

I kept telling myself that as we left the agency, riding west under the light of the moon. Little El was riding at the front of the group alongside our leader, a feller named Richard Dooley. I stayed near the back, though it meant breathing in the dust of all the other horses. There was a good bit of dust, too, for we were riding as fast as the darkness and the roughness of the trail would allow. We rode until the moon set in the early hours of the morning, and then Dooley reined in his horse.

"No point going on in the dark," he said. "Lay out a bed roll if you've got one, and let's get some sleep."

I didn't sleep. The tree root poking me in the back wouldn't let me—or was it the memories of the last time I'd seen Little El? If I turned my head just a little, I could see the dark lump he made against the summer-dry grass. Why did Major DuVal trust him? Based on my dealings with Elwin Root, Jr., I'd figure him more likely to join up with the war party than to talk them out of fighting. But Major DuVal was the Indian agent, and he hadn't asked for my opinion. I was just a big man with the look of a scoundrel—a good match, I thought, for the black notions in my heart.

I was glad when Dooley whistled and we were back in the saddle, riding with the pink streaks of a new dawn at our backs. We caught up to the war party late in the afternoon. I don't know what I'd expected from a war party, but this looked like just an ordinary group of men riding together. It was clear they were angry, though, from the way they protested when Dooley told them we were sent from Major DuVal to turn them back from their purpose. A man I guessed must be their leader urged his horse out of the pack toward us, and he shouted at us in their strange language, waving his arms and pointing, especially at Little El, who then took his turn speaking. They went back and forth for a while, both of them so heated I half expected one of them to raise a rifle and shoot the other dead off the back of his horse. The war party's leader suddenly whipped his horse around and rode back into the center of his group. With a loud shriek, they all rode off.

"So what was all that?" Dooley asked Little El.

"They say your government has failed to give them satisfaction in this matter."

"So they are going on to Osage territory?" Little El shrugged, and Dooley snapped at him. "Do we follow them, or not? What did you tell them?"

Little El smirked, that arrogant look I knew all too well. "I gave them the message your agent trusted to send by me. I would not betray his trust."

Dooley sighed and looked over at the rest of us before turning back to Little El. "Do we follow them, or not?" he asked again, a little nicer this time.

"To do what?" Little El said. "The message has been given. If we follow, all we can do is give the same message again—unless you plan to engage them in battle yourselves to stop them."

The men around me stirred a little, muttering, and Dooley took off his hat to scratch the back of his head.

"Well," he said, "Major DuVal didn't say anything about fighting them. I myself ain't too keen on picking a fight with 20 armed Indians when we've got six men." He set the hat back on his head. "He said to give them the message, and I reckon we've done that. Come on, boys, let's head back."

⅔ ⅔ ⅔

We set up a real camp that evening, next to the river. I had just started smoothing a spot to sleep on when Dooley barked out another order.

"McKellar! Root!" He handed Little El a hatchet. "Go rustle up some wood for a fire."

The two of us looked at each other for a moment, then I turned quickly and headed out of camp toward the river. I could tell by the crackle of brush behind me that Little El was following. Once we had reached the river bank and were out of hearing distance of the camp, I whirled around to face him.

"You don't have to follow my footsteps," I growled. "There's plenty of wood washed up around here for the both of us. Go someplace else."

"There's only one hatchet." I didn't like the way he was grinning. "Unless you're stronger than last time we met, you can't break up wood with your bare hands."

"I'd like to break something else with my bare hands," I muttered, bending to pick up a couple of good-sized sticks and snapping them across my thigh. Little El moved away a few paces and began to hack at a fallen branch.

"I heard you had gone to Lovely's Purchase," he said. "Why didn't you stay there?" I didn't answer, just picked up more sticks, bigger ones, and broke them. I had to bear down hard enough to do it that I knew there would be a bruise on my leg in the morning, but I wasn't asking him to chop a single stick. He threw a piece of the branch into a clear area, and then moved closer to where I was. "How are Maggie and Penny?"

Anger surged in my chest, but he had a hatchet and I had an armload of half-rotten sticks. I bit back the curses I wanted to sling at him.

"It's none of your affair."

151

He shook his head. "I don't understand you, McKellar. I'm being polite in asking about the health of your family, like any man would do, and you act like I've insulted you. What is your grudge against me?"

It was time, I figured, to lay it all out. I straightened to my full height to look down at him, holding his gaze eye to eye.

"I don't like the way you look at my wife," I said, trying to keep my voice low. "I don't like the way you smirk when you see her, like she's still naked in the creek, like you have some right to stare at her—"

"For God's sake, McKellar!" he broke in. "That was years ago! I was a boy then."

"And now you're a man," I snapped. "But you're still looking at her that way, like she don't already have a man."

He smirked. "You think I want to—"

I moved a step closer. "Don't you?"

He narrowed his eyes. "I see. Since I'm Indian, you believe I don't have any control at all over my desires. I'm just a savage with no morals or sense of what is wrong or right, with no restraint. I'll take any woman, especially any white woman, whether she wills it or not." He spat on the ground. "You're a fool, McKellar! Adultery is adultery, among my people as well as yours. I would not take Maggie so long as she is your wife."

"Well, there's some comfort," I snapped, turning my back on him and reaching for another stick.

The next thing I knew, the hatchet was whizzing past my head. I gasped and stumbled backward, blood pounding in my ears. The blade hit the ground near where my hand would have been.

"What in the hell!" I sputtered.

Little El stepped forward and used the hatchet to rake something off to the side. He leaned forward and picked up the body of a snake, still writhing. It was a sickly brownish-black and thick as my forearm.

"That's a cottonmouth." I suddenly felt like I might puke.

"Big as I've ever seen," he said. "Lots of poison in that one. You nearly picked it up."

My hand was shaking as I wiped it across my mouth. Hell, my whole body was shaking.

"I reckon I owe you thanks," I said.

He shrugged and awkwardly threw the snake's body toward the river. It hit the water with a dull slap. I laughed weakly.

"I thought—well, I mean—"

"You thought I would strike you down to clear a way to Maggie? You really are a fool of the worst kind, McKellar. I don't understand at all what she sees in you." He bent to wipe the bloody blade on some weeds. "I do like Maggie. She's one of the few white women who don't recoil when I'm so bold as to even glance at them, like I'm some kind of beast about to attack them. But she's your wife, and I know how she feels about you—though God knows why. I'm not going to do anything to try to change that. My people have honor."

He went back to chopping at a hunk of wood, and though my legs felt like they had turned into piddly vines, I picked up a good-sized armload of wood and carried it back to camp.

We didn't speak anymore that night or on the rest of the way home the next day. He rode at the front of the party, beside Dooley, and I rode at the back, just as when we'd left Dardanelle. For the whole day's ride, watching his back ahead of me, I pondered what had happened. No doubt, he'd saved my life—twice now. That irked me, irked me bad. But I couldn't say I'd rather he hadn't done it. And I couldn't say why he'd done it. Elwin Root, Jr., was my enemy, my rival. If the hatchet had been in my own hand, would the outcome have been the same?

Major DuVal was waiting when we got back to the agency, and after Dooley reported on our trip, we lined up on the porch to be paid. Little El was first to get his share. He pocketed the money and turned to go, but as he came close, I took a half-step out of line and he stopped. He looked up at me with those black eyes, with that same prideful smirk that always boiled my blood. His muscles tensed as I raised my hand, and it seemed to me like every other man in the group was leaning in so they might hear anything I meant to say.

But I said nothing, just touched my fingers to the brim of my hat. Little El's smirk twisted a bit, almost into a smile, and then he left.

⁂

I saw Maggie when I got home before she saw me, and I paused a minute in the road to watch her. She was alone on the porch, her eyes

153

turned down to shelling beans. She looked like she always looked, like any other woman doing household work. But she looked up then and her eyes caught sight of me and she smiled, and she looked to me like no other woman ever had or ever would.

"I'm back," I called to her, taking a step and then breaking into an easy lope to cross the distance between us. Each step felt better, like chunk of a heavy weight that had been pinning me down was cut away and flying off and I was finally free again. She stood to meet me, but I scooped her off the porch and held her in my arms like she was as little as Penny.

"I'm back," I whispered.

Chapter 14

The war party came back without going to Osage territory, so for a time it seemed tempers had cooled. But the territory was like a pot of water over a hot fire, at the stage of simmering before breaking into a boil. The Cherokees heard the rumors that the government wanted to approach them about trading their land for land in the western part of the territory. Although Major DuVal assured the chiefs he hadn't heard anything formal to support the rumors, the Cherokee council voted to give the death penalty to any man who negotiated a land trade with the United States.

Fall was especially tense. In October, the territorial legislature was tired of waiting for the U.S. government to decide the fate of Lovely's Purchase, and they used their authority to create a new county in the territory, Lovely County. I borrowed the *Arkansas Gazette* from Major DuVal and took it home to read the news to Maggie.

"'Be it enacted by the General Assembly of the Territory of Arkansas that all portion of the county of Crawford called and known by the name of Lovely's Purchase, and all that section of country adjacent to said purchase, which has heretofore never been apportioned to any county in this territory, bounded as follows, to wit'—now it gives the boundaries—'be laid off and erected into a separate county, to be called and known by the name of the county of Lovely.'" I laid down the paper. "I reckon Thomas Mallory was right—looks like the white folk got their foothold in that country. Do you ever wish we had stayed?"

"I don't. I'm glad we left." She gave an aggravated little puff of breath. "Thomas Mallory can have the whole of Lovely County, for all I care."

Everybody seemed to be aggravated that fall. I spent a good bit of time writing from Major DuVal to George Hammatrack, the agent to the Osage, trying to smooth over a misunderstanding that came up between them, when Major DuVal didn't bring a Cherokee delegation to a council with the Osage back in the summer. Even the leaders of the territorial government couldn't be civil; in November, we got word that the former territorial secretary, Robert Crittenden, had killed the territorial representative to Congress, Henry Conway, in a duel. The candidates to replace Conway in Congress built their campaigns on removal of the Indians from the civilized part of the territory, which kept the Cherokees coming in to the agency with sour moods and anxious questions.

Home was like an island of peace in the midst of all the storms of politics. There were no more worries about money. We even had a good bit of money put away by now, and my plan was to find and buy some land during the early part of the new year. Maggie was looking better than I'd ever seen her look, rounded out instead of being so skinny. Penny was a little girl now, not a baby, completely weaned and coming up on three years old. She tracked Maggie's every step and repeated just about anything either one of us said. I thought it was funny to teach her the names of the Cherokee chiefs and the government officials, especially to listen to her little voice trying to say Hammatrack's name.

"What use does a girl have knowing such as that?" Maggie said. "She ain't ever going to be meeting them fellers."

"I know," I said, bouncing Penny on my knee while she squealed with laughter. "Ma would say the same. But the Territory is different from the States. No telling what a girl might need to know out here." I tickled Penny's solid sides, and she giggled and squirmed. "You may have to send a letter to President Adams for your old pa someday, right, my girl?"

"John Qincy Adums!" she shouted, and even Maggie couldn't keep from laughing.

One cold morning in November, everybody at the agency was rushing around with an excitement I hadn't seen in the months I'd worked with Major DuVal. The Grand Council of the Cherokees— the most important of the chiefs—was gathering at the agency. I spent all day over a sheaf of paper, listening to the Cherokees talk angrily in their own language, then trying to record word for word the translation John Rogers gave. By mid-afternoon, I could tell all the talk was coming down to one thing—the Cherokees wanted a meeting with the Secretary of War, face to face. Major DuVal sat silently behind his desk, his expression grave, as the Council decided to leave for Washington City in December, only a few weeks away.

It was nearly dark when the chiefs finally left, and I sat behind Major DuVal's desk, recopying my hasty notes into a more presentable report as he saw the Cherokees off. Then he came and sat on the edge of the desk beside me. He sighed deeply, and I looked up.

"Something wrong, Major?"

He was rubbing his temples. "Bring me a bit of brandy, Josiah. And one for Mr. McKellar, as well." He glanced at me as Josiah left. "I suppose I should have asked if you drink brandy." I shrugged, and he smiled, a smile that didn't make it to his eyes. "Remind me, Mr. McKellar, of the topics the Council wants their delegates to bring before the Secretary."

I looked through my notes. "Securing payment of the annuities that are overdue. Arranging for a survey of their lands in the territory. Presenting a case against white settlement in Lovely's Purchase. They emphasized—"

He cut me off. "Under no circumstances is there to be any discussion of a cession of their land to the United States." He sighed again as he took the brandy from Josiah. "The Cherokees don't want to talk about that topic, but I'm certain that will be foremost on the mind of the Secretary. I'm in a difficult spot, Mr. McKellar. I'm sworn to represent the interests of the Cherokees, but I hold my position at the pleasure of the Secretary of War, the Congress, and the President. At times like this, I feel the pull of those different obligations will leave me drawn and quartered." He sipped his brandy and glanced idly at the finished page of notes.

"You do good work, Mr. McKellar," he said. "I should speak to the Secretary about providing me with funds to increase your salary. Perhaps it won't be too difficult to convince him. I'll introduce you to him while we are in Washington City."

I choked on my brandy, a gulp bigger than I'd meant to take in. "We?" I managed to squeeze out between coughs. "You mean I'm going with you?"

He smiled. "I shall need a recording secretary."

I stared at him. Me, go to Washington City? The capital of the United States—the heart of law and politics and decision-making. Even my Uncle Abner, in all his years of practicing law and with all his love of everything about politics, had never been to Washington City.

Major DuVal laughed. "I see you are speechless. Go home and talk with Mrs. McKellar about it. But I certainly hope you will agree to come. I will need a man as competent as you are to help with the records and correspondence necessary for such a trip."

Maggie was just as speechless when I told her as I had been in Major DuVal's office. I took one of my law books from the box under our bed and opened to the map of the country.

"Here we are, in Arkansas Territory." I pointed to the spot on the map. "And here's Washington City."

"That's far off," she said solemnly.

"It is."

"How long would you be gone?"

"I would think it would just be a matter of weeks, most of it travel time. The Cherokees just want a meeting with the Secretary of War, so we wouldn't be in Washington City itself for that long a time, maybe a day or two. If we leave in December like they want to, I figure we'd be back for sure by the first of February."

She was silent, staring at the map and rubbing her hand across her apron, smoothing it against her belly. Finally, she looked up at me.

"Do you want to go?"

"I don't know," I said, honestly. "It would be something to see. And Major DuVal says he needs me to come along. But I don't like the thought of leaving you and Penny here alone, even for just a couple of weeks."

"I don't like it, either."

I clapped the book shut. "I'll tell him I can't go, then. There's bound to be fellows in Washington City who could take his notes."

"I don't like it," she went on, like I hadn't said anything. "But I reckon nobody promised we're going to like everything that happens to us in life. Like you say, it's only for a little time. I reckon you ought to go."

I slipped my arms around her. "I don't have to go, Maggie. I'll just tell him to find someone else. I won't leave you here alone." She looked up with a little grin twisting her mouth.

"He'll pay you to go, I reckon? Enough to for sure get us a good-sized piece of land?"

⁊⁊ ⁊⁊ ⁊⁊

So it was decided. The days until we were leaving Dardanelle rushed past, filled with helping Major DuVal prepare for the trip and with helping Maggie be ready for the stay without me. In the daylight hours when I wasn't busy at the agency, I cut and split firewood until the stack was more than halfway up the wall the full length of the cabin. I took some of the money we had saved and bought a big ham, a whole keg of salt pork, and two bags of cornmeal to store in the attic under the eaves. Maggie laughed at me.

"How much do you think I'm going to eat while you're gone?" she asked. "Or are you counting on Penny to eat that keg of pork?"

"You won't have money coming in while I'm gone," I reminded her. "I just don't want you to run short of anything."

I asked Joseph Brearley to look in on Maggie now and then while I was gone to see if she needed anything, and he agreed he'd do it. But a week before we were to leave, I stopped by the store for a stock of beans, salt, and sugar, and he had forgotten already.

"Looks like you're planning for a hard winter, McKellar," he joked. "Are you afraid snow will be so deep you'll not be able to get to the store? You're sure laying in a cabin full of supplies."

"I'm going with Major DuVal and the Cherokees to Washington City," I said. "I asked you to look in on Maggie, remember?"

His face instantly changed from smiling to guilty. "Oh, right," he said. "I remember now. Sorry, McKellar. We've been so busy lately, with everybody trying to stock up for winter. But I won't forget again."

"It's all right," I said. But as I walked home with the box of supplies, I knew I had to think of another plan. Joseph Brearley was a good fellow, but he had his own concerns to look after. Every man in the Territory had his own concerns to look after. If I'd been back home in Campbell County, I could have gone to my brothers. Any one of them would have stepped in to give Maggie whatever help she needed, without a second thought. But I'd made my choices, and my brothers weren't here.

"I don't need them," I told a hawk flying overhead. "I'll find some other way."

I did think of another way, soon after, but the idea was so daft I put it out of my head—until a couple of days before our party was to leave for Washington City. I was going through the supplies in the cabin, one last time. Penny was fretful, with a case of sniffles.

"Watch her for a bit," Maggie said. "I need some pine needles to make a tea for her, but I don't want to take her out in the cold with me."

I sat by the fire snuggling Penny on my lap, with her cheek against my chest. She wasn't really sick, I knew that, not from sniffles. But she could get sick while I was gone—young'uns got sick all the time. What would Maggie do then, alone?

As Maggie hung her cloak on its peg, I set Penny on the bed and took down my jacket.

"Where are you going?" she asked, surprised.

"I'll be back for supper," I promised. "I nearly forgot something."

The information I got from the Cherokees hanging around the agency led me to a small cabin in the woods north of Dwight Mission. An old Indian woman was on the porch, splitting a chunk of rich pine into kindling. I stopped at the edge of the porch and, for some reason, took off my hat.

"I'm looking for Elwin Root, Little El," I said. "Folks told me I could find him here."

The woman stared at me for a minute, then shrugged and went inside the cabin. I stood still in the yard with my hat in my hands, unsure whether she was going to come back out or whether I should give it up as bad luck. I was just about to remount the horse I'd borrowed from Joseph Brearley when Little El came through the door. He stopped dead still when he saw me, and then he started laughing.

"She said there was a white man out here, but I have to say you are the last white man on earth I expected it to be," he said.

I grinned at him a little sheepishly. "I had something to talk to you about. The folks around the agency said you would probably be here, studying with George Guess."

"Sequoyah," he corrected me. "Come in, McKellar. We can talk in front of the fire."

I cleared my throat. "It's something of a personal matter," I started, but he shook his head.

"Neither of them speak English. Whatever you have to say will be as private as if you said it into a well. Come in."

The cabin's ceiling was low, and I had to stand with my shoulders hunched uncomfortably to keep from knocking my head against it. It was dark, as well, with only the light from the fireplace. A thin old man sat by the hearth, dressed in what I'd come to know was the old-time garb of the Cherokees. He was surrounded by pieces of bark on which were scrawled some kind of strange pictures.

"This is what I'm studying," Little El said, taking up one of the bark pieces. "It's the Cherokee language, written down. Sequoyah is the master who created it, and if our people learn it, we will have the same power in writing that white men have." He tapped me on the arm with the bark. "But you are not here to learn about that. You have a personal matter to discuss with me?"

He squatted by the fire and motioned for me to do the same, so I squatted awkwardly, leaning on the balls of my feet to keep from knocking over the piles of bark. Now the time was come, I wasn't sure of how to say what I had come to say, and I turned over several openings in my mind, none of them right. Little El waited, staring at me with frank curiosity, which made it even harder.

"Mr. Guess – Sequoyah – is going with Major DuVal to Washington tomorrow," I started, and Little El nodded. "I'm going too, as a recording secretary." There was another long silence while I wrestled with words in my mind, which refused to string them together in a way that made sense. Finally, I just spit it out, plain.

"I wondered if you would look after Maggie while I'm gone."

Little El's expression didn't change, but I could tell by the slight widening of his nostrils that I'd near toppled him over with my request.

"You're wondering why I'd ask you, of all people," I went on, in a low voice, though he'd said the old man and woman couldn't understand us. "I wonder myself if I'm plumb mad. But the men around Dardanelle, they're all busy with their own doings, busy enough that they might forget about her, out away from town like we are. I've tried to set her up so she won't need anything, but a man can't guess all that might happen, and I don't want her and Penny to have to do without. I know you won't forget about her."

He looked down at his hands, rubbing them together slowly. "You trust me with her now, McKellar?"

I stared at the neat little piles of bark pieces. "I won't be gone that long, only a couple or three weeks, and like I say, I've set her up—" I suddenly stopped and met his eyes. "I trust you with her. I wouldn't have asked if I didn't."

I was keenly aware of the crackling of the fire, of the painful pressure in the balls of my feet, of the smell of greasy dishes. It seemed like time had frozen until Little El suddenly stuck out his hand toward me. I took it, and his grip around my hand was firm.

"Have no worries," he said. "I will take care of anything Maggie and Penny might need that you haven't planned for."

I stood, forgetting about the low ceiling, and got a good cracking on the back of my head from a ceiling beam. Little El saw me out to the porch, and I thought there was something different about him, a higher tilt to his chin, maybe, or a brightness to his eyes. He watched as I mounted the horse, then he lifted one hand in a wave.

"I hope your journey is safe, McKellar," he called, "and that the chiefs are successful in settling the questions with your government."

"So do I. And I thank you for looking out for my family."

"I will care for them like sisters," he promised. "And if God wills something to happen on your trip, a steamboat accident or an illness, and you don't return—" I stiffened in the saddle, and he laughed. "I'm joking, McKellar."

❧ ❧ ❧

We waited to pack my bags until the last night, after Penny was sleeping and Maggie could use the sad iron without worry. She brought out the suit coat that I hadn't worn since we'd been in Nashville, four years ago, but it was a little tight in the shoulders and a little short in the sleeves. Maggie sighed as she helped me out of it.

"Either you've grown some since you wore this last or it shrunk when I washed it," she said. "I might could let out these hems on the sleeves, but it's still going to look too tight. We should have took some of the money and got you a new one."

"There's nowhere to buy a suit coat in Dardanelle. Don't worry about it—the chiefs probably don't have anything any better."

"But you're helping Major DuVal, and he will." She laid the jacket aside and spread a shirt across the table. "And you'll be talking to all those fancy fellers from the government."

"I won't be doing the talking—I'll be at the end of the table taking notes. They probably won't even notice me." I watched her move the hot iron across the collar of the shirt, smoothing out the wrinkles. As she set the iron down to reposition the shirt, I caught her hand. "I need to tell you something. Nothing bad," I added quickly.

She pulled a chair around beside me and sat.

"I've tried to think what all you might need while I'm gone," I started. "You should have more than enough. But I've asked a couple of fellows to check in and see if you're needing anything."

"Who?"

"Joseph Brearley, and—" Suddenly it was harder to say than I had thought it would be. I took in a deep breath. "Elwin Root. Little El."

She stared at me without speaking.

"I asked Brearley first," I explained, stumbling over my words a little in my hurry to fill the silence. "But you know he's busy with the store, and I don't want you and Penny to be forgotten and in need. Little El's not doing anything but studying that language the Cherokees have made up. He'll have plenty of time to help if you should need anything."

She was looking at me like she thought I might have gone mad. "You're sure you want that?"

I took her hand and touched my lips to her fingers. "You were right about me before. I was a fool then." Her face relaxed.

"It's all right, then, I reckon." She laughed. "At least you ain't dumping us at Dwight Mission this time."

She started to stand, but I tightened my hold on her hand.

"Maggie—" I swallowed hard. "If something should happen, an accident or some such—"

But she wouldn't listen to that. She pulled her hand away and went back to the iron.

"Nothing will happen," she said. "I'll be praying for you every day till you're back home. You'll be fine, and back home before—" She suddenly stopped.

"Before what?"

"Before you know it. Before time to plant corn." I was sure that was not what she'd meant to say, but she went back to smoothing the wrinkles from a sleeve. "You ought to pray for us, too, you know. I ain't seen or heard you pray in a long time, John David. You will pray for us, won't you?"

"Of course," I said.

⁂

The next morning, I eyed the steamboat with a nervous flutter in my gut as the delegation was loading the baggage. I wished now I hadn't read all those accounts in the *Arkansas Gazette* of steamboat explosions that caused a whole boat and everyone on it to sink into the depths of the Mississippi River in a matter of minutes. Maggie and Penny had walked with me into Dardanelle, and my eyes teared up a little as I held them close for goodbye.

"It's time to board, Mr. McKellar," someone called, and I tightened my arms around Maggie.

"I love you," I whispered into her ear. "Take care."

Her lips were warm and soft against my cheek before I pulled away and started up the gangplank toward the deck. I settled myself at the railing, finding them in the wad of people on the shoreline. They waved at me, and I waved back as the gangplank was pulled on board and the captain blew the deafening whistle that meant the journey was starting. I kept my eyes on Maggie while the big wheel on the boat slowly churned into action and the boat began to pull away. She looked away then, and I saw that Little El was speaking to her. She turned back to look at me, then I saw her nod, and the three of them—Maggie, Penny, and Little El—started away on the road back toward our cabin. She wouldn't have to be a lone woman walking on the road, and I was glad of that, but still—

"Damn you, Elwin Root," I murmured. "Don't stay for pie."

Chapter 15

Traveling down the Arkansas River on a steamboat was better than poling a keelboat up it had been, but sometimes it seemed to me we weren't making any more progress in a day than the keelboat had. Then there was a wait once we'd finally come to the end of the Arkansas River, until we could catch another boat going north up the Mississippi. We chugged our way up the Mississippi and up the Ohio to Wheeling, Virginia, where we finally left river travel behind. Major DuVal secured spots for us in a pair of stagecoaches traveling toward Washington City on what they called the National Road. Being from Baltimore, Major DuVal had brought along his wife and children to visit family while we were in Washington. I ended up riding in the coach with them, while the Cherokee delegation rode in the second coach.

After a couple of days of jolting along in the stuffy coach, listening to Major DuVal's young'uns fuss, I moved out to sit with the driver, even though it meant being out in the cold. The driver was a friendly sort, and he told me all about the countryside as the miles rolled along. We cut through mountains as dark and steep as the ones I'd grown up in and over rolling fields covered in snow. For the first time in my life, I passed over a river on a bridge, not a ferry or a ford, and I have to admit I was uneasy until the coach was back on the solid ground. The road was busy, even in winter. Several times, we caught up to herds of cattle or hogs moving along the road with young boys walking behind, carrying sticks or limber switches to keep the animals moving. Sometimes we would be stuck behind other stagecoaches, breathing in the dust of the road for miles.

What worried me, though, was the traffic we met going the other way. Plenty of folks passed us heading west in wagons with canvas-covered frames overhead. I saw others who were like Maggie and me, walking with a pack animal loaded with everything it could carry. At the stations where we stopped to change out the teams of horses, everyone was talking about the West. It seemed to me the whole East Coast was emptying out with folks going west, and some days, I was gripped with anxiety that I wouldn't get home in time to buy a piece of land before all these folks had beat me to it.

I quickly came to see this trip was going to take longer than Maggie and I had planned. The journey itself took nearly six weeks. It was mid-February when the coaches finally moved into the streets of Washington City. I had spent most of a year in Nashville and thought at the time that I managed city living well enough. But Washington was bigger than Nashville, with streets that ran at strange angles, and I was soon lost in trying to make sense of the path we were following. The coach driver pulled up in front of a set of tall brick buildings standing side by side in a row. I stood beside him as he held the door for the DuVal family to leave the coach.

"I don't see how a man finds his way through this city," I said, lightly, like I was making a joke. "The streets twist themselves into knots."

"Aye, that they do," the driver agreed. "But you got the luck to be staying on the one street where you can always find your way— Pennsylvania Avenue, they call it."

"What makes this one so easy to find?" It looked like any of dozens of muddy streets we had been in that morning. The driver laughed.

"Raise your chin, McKellar, and you'll see it. Your hotel is set between the Capitol building on one hand and the president's mansion on the other."

I stepped to the other side of the coach, and there I could see them – two huge buildings of white stone, set at opposite ends of the avenue, but with a clear sightline between them. I'm pretty sure my mouth was hanging open in wonder when Major DuVal called to me.

"Mr. McKellar, can you give us a hand with the baggage?" I pulled myself away from the sight and took the first of the DuVals' trunks that the driver was handing down. Major DuVal took one handle of the trunk, and he smiled as we lugged the trunk to the board sidewalk in front of the hotel.

"Quite a sight, isn't it, Mr. McKellar?" he said. "There's no city quite like Washington."

⁂

Major DuVal sent a messenger to the Secretary of War's office that afternoon to let him know the Cherokee delegation had arrived. I was hopeful that evening as we sat in the tavern of the Williamson Hotel. The delegation's business couldn't take more than a couple of days, and travel down the rivers was likely to be a lot quicker than coming up. I figured I'd be back in Arkansas Territory by early March, plenty of time to scout out some land and get at least one field ready for corn. I looked around at the chiefs, who sat drinking whiskey with the same dignified posture they had during a council meeting. They didn't say much, but it was clear they were the center of attention in the room. Some of the other guests were trying to strike up conversation through James Rogers' translation. Others sat and simply stared. I leaned forward and poured a little more whiskey into my glass, then offered some to John Flowers and David Brown, the secretaries for the Cherokees and the men I'd be sharing a room with until we left the hotel. Flowers held out his glass, but I wasn't surprised that David Brown refused; he was some kind of preacher for the Cherokees.

"Here's to a quick meeting with the Secretary of War," I said, raising my glass, and even Brown, though he wasn't drinking, raised a glass to click against it.

Two weeks later, we were still sitting in the tavern every evening, waiting for some word from the government. The mood was considerably different. The other guests' curiosity had been satisfied, and they mostly left us alone at the tables near the back of the tavern. The chiefs still didn't say much, but they didn't sit quite so stiff and dignified anymore, and I'd noticed a couple of them had taken to drinking a good bit of the whiskey the U.S. government was so generously supplying for us. I hadn't seen much of Major DuVal during the past weeks, as he had been taking his family to visit relatives in the area. Most nights, I sat at the end of the table drinking while the Cherokees talked around me in their own language. I didn't

167

have to understand the words to know the chiefs were beginning to get impatient.

It was the end of March before a response came from the Secretary of War. I sat at the back of the room while Major DuVal read the letter to the chiefs, slowly, so James Rogers would have time to interpret.

"'The Secretary of War has received and read attentively the letter of the Cherokee Deputation now in this City. It may suffice for the present to state in reply that it is the full determination of the Executive to fulfill all the Treaty and other obligations to the Cherokees. Causes have hitherto existed in regard to the ascertainment of the quantity of lands ceded by the Cherokee in Georgia, Alabama, North Carolina, and Tennessee, which have prevented the Executive from giving to them a like quantity in Arkansas.'"

Flowers snorted. "There they go with that excuse again." Major DuVal ignored him.

"'But the obligation is not considered as being impaired by the delay. The Faith of the United States as pledged to the Cherokees the Executive will maintain. The Secretary of War wishes the Delegation distinctly to understand this.'" He paused a moment to let Rogers catch up. I looked around at the faces of the chiefs, clouded with suspicion. They had heard this before.

Major DuVal cleared his throat and went on. "'It is believed, however, that a new arrangement may be made as to boundaries, which shall not only embrace all the lands as to quantity which the Cherokees may have a right to, but essentially benefit themselves and their posterity; and at the same time, such an arrangement being agreed to, the other subjects submitted by the Deputation could be provided for. With the view of ascertaining the disposition of the Cherokees on the subject of the foregoing suggestion, the Secretary desires to be informed if they have any objection to open a negotiation upon a basis which shall give them lands, for quantity, west of the Western boundary of Arkansas, that boundary being fixed to run forty miles east of its present location—in exchange for those to which they are now entitled—'"

The quiet in the room exploded into sounds of protest as Rogers finished his interpretation.

"We are not here to negotiate trading land!" Thomas Graves

growled, and I thought he looked like a man who could murder someone.

"The council said we are not to talk about land trades," Black Fox said, standing. "We will go home with no meeting before we talk about land trades!"

Major DuVal was pale, I thought. "There's no need to talk of going home just yet," he said. "We should first respond to the Secretary's letter and tell him you are not authorized to discuss land exchanges. I will send such a letter this afternoon."

"Ask for a meeting face-to-face," Graves said. "We'll make it clear why we are here."

Major DuVal had me fetch my quill and paper right then, and that satisfied the chiefs enough that they left us to write the letter while they went to the tavern. I sat with the quill ready to go into the ink, waiting while Major DuVal paced around the room, his hands folded like he was praying. Finally, he turned and looked at me.

"I must be careful with my choice of words in this letter, Mr. McKellar. Take down a draft and then we will revise a final copy to send to the secretary." He sighed deeply. "To James Barbour, Secretary of War—"

༞ ༞ ༞

I heard John Flowers and David Brown arguing through the door when I went to our room after finishing Major DuVal's letter.

"It's a trick," Flowers was saying. "They don't want to talk about surveys. And they won't want to talk about Lovely County."

"We have to meet with them in good faith," Brown answered. "Nothing will be accomplished if we go in with our shields up."

"You are too willing to trust them! Sometimes I think it's true what some folks say about you, Brown—going to those missionary schools made you gain Greek and lose Cherokee!" Flowers threw the door open and nearly bowled me over as he charged out. "Watch where you're going, McKellar!" He stormed down the hallway toward the staircase.

David Brown looked a little flustered as I came into the room, but he smiled at me.

"Did Major DuVal get a reply off to Secretary Barbour?" he asked.

I nodded, crossing to set the writing tools in the trunk I'd borrowed from the DuVals for the trip. "Maybe that will set straight paths for the discussions."

"Maybe." I turned to look at him. "I don't understand it, Brown. You're a Cherokee, but you want to meet and negotiate with the U.S. government. Flowers is a white man, but he doesn't trust the whites."

"John married John Rogers' daughter," he told me. "They are a powerful family within the western nation. I think he sees more possibility for importance as the son-in-law of John Rogers than as just another white man under your government."

"What about you?" I asked. "What's that he said about you losing Cherokee?"

He pondered a minute before answering. "I am proud of what I learned at Andover. I am also proud of my people, and I want us to prosper. But I don't hate white people. We are brothers under God. It is my hope that we can all come to see that, in time."

I closed the trunk and reached for my jacket.

"Are you going to the tavern?" he asked. I shook my head and left him sitting at the desk with his notes on the translation of the New Testament, which he was putting into the Cherokee language.

I passed by the tavern where the chiefs were grumbling in low voices over their whiskey. I stepped out into the chilly twilight and walked down Pennsylvania Avenue toward the Capitol building. Everywhere around me were the sounds of the city—talking and laughter, the squeal of a fiddle, the clop of horses' feet and the creaking of carriages. It was late March. At home, peeper frogs would be shrilling in the mud along the river and the wind would be sweet with the smell of fresh grass. Penny would be having a birthday in another week, her third. Maggie would be rocking her to sleep now in that crooked chair, singing so softly it could barely be heard. In my mind's picture, Maggie's hair was loose, falling around her shoulders in soft, brown waves—

"Hey, fella," a woman called, stepping from the shadows into the yellow light from a tavern window. "Want a drink? Need some company?"

I shoved my hands deep into my pockets and walked on.

❦ ❦ ❦

The delegation met with Thomas McKenney, the Superintendent of Indian Affairs, a few days later. Sitting in the back of the room, taking down notes for Major DuVal, I thought Mr. McKenney seemed ill at ease. He hardly looked at the Indians as he put forward the government's proposal. The government was willing to give the Cherokee land west of their current holdings, acre for acre. It would, he said, help the Indians avoid being penned in by white settlers and would give them a permanent outlet to the hunting grounds in the west.

The chiefs sat in stone-faced silence as Mr. McKenney talked about the proposal. Once he had finished, John Rogers turned to his son and said something in Cherokee. James stood.

"You say your government will give us acre for acre what we give up. That is the same promise that was made when we left our lands in the east, but your government has not yet honored that treaty."

Mr. McKenney flushed red up to the roots of his white hair.

"Ah, yes," he said. "That survey of the land in the east has not been completed. The exact acreage is unclear—"

"We will not talk about trading land," Black Fox said. "Your government needs to complete the survey of the land in the east and give us what is due. Drive the white settlers out of Lovely's Purchase and let us have that land as part of what the treaty promised."

"There are many considerations," Mr. McKenney began, but John Rogers stood and spoke again in Cherokee. Black Fox nodded.

"We are anxious to bring this business to a close as soon as possible," he said. "We are ready to return home."

Home was the main topic of talk over supper, but Major DuVal silenced the talk with one sobering statement.

"We have no appropriation for a return home."

The chiefs who spoke only Cherokee leaned toward James Rogers, who repeated Major DuVal's words for them. They sat back slowly, and every face around the table was stunned.

"We can't go home," John Flowers murmured.

"Not unless we use our own money," Major DuVal said. "Do any of you have means with you to pay for fare back to Arkansas Territory?" James Rogers mumbled the translation, and the chiefs shook their heads.

"Hostages," Flowers said. "We're a bunch of damned hostages until they get what they want."

❦ ❦ ❦

There was much drinking in the tavern that night and little talk, not even in their own tongue. Yet the next letter the delegation sent to Mr. McKenney firmly declined his offer of a trade. For the next week or so, correspondence fluttered back and forth over the amount of land due to the Cherokees based on what they had given up in the east. Then in the middle of April came a letter from Mr. McKenney that deepened the worry lines in Major DuVal's brow as he read it to the delegation.

"'Friends and Brothers, I am directed by the Secretary of War to state that he has submitted the entire subject, as embraced in your letter of the 28th of February last, to the President of the United States, together with the subsequent correspondence in relation to the proposition made to you by him for an exchange of your location. The President, I am directed to say, after mature deliberation, has concluded to order a permanent Western line to be run, to embrace the quantity of land to which you are entitled in Arkansas, in exchange for that ceded by you in Georgia, Alabama, North Carolina, and Tennessee.'"

The message went on to say the Cherokees were entitled to a little more than 3 million acres and that the President would order the survey 'without delay.' On every other request the Cherokees had made, however, the President deferred to Congress as the final authority, which we all knew meant they would get no satisfaction. The chiefs grumbled together as they left, and the worry lines in Major DuVal's face deepened as he watched them go.

"The President is involved now," he said to me. "That means Secretary Barbour and Mr. McKenney want this business over with. Secretary Barbour is leaving office in another month or so. If I can't persuade the chiefs to negotiate soon, I fear the government will simply force them to leave, with no compensation at all."

To make matters worse, late one morning we learned from a clerk in Mr. McKenney's office that Arkansas' territorial representative to Congress, Ambrose Sevier, was complaining loudly about any deal that would force white folks out of Lovely County. Though Major

DuVal was sick that day, he called me to his room at once and dictated a letter to Mr. McKenney.

"Very few things astonish me nowadays, or I should be greatly surprised at what you say has been communicated by Mr. Sevier to the Secretary of War. I say, without hesitation, and I would write it in the presence of Mr. Sevier, that there is not even the shadow of truth in it: No—not the shadow. Emphasize that last," he ordered. He lay back on the pillows for a few moments, gathering the strength to go on. "Be as liberal as justice to the U.S. will allow you to be in the inducements you may offer for the exchange, and it will still remain a matter of difficulty and doubt. I should render myself fairly obnoxious to reproach for gross dereliction of duty were I to connive at terms that were either unreasonable in themselves, or unexpected by the Cherokees."

He waited while I scratched down the words, but when I looked up, his arm was thrown across his eyes.

"I fear I've failed them," he said quietly. "All I can do now is try to get them to accept the deal and get the best they can out of it." He struggled to sit up, then collapsed back into the pillow. "Mrs. DuVal is away visiting family. Can you please help me up, Mr. McKellar?"

I helped him into a robe, and he leaned on me as we went into the front room of his chambers.

"Are you sure about this?" I asked, as he dropped into the armchair, panting like he had run a mile. He nodded, motioning for the chamber pot, and I fetched it quickly. He puked into it, then wiped his mouth delicately and leaned back into the chair.

"Send up James Rogers, and then ask the chiefs to come up individually," he murmured. "And please be sure that letter is sent to Mr. McKenney today. We must counteract Sevier's poison before it has time to spread."

Throughout the afternoon, he met with the chiefs one by one. By evening he was so exhausted he sagged against my arm as I helped him back to his bed, but he seemed a little easier in his mind.

"Perhaps it will be over soon, Mr. McKellar," he said as I pulled the covers over his shoulders. "Perhaps you'll soon be able to see your pretty wife again."

I didn't go to the tavern that evening, for the chiefs were arguing among themselves. Instead, I took a bottle of whiskey out to the courtyard behind the hotel and sat in one of the chairs meant for the kitchen servants. I poured a healthy portion of the whiskey into the glass the serving girl had given me. The night air was warm and fresh with spring, except when the breeze carried the stench of the privy my direction. I took a long swallow of the whiskey and looked up at the moon above the three-story building, a waxing moon, bright enough that I could read the label on the whiskey bottle without much trouble. By the size of that moon, I figured I'd missed my best time to plant corn. I wondered if Maggie would be able to plant a garden under the growing moon, like it ought to be done. Little El might help her put in a garden, that I could hope for, but no one was going to plant a field of corn for me. It had been five months since I'd left, much longer than either he or I had planned when I asked him to look in on her. Was he tired of the job? Or was he liking it too much? Did Maggie even miss me anymore, or was my being gone something she'd grown used to, like a splinter that had callused over? I regretted now that I hadn't written a letter to her in all these months. But she couldn't read it herself, and I didn't fancy the idea of Little El reading aloud to her the things from my heart.

I heard a door open, and then footsteps, and I looked around to see David Brown.

"Mind if I join you?" he asked. I shrugged and took another drink. He pulled another chair near to mine, and for a while we sat in silence.

"So what do the chiefs say?" I asked. "Did Major DuVal's talking change anything?"

"They will agree to the treaty," he said softly. "What other choice is there? We will leave our farms and our houses to go west and clear new ground. We'll build new cabins and start over, again."

"Will your people in the Territory honor the treaty? There wasn't supposed to be any negotiation over land trades on this trip."

"They will be angry. But they will go west. We have no choice, Mr. McKellar. Your people are too powerful and too many." He sighed. "I would like to see the time when Cherokees and whites can live side by side as brothers in Christ. But that time has not come."

Unbidden, the terrified face of the pregnant Cherokee woman in Lovely's Purchase came into my mind. I took another hefty swig of the whiskey.

"When I got to Arkansas Territory, I thought you folks were a nuisance," I said. "I wanted you all gone. But I didn't think about it happening this way."

"It's the way of your government," he started, but I cut him off.

"It's not the government. It's me. The government is just doing what I want, me and all the other white folks pushing into new country. We say we'll use the land proper, not like you 'savages,' but then we come across your people with farms that aren't a whit different from our own farms. So we change to some other excuse. Folks say you red men are simply an inferior race by nature." I gave a bitter laugh. "But look at us, David Brown, you and me. There's you on the one hand. You've studied Greek and Hebrew in a seminary out East and you're translating the New Testament into a new language, the whole New Testament. Then there's me." I took another quick swig. "I quit my law studies, and I've never had steady work of any kind until Major DuVal took me on. I've always been a hacker of brush, or a loader of boats, or a killer of hogs." I held my bare forearm out against his. "But because my skin is one shade lighter than yours, I'm the better man."

He reached over and took the whiskey bottle from me and set it carefully on the ground on the other side of his chair.

"Are you married, Mr. McKellar?" I nodded, and he smiled as he looked up at the moon. "So am I. Rachel's her name and we have a little son named John. Do you have children?"

"A girl, Penny."

"That's nice." He leaned back with his head cradled in his hands. "When I was young, my parents sent me to a mission school where we were forbidden to have anything to do with Cherokee ways, or even to speak in our language. I was a good student, an eager student. Some of my people think I am a betrayer because of my studies and because I am a Christian. They think there's no place for white ways in a true Cherokee life. But in the long run, what do we all want, whether we are Cherokee or white? To take care of Penny and John, and to be right with our God, would you agree? We are the same inside, and I believe it is God's will that we live together in peace."

"Well, it's not the will of the U.S. government," I said. "Keep us separate, that's what the President—and most white folks—want."

"For now," he said. "But the will of God cannot be recalled." He stood. "Don't drink too much, Mr. McKellar. You don't want to be ill when we meet with Mr. McKenney again, and I believe that will be soon."

I sat for a while longer in the dark, thinking about the treaty. It was going to happen. They would sign, and then my way was clear to the land north of the river that I'd coveted since the first time I'd set foot on it. Little El and his pa would have to leave it, same as Maggie and I had. For a long time, I'd wanted that, and I'd even dreamed of being there to see it, sitting astride a horse and watching Elwin Root and his whole family ordered off the land, just as he'd watched when the 7th U.S. Army Infantry had evicted me. But tonight, under the waxing spring moon, the thought didn't bring me much pleasure. I thought of George Guess, past his prime and half-lame to boot, and I wondered how he would manage to start over in rough new land.

I sighed deeply and drained the last of the whiskey in my glass. Whatever my part in starting it, removal was coming, like a flash flood down a narrow creek. Nothing could be done now but ride it out.

Chapter 16

Once there was the smallest indication that the delegation might be considering the land exchange, the Secretary of War's office began putting on paper possible conditions of a treaty. Major DuVal, still weak from his sickness, dictated a letter pressing for some sort of monetary compensation for the Indians.

"Take this down," he said, leaning his head against one hand. "They would get, by the exchange, of what is termed 'Lovely's Purchase,' together with the lands laying on the waters of Grand River, about two millions of acres, which may be supposed equal, but certainly not superior, to the lands they now occupy. The residue—say four millions of acres—would consist of lands, mostly naked prairies, which, acre for acre, is scarcely of half the intrinsic value of that they now hold." He sat for a minute while I waited, quill poised above the ink pot.

"Is this nothing to them?" he suddenly exclaimed, and I set about writing it down. "No, Mr. McKellar," he said quickly. "That was not meant for the letter."

"I'm sorry, sir. I'll recopy—"

"No," he said, and his voice was stronger than it had been in days. "On second thought, keep it. Let's resume. Is this nothing to them? An exchange would compel them to leave their opened fields and improvements, which they have been making and toiling on for year—a great many of them with fine peach and some with apple orchards, and again settle in the forest, comparatively remote from many of the conveniences which they now enjoy, and create every thing, requisite to ordinary comfort, anew. Is it supposed that these things are not thought of by them?"

Correspondence passed between the Secretary of War's office and the hotel every day the last week of April as details of the treaty were worked out. A draft was sent to us, and Major DuVal went over it carefully before giving it to John Flowers and David Brown to translate into Cherokee for the chiefs who didn't know English. In answer to Major DuVal's request, the Secretary had added "gifts" for some individual members of the delegation. George Guess was to receive $500 in recognition of the "beneficial results" of the alphabet "discovered by him," as well as a salt spring to replace the one he would lose in Arkansas. Thomas Graves was awarded $1,200 for "losses sustained in his property and for personal suffering endured by him when confined as a prisoner, on a criminal but false accusation."

At the end of the week, the delegation asked Mr. McKenney to arrange a meeting with the President. When we heard the request was granted, Major DuVal tried to act like it was just another part of his job, but I knew he was about to bust with the excitement.

"Not everyone gets an audience with the President. Of course, it's natural that he, as head of state, would want to sit down with the parties to a treaty the United States is entering into," he told me that evening when we were checking over all the correspondence related to the treaty.

"That's quite an honor for the Cherokees, I reckon," I said. He suddenly turned on me with a broad grin.

"Oh, you're coming with us, Mr. McKellar. You've been part of this process for more than a year. You certainly have earned the chance to visit the White House."

"Me?" He nodded, and I laughed. "What will Maggie and Penny think? I'm going to meet President John Qincy Adums."

"Quincy," he corrected quickly.

Mrs. DuVal took us all in hand in the days before the meeting, making sure we'd all be presentable enough to see the President. She frowned a little and tilted her head to the side when I showed her my suit jacket.

"That won't do, Mr. McKellar. It's a bit faded, and that style is several years outdated, besides. You'll need a new one."

I didn't want to spend my land money on a jacket I'd wear one time, even if that one time was to meet the President. "How much will it cost?" I asked.

"Don't be concerned with that," Major DuVal said from the other side of the room. "I'll put it in the expense report, and the government will pay for it. Ellen, dear, see to it he gets a cravat and a nice pair of shoes, too."

"Shoes? For those big feet?" she exclaimed, and then she blushed as she looked up at me. "I didn't mean that as it sounded, Mr. McKellar. But Edward, no merchant will have that size—we'll have to find a cobbler who's willing to work quickly."

Mrs. DuVal also insisted I needed a haircut, so the afternoon before we were to go to the White House, David Brown, John Flowers, and I went looking for a barber to give us all a haircut and a close shave. We were glad to find a shop a short way down Pennsylvania Avenue, since none of us had been brave enough to wander off that main street during our time in Washington City. The barber, though, took one look at David Brown and waved the razor in his hand toward the door.

"I don't do business with his kind."

"We have cash," I started, but the barber turned his back.

"I won't do business with red men for any amount of cash."

"You son of a bitch," Flowers growled. "I'll teach you a thing or—"

"Come, John," Brown said. "We'll find another barber."

Flowers was still turning back to look toward the shop, muttering threats, as Brown steered him into the street.

"You should stand up for yourself, Brown," he said. "Why should he get away with treating you that way?"

"Would threatening him and forcing him to serve me change his heart?" Brown said. "You know it wouldn't. And a display of force would only harden his notion of me as a savage. It's better to find another barber."

We had to leave Pennsylvania Avenue and try several shops before we found a barber willing to serve us all, a free Negro in a small, simple shop. Mrs. DuVal inspected us when we finally got back to the Williamson Hotel, and she announced herself satisfied that we looked worthy of the honor the President was extending.

May 1 was a rainy day, so Major DuVal ordered a closed carriage to take us the short distance down Pennsylvania Avenue to the White House. My heart was beating fast under my new suit jacket as we waited in the hallway for the aide to announce our arrival to the President. The Cherokee chiefs, however, looked as impassive as if they were waiting to walk into Walter Webber's store back home.

The aide led us into an office where the President rose to greet us from behind his desk. My first impression, to be honest, was a quick disappointment that the leader of our country was such a very small man. He was hardly taller than Maggie, with a bald head that stretched high above a thin, long nose. He glanced around at us with a stiff smile, and for just a moment, his eyes rested on me, the tallest man in the party. Then Major DuVal stepped forward to shake his hand and introduce the chiefs and other members of the delegation. I took a step backward, toward the door, trying to fade into the wallpaper, as fit my position with the party.

"It is a pleasure to meet my Cherokee children," President Adams said. "I desire to do everything for you that is in my power to do. I particularly hope the treaty prepared to be signed by the Secretary of War and you will be satisfactory to you. I am well aware of the promises made to your people by President Monroe and Mr. Calhoun in 1819 concerning a permanent home. I assure you we will take every proper measure for giving those promises substantial effect."

When he was finished speaking, he motioned toward the delegation as if giving them permission to speak. As the chiefs had decided last night, Black Fox stepped forward. He stood straight, a perfect picture of dignity, and a little shiver ran down my backbone at the sight. He looked like the leader of a nation.

"I thank the Great Spirit for giving to me and my brothers the chance to hold talks with the great father of the United States."

The President then spoke for a time about the benefits of the treaty, while the Cherokees listened without moving. When the President stopped, Black Fox gave a slight nod.

"We wish not to make a hasty decision, but to take time to consider all these things."

"Certainly, certainly!" President Adams said. "I want you to take all the time you desire to think about this treaty, and I hope you will be frank in letting me know all that you think and want."

He shook hands with all the Cherokee again as Major DuVal repeated their names. As he shook Sequoyah's hand, the aide leaned and whispered something in the President's ear.

"Ah!" President Adams said. "Mr. Guess! The inventor of the Cherokee alphabet! You have rendered a great service to your nation, in opening to them a new fountain of knowledge."

There was a moment of awkward silence, since Sequoyah couldn't understand what the President was saying. The President smiled stiffly and moved on to shake hands with the next man in the delegation while someone muttered a translation to Sequoyah. The aide then ushered us all back outside the office, and the door closed quickly behind us. I drew in a deep breath for the first time since we'd walked in the White House, and Major DuVal heard it. He gave me an eager smile.

"So, Mr. McKellar, what do you think about your brush with the power of the presidency?"

An aide came just then to announce our carriage was ready, and I was spared having to answer.

🦎 🦎 🦎

It took another five days of talking and waiting and drinking in the tavern, but on May 6 the chiefs signed the treaty. The boundary line between Arkansas Territory and the Cherokees' new land was established, and it was agreed the Cherokees had until the middle of the next year to leave Arkansas and make their homes to the west of that boundary. The Secretary of War hired James Rogers and Thomas Maw to go to the eastern Cherokees and talk about the advantages of the treaty, including enticements to join the Arkansas Cherokees in relocating—a rifle, a blanket, a kettle, and five pounds of tobacco for the head of any family that would move.

After months of sitting and doing nothing, suddenly everyone was moving. Several members of the delegation had suspicions— probably well-founded—that the members of the council back in the Territory wouldn't be too pleased with them for signing, so they also went to visit the eastern Cherokees. Major DuVal said that rather than returning immediately to Arkansas Territory, he would take the opportunity of being in the East to visit more family. I wondered if he, too, was afraid of the reaction of the Arkansas Cherokees to his part in bringing about this treaty.

He understood, though, that I was eager to get home, so he provided me with tickets for the stagecoach and money for steamboat

181

fare. By the end of May, I was packed and ready to leave the hotel. Major DuVal gave me my wages for the months in Washington, as well as some extra money he called my "appropriation for return travel." The morning I was to leave, he walked with me out to the stage and watched as the driver and I added my bags to the others on top. He stepped forward to shake my hand, and it seemed to me something a little sad was in his expression.

"I suppose our association is at an end now, Mr. McKellar," he said. "When the Cherokees move west, the agency will go with them. You will, I'm sure, want to stay in Arkansas Territory and finally get that farm you've so longed for."

"I reckon I will," I said. He smiled and shook my hand a final time.

"It's been a pleasure to work with you." He was walking away, back into the hotel, and a memory suddenly came to mind of the first time I'd seen him in his fine clothes on the streets of Dardanelle, and of myself standing in britches caked with the blood of hogs.

"Major DuVal!" I called after him, and he turned. "I want to thank you, sir, for—well, everything. I don't know what would have happened to Maggie and me if you hadn't hired me on."

"I never regretted doing it," he said. Then he touched the brim of his hat and went into the hotel. I climbed up beside the coach driver, who flicked the whip above the team, and the coach jerked forward, away from Washington City and toward home.

⁂ ⁂ ⁂

It took six weeks to get back to Dardanelle. The last miles were agonizing. The river was low enough that the steamboat had to go careful and slow, so slow I was sure I could make better progress upriver by swimming. I spent my time pacing the deck, watching the passing of the towns and stretches of woods along the banks and trying not to think too much about Maggie. The closer we got, the harder that became. It had been about six months since I'd left, and I leaned against the boat's railing, picturing her face, remembering her soft kisses, until I felt nearly mad with my need to be with her. My only relief was walking, and I'm sure the other passengers thought I was an odd one as I circled the deck time after time.

We finally pulled up to the dock in Dardanelle on a July afternoon that was muggy and hot as only a summer day in Arkansas Territory could be. I'd left the DuVals' trunk with them and bought a couple of bags for my belongings, and as soon as they were unloaded from the boat, I swung them over my shoulder and started at a brisk walk toward the road leading to our cabin. As I walked through the town, my insides were trembling. What if six months had been too long? What if she'd come to depend on Little El, to think of him as something more than a helpful neighbor? What if, despite his promises, he had pushed the advantage of being here with her while I was on the other side of the country?

"Want a kitten, Mister? Only a half disme!" A dirty little boy was running beside me, with a gray striped kitten squeezed between his hands. He pushed the kitten toward me, and it squalled in protest. I stopped, and the little boy stopped too, panting. "Want her? Her ma's a good mouser."

"Sure," I said, "I'll take her for my daughter." I reached into my pocket and pulled out whatever change was there, two bits, and the little boy handed over the kitten, marveling at the fortune she'd brought. I stuffed the kitten inside my shirt and slung my bags across my back, walking on before he had a chance to say another word.

I'd never traveled the distance from Dardanelle to our house as fast as I did that day. I could finally see the cabin, and I took off running, the bags bumping against my back and the kitten yowling against my belly. They were in a garden—Little El must have broken some ground for her. Maggie was squatted down picking something that she handed to Penny, who carried it to a basket sitting nearby. On one of her trips to the basket, she saw me, and she stood for a minute, staring.

"Penny!" I called. "It's me, Pa!"

Penny turned to Maggie, who looked over her shoulder and nodded with a big grin. That was enough for Penny, who came running at me as fast as her legs would carry her. I scooped her into my arms and held her close, nearly weeping with the joy of seeing her again. The kitten was yowling even louder and scratching my bare skin, and Penny bent down in my arms, trying to see what was making such a commotion.

Maggie was coming toward us, more slowly. I just about dropped Penny as I looked up and caught sight of her. She was heavy with child, her belly high and rounded, her bosom full. She was laughing as I set Penny down.

"Didn't I tell you he'd be surprised, Penny?" she said. Penny giggled and reached her hands up toward the wriggling in my shirt.

"It's a baby wriggling under Ma's shirt," she said. "But what you got under your shirt, Pa?"

Still unable to speak, I reached inside my shirt and handed the kitten to Penny. She immediately sank to the dirt with it, cooing and loving on it.

"I'm glad you're home," Maggie said, stretching up to kiss my cheek.

An ugly, black thought shot through my mind, but my reason wrestled it down before anything came out of my mouth.

"I was beginning to wonder if you'd get here before the baby does," she said. "It won't be much longer, maybe just another month, if my figuring is right."

"A month?" I managed to say, as my mind raced to count back the time. "You knew, then, before I left."

"I had suspicions." She bit her lip. "Well, to tell the truth, I was pretty sure."

"But you didn't tell me."

"I nearly let it slip once, the night before you left. But I knew if you knew, you wouldn't go. I thought a few times about having Elwin write a letter for me to tell you, but the longer you were gone, the more I thought you must be on your way back and a letter would miss you, anyway." She laid my hand against her belly, and I felt the strong movement of the child beneath it. "I was afraid you'd be worried if you knew, and there ain't been anything to worry about this time, John David. I wasn't even too bad sick with this one." She looked up, a little smile on her lips. "I knew you'd be surprised, but you look almost overcome by the news. Come in and sit down, and let's hear your tales."

⁂ ⁂ ⁂

Our cabin was buzzing with talk all the evening. Before I told any of my tales, I insisted on hearing theirs and knowing how they had fared over the winter. Little El had been true to his word—they hadn't been without firewood or meat the whole time I was gone. They took me out to see the garden spot he had plowed for them, and then they showed me the field of corn he had put in for us.

"I can't believe he'd do all that work for us," I said, shading my eyes against the sun so I could see how far the corn stretched. "I'll have to pay him for it."

"He said you would say that," Maggie said. "But he said to tell you he don't want pay."

"Well, he's getting some. I don't like being beholden to—"

"To an Indian?" Her voice was sharp, and I looked down at her. "To any man."

The look on her face softened a little. "He meant it as a gift, John David. To pay him for it takes that away. Accept it, and thank him for it, but don't even offer to pay."

I looked across the corn again, but my eyes weren't seeing it. Instead, my mind was painting a picture of how it must have been here while I was so far away in Washington City. Maybe Little El had been true to his word about adultery, and maybe Maggie had been true to her word about faithfulness. But some part of her heart had gone over to him these past months, that was clear enough. The black part of my soul started to rise again, but I took a deep breath and pushed it down. We should live together as Christian brothers, David Brown said. With no family of our own here, Maggie needed a brother.

"All right, I won't." I plucked Penny up from the ground and set her on my shoulders. "You're getting to be a heavy girl. How much longer will your old pa be able to carry you like this?"

She kicked her heels against my chest. "Giddy-up!"

Maggie took my hand. "You've seen everything here now. Are you finally ready to tell us about Washington City?"

※ ※ ※

After supper, Penny sat on my knee with her kitty clutched in her arms, her eyes wide and round as I described the things I'd seen in Washington.

"How big was that White House, Pa?" she asked. "The one that Mr. Adums lives in?"

"Huge," I said, "so big if you lost your kitty in one end, she would be full-grown by the time you found her."

"Was he a nice man, Mr. Adums?"

Maggie laughed. "Pa's already told you that, little missy. I think you're just trying to put off going to bed."

I scooped Penny into my arms and stood. "Reckon where I ought to put her?" I asked, pretending to head to the door. "In the bean patch or the corn patch?" She giggled as Maggie stooped to pull the trundle from under our bed. I laid her on the bed and she wiggled out of her dress, trying to keep the kitten from escaping.

"Can I sleep with the kitty?" she begged, and we left the two of them curled under the blanket as we stepped out to the porch.

"If that kitten survives all the loving it's getting, it'll be a miracle," Maggie said, grunting a little as she sat on the edge of the porch. I sat beside her, and for a while, we didn't say anything. The evening was still warm, and the peeper frogs were loud along the creek.

"It's good to be home," I said.

Maggie took my hand. "Did you miss us? Or did Major DuVal keep you so busy you didn't have time to think?"

"I missed you every day. Those last few miles up the river, you and Penny were all I could think about." With my free hand, I touched her soft cheek. "Mainly you. You might be scandalized if you knew the things I was thinking about you all the way up the Arkansas River."

Her laugh was low and soft. She scooted herself closer, so she could lay her head on my shoulder. "I doubt that. You ain't the only one who's been lonely all these months, John David."

We sat like that as the sunlight began to dim and as Penny's murmuring to her kitty slowed and then stopped altogether. It was good to be home, but I felt different about it, knowing that while I sat here with my wife, other fellows and their wives were faced with leaving what they called home.

"They signed a treaty," I said. "The Cherokees signed a deal that will move them west. Once the boundary is set, they'll have three months to leave the Territory. You know what that means." She looked up.

"Nobody will be living on that place north of the river? Elwin and his folks will have to go?"

"Yep."

She was quiet for a minute. "Will we be able to get that spot?" she finally asked. "That exact spot?"

"I can try for it when the land is surveyed. There's a chance we could get it, a good chance, maybe."

She stroked my hand. "So we'll finally get what you've wanted all this time. I reckon everything's worked out for you."

I scooted out from under her, off the porch, and took a couple of steps into the twilight. I could still remember the lay of that land north of the river, the smell of it, the feel of it, and I knew it was still the same, still what I'd always hoped to have. But it seemed like a different man who had been so sick with longing for it, all that time ago.

"You should have seen how the government treated them, Maggie," I said. "They wouldn't let the chiefs leave until they gave in and signed the treaty. I wanted the land, still want it, but cheating them feels wrong." I turned to look at her. "I feel like a thief, Maggie."

She heaved herself off the porch and came to put her arms around me. "You ain't a thief. Lovely's Purchase proved that. You're an honest man, John David. When the time comes, you'll know the right thing to do, and you'll do it."

I looked up into the purple-gray of the sky, where a few stars tried to mark their places. They were outnumbered by the tiny, bright flashes of the army of fireflies above the field. Summer was in the air, the smell of hot grass and the mustiness of creek water. It was like any other summer in Arkansas Territory, but I could feel change coming, and soon.

"I don't know," I said softly. "I just don't know."

Chapter 17

Maggie delivered a son in mid-August. She named him Jacob, after my pa, but from nearly the beginning of his life we called him Jake. He was as different from Penny as any baby could have been, suckling placidly at Maggie's breast until he fell asleep, then sleeping for hours under the dishcloth Maggie insisted on draping over the cradle.

During the months after the treaty, I often thought that Arkansas Territory would have been better off if everybody was turned like Jake. Passions seemed to be riding high on every side. Word was, the Cherokees had put up poles in front of the houses of the delegation members, ready to hold their heads when the death penalty was carried out for negotiating the treaty. I might have laughed that off as some wild tale, except I had seen the pole in front of Thomas Maw's place.

The whites, on the other hand, were giddy with the prospect of new land opening. Major DuVal was not yet returned from the East, but the business of carrying out the provisions of the treaty wouldn't wait. I may have thought, when I left Washington City, that my dealings with the Cherokees were over, but I was scarcely home for a week before Reverend Finney came to visit, asking if I would be willing to help with the job of recording the value of the land and improvements the Indians would be leaving behind.

"Major DuVal recommended your work when he sent my letter of appointment," he explained. "He felt, as do I, it would be useful to have someone familiar with the records of the agency."

So I divided my time that summer and fall between my cornfields and the agency office. Reverend Finney and Radford Ellis listened to the claims for compensation from the government for the buildings and fields of corn and peaches the Cherokees would be leaving behind. My job was to record their decisions in a journal so we would have good records once Major DuVal was back with the money from the government to pay those claims. One evening as I scratched the day's entries into the journal, I paused.

"Here's a claim for 100 acres on the east bank of the Illinois river, just a quarter-mile north of the salt works George Guess owns," I said. All three of the other men in the office looked up—Reverend Finney, Radford Ellis, and the secretary working with Ellis, Wilber Fleming.

"What of it?" Reverend Finney asked.

"I think someone's already put in a claim for that spot." I ran my finger back over the list of entries, going back three pages before I found it. "Here it is—a claim for 100 acres, the eastern bank of the Illinois River, one-quarter mile north of Guess' saline. Two buildings, 70 acres of cleared land—same as for the claim today."

Fleming laughed. "Some sneaky bastard is taking advantage of the U.S. government's generosity."

Reverend Finney didn't seem to think it was funny. "Strike today's entry, Mr. McKellar," he said. "I'll check the records tonight for any other attempts at fraud."

He reported the matter to Mr. McKenney, and instructions came from Washington City that we were to give each person who made a claim a numbered certificate that would match with the record in the journal. Trying to explain the importance of that certificate to the Cherokees was no easy task—especially when they didn't speak English.

Most times, the Cherokees brought in someone to interpret for them, and many times, that someone was Little El. He hadn't been by the cabin since I'd come back from Washington City. The first time we worked together at the agency, we kept ourselves turned to the business at hand while I copied down all the improvements the fellow said he had made on his land. Little El read the list back to him, and the man seemed satisfied as he left. Little El stayed back, though, until only the two of us were left in the office. He didn't say anything just stood with his hat in his hands, looking out the window.

"I want to thank you for putting in a corn crop for us," I said. "That was more than we bargained for back in December. You didn't have to do it, but I'm grateful you did."

"How are Maggie and Penny?" he asked, still looking out the window like there was something as interesting as Washington City out there instead of the sleepy streets of Dardanelle.

"Good," I said. "You cared for them well, and I thank you for it."

His black eyes darted to me for just a minute. "The baby?"

"A boy. We call him Jake."

"A son, that's good." He turned the hat over in his hands and then back again. "When I found out she was with child, I considered writing to tell you I couldn't take care of them anymore. She said you didn't know, and I was afraid you might think—" He let the thought drop.

"It never crossed my mind." He glanced up at me as I lifted the blotter from the papers. "He's something, I tell you. He's got McKellar feet, the biggest on any baby I ever saw. Maggie says she expects he could end up taller than I am."

His shoulders relaxed suddenly.

"Just what the world needs," he said, "another damn giant McKellar." I laughed and he smiled with that cocky smirk. "I know they're glad to have you back."

"You should come see us sometime," I said, shuffling the papers together and sticking them inside a drawer. "Penny asks about you. She'd be pleased to show you her little brother, though I think she's prouder of her new kitten."

"I might. Give them my regards." He put on his hat and waved as he left.

⚹ ⚹ ⚹

He never came, though, and before long, other business crowded the invitation out of my mind. Early in August, Joseph Brearley was hired to survey the line that would be the boundary between Arkansas Territory and Indian Territory. Once the boundary line was set, both the whites and Cherokees had ninety days to get on the right side of that line. To appease the white folks who were upset that Lovely County had gone to the Cherokees as part of the treaty, the government was offering two sections of land in Arkansas Territory to white settlers who were having to move east of the boundary. It became part of the agency's business to help record those claims, as well, and people flooded into the office to get their name on the list.

I learned quickly to keep a wary eye on the claims.

"I'm Harley Brooks, lately of Lovely County," one man started, as they all did. "My son and I both had claims, so we're entitled to four sections."

"What is your son's name?" Reverend Finney asked. "Is he of age to own property?"

"George Brooks, and he's over 21." The man's gaze shifted for just a moment outside the window. I followed it to where a boy was throwing rocks against the side of the building. The boy had the same red hair as the man, and he couldn't have been more than 10. I laid down the quill and went to the door.

"Hey, George," I called. "Come in here a minute."

The boy sidled into the building, shuffling a little to keep a pair of too-big moccasins on his feet.

"How old are you, George?" Reverend Finney asked.

"I'm over 21, sir." Reverend Finney looked at me with a slight frown. I went to stand right beside George.

"You're crowding him," Brooks said, but I didn't budge.

"Let's have a look at those shoes, George," I said.

"Now, what kind of a fool notion—" his pa sputtered, but Reverend Finney ignored him.

"Take off your shoes, George," he ordered

The boy kicked off the moccasins and stood with his jaw jutted out. I picked up the shoes and gave them a shake. A scrap of paper fluttered out of one and into my hand. The number 21 was scrawled on the paper with charcoal. I laughed and showed it to Reverend Finney.

"Technically, he's telling the truth," I said. "He was over 21."

"We are not interested in technical truth, but actual truth," Reverend Finney said. "Greed will get you nowhere, Mr. Ellis. Write him down for two sections, Mr. McKellar, and note he attempted to defraud the government with a false claim."

❧ ❧ ❧

'Greed will get you nowhere.' Yet greed was everywhere around in Arkansas Territory that fall. Some greed showed itself in lies, like the ones told by the boat captain and his crew who had never lived in Lovely County but who made a trip up the river so they could camp one night on the land and come back to make a claim for the government's grants. Some greed showed itself in impatience, as when people chafed that Joseph Brearley was taking so long to survey the line, since no one could begin to claim specific pieces of land until the Cherokees were moved out and their land had been surveyed by the government. Some folks were not willing to wait that long, and a few times, a Cherokee family would come to the agency to complain of harassment—horses were stolen, livestock driven off or killed, outbuildings burned.

I resisted the greed as best I could, laughing as I told Maggie the boldness of the lies people were willing to tell. But one evening as I was leaving for home, I ran smack into greed, in the person of my old hog-killing partner, Levi Webster.

"Are they closing up for the day?" he asked, peering around me to look in the window. I nodded, and he cursed. "I'll have to come back tomorrow, then."

"Are you making a claim? You never lived in Lovely's Purchase," I reminded him. "You backed out of the party at the last minute. If you try to make a claim, I'll be duty-bound to tell Reverend Finney it's a false one."

He shot a look of pure contempt at me. "Sure you'll do that," he spat. "More for you if I don't get any."

"What are you talking about?"

"I'm sure you've made your claim. You'll probably get your choice of land, too, working in this office, all friendly with that reverend and the Indian agent." He rubbed his hand across his eyes. "I've got to take advantage of this chance to get a good start here, McKellar. So many folks are talking about their claims and the land they'll get once the Indians are gone—Arkansas Territory's filling up. And you know it's not just regular folks like me who are making claims on the land. I bet half the fellows who've been in to claim land don't even want it for themselves—they're land speculators who are going together to get big chunks of cheap land from the government that they can sell for a high price to the rest of us. You know they'll get the best land, too. I'll never get a place if I can't get one of these grants."

"There's plenty of land to go around," I said, but Webster noticed my tone had weakened. He stepped closer.

"There ain't, and you know it, too. Things will go as they always do—the rich will take care of the rich. Well, I'll be damned if I won't at least try to take care of myself!"

"Get out of here!" I ordered, giving him a little push.

He left, muttering a new threat or complaint with every step, but instead of starting toward home myself, I stood on the porch, thinking about what he had said. We had recorded a lot of claims, on both sides. But maybe Webster was right, and the balance of claims was tipping toward the whites, getting a promise from the government to give away more land than the Cherokees were turning over. He was wrong, though, about me being able to get a claim just through a connection with the office. Reverend Finney and Radford Ellis both were letter-of-the-law men who would think my wages were plenty of compensation for helping them—they wouldn't give me the advantage of a claim certificate. I would be competing for land with all the Harvey Websters flooding into Arkansas Territory since word of the treaty had hit the newspapers in the East. I had some money saved, but would it be enough? Maybe not, if I had to pay speculators' prices—

"Did you forget something, Mr. McKellar?" Reverend Finney asked as he paused to lock the agency door.

"I believe I did."

He pushed the door open a bit. "Go back and get it. Then if you will, lock the door when you leave." And he walked away, leaving me alone on the porch with Greed.

Everything in the office was shadowy and gray in the early twilight, but I didn't light a lamp. I went straight to the desk and sat in Reverend Finney's chair. I deserved a claim on the government land, more than any of these newcomers who were rushing into the Territory. I'd been here nearly five years now, built a home, lost it, raised several small crops of corn on other folks' ground. Surely it was time I had my own fields, that Maggie had her own house. And unlike some of these folks making claims, I had actually lived in Lovely's Purchase. I wasn't living there now and wouldn't be losing my home when the Cherokees moved in, true, but I had lost my home there, in a manner of speaking. I was due compensation for that loss.

I went to the window and peeked through the crack between the curtains. Reverend Finney was already a hundred yards or so down the street, not even turning back to be sure I was locking up. I turned back to the table and sat down, in my own seat this time. I took a piece of fresh paper off the stack and dipped the quill in the ink. I knew exactly what to write—I'd copied so many claims over the past weeks.

"I, John David McKellar, being of age 26 years, present the following claim to the United States—"

This is where I would give the description of the property I was losing in Lovely County. I paused for a moment to recall the particulars of the farm in Lovely's Purchase. But instead of my own corn field, another came to my mind, a ruined field with beautiful ears of corn stripped and dangling crookedly from the stalk. And close after, the picture I couldn't seem to escape—the tear-streaked face of a desperate woman, shielding the child in her belly—

A drop of dark ink had fallen from the quill onto the pure white of the paper, and it was slowly spreading. I suddenly crumpled the paper and pushed it into my pocket. I took another sheet and without any pauses wrote a different note.

Reverend Finney,

I regret to say I will no longer be able to serve as your recorder for the claims regarding the transfer of lands.

Respectfully yours,

John David McKellar

❧ ❧ ❧

"You're quiet tonight," Maggie said as I sat at the table holding Jake so she could fix supper.

"I quit the job at the agency." She turned to look at me in surprise. "Why?"

"I'm an honest man," I scoffed. "I finally had my can full of all the false claims and the tricks people are trying, just so they can get their hands on a few acres of land."

She studied me for a minute, then the ham smelled like it might be getting too done, and she turned back to the fire.

"Well, it's for the best, I reckon," she said. "The last of the garden's ready to harvest, and I could use your help. Seems like Jake is hardly through nursing before he's hungry again. I swear I spend the better portion of my day feeding him."

"I won't look for new work right away, then."

Maggie handed the plate of ham to Penny. "Set that on the table by Pa, sweet." She brought over a steaming kettle of beans herself and set it in the middle of the table. Then she laid her work-roughened hand against my cheek.

"You are an honest man," she said softly. "Things will work out. As Sarah always said, God will provide. You believe that, don't you?"

"Sure," I said.

※ ※ ※

I spent a couple of weeks around the cabin helping Maggie and harvesting the corn crop Little El had planted for me. When I took the corn to be milled, I got the idea that I might be able to make some money hauling cornmeal. I used some of my wages from the agency to buy a team of mules and a wagon and within two days I had steady work with the grist mill, hauling in folks' corn to be ground, filling bags with cornmeal, loading the bags and hauling them either back to the farm or to the Dardanelle wharf. Within a month, I'd made enough to more than repay what it had taken to get the team.

One November evening I was late coming in from taking a load to an outlying farm, and I hurried to unhitch the mules in the growing twilight. As I led them to the stable, a strange feeling came over me, like someone was watching me, and the hairs on my arms prickled as I looked around, straining to see through the thick gray dusk.

"Who's there?" I called out. The lead mule snorted as Little El stepped out of the shadow of the stable. One of his arms was hanging in a makeshift sling, and although it was hard to see clearly, it looked to me that a dark bruise covered his cheek.

"Elwin? What in the hell happened to you?"

"I need to talk to you, McKellar," he said, with no kind of greeting. He looked around like he thought someone else was lurking in the dark. "Not here."

"Well, go on in," I said. "I'll get the mules settled first."

But when I came to the front step, he was there, leaning against the wall of the cabin.

"Why didn't you go in?" I asked. "It's cold out here." I stuck my head in the door. "Maggie? Are you decent? We got company."

She gasped as Little El stepped into the candlelight, and I reckon my mouth dropped open too. There wasn't just the one bruise on his face; it was clear enough someone had pummeled him good. One eye was puffy and purple, and his forehead had a scraped area below a lump the size of a small egg.

"What happened?" I asked again, pulling out chairs for the two of us to sit. "Who did this to you?"

"I don't know them." He sat in the chair like he had grown years older, and he leaned his head against his hand. "They must be new in the Territory."

"There are a lot of new folks around, especially since Brearley has finished the survey," I agreed, but I was wondering why he had come to our house. "What happened? Did they try to force you off your farm? If you need me to take down a complaint for Reverend Finney, I reckon I can, though I don't work with him anymore." I looked up at Maggie, who was hovering behind my shoulder. "We got any paper?"

"It's too late for that, McKellar," Little El said. Something in his voice made me turn back to him. He shook his head. "It wasn't our place, anyway. They had been to the Killfox farm."

"Killfox," Maggie said. "Ain't that the name of your bride-to-be?"

"You're getting married?" I blurted out, and Maggie pinched my ear, hard, but Little El didn't seem to care, or even to notice.

"Julie," he said quietly.

"Is she all right?" Maggie asked. "Did they hurt her or her folks? They didn't—" Her voice dropped low. "They didn't kill someone?" Little El suddenly turned his face into his hand, and he was shaking all over.

"She's alive, but nothing is all right," he said.

"What happened?" I asked, one last time, though I suddenly wasn't sure I wanted to know.

He took in a deep, shuddering breath, and when he finally spoke, his voice was low and hollow.

"It was pretty weather this afternoon, you know, so we'd been out walking. We were on our way back when we smelled smoke, so we were hurrying through the woods toward the cabin, and we ran right into them. There were five men on horseback, laughing and celebrating, and they must have just left the farm. I knew they were trouble. We were getting into the brush along the edge of the path to hide and let them pass, but one of them saw us." He shook his head. "They were on us before we could even turn around. They held me there and made me watch what they did to her, made me watch them violate her, and I couldn't stop them—I pulled my shoulder out of its socket trying to get to her, but I couldn't stop them—" His voice cracked, and he was silent.

Maggie's hand was like a vise on my shoulder, and I closed my eyes for a moment. I didn't know Julie Killfox, but the thought of any woman in the hands of men drunk with power sent a sick feeling through me. And the shame her man would feel from being powerless to help her—how could any man bear that? I stood.

"Let's go to the sheriff. Rape's a capital offense. We'll find those bastards and see them hang."

But Little El was shaking his head again.

"It's hard enough for a white woman to win such a case, McKellar. No one will believe a Cherokee woman, not the sheriff, surely not a jury of whites. Sit down. I didn't come here for your advice." I slowly sat down, watching as he rubbed his hand over his forehead. "We're leaving tomorrow for the west. Julie's family was burned out, so they have no reason to stay. I talked Father into going with them. He wanted to stay till the end, make the soldiers have to force us off, but I changed his mind. Brearley has finished the survey of the boundary line, which means we were going to have to go soon, anyway, so we're going now." He suddenly looked straight into my eyes. "I'm here because I want you and Maggie to take over our farm."

I stared at him, hardly sure I'd heard him right. Something was unreal about the whole moment, sitting in the dim candlelight, talking in hushed voices so we wouldn't wake the young'uns, looking into the battered face of the man I'd hated as an enemy and feared as a rival, and he was simply giving me what I'd wanted all this time. The moment wasn't at all what I had dreamed it would be; there was no rush of pleasure, no sense of justice or revenge, just a numbness that spread through my mind and body.

"We built the cabin where you had started it," he was saying, "since there was a start on a solid foundation. Over the years, we've cleared probably thirty acres for corn and another ten for peach trees."

"Peach trees?" I murmured.

"Father brought them from Georgia. Another year or two and they will bear fruit. They do better on the higher stretches of land, since cold air settles in the valleys in springtime. You'll need to prune this spring—that's one thing we were planning to do."

"Elwin," Maggie interrupted, "why are you doing this?"

He sighed. "We have to leave it. There is no choice. Some white man will take what we've built up and do with it as he will." He glanced up at Maggie and then at me. "It's as you said to me once, McKellar. I trust you with it. I know you care for that land and that you will tend it with respect, not rip at it to grasp from it whatever profit you can as fast as you can. If it has to go to a white man, I want that white man to be you."

The room was silent except for the hissing of the fire.

"I don't know anything about peaches," I said. Elwin smiled, slowly, like it hurt him.

"I'll leave instructions on the mantel."

"Well," I said, standing. "There's just one thing left to settle."

I went to the hearth and moved the empty stewpot to the side. With a grunt, I tipped back the loose rock from the hearth enough that I could stick my hand in the slot it left. Carefully I pulled out the little cloth bag Maggie had made, and I set it on Elwin's knee.

"What's this?" He looked surprised when the bag clinked as he lifted it. With his good hand, he awkwardly loosened the drawstring and poured a small part of the coins from the bag out onto the table.

"It's yours," I said. "The government says the Cherokees are to be compensated for the land and improvements they give up in Arkansas Territory. If you'll wait a minute, I'll find some paper and write up a bill of sale."

He didn't say anything as I hunted for a quill and some ink. We didn't have any paper, though, so I tore a blank end paper from one of my law books. I wrote out a bill of sale for land, putting down everything I could remember should be on such a document. Elwin described landmarks that were the boundary of what his father claimed as their farm, and together we counted out the money Maggie and I had been saving all this time. I put the total down as the sale price, and then I signed it and handed the quill to Elwin.

"When he's done, Maggie, you put your mark and I'll sign for you as a witness," I said, but she shook her head. Elwin smiled at her, a real smile, and handed her the quill. She bent over the paper and slowly, carefully, scrawled her full name beneath mine. Then she stood up with a triumphant grin and handed me the quill.

"Elwin taught me while you were in Washington City," she said. "I meant to tell you, but Jake came along and I forgot about it. But I won't be needing anyone to sign for me now."

"I should be going," Elwin said, standing and tucking the money bag deep into his sling. "Tomorrow will be a busy day for us."

"Will you need help packing and loading your goods?" I asked. "You won't be able to do much with your shoulder that bad."

"We probably will need help, McKellar, but it shouldn't come from you." He started for the door. "Father wouldn't like that. It's better if he doesn't know I came to you at all." He lifted his good hand. "Goodbye, Maggie."

She smiled in that way I knew meant tears were about to spill over the edges of her eyes. I stepped forward quickly to shake his hand, before she did something like hug him.

"Goodbye, Elwin Root," I said. "I hope your people will be left alone now. I hope it is as the treaty says, a permanent home."

"I don't know about that," he said. "Your people are greedy and powerful." He smiled. "But, to be fair, I must add that some keep their greed in check better than others. You are a better man than I once thought, McKellar."

"Thank you for giving us the chance to get the land," I said. "You didn't have to do that."

"No. You could have come to take it from us, though." He patted the bulge at his elbow. "Thank you."

Maggie came to me as the door closed behind Elwin, and I wrapped my arm around her shoulders.

"Do you believe that?" I said. "It's ours, Maggie. There was a time when I thought we'd never step foot on that land again, and now it's ours."

"Bought and paid for!" she said.

I looked at the hole in the hearth. "With every penny of what we'd been saving—maybe I shouldn't have given it all to him."

She put her arms around my waist and looked up at me. "I'm glad you gave him all the money—it was the right thing to do. I sure hate how we came by the chance to get it, though. Poor Julie Killfox." She leaned her cheek against my chest.

"Yep." I waited what I hoped would be a respectful moment. "You'll need to start packing tomorrow while I'm at the mill. We'll give Elwin and his folks till the end of the week to get out."

She pulled away and looked up at me again. "We're moving there now? It's coming on to winter, John David!"

"There's a cabin to move into—we better get there before somebody comes along and thinks it's an abandoned farm and moves in themselves." I tweaked her chin. "It's ours now, Maggie, and I'm doing whatever it takes to keep it. I'll be damned if I'm losing it again."

❧ ❧ ❧

Some things had changed, of course, since we'd been on the land. There was a wagon path now, with a ford crossing the creek and leading into the yard of the cabin. The cabin wasn't what I'd had in mind to build for Maggie—it was small and plain, a man's cabin, but it was solid and tight against the wind. At least they had left the shade trees in the yard.

We'd got there in the middle of the afternoon, so we unloaded the wagon as quick as we could before the early darkness fell. When I set the last bundle on the floor of the front room, there was still sunshine left in the day.

"Come on," I said to Maggie, who was already unpacking dishes for supper. "Let it wait. Let's go have a look at it before dark."

She swaddled Jake in a blanket and carried him under her shawl while I carried Penny piggyback. We started out to the north, toward the mountains. Elwin and his pa had cleared enough trees that we could easily see the mountains from the yard, just as I had thought to do when we'd been there before. The late afternoon sun highlighted the western slopes so they stood out from the rest of the landscape, and a swelling happiness filled my chest. I'd told myself for these years that it didn't matter where we lived, so long as I could feed my family. But seeing the bright mountains there before me, with the deep blue shadows of the valleys cutting through, I knew I'd been wrong. I was meant to be here. Not Lovely's Purchase, not Dardanelle, not any place south of the river. Here.

"Look at the mountains, Penny," I said, not really caring if Maggie noticed the quaver in my voice. "Pretty, aren't they?"

"They sure are, Pa. Do they belong to us?" Maggie laughed at her question, but I squeezed her shin where it rested against my shoulder.

"They do, my girl. They surely do."

⁂ ⁂ ⁂

We took a quick look around the place, the garden patch, the barn and smokehouse, the empty cornfields. The strangest sight was the orchard of peach trees. The trees were stubby, not much taller than me, and laid out in rows like a field crop. They stretched out across the top of the little rise as far as our eyes could see, slender and black against the rosy orange of the sunset.

The young'uns were cold and Maggie was anxious to get supper cooking, so I let them take me back to the cabin.

"The chimney draws good," I said as I built a fire on the back of the hearth. "It's a good thing we thought to bring the woodpile, though, and had room for it. They took everything that wasn't rooted to the ground."

"It was theirs to take," Maggie said. "Now, where did I pack the spoons?"

Supper was simple, and Penny was so tired from the excitement of the day that she fell asleep before we were finished with it. Maggie pulled out the trundle bed, and I laid Penny in it, tucking the quilt up under her chin. I stretched as I stood, and my head banged into a joist. Maggie laughed.

"Elwin and his pa should have been more considerate when they built this cabin," she said. "Putting those joists low enough for you to bump your head was just unneighborly."

201

I grinned. "I can take care of that. I'll build another room on the other side of that wall and put the joists as high as I want them."

"A two-room cabin like your folks have—I never dreamed I'd have a two-room cabin."

"Not even after I promised you one? Didn't you believe in me?" I teased. She shrugged, and I laughed as I sat down. "Don't feel bad about it. I'd given up on that dream too. I thought I'd never set foot on this place again."

"You quit believing? Even after what you said?" I looked at her, confused, and she laughed. "You don't remember? It was when we first decided to stay in Arkansas Territory. It was a verse from the Bible, something about 'The Lord will make me walk on high places.'"

"Habbakuk," I said, "'The Lord God is my strength, and he will make my feet like hinds' feet, and he will make me to walk upon mine high places.'"

"Well, it happened, I reckon. Just not when we wanted it to happen."

I grinned. "That's for sure. My hinds' feet have walked through a lot of places these past years."

"That they have." She smiled as she lifted Jake from the cradle for his evening nursing. "I reckon it just wasn't the right time before."

"No," I agreed, sobering suddenly. "It wasn't the right time. I had some things to learn first."

Chapter 18

That winter was a happy time. The cabin was snug against the wind, and the floor was smooth enough we weren't afraid to let Jake down on it when he started scooting around. I had to admit Little El and his pa had done a fine job with building. I was pleased well enough, too, with the way they had laid out the farm. As winter turned the corner into March, I began to itch to lay my hand on the handle of a plow in the corn field they had started.

I didn't have a plow, though, so I spent a couple of weeks riding back and forth to Dardanelle to pick up whatever work I could find to earn enough to buy one secondhand. It was on one of those jobs that I heard the news I'd been waiting for. I pushed the mule hard all the way home that evening and hurried through tending to him so I could get in and tell Maggie.

She was nursing Jake when I came in, so I dished up my own supper from what she was keeping warm over the fire. But I set it on the table to wait and pulled my chair close to hers.

"They were saying today in Dardanelle that the government land office has ordered a survey of the Cherokee lands," I told her. She didn't say anything, just kept patting Jake's bottom, but her eyes smiled. "They didn't say when. I'm not sure any date's been set. But I bet they'll start come late spring when the weather's better." I squeezed her knee. "You know what that means."

"The land will be ours, legal."

"Yep!" I whooped, and Jake jerked, like I'd woke him. I stroked his head and lowered my voice. "We ought to be able to assert squatter's rights and make our claim solid."

"That'll be a pure relief," she said. "After all the moving around we've done, to be settled on our own place that nobody can take out from under us—that will be a blessing." I started to say something else, but she laid a hand over my mouth. "You need to eat before your supper gets cold."

Knowing the survey was coming seemed to take some of the tenseness out of both of us. I took more pleasure than I ever had in my work, knowing it was work that was going to build up our own place. On the chilly March afternoons, I went through the peach trees and trimmed away branches until each tree looked like a hand cupping a piece of fruit, just as Little El said it should. Although I was sure I hadn't done the job as well as he would have, I liked working with the trees, and when they bloomed in early April, I thought I'd never seen anything so pretty as that hillside covered in a blanket of pink. Once the days began to get warmer, I spent all day in the fields, plowing. Watching the dark soil roll away from the point of the plow, feeling the sunshine warm on the back of my neck, listening to the birds singing in the trees along the edges of the field—I couldn't remember a time when I'd felt so content.

One afternoon as I followed the mules around the field, I was singing out loud, some song that hadn't passed my lips since I was a boy in Campbell County. As I turned the corner, though, I broke off quickly. A man was sitting on horseback at the end of my field. Slowly, I pulled the reins from over my shoulders and left the mule and plow in the middle of the row. As I made my way toward the man, I could see my eyes hadn't been fooling me, even from the distance—it was Thomas Mallory, sitting astride his fine stud horse.

"Howdy," I said, scanning his hands and saddle for a gun. I couldn't see one, but that didn't give me much relief.

"It's been a long time, McKellar."

"It has. I see you found your stud."

He stared out over my field. "I see you're back north of the river. How'd you manage that?"

"Good fortune."

He snorted and his eyes suddenly came to rest on me.

"I heard about you in Dardanelle," he said. "Working with Duval and the Cherokees. I ain't surprised. Once an Indian lover, always a dirty Indian lover."

I forced my voice to keep calm and low. "What are you doing here, Mallory?"

"We got tossed off another piece of land. We were on the wrong side of that line they drew through Lovely County. But you know that. I heard you were part of the group that went to Washington and betrayed good white folks in favor of them damned Cherokee bastards."

There was no point answering him. If he wanted a fight, he'd make one out of anything I said. My muscles tightened, waiting for the moment he would leap down from his horse and come at me. But he sat looking over my field, the way it curved gently toward the creek with the strips of dirt turned up.

"This is a mighty pretty piece of property," he said. "Looks like you was richly rewarded for your part in the deal, McKellar."

"I wasn't part of the deal," I started, but he ignored me.

"How many acres did you get, McKellar? Forty? Fifty?" He shielded his eyes against the sun and half-stood in the stirrups to see the far end of the field. Then he sat back with a smirk.

"What I'm doing here is scouting land," he said. "The territorial government is getting ready to do a survey of the Indian lands north of the river in preparation for opening those lands for sale. But I don't have to buy anything. To repay us for the trouble of having to leave Lovely County, the government is giving us a grant of land in Arkansas Territory. This is a mighty nice piece of land, yes sir. Yes, sir," he repeated, slowly. "I like it. I surely do."

It seemed like everything around me started to whirl slowly, gaining speed as I stared up at Thomas Mallory. The whirling grew into a tight ball and lodged in my chest, hard and hot.

"You son of a bitch," I said. He laughed and lifted the reins, turning his horse to ride away from me.

"You'll see how it feels," he called over his shoulder.

I squatted to pick up a rock and let it fly after him. Mallory's horse jumped when the rock nicked his hindquarters, and then Mallory was gone, down the draw toward the path crossing the creek. I crossed my hands behind my neck and squatted there a minute, my eyes closed. It was slipping away, all of it, once again, and nothing I could do could stop it.

I felt too weak to keep plowing, so I unhitched the mule and led him back to the barn. Maggie was washing clothes in the shade of the hackberry tree, and she glanced up as I came into the yard. Her face went from contented to worried in one blink, and she dropped the wooden paddle into the washpot and rushed over to me.

"Are you hurt? What's wrong?"

I took her hand. "Come inside. We need to talk."

She gathered up the young'uns and followed me into the cabin. I sat heavily in a chair near the table as she set down Jake on the floor.

"Mind your brother, Penny," she said, "while I talk to Pa. Don't let him get in the fire." Then she came and laid her hand on my shoulder. "What's wrong?"

I didn't try to pretty it up. "Thomas Mallory came by. He got tossed out of Lovely County for being on the wrong side of the boundary line. The government's going to give him a piece of land for being moved out of Lovely County, you know." My throat was tight, and I swallowed hard. "He wants this piece, Maggie."

I lowered my head to the table, and Maggie dropped into the chair next to me.

"He can't have it, though," she said. "We bought it. Elwin has the deed you wrote out. We could find him—"

"That deed won't stand in a court of law," I mumbled. "I wrote it mainly to benefit Little El, so no one would accuse him of stealing the money. The government will claim as its own all the land the Cherokees leave so it can get the money from the sale. There's no private ownership by Indians in the Territory, anyway—the tribe owned the land. The Root family never had the land to sell."

Penny's happy chatter as she bossed Jake seemed miles away. Maggie and I sat in silence for what seemed like a long time. She laid her hand on my head, and I raised it to look at her.

"What can we do?" she asked. "There has to be something we can do. Can't we buy it again?"

"With what? I gave everything we'd been saving to Little El." I hit my fist against the table. "I shouldn't have done that! He was going to have to leave anyhow—"

"No!" She grabbed my fist. "You were right to give it to him, and you know it! It was the honest thing to do." I didn't answer, and she squeezed my hand. "You know it."

We didn't speak for a while.

"We'll just have to sell something," she said.

"Public land's a dollar and a quarter an acre," I said heavily. "The smallest parcel they'll sell is 80 acres. That's one hundred dollars, Maggie. Even if we sold everything on this place—the wagon, the mules, the plow—I doubt we'd get a hundred dollars. Especially since most of it was secondhand to start with."

I laid my forehead back against the table, and she stroked my hair, but that didn't calm me like it usually did. Bitter bile was swirling in my belly. This month marked five years in Arkansas Territory. Five years, and we were about to be right where we'd been when Suzy had stolen our money in Arkansas Post. How many times could a man pick himself up? How many times could I keep trying?

"I wish your folks would have helped," Maggie murmured. "Looks like they would have."

What was the use of keeping it from her now?

"Don't be blaming them," I said. "I never asked them for help."

Her hand on my head stilled. "What? But you sent letters!"

"With news, that's all. I never asked for any money."

The young'uns were fussing behind us, and Maggie stood quickly and swept away from me, her skirt whipping against my leg.

"Hush, now!" she scolded, meaner than she usually spoke to them, and I knew Penny was getting the temper that was meant for me. "Penny, go sit on the bed."

"I told him he can't go outside, but he won't listen to me, Ma," Penny wailed. "He just won't!"

"He comes by it honest," Maggie snapped. "He's just like his pa."

I sat up as she came back to the table with Jake wiggling on her shoulder, and I motioned to Penny to come from the bed. She ran across the floor to me and climbed on my lap, sniffling and pushing her cheek against my chest.

"I'm sorry," I said to Maggie. "I thought I could take care of you on my own. That's what I wanted to do. I didn't know at the time I'd be such a failure at it."

She sat for a moment, calming Jake, and when she finally spoke, her voice was kinder. "You're only a failure if you quit trying." She looked straight into my eyes. "Since you never asked, they ain't ever said no. I reckon it's time to ask."

I opened my mouth to protest, but something in her eyes told me the kindness was only a thin layer over her aggravation with me.

"You can write to them today. And John David—" Her eyes narrowed. "Elwin taught me to read a little, too."

I sighed. "There's not time to write, Maggie. By the time a letter gets to Campbell County, and they have time to talk it over and get some money here, the land could already be surveyed and sold."

"Then I reckon you'll have to go yourself."

I stared at her. "Go? I can't go. I can't leave you here alone with two young'uns—"

"You could make it a fast trip and be back in a month or so. You could take a steamboat—"

"We don't have money for steamboat passage," I interrupted. "There's nothing we could sell that could buy me a ticket."

She was quiet for a minute.

"There is," she said. With her free hand, she reached inside the neck of her bodice and pulled out the little gold locket I'd given her all those years ago on the day when I'd asked her to stay with me as my wife. She pulled it over her head and laid it on the table. It was burnished to a soft sheen from lying against her skin. A lump started in my throat.

"No," I said. "We've been through this once." But she shook her head.

It's a pretty trinket, John David, that's all. There was a time I needed it to help me feel close to you, but look what I've got now." She patted Jake's wiggling bottom. "I've got two fine young'uns that have pieces of you all through them. If the locket can help us get this land for our home, if it helps us stay here, then I'm glad to part with it."

I took the locket in my fist and bowed my head, swallowing back the aching in my throat. She was right, of course.

"I could ride in to Dardanelle this afternoon and see what I could get for it," I said. "Maybe I could be on a steamboat by the end of the week."

She smiled as she took the locket from me and opened it. Penny leaned forward to coo over the lock of my hair and the faded little flower inside.

"Pretty, Ma!"

"I do want to keep these," Maggie said. "I doubt they would add anything to the price, but they do mean something to me. Where should I keep them now?"

She stood, but I caught her hand.

"I'll get you another one someday."

She smiled. "Just get to Campbell County and ask your folks for enough money to buy this place. I'll give up the locket, and gladly, but I want a home—a permanent home, like you told Elwin—in exchange."

⅔ ⅔ ⅔

I flat-out told Joseph Brearley the price for the locket was steamboat fare to Nashville, no more but no less.

"I don't know," he said. "Maybe it's only silver plated with gold. Maybe it's not worth that much."

"It's real," I said. "I paid more in Jacksborough than I'm asking from you, and that was in settled country. In Arkansas Territory it's worth more. How many gold lockets do you see in Arkansas Territory? You can ask whatever price you want."

"I don't know." He pretended to be pondering. "It might sit in the store a long time."

"Look," I said. "You can pay what I ask, or I'll take it to another store owner and it can sit in his store. Someone's going to make money off this locket. I wanted to give you first chance, because your family's been good to us. But I need the price I'm asking, no less, and if you won't give it to me, I'll go to someone else."

That changed his tune. He paid just what I'd asked and even threw in a stick of candy for Penny.

"Need anything else?" he asked.

"How much would you take for that cur?" I pointed to the half-grown black pup lying outside the door.

"Hell, I'd pay you to take that damn thing. It barks at every customer all day long and at every rustle of the wind all night long."

"You got any scrap twine?"

He gave me a piece of twine, and I straightened it as I walked toward the dog. He growled. I pulled the cornpone Maggie had sent

209

for my dinner from my pocket, broke off a piece, and tossed it between the dog's front paws. He licked his chops, but he didn't eat the pone. His eyes stayed on me as I came a step closer.

"Does this dog bite?" I called to Brearley.

"I never get close enough to find out."

I turned half-away from the dog and pretended to study the handbills on the side of the store. But I watched from the corner of my eye as he devoured the pone in one bite. Still facing the handbills, I tossed another chunk toward him, just past his tail. He had to get up to reach this chunk, and while his back was to me, I pounced on him. I slipped the rope around his neck and held him tight while I tied the twine into a noose. He growled and snapped at me, but I kept him at bay with a stick while I dropped the last piece of pone on the ground.

At first he ignored it, but hunger won over fear, and he bent to snatch it off the ground. I laid my hand on the top of his head between his ears for just a minute.

"Come on home," I said softly, so only he could hear. "We'll fatten you up. I just ask that you give Mallory that kind of greeting if he happens by the place while I'm gone."

※ ※ ※

We were lucky enough that a steamboat was leaving in three days, so we had a hurried time getting everything ready for me to go. I spent two of those days plowing from sun-up to sundown, getting the fields ready for corn I wouldn't be around to plant. It was only a half of what I'd hoped to have ready, only a part of what Elwin and his pa had cleared, but I knew if I waited for another steamboat to leave Dardanelle, those fields and the corn in them might belong to someone else by harvest. The thing that fretted me most was that Maggie would have to plant the corn. It was still early enough in April there was the risk a frost would kill the young plants, so I couldn't have planted the crop myself, even if I had time to do it.

"How will you manage the planting?" I asked, once we'd gone to bed after the second long day. "I don't see how you can do it, with two young'uns to watch over."

"Take some time before you leave tomorrow to make a little pen. I can set them in the shade at the edge of the field while I'm working.

Penny will have to keep up with Jake. And I'll just have to take it a little at a time. It won't be like having you plant it, but I'll get a crop in the ground."

"I know you will." I shifted to take her in my arms, and she laid her head on my shoulder. Already, that ache of missing her that had plagued me so in Washington City was settling heavy in my chest.

"I don't want to go," I said.

"I'll miss you." She lifted her hand to stroke my cheek. "Still, you'll be glad to see your folks." I didn't answer, and she raised up to look at me. "Won't you?"

"I wish I didn't have to ask for money. I wish I could walk in an independent man instead of like the prodigal son, come to throw himself on the mercy of his family. That's what Ma said would happen, remember?

The look on her face said she did. "Well, that's what family is for," she argued. "Family is who you can turn to in trouble."

"I reckon. I still hate to do it. Speaking of family—want me to tell your pa you say howdy?" She let out a hot little huff of breath, and I laughed.

"You rascal!" she said, but then she laughed too. "It would be good to know how all the young'uns are doing, though."

"I'll try to go see them," I promised.

She settled back close to me, soft and warm. Her hair tickled against my cheek with every in and out of her breath.

"I don't want to go," I whispered.

"I'll miss you," she answered.

⁂

First thing in the morning, I fashioned a little fence from sticks and twine to stretch around a spot as big as a quilt, and I attached an extra length of twine so Maggie could easily move it from one spot to another as she worked a different part of the field. Then I had to leave so I could be sure of getting across the river before the ferry quit running for the day. I would camp at Brearley's so I could catch the steamboat early the next day.

Maggie and the young'uns watched as I shouldered the bundle she had packed for me, and they walked with me across the yard and down to where the road ran across the creek. Then we stopped, and I hugged each of the young'uns.

"Be good," I said to Penny as she wrapped her arms around my neck. "Help out your ma, especially with Jake."

"I will, Pa," she promised, planting a sticky kiss on my cheek.

I was glad the young'uns didn't understand how long I'd be gone. They played with the dog, happy as ever, while Maggie and I held to each other like cockleburs in a horse's tail. I didn't trust my voice to say anything, and when she finally pulled away from me, Maggie's eyes were shiny with tears.

"Get on with you," she said. "Tell your folks all about the young'uns." I nodded, and she leaned in for one last kiss. "God be with you," she whispered.

"You, too," I managed to choke out.

She stepped back to stop Jake from pulling on the dog's floppy ears, but then she turned back to me with a smile.

"One thing I can promise you," she said. "This time when you come home, you won't find a surprise like you did last time."

I laughed because I knew it was what she wanted me to do, and with a last wave, I turned away from them and started down the road, though every step tore a piece from my heart, stretching and snapping like the strands of a cobweb caught by the wind.

Chapter 19

Pa's cabin looked just as it had all those years ago when I'd first brought Maggie off the mountain. I stood for a minute on the path, bracing myself for what was coming. This wasn't the first time I'd come home after getting into some kind of trouble, and though my folks weren't harsh, they were stern, and I knew I could expect a tongue-lashing at the least. It rankled me to think Ma would drag up her long-ago prediction that I would come back defeated and in need of their help.

It rankled me, but it was true, and nothing was to be gained from pride at this point. I shifted the bundle on my back and started across the clearing.

"Remember," I muttered aloud, "'Father, I have sinned against heaven, and in thy sight, and am no more worthy to be called thy son.'"

A hound with a graying snout raised its head as I stepped on the porch, and with a little jolt I realized it was Rounder, grown old. He wagged his tail feebly as I squatted beside him and scratched behind his ears, just as I'd always done.

"It's been a while since either one of us has done any hunting, I reckon," I said, and he laid his muzzle against my knee. For a while, I smoothed the wrinkles on his head, but I knew I was only delaying the moment that had to come. With a sigh, I stood and knocked on the door.

Ma's face was curious when she opened the door, but in an instant, her expression changed to one of pure disbelief.

"Oh, my Lord!" she gasped, staggering back a step. "Is it really you?"

"It's me, Ma."

She seized me in a tight hug, and her whole body was shaking. She pulled back to look at me, then hugged me again, then pulled away again, wiping her face with the dishrag in her hand.

"I can't believe it! We hadn't heard anything from you in so long. Come in, come here, let's go tell your pa!"

I followed her across the front room toward the door of their bedroom, which struck me as strange. It was mid-afternoon. Pa should have been in his fields on an afternoon with good spring weather.

But he was in bed, and for a minute, my heart leaped into my throat. He looked dead, lying there with his eyes closed and his hands crossed over his chest.

"Jacob," Ma said softly. "Wake up, love. Someone's here to see you."

She pulled on my arm, and I moved forward. Pa's eyes opened, but there was no recognition in them.

"Sit on the bed," Ma whispered, "so he can see it's you."

As I sat down, he suddenly smiled and moved his hand to my arm.

"John David," he said. "You're home." He clasped his hands together and closed his eyes. "Oh, hallowed Father," he prayed, "I give thee thanks for bringing my boy home, for thy kindness in allowing me to see him again before I pass from this earth. Amen."

"Amen," Ma murmured. Pa opened his eyes again and tried to sit up. His grip on my arm was weak as he held to me.

"Help with the pillow, will you, Malinda?" he asked. "I'd like to sit up to talk."

It took some time to get the pillows just right and to help Pa scoot up in the bed until he was leaning back on the pillows to look at me, every part of his face a smile. I smiled back, though my insides had become a heavy knot of misery.

"Tell me about Arkansas Territory, son," Pa said. "Zeke says there's been a treaty signed to give the eastern portion to white settlers."

I nodded. "The last of the Cherokees are moving west this summer. That opens up some fine land north of the Arkansas River."

"Where are you settled?"

"North of the river." I paused and looked at my hands. I hadn't meant to tell him the whole of the situation, but how could I deceive him when he was looking at me with such pride shining through those watery, old man's eyes? "Truth be told, Pa, we're squatting there—illegally, I reckon. It's a long story how we came to be on that spot."

A little of the old twinkle sparked in those weak eyes. "Start to telling, then," he said. "I reckon I've time enough to hear one more tale."

Ma made me wait to start, though, until she called Trisha and Paul from the garden. They all crowded into the bedroom while I told the story of the path my life had taken since I'd left Campbell County. But I hardly noticed they were there, because this story was for Pa. I didn't leave out any part, not even the things I'd done that I was ashamed of. I tried to put into my words the beauty of the land, so he could see it and maybe understand what I couldn't put into words—the hold it had on me, why I was willing to break the law to have it.

He didn't say anything until I'd finished telling about the threat from Mallory, and then he broke in.

"You came home to ask for money, didn't you, son?"

I bowed my head, but I had to admit it to them, sooner or later. Sooner was better. I only wished Trisha and Paul weren't there to hear it.

"I did." I turned to look up at Ma. "It's like you said. I'm here to throw myself on the mercy of my family."

"What?" she said, but Pa spoke before I could explain.

"How much would it take to make your claim legal?"

"The government price is a dollar and a quarter an acre. I'd need to have enough for eighty acres. That's how much land they sell as a parcel. I can't buy less than eighty acres."

"That's a lot of money," Trisha said with a huff. I kept my eyes on Pa.

"It is a lot," I said. "One hundred dollars."

Pa nodded and looked at the ceiling.

"You say the Cherokees had put peach trees on the land?" he asked. "How many acres?"

"Ten, at least," I answered.

"How much is in corn?"

"Maybe another ten that I had time to put in this spring. But the Indians living on the land had cleared probably forty altogether."

"That's a good start," Pa said. "You can feed your family and more on forty acres of corn."

"It should give us enough to get by."

He looked back at me and smiled.

"I'll give you the one hundred dollars and then some," he said. "I want more for you than just enough to get by, son."

"You don't have to do that," I said quickly, since Paul and Trisha were listening.

"I want to do it," he said. "I want to know my sons are set up to prosper once I'm gone on. I've given something to all the others, and now it's your turn, John David. I'm proud to do it."

"Thank you, Pa," I said, pushing my voice past the lump in my throat. "I aim to make you proud. You can be proud to know all your sons—even the boneheaded youngest one—are following in your ways."

"Except Matthew," Trisha said, and I was surprised, both by what she said and by how both Ma and Paul shushed her. But I quickly saw why. All the joy that my visit had brought to Pa's face drained away like water from a bad bucket.

"Aye, Matthew," he said, and something like a sob caught in his voice. He suddenly gripped my arm. "But you can do it, John David. You were always closest to him. You can save your brother."

"Save him? From what?" I asked. Ma was tugging on one elbow, but Pa's grip tightened on my other arm.

"You have to save him, John David. That's the condition on the money. You have to save your brother."

"Come," Ma said, close to my ear. "He needs rest now." But as I tried to stand, Pa struggled to stand, too, like he meant to rise from the bed and follow me.

"You have to save him!" I sat back on the bed and gently pushed Pa back to the pillows.

"I'll save him, Pa. I'll do it. Just rest easy now."

"You'll do it?" He was staring into my eyes.

"I will. You can set your mind at ease."

He let go of me and dropped back to the pillow, breathing like he'd run a mile. Ma pulled me out of the bedroom and shut the door. Trisha stood in front of the fireplace, her hands on her hips and a defiant look on her face.

"It slipped out," she said. "Don't be blaming me."

"What's going on?" I asked. "What does he mean, save Matt?"

The women both looked at Paul, and he sighed.

"Bess died about a year ago," he said. "Matthew hasn't been right since then."

"Is he sick?" I asked.

"Sick with grief," Ma said.

"Crazy with grief," Trisha said, and Ma gave her a sharp look. "It's true!" she said, sticking out her chin. "He's a lunatic nowadays."

"A lunatic?" I asked, but Ma frowned and started to punch down the bread dough that had risen over the edge of the bowl while they'd listened to my story.

"He'll be fine," she insisted. "Maybe having you back, John David, will bring him out of his grief and help him see the good in life so he can start living again. That's what your pa hopes for. That's what he wants you to do."

"All right," I said. "I can do that."

"Well, you have to now, don't you?" Trisha said, and I turned to look at her. She smirked. "You heard Pa—it's the only way you'll get that money you came all this way to get."

I said nothing.

※ ※ ※

The next morning I saddled one of Pa's horses and rode over to see Zeke's family. It was a bigger family now than when I'd seen them last, with another little girl and a baby boy besides Hannah and Lily, who were grown so I hardly recognized them. There was another girl, too, the same size as my Penny, with curly, dark red hair, and I knew right away she was Matt's daughter—she was the picture of Bess Clardy.

Zeke and Sarah dropped all their work to sit at the table with me and catch up on six years of news. But there was one bit of news I wanted to hear more than any other, and finally I had to flat-out ask about Matthew, since they weren't saying anything about him at all.

"Ma says he's sick with grief," I said, "but Trisha says he's a lunatic."

Zeke and Sarah exchanged a quick glance.

"Much as I hate to say it," Zeke said, "Trisha may be closer to right. I don't believe in demon possession in these times, but if I did, I'd say Matt's been took over by one."

"His heart is so broken," Sarah said softly.

"What happened?" I asked. "I've heard tell of men mourning over the loss of their wife, but none I'd say are still crazed with grief a year later."

Zeke looked at Sarah again, and she patted Hannah's hand.

"Take the young ones outside to play," she said. "See if thou can find any ripe strawberries, and we'll make thy uncle a special treat."

Zeke waited until the young'uns were all outside, and then he turned to me with a grim face.

"Matt is convinced he killed Bess."

"But it was an accident," Sarah said quickly. "We've all tried to get him to see that."

"What happened?" I asked, a little thrill of apprehension running down my backbone.

"They used to go riding for fun," Zeke said. "They'd take Bessie— you saw her, the little redhead—to either Ma or to Bess' folks, and then they would take a ride, just the two of them. One afternoon they were on their way back to get the baby and they saw a fox, out in the daylight and stumbling around. Matt figured it was mad, so he shot it."

"My God, he didn't shoot Bess," I said. "Or did he?"

"He didn't. But her horse spooked at the gunshot and threw her off. Nobody's sure what happened then, because we can't get a straight story from Matt, but best we can figure, her foot or maybe her skirt caught in the stirrup, which threw the horse off-balance. He fell on her and crushed her. I reckon she was hurt pretty bad inside. Matt got her back home, and she lingered for a couple of days before she died. It was terrible to see. She was in awful pain and had to fight for every breath. She went down pretty fast at the end."

"That was the saddest thing I've ever seen," Sarah said, wiping her eyes. "Matt was leaning over her, begging forgiveness, and we had to pull him away because she was gone."

"He was crazy with grief and guilt," Zeke said. "We couldn't leave him alone for fear he'd shoot himself." He shook his head. "We thought he'd get better with time—folks usually do—but I swear, John David, he's nearly as bad now as he was the day she died."

"Zeke and thy pa took away all his weapons so he can't harm

himself," Sarah said. "Every gun, every rope, every knife, even the paring knife. But he's found other ways to cause himself harm."

Zeke sighed. "I don't know if anyone will be able to get through to him."

"Pa thinks I can," I said. "In fact, I have to. I need money to pay for land in Arkansas Territory, and Pa says the only way he'll give it to me is if I'll save Matt."

"Pa's desperate." Zeke shook his head. "He doesn't want to die leaving Matt in this condition."

"Who knows?" Sarah said. "Maybe thou are the answer to our prayers, John David. Maybe thou can be the one who reaches him."

"How's he trying to harm himself now?" I asked.

Zeke stood. "Come see for yourself."

❧ ❧ ❧

By my first sight of the cabin, I thought Matthew might have succeeded in doing away with himself without anyone knowing it. Everything was still and overgrown; not even a chicken hunted for food in the tall grass that grew all the way up to the porch. It had been a nice cabin, too, with two glass windows on the front, just like I'd promised Maggie we'd have once upon a time.

"Matt!" Zeke called, getting down from his horse. "I brought someone to see you."

A string of curses was the only answer. I dismounted and threw the reins over the railing of the porch.

"Matt," I said, "a man who comes all the way from Arkansas Territory ought to get a better greeting than that."

I started to step onto the porch, but Zeke threw out his arm to stop me. We waited in the yard until Matt appeared in the doorway.

"My God," I murmured, and Zeke squeezed my shoulder.

Matt squinted at us from behind a shaggy mass of hair that hung nearly to his shoulders and a scraggly beard with two matted tracks running down from the corners of his mouth. He was only half-dressed and barefoot, and in one hand he held a jug.

"Look who it is," he said, and his voice was heavy and slurred. "The prodigal son come back from the wilds." He took a long swig from the jug.

I glanced at Zeke and he nodded, so I stepped on the porch.

"I wanted to see you," I said. He laughed, a hard, bitter laugh.

"Come to see the curiosity, have you? The big brother gone bad?"

"No. The big brother I love." It was hard to tell beneath all that hair, but I thought his face hardened. I took a deep breath. I had to say something to get through to him. My claim north of the river was riding on it. "Come sit down here and let's visit."

He stood for a minute longer in the doorway, then he shuffled across the porch and sat on the steps. I sat by him, and Zeke leaned against the railing.

"I'm sorry to hear about Bess," I started.

"Everybody's sorry," he said.

"I understand how—" He cursed violently.

"You don't understand."

"I do, better than you know. I reckon Zeke told you our first baby died—"

"It's not the same," he interrupted. "You never held that baby in your arms. You never saw it smile, or heard it laugh—oh, God!" He suddenly broke into weeping. He swung the jug up to his mouth, but he choked as the whiskey gushed into his mouth and down his beard. I looked up at Zeke, and he shook his head.

"Matt," I tried again. "You can't let this ruin your life."

He had gotten to his feet. "It's my life to ruin," he said between coughs. "It don't have anything to do with you."

It does, I thought. If I can't talk you out of ruining your life, my life is ruined. But I didn't say so. I stood and put my hand on his shoulder.

"Bess wouldn't want this—"

It was exactly the wrong thing to say. He whirled around and landed his fist right in my gut, hard. I tried to step away from him, but he was all over me, and before I knew it, he'd tripped me and we were sprawled in the dirt, scrabbling around like we used to do when we were boys.

"You don't know a thing about her," he snarled as he pummeled me.

"Zeke!" I gasped as I tried to ward off his fists. "Get him off me!"

It seemed Zeke was mighty slow to move from his perch against the railing. He pulled on Matt's shoulder and held him back enough that I could scoot myself away. Matt shook off Zeke's hand and crawled to where he'd dropped the jug. He dusted it off and then raised it to his lips again.

"To hell with you both," he said, as he got to his feet and staggered around behind the cabin.

"Seen enough?" Zeke asked.

We didn't talk on the ride back to Zeke's cabin. I sat at the table while Sarah cleaned the scratches Matt's fingernails had left on my face.

"What am I going to do?" I fretted. "I've got to get money or I'll lose the land in Arkansas Territory, and I'll be right back where I was when we first got to the Territory. But Pa won't give me any money unless I can bring Matt around. And that sure don't seem likely to happen."

"I'd give you the money if I had it," Zeke said. "But having more young'uns takes more and I don't have any to spare."

"I know," I said. "I wouldn't ask it of you, anyway."

"He'll come around in time," Zeke said.

"I don't have time." I sighed. "There's someone else waiting to snatch the claim if I don't get it first."

"What seems impossible for man is possible with God," Sarah said. "Thou must add thy prayers for Matthew to ours."

"That won't help," I said. "It's been a long time since God's paid any attention to me."

She gave my cheek a little tap that was almost sharp. "Whose fault is that, then? Thou know He's not changed. He's ever the faithful Father, awaiting the prodigal's return."

"There it is again," I said, hiding my annoyance with a laugh. "Everybody's determined to make me out to be the prodigal son."

She patted my cheek again, softer this time. "Well, it's not the fatted calf, but I did kill the old stewing hen. Thou will stay for supper?"

⁂

I stayed, but I didn't linger long after, for I felt uneasy about Pa, like he might have died during the day while I was gone. But he was sitting up in the front room when I came in after putting away the horse and tack.

"You're just in time, son," he said. "Paul's about to read for us."

"We're reading through the Psalms again," Paul told me as I sat on the bench. "Tonight is Psalm 40." He cleared his throat and began to read. "'I waited patiently for the Lord, and he inclined unto me, and heard my cry.'"

Within a few words, my mind was wandering back to the sight of Matthew walking away after beating on me. How was I going to save someone who didn't want saving? I'd been waiting patiently on the Lord for six years, and now he'd thrown another obstacle in my path, just when I'd thought the way was clear. Why should I have to be the one Pa laid the burden on? And why couldn't Matt just get over losing Bess? It had been a year. That was more than enough time to grieve. In fact, it was an indulgence to grieve so long. Damn him.

I almost said it aloud, but caught myself just in time. I turned my mind back to Paul's voice.

"'…mine iniquities have taken hold upon me, so that I am not able to look up; they are more than the hairs of mine head; therefore my heart faileth me. Be pleased, O Lord, to deliver me; O Lord, make haste to help me.'"

The words hit me as hard as Matt's fist landing in my gut earlier in the day. 'Mine iniquities have taken hold upon me…they are more than the hairs of mine head.' If I was honest with myself, I knew it was true. I hadn't waited patiently these six years. Since stopping in Arkansas Territory, I'd squatted on the land, trying to steal what rightfully belonged to another—not just once. I'd lied to Maggie—not just once. I'd harbored envy and hatred in my heart, and one ugly night in Lovely's Purchase, I'd ridden out with Thomas Mallory to act on it. Now, I was back home, not because I'd wanted to see my folks, but because I wanted money from them. And I couldn't even spare sympathy for my closest brother's deep hurt. How could I blame him for acting so over losing his Bess? I'd had murder in my heart when I thought I might lose Maggie to Little El.

I bowed my head and listened to the last of the psalm, and then I kissed Ma good night and squeezed Pa's shoulder before heading up to the attic where Ma had laid out a pallet for me. I lay on my back and watched the shadows of the candlelight from downstairs flicker across the rafters.

I'd made a mess of things, for sure. I couldn't turn back what I'd done—the Cherokees were already out of Arkansas Territory for good, by treaty. That wasn't all my fault, but I would have to live the rest of my life knowing I was partly responsible for rooting them out. But it was done, and now I had the duty to provide a home for Maggie and my children. The only way to do that—the right way to do it—was through Matt. Wild, dirty, drunk, grieving Matt. How would I ever reach him?

The last words of the psalm came into my mind, and I whispered them aloud.

"'I am poor and needy, yet the Lord thinketh upon me; thou art my help and my deliverer.'" Suddenly I closed my eyes and clasped my hands together, just like Pa would do. "I am poor and needy," I murmured. "I know I don't deserve it, but I need a deliverer, Lord. Please show me the way to get through to Matt." I paused, and then added, "And as the psalm says, 'make no tarrying, O my God.'"

Chapter 20

I wasn't blessed during the night with any ideas about how to handle Matt, so I decided I'd go up the mountain to see Maggie's family. The Boons' place looked more prosperous than the last time I'd seen it, the day I came to take Maggie away from it. The smokehouse had been rebuilt so it was straight, and it looked to me like another room had been added to the cabin. A young woman was in the yard working over a washpot, and I could hear children's voices behind the cabin. I dismounted and walked over to the woman.

"Is this still the Boon place?" I asked.

The woman jumped a little, like I'd scared her, and threw a quick glance at me over her shoulder. Then her wet hands flew up to her mouth, and she turned toward me eagerly.

"Is Maggie with you?" she asked, trying to see around me.

"No, it's just me. Maggie stayed behind in Arkansas Territory." The eagerness left her, and she half-turned away from me, but not before I saw that the lower half of one side of her face was marred by a thick, raised pink scar. It was a shame, for I recognized her now as the pretty sister just younger than Maggie. I couldn't remember her name. "Are your folks here?"

She carefully kept the damaged side of her face turned away from my sight. "Ma's in the house. Pa's dead, though."

"He is? When?"

"It wasn't all that long after Maggie left, just a couple of years." She waved me toward the house. "Come on, I'll tell them you're here."

I followed her into the cabin. Maggie's ma sat in a rocking chair by the fire, and another woman I figured must be the next youngest sister sat at the table, holding a young'un.

"Ma," my guide said, "look who's come for a visit. It's Mag—"

"That fancy McKellar boy," Mrs. Boon interrupted, like her daughter wasn't even speaking. "It's been a long time since you darkened this door. Is Maggie with you?"

"No, she stayed back home in Arkansas Territory."

The woman with the baby gaped at me. "Arkansas Territory? Where's that?"

"It's out west," I told them. "Past the Mississippi River." I could tell they had no idea what I was talking about. "It's a long way off."

"So you stayed with her." Her ma laughed. "We sure never expected that."

Her laugh triggered a surge of anger through me, but I didn't say to her what I wanted to say.

"We're doing well," I said instead. "We've got two young'uns now, and we're taking up a claim on the land the Cherokees traded to the government."

"Prospering, are you?" She had that greedy look I remembered.

"Well enough," I said. "Looks like you all are prospering, too."

"That's my doing," the one with the baby said. "It's thanks to my husband. He come in and took over when we was doing so poorly after Pa died. He's a good, solid man, not like some I've seen." She threw a triumphant look toward the sister with the scarred face, who shrank even farther into the corner by the fireplace, like she didn't want anyone to notice her. It didn't work.

"Mary!" Her ma snapped. "Are you done with the washing yet?"

"No, Ma."

"Then why are you lolling about in the house?"

"I wanted to hear about Maggie—"

In one quick move, her ma rose from the rocking chair and slapped Mary across the face.

"Don't you mouth back to me!" she snarled. "Get back to the washing!"

I should have said something, but I only stepped to the side so Mary could get through the door. She kept her face turned from me, but I could see her lips were quivering, though she had them pressed tight together.

"How much land you got?" her ma asked, like none of that had happened.

"We're still waiting on the survey," I said, watching through the door as Mary went back to the washpot. "I expect to get eighty acres. What happened to her face?" I asked, turning back to them. "I want to take word of you all back to Maggie."

"The clumsy dolt tripped while she was carrying hot lard and it splashed on her face," the sister with the baby said. "You can tell Maggie that Callie—that's me—got herself a good husband and a pretty baby boy."

"I'll tell her." The other young'uns were coming into the cabin now, and I started to feel closed in like a trapped animal as they filled the small front room.

"Mary's the only one had any misfortune," Maggie's ma said. "The rest of the young'uns are growing up fine. Billy, now, he took off about a year ago, soon as he turned 16."

"He didn't like Adam—that's my husband," Callie added. "He was jealous that Adam got to be the man of the house once we married. But that's how it ort to be—Adam's full a man and Billy was just a rawboned boy."

"Who's he?" one of the younger girls asked, pointing at me.

"I'm Maggie's husband," I said, turning toward her. But their ma laughed again.

"She don't remember Maggie. She don't know there ever was a Maggie."

The urge to leave came on me hard and sudden.

"Well," I said, "I reckon I'll be going. I just wanted to have some word of you all to take back to Maggie and to let you know she's doing fine. I know we left Campbell County pretty suddenly and I always hated it that she didn't get to say goodbye."

"We'd heard you left," her ma said. "Bob Dunlop brought that word, said you had a big fuss with your folks and said you was going to Texas. We always figured you tired of Maggie once you got on the road and you left her someplace along the way. We figured you'd be back in Campbell County someday without her."

"I'm not here to stay," I snapped. "I'm going back to her in Arkansas Territory quick as I can—"

I shut my mouth quick before I confessed I was back in Campbell County to get money.

"Goodbye," I said, and I stepped out of that suffocating cabin into the clearing. Mary threw a quick glance at me over her shoulder, and I waved a hand at her, awkwardly. I wanted to say something, but what was there to say? That I was sorry for how things had turned out for her? That it wasn't fair she was scarred and ill-treated while her closest sister was happy and well-loved? With a heavy heart, I swung into the saddle. Maggie's sisters and brothers came outside to watch as I rode away. I waved to them one last time, then I set the horse to as fast a pace as he could safely manage over the rocky trail.

I half-wished I'd never come. Maggie would be glad to know, I suppose, that they were healthy and well-fed, but there were plenty of things that would grieve her, too. Like that her ma hadn't even asked how old our young'uns were, or even whether they were boys or girls.

"Mr. McKellar!" The voice behind me sounded desperate, and I reined the horse quickly, looking over my shoulder. It was Mary, running over the rocky path, waving her arm. I waited for her to catch up, and then I waited some more for her to catch her breath to talk.

"Mr. McKellar," she said again, before she was even beside the horse. "Please take me with you."

The shock I felt must have showed on my face, for she grabbed my stirrup and turned her ruined face up to me.

"Please," she begged. "I want to go to Arkansas Territory with you. I could be a big help to Maggie, I'm a real hard worker, and I know she's probably got her hands full with two young'uns. Please take me with you."

"Mary," I said, "I can't take you."

"Please!" Tears were streaming down her cheeks, unevenly, for on the one side they hit the raised scars and ran crooked off the side of her face. "You don't know what it's like here, living with them—"

"I have a pretty good idea," I interrupted.

She was sobbing now. "If I could only get a new start, leave all this behind me, I know things would be better. I could feel better, more like myself again. I could live better with what happened if I had some hope. Arkansas Territory could be a new start. I don't care if I have to work real hard and if you want me to sleep up in the attic, or even in the barn—I could help Maggie a lot—Please let me come to Arkansas Territory with you!"

I couldn't watch her, hanging on to my foot like I was some angel come to rescue her from the fiery pit.

"I know your life is hell," I said, as gently as I could. "But Mary, I can't take you with me. Truth is, we're barely holding on out there ourselves. I know you'd work hard and be a help to Maggie, but I can barely feed the four of us, much less another adult."

"I'll work in the fields!"

I shook my head. "I'm sorry, but I can't take you."

Her hands dropped from my foot and she took a deep, shuddering breath.

"All right. I understand."

I watched as she walked away, back up the road toward the cabin. Her head was bent, and I was sure her shoulders heaved with more sobs.

"Damn it!" I muttered. "I wish I'd never come here today." I kicked the horse's sides, a little harder than I needed to, and she took off at a fast trot that made my teeth rattle. But I didn't try to slow her.

It was the right choice, I told myself. Everything I'd told her was true—without land, I couldn't do more than keep food on the table a day at a time. And though I didn't want to admit it, I was beginning to fear this trip had been for naught, that I wouldn't get the money for our land. Pa didn't change his mind, once he'd settled on something, and he wouldn't give me a disme if he couldn't be convinced I had saved Matt. But saving Matt—I couldn't see any way that was going to happen—

A little branch whipped across my forehead with a stinging pain, knocking my hat to the ground. I pulled the mare to a stop and dismounted so I could go back for it, and then it was like something else hit me in the forehead, so hard I nearly reeled.

If I could only get a new start, leave all this behind me, I know things would be better. I could almost hear Mary saying the words. *I could feel better, more like myself again. I could live better with what happened if I had some hope. Arkansas Territory could be a new start.*

"Of course!" I said aloud. "He can't get past his grieving sitting in that cabin full of his memories. That's what I need to do—take him to Arkansas Territory so he can start over!"

My heart was light as a feather as I climbed into the saddle and started the mare back down the mountain. I could convince Pa it was a good plan, I was sure of that. The hard part would be convincing Matt, but I didn't much care if he liked the plan or not. I needed that money, and if it meant taking Matt kicking and screaming all the way to Arkansas Territory, I would do it.

The horse hadn't gone more than three steps more, though, before something else hit me hard, this time straight in my heart. The Lord had answered my prayer, with no tarrying, just like I'd asked, in the form of a maimed woman's desperate plea. Mary was the deliverer I'd asked for—how could I take her help and then just ride off to leave her in the misery of a life as a slave to those hateful Boons? Mary needed saving, same as Matt did.

"Oh, God," I groaned. But I couldn't bear the burden of another guilt. With a jerk of the reins, I turned the horse on the path and headed back up the path toward the Boons' clearing.

I left the mare in the woods about a hundred feet from the clearing. Mary was still working alone at the washing, twisting the wet clothes to wring out the water. I crept as close as I dared in the brush at the edge of the clearing.

"Mary!" I hissed. "Mary!"

Her puffy, pink eyes brightened a little when she caught sight of me. With a quick glance back at the cabin, she brought the basket to the brush and started hanging clothes over the branches.

"You're sure you want to go?" I asked. She turned to me quick, and hope was shining in her whole face, even the ruined part. She nodded. "Get your stuff together, then, and meet me down at that place where a flat rock juts out over the creek. You know the place?"

"I know it," she said. "But I've got nothing I care to bring with me." She dropped the clothes hanging over her arm back into the basket and stepped into the cover of the woods beside me. "Let's go."

❧ ❧ ❧

I stopped first at Zeke's, to try out the idea on him before taking it to Pa. After one quick look at Mary's scarred cheek, Sarah stepped forward to take her hand.

"So thou are Maggie's sister. Welcome. Would thou like something to drink after thy trip?"

Zeke and I left them and stepped out on the porch.

"What in God's earth are you thinking now?" he asked.

"I know," I interrupted, before he could tell me how foolish I was. "But I've got an idea now of what to do about Matt. I'll take him back to Arkansas Territory. Maybe if he's away from all the things that remind him of Bess, he'll come back to himself."

"I see. And how does Maggie's sister figure into all this?"

"She gave me the idea. She asked to come, and I didn't feel right about leaving her after she helped me figure out what to do. But that's a side matter—do you think Pa will go for this?"

"You'll just have to ask. He's desperate, though, to see something done before he passes on." He smoothed his beard for a minute, like he always did when he was thinking. "The bigger question may be, do you think Matt will go for this? You saw him."

"If Pa is willing, Matt's coming with me, willing or not," I said grimly, and Zeke suddenly laughed.

"It's as it ever was," he said. "Matt could never out-stubborn you."

"And he won't this time." I was quiet for a minute, looking out toward Zeke's well-tended garden. "But reckon it will help him, to come west?"

"It can't make things worse," Zeke said softly. "I fear he'll grieve himself into an early grave if he stays here. Maybe going west will get his mind to work on something besides his loss."

"I hope so." I suddenly laughed. "Poor Maggie! She has no idea her household is about to include her sister and my damned lunatic brother."

"And little Bessie," Zeke added. "Lunatic or not, Matt's her pa."

I groaned, and Zeke laughed and clapped his hand on my shoulder.

"I reckon it's God's providence you brought Mary," he said. "She can mind Bess, since you'll have your hands full with Matt."

"I'll have the worst of it," I muttered. Zeke grinned.

"You'll make it all right. Matt might think he could beat you in a fight, but you always stayed in it till the end, just like a bear dog with its teeth sunk in." He slapped my back and laughed again. "I bet you've worn out your welcome at the Boons' place, brother. Every time you visit, you take away another of their daughters."

"This is the last time," I said. "If I make it back to Arkansas Territory with these three and we're all still alive, I'm staying."

Mary stayed behind with Sarah when I rode off toward home. It was nearly dark by the time I was finished turning the mare out to pasture and putting away the saddle.

"How's Pa?" I asked as I came into the cabin.

"Sleeping," Paul said, and I nodded. I was halfway glad, for on the way from Zeke's, my mind had started to fill with doubt about my plan. Could I really expect Pa to agree to something that would take another son away, something that might not even work?

"I'll speak to him in the morning, then," I said. "I might have an idea of what to do about Matt."

I was started up the stairs to the attic when a feeble voice came from Pa's room.

"Is that you, John David?"

I hurried to his bedside. He looked more frail than he had this morning, and his breathing was hardly more than a flutter. I swallowed hard against the lump in my throat.

"I'm here, Pa."

"Did I hear you right? You have a way to help Matt?"

"I hope so." I sat on the stool beside the bed and took his knotty hand in mine. So many times that hand had closed around mine, showing me how to fire a rifle or guiding my fingers as I learned to whittle an axe handle. Many the time I'd felt the power in those hands as they wielded a strap against my backside when I was a stubborn cuss of a boy. But now they were trembling and weak.

"I'd like leave from you to take Matt back with me to Arkansas Territory," I said. "He's in that cabin where everything around him reminds him of Bess. Maybe the only way to get him over it is to take him out of there and give him a fresh start. That's what I think. But what matters is what you think."

Pa didn't answer me. In fact, he closed his eyes, and I figured he hadn't heard any of what I'd said. I sat a while longer, holding to his hand, until Paul spoke behind me.

"That's your plan?"

"It is. I don't know that it will work, but it's worth trying."

"Worth trying!" Trisha scoffed. "You know what he'll do, Paul. He'll take Pa's money and then leave Matt drunk in some tavern along the way—"

"He's my brother," I snapped. "I'd not do that to him. If Pa gives me permission, I'll get Matt to my farm in Arkansas Territory if it breaks us both."

"Sure you will," she said. "You've never stuck with anything that was hard to do, not in your whole life."

"Shush!" Ma scolded. "Have respect for Jacob, both of you! Take your fighting someplace else."

Pa was squeezing my hand.

"Malinda," he said. "Shut the door. I want to speak to John David alone."

I heard Trisha muttering as Ma shooed her back into the kitchen, and then the door shut softly, leaving the room dark but for the light of a candle on the table by the bed. Pa struggled to sit up, so I helped raise his shoulders and adjusted the pillow so he could lean against the headboard.

"Trisha thinks you're still the boy who left here in anger all those years ago," he said. "But I see the new country you've lived in has made you more than that, son. There have been some hard lessons for you in all that's happened since you left home."

I nodded.

"Remember that the Lord says, 'No chastening for the present seemeth to be joyous, but grievous; nevertheless afterward it yieldeth the peaceable fruit of righteousness unto them which are exercised thereby.'" He quoted the scripture easily, as he had done all my life.

"Yes, Pa."

He lay against the pillow quietly for a while, his eyes closed. Then he opened them again and smiled at me. "I never told you younger boys much about when your ma and I first settled in Tennessee. I look at you, son, and see myself of nearly fifty years ago. So young, so determined to get a foothold and have a home of my own. That struggle shapes a man's soul. It knocks him down, it trips him, it batters him—but it can't defeat him unless he gives in to it. You know my struggle like none of my other sons, John David. Paul can't understand you, and Zeke, though he loves you, doesn't know you as he once did. But I know you—better now than ever I did when you lived under my roof." He squeezed my hand again. "I'll not be much longer on this earth, son. I'm going ahead of you all into new territory. But I'm pleased to leave knowing at least one of my sons truly understands the life I've lived on this earth."

Tears were rolling down my cheeks, but I didn't want to let go of him long enough to wipe them away.

"Don't grieve," he said. "I've lived the threescore years and ten our Lord has been gracious to give me. It's been a good life, and I've been greatly blessed." He raised his free hand and pointed toward the cupboard in the corner of the room. "There's a small crock in the bottom of that cupboard—fetch it for me."

The crock was heavy, and though I didn't look in it, I knew it was filled with coins. As I sat it on the bed beside him, I felt like I might start bawling. Here it was, the money I wanted and needed so badly, yet why did my heart feel heavier inside my chest than the little crock felt in my hands?

"I can't see well enough," he said, "so you count out what you'll need for your eighty acres."

I counted out the coins and laid them on the bed beside him.

"You have a money bag?" he asked, and I pulled the limp buckskin bag from my pocket. I held it open while he picked up the coins and dropped them in. With each click of one coin against another, I felt more like a thief. He couldn't see to tell the difference between the coins, but I reckon he could read my face, for as I pulled the drawstring to close the bag, he laid his hand over mine.

"Don't feel bad to take it, John David," he said. "A family takes care of its own. I'm glad you gave me the chance to help you instead of putting yourself in debt to worldly lenders."

"I'm glad, too," I murmured.

"Paul said you've been riding the black mare."

I got up to take the crock back to the cupboard. "She's a fine horse—she has a nice, smooth gait."

"She'll foal late in the fall. I want you to take her with you, too."

"I can't do that," I said, coming back to his bedside. "It's too much." But he took my hand again.

"Take her—as a remembrance of your last trip home."

"Thank you," I started, but my voice choked off in my throat. "Oh, Pa—I—" I couldn't hold it any longer. I laid my head on the side of the bed and cried like a young'un.

He laid his hand gently on my hair until I had myself back in control and sat up.

"I'm glad we had this time," he said. "I was afraid you'd never know how proud I am of you. I know I was hard on you when you were younger, but it never meant I wasn't proud of you."

"I did plenty to disappoint you, I know." I wiped my eyes with my sleeve. "But it never meant I didn't love you. I do, Pa."

"And I love you." His pillow slipped a little as he raised his head, and I pushed it back straight again. "I know it won't be easy to deal with Matthew," he said, looking up at me. "But you must get through to him."

"I will," I promised. "Somehow. I won't give up on him."

His eyes were drooping closed.

"You're tired," I said, starting to stand. "I'll go now and let you sleep." But he still gripped my hand.

"Not yet. Stay a while longer." So I sat back down, and he smiled. "Tell me about your land, John David. What does it look like in Arkansas Territory?"

I closed my eyes a moment to picture it better, the cabin, the creek and the woods, the gentle rise of the cornfields, the acres of stubby peach trees in bloom covering the hillside with a blanket of pink, Maggie smiling and holding our Jake with Penny at her side. A lonely pang stabbed through me, and I wondered how a man could be homesick for two places at one time.

"We can see the mountains off to the north," I started, "low compared to your mountains, I suppose, but blue and so pretty I just stop sometimes in my plowing to stare at them a while."

I talked until I was sure he was asleep this time, and then I carefully pulled my hand away and went back to the kitchen where Ma was sitting alone by the fire. Her eyes caught mine, a little fearfully, I thought.

"He's sleeping," I told her, and her face relaxed.

"I'm glad you're here to see him," she said. "He never said a word, but I knew he was longing for it before he goes."

I knelt to put my arms around her.

"I'm glad, too, Ma. Mighty glad."

Chapter 21

Two days later, Zeke and I rode over to Matthew's place. We brought along Sarah and Mary, leaving the young'uns behind with Ma. Zeke looked at the length of rope looped across my chest and one shoulder.

"Maybe you won't need that," he said. "Maybe he'll be in a more cooperative mood today."

I shifted the rope higher on my shoulder. "Maybe. I'm not leaving it to chance."

The cabin was silent in the spring morning.

"What if he's sleeping?" Sarah whispered. I looked at Zeke and shrugged, and then I dismounted and walked across the porch to open the door.

The sour smell from inside the cabin hit me like a powerful fist before my eyes adjusted enough to the dim light to let me see what I was facing. Matt wasn't sleeping. He was sitting at the table with his head leaning on one hand and a jug in the other. I checked to see that Zeke was right behind me.

"Good morning, Matt," I said. He looked up, startled. "I've got a proposition for you."

"Go to hell," he muttered. So much for a cooperative mood.

"No, I'm going back to Arkansas Territory. And you're coming with me."

He started to rise from the chair, but Zeke and I were quick, and we each had one of his arms before he could move away from the table. He howled and twisted against us, but we held him tight and half-carried, half-drug him out onto the porch.

"Are you going to come along nicely?" I said, as close to his ear as I dared to put my face. "It'll make things easier on you if you do, but I'm prepared to take you, even if you don't want to go."

"This is kidnapping!" he screamed. "Get out of here and leave me alone! I want to be alone!"

"Take him," I said to Zeke, and he pinned both Matt's arms tight against his body with a giant bear hug. I lifted the rope over my head and wound it around Matt several times, low around his belly so he couldn't move his arms. He cussed us with every breath, bucking against Zeke's hold, but finally the rope was secure and Zeke let him go. We took him over to a chair and sat him down. Zeke motioned to the women, and with quiet, determined faces, they came on the porch, and the three of them went into the cabin.

"What are they doing? What are they doing?" Matt howled. I sat on the porch railing beside him.

"I don't like this anymore than you do, Matt," I said. "Taking you by violence, like you're some kind of animal. But we've got to do this for your own good. You'll sit in that house and drink yourself to death—"

"I want to be dead," he spat at me.

"Well, that's unfortunate," I said, calmly. "None of the rest of us want you to be dead. So we're not going to let it happen."

Zeke came out of the house with several jugs cradled in his arms.

"Where did you get all these, Matt?" he asked. "You must have cleaned out Sparky Wooten's whole supply." He handed a jug to me, and I poured it out on the ground beside the porch.

"You can't do that!" Matt was struggling to stand, and he fell, face first, to the porch. I stopped pouring and lifted him back into the chair.

"No more drinking for you, Matt," I told him, starting to pour again. "When a man can't stop with one cup of whiskey, it's time to cut it out altogether. It's probably for the best, anyway—I don't have any liquor around my place in Arkansas Territory."

"I'm not going anywhere with you!"

"You'll like Arkansas Territory, once you've come to your senses." I tossed the empty jug into the yard and started on the next one. "Life is still pretty rough out there, but the land is good, and if we work together, we ought to be able to prosper. I figure you can take up a claim next to mine and we can work them both. We'll be the western branch of the clan McKellar."

"Go to hell!"

He stayed agitated the whole time, throwing out a string of curses at Zeke and even the women as they carried his goods out of his house. Zeke fetched Matt's pair of mules from the pasture behind the cabin. I left Matt alone on the porch to help Zeke hitch the team to the wagon sitting by the barn, and then we loaded everything from the house and cleared the barn as well of what equipment we could fit.

"That's a good plow," I said, bending to look at the curved blade of it. "Better than the one I have."

"It's a shame you can't take it," Zeke said. "But it won't ride well in the wagon."

"Oh, I'll find a way to bring it. We need good tools too bad in the Territory to leave it behind."

In the end, I tied together a pair of wheels from a handcart to either side of the plow, and the contraption was just high enough to keep the point from scraping the ground. I saddled Matt's stallion and attached a rope to each stirrup strap so the horse could pull the plow behind. He didn't like it, of course, but I didn't care. Just like Matt, that plow was coming to Arkansas Territory, like it or not.

※ ※ ※

Matt had calmed some by the time we pulled into the yard at Pa's. Whether he was truly calm or just worn out from the struggle, I wasn't sure, but I hoped he would behave himself long enough to allow Pa to say goodbye. Zeke and I lifted him from the wagon, and I held him by the shoulder and bent so he had to look into my face.

"We're here to say goodbye to Pa," I told him. "We'll take you out of the ropes if you'll promise to act decent."

He cursed me again, loudly and in front of Ma and the young'uns. I leaned closer as we walked him to the barn.

"Cuss me all you want, with every breath all the way to Arkansas Territory, I don't give a damn," I said. "But give Pa a chance for a proper goodbye, hear me?"

We removed the ropes, but Zeke kept a good hold on him while I wrestled him into a clean shirt and britches, which helped some with the smell. Sarah brought a rag and gently wiped his face clean and flattened his wild beard.

"There's no time to clean thy hair, though," she said.

"I don't want it clean," he growled.

"Don't worry over it, Sarah," Zeke said. "Pa knows the way things are." He looked across at me. "Ready? Paul, step in here to block him if he tries to break out behind us."

Ma had brought Pa to sit in the rocking chair in the front room, and she tapped his shoulder gently to wake him when we came in.

"The boys are all here, Jacob."

For a minute, his eyes were dim and seemed unable to see anything, but he suddenly smiled and held out his hands toward us.

"Matt and I are leaving for Arkansas Territory today," I said. "But we wanted to say goodbye first."

"I'm glad." He leaned forward toward Matt, liked he wanted to touch him. I gave Matt a hard jab with my elbow, and with a little growl in his throat, he stepped forward enough Pa could take his hands. Every muscle in my body was tense as I held myself ready for whatever Matt might do—try to shake off Pa's hands, whirl around and break out of the room. But he didn't move, didn't say anything, didn't even look down at Pa.

"You ass," I muttered, under my breath.

I knew by the way Pa's smile faded that he had noticed too. But he still held to Matt's hands and looked up into his stony face.

"Your soul is deeply wounded, son," he said. "You've been through terrible suffering, but remember, the Lord works all for the good of those who love Him. I pray the Lord will bring you healing in the new land."

Matt didn't respond at all, and I stepped in quickly to take Pa's hand.

"I don't want to rush your goodbyes, but we probably should be starting," I said. Pa nodded, still looking at Matt.

"What a blessing it is to have all my sons under my roof again before I die," he said, "a blessing I never thought I would have. It's as the scripture says, 'As arrows are in the hand of a mighty man, so are children of the youth. Happy is the man that hath his quiver full of them.' Just look at our boys, Malinda!"

"Yes," Ma said, coming to stand beside him. "They are fine men."

"Two stay and two go," he said. "Such is the march of life."

Matt shifted beside me, and I was certain he was nearing the end of his good behavior. I shot a look at Zeke, who nodded and gripped Matt's arm. I squeezed Pa's hand a last time and then let it drop.

"We'll be going now," I said. "Goodbye, Pa."

"God bless you!" he called after us as we steered Matt back onto the porch.

"All his yammering about God," Matt scoffed. "God doesn't care about us."

"Come on," Zeke said roughly. "Back in the wagon with you." He looked at me. "Do you want me to tie him?"

"Probably should," I said. "I don't trust him yet to go free."

Matt sat fuming on the wagon seat while I got the money bag and my bundle from Arkansas Territory and while we tied the black mare alongside Matt's stallion at the back of the wagon. Once we had everything ready, Sarah brought her girls and little Bessie from the back yard where they'd been playing, and Zeke set Bessie in the wagon box with Mary. As I lifted the reins to start the mules, Bessie went into a crying fit.

"No! No!" she screeched. "I don't want to go! I want Aunty Sarah!"

"Come, come," Mary said soothingly. "We're taking you to a new home with your pa."

Matt's laugh was bitter as he turned to look back at them. "Yeah, you're coming to live with me. The crazy man they have to tie up."

Bessie's spoiled crying suddenly turned into screams of terror, and Matt made like he was going to lunge toward her.

"Stop it!" I said, slapping the ends of the reins across his thighs. "I'll make you walk every step to Arkansas Territory, back with the horses, if you're going to do such as that."

"Bessie," Mary was saying, "sit down, sweetie. He's only playing a game. Come sit with me."

"No!" Bessie screamed. "I don't want him! I don't want you! You're ugly! Ugly!"

I glanced back then, half fearful Bessie might be trying to jump over the side, but Mary, her own face tight with pain, had caught the thrashing little girl and was holding her close, rocking her and gently patting her back. I sighed and turned back to the road before us.

"My God," I muttered. "What have I gotten myself into?"

❧ ❧ ❧

About the time we stopped to set up camp that night, Matt took sick, shaking so bad he could hardly stand and bending over with dry heaves every few minutes. He kept trying to swat at his face, though he couldn't with his hands tied.

"I feel like ants are crawling all over me," he said, shuddering. "There's not anything on me, is there?"

"Nope." I figured there was no danger of him running off in such a condition, so I set him free of the ropes. He immediately grabbed the front of my shirt in both fists.

"I need a drink," he said, desperately. "To calm my jitters."

"Nope." I pulled my shirt out of his hands, but he grabbed it in different places.

"I need it, John David! You don't understand how bad I'm feeling."

"You're in for a bad night," I agreed, "but you'll just have to get through it. There's no more whiskey for you, brother. Ever. I'll not have it around my young'uns."

He let go of me with a push and a frown. "You sound like Pa."

I laughed. "Why, that's the nicest thing you've said to me since I got here."

He was taken with another fit of retching, and I left him to go help Mary with setting up camp. She looked over at Matt, and then at Bessie, who was huddled against the wagon wheel.

"I've seen sickness like his plenty of times," she said. "Pa would get like this every time he had to quit drinking because there was no money for whiskey. If you want, I'll tend him while you see to little Bessie."

"That sounds fine," I said. She went to fetch a dipper of water for Matt, and I turned toward Bessie. It was a wonder how much she looked like her pretty ma, even as such a little girl. But right now she looked scared and tired, and I was sorry for her. She'd had a bad day, for sure. I sat on a rock near her.

"I have a little girl," I said, glancing over at her. "Penny is her name. She's just about your size. She'll sure be happy to meet a girl cousin and have someone to play with. All she has right now is a little brother to pester her."

She didn't say anything, but she was still looking at me. I picked a yellow flower from a weed nearby and held it out to her. After a minute, she took it and held it close to her nose.

"Want to help me find sticks for a fire so we can cook some supper?" I asked, and she nodded.

I may have won Bessie over on that night, but truth is, I don't know how I would have managed with her on that trip without Mary. Besides cooking a hot meal for us every night and keeping us clean enough to be respectable, Mary coddled Bessie, who cried herself to sleep every night. Bessie would seem to be getting used to the idea of leaving Sarah and her cousins behind, then she would have a night where Mary had to rock and soothe her for a long time before she would fall asleep. We had one of those bad nights when we were just past Nashville. Long after supper, Bessie fussed and whimpered, no matter what Mary tried. Matt was having another bad night, too, and after a while, he scrambled to his feet and started pacing around the clearing where we were camped.

"Good God!" he exploded. "Can't you get that child to shut up?" Of course, that set Bessie to wailing loud again.

"A lot of good that did," I said, leaning forward to poke a stick deeper into the fire. "Now she's probably so scared she'll cry the rest of the night."

He came back to sit again with me by the fire.

"Why didn't we leave her with Sarah?" he grumped. "She just cries all the time—"

But Mary, who was usually so quiet and mild, had turned on him with eyes blazing hotter than the campfire.

"You can't blame her—she's had everything in her life upended," she said, her voice low but hard. "Poor little thing."

"She's not the only one," Matt spat back at her.

"No, she's not," Mary said. "But neither are you."

His eyes narrowed. "You don't know what I'm—" he started, but she cut him off.

"I do—I know suffering. I know what it's like to be alone. I had a husband, but he left me when I got burned and took our baby with

241

him, and I've never seen my son again. You lost your wife, true, but at least you have this little one left with you as a part of her, to remember her. You have this little girl who would love you, but you'd rather hide behind that nasty hair and hug on your hurt when you could be holding your precious daughter."

Matt sat with his mouth open while Mary bent back over Bessie, humming in a low voice that was just a little off-key. He looked at me, and I shrugged.

"I'm not taking your part, brother," I said. "She's right."

With a huff, he got up and stalked off into the darkness, which meant I had to get up and follow him around—at a distance, of course—until he was ready to come back to camp. By now, for the most part, he had quit fighting coming along on the trip and had instead sunk into a sullen silence that I thought was more dangerous, because I couldn't know what he was thinking. For all I knew, he could be plotting how to leave us. Part of me wished he would leave, and soon—I had the money now, and I'd made an honest try to help him. But I'd made a promise to Pa that I meant to keep, and that promise made me get up from my comfortable spot at the fire every night to follow Matt through the dark to make sure he couldn't go.

I couldn't say just what it was, but he was different after that night. He was still sullen and silent, but I thought it seemed he was watching Mary and Bess all the time now. A couple of times I caught him at it, and something in his face could have passed for interest. But he turned and saw me looking at him, and in a heartbeat, it was gone, and he had slipped back behind his scruffy beard. I didn't say anything. Whatever thought was sending out tender roots in his head, I sure didn't want to trample it.

We went as many miles in a day as Bessie could tolerate, and by the beginning of June we were ready to cross the ferry at Memphis into Arkansas Territory. We camped by the big river that night, ready to catch the first run of the ferry in the morning. It was too warm to need a fire, but I built one anyway, with green wood that would smoke a lot and maybe keep the mosquitos away. Mary and Bessie bedded down in the wagon, but Matt and I sat for a long time around the fire, not even talking, just sitting. It was strange to be that way with him. As long as I could remember, Matt and I had been close as brothers could be, coming at the end of the family as we did and separated by so many years from Paul and Zeke. I'd followed him into more fun and more trouble than I'd want to admit to anyone, but we'd always shared the consequences, be they good or bad. But now he was as strange to me as one of the stars in the dark sky and seemed just as far away.

I couldn't do anything about that, though. I stretched out on my back and made a pillow of my arms so I could look up into the stars comfortably. Arkansas Territory tomorrow. Of course, it was still a long way on the roughest roads we would face, but I figured within three more weeks we could be home. I pictured the way it would be, stepping off the wagon and into Maggie's arms, holding her close and kissing her—except there would be a slew of folks watching now—

"Reckon Bessie remembers her ma?" Matt's voice cut into my daydreaming. I leaned up on one elbow to look at him.

"Maybe."

"I don't think she does." His voice was hollow with sadness. "She was too young when—" He didn't finish the thought.

I figured he was right, but I wasn't going to say so. I lay back on the ground.

"I don't think she remembers me, either," he said after a while. That I did have an answer to.

"It's because you're not the Pa she remembers," I said, turning my head to look at him. "Think about it, Matt. I hardly recognize you myself. You don't look like you used to, and you sure don't act like it."

He didn't answer, just stared into the fire. I lay down again and tried to bring back my daydream of Maggie, but just as I had her face clearly in my mind, he broke in again.

"Did you ever have something that was perfect, just so perfect you knew it was the right thing for you? And then it's gone and you're sick inside with wanting it back, so sick inside—"

I knew the feeling he meant. Hadn't I gone through several bouts of it mourning for the land north of the river? Of course, land wasn't the same as a woman, and I was getting a second chance, but—

"Yeah," I said softly. "I know that feeling." He moaned a little and wrapped his hands around the back of his neck, pulling himself forward into a ball of misery.

243

"Let me give you a piece of advice someone gave me once," I said, staring up into the soft black sky. "That feeling is like heart rot in a good oak tree. If you leave it alone, don't fight it, it's going to spread and eat away all the good parts inside you. Before long, you'll have just a thin shell of good wood left and inside will be nothing but that black rot."

"I'm already filled with black rot," he murmured.

"There's bound to be something good left inside you, Matt. The brother I remember was a mighty strong oak. There's got to be a way you can grow a burl around the rot, keep it from spreading more. If you can't do it for yourself, do it for that little girl. She needs her pa— not me, not Maggie, not Mary—you."

He was quiet for a long time, and I had begun to ponder whether it was worth getting up to make a bedroll or if I felt too drowsy to move from the spot I was in. Suddenly I was aware he was standing over me, and my heart jumped and began to thud.

"I want your knife," he said. "You have mine."

I sat up. "Now, Matt, don't do anything hasty—"

"I want your knife. Mary said Bessie is afraid of my hair—I want to get rid of it tonight. Then maybe in the morning she'll see the pa she remembers."

My heartbeat slowed, and I grinned at him.

"Sit down close to the fire," I said. "It's probably better if I do the cutting. I can't promise you'll look much better, but we'll try."

༚ ༚ ༚

When Mary caught sight of Matt the next morning, she went right away to find the scissors from the sewing kit they had brought out of Matt's cabin. Bessie sat on my knee and we watched while Mary evened up the rough haircut I'd given him in the dark.

"I can't believe you did this!" she kept saying, but I just laughed.

"I still have all my fingers, and Matt still has both ears," I said. "I'd say it was a success."

Something that looked a little like a smile crossed Matt's face. "I'm glad you decided to let the beard go till morning, though," he said.

"How much of it do you want me to take off?" Mary asked, lifting the tangled mess.

"We don't have time for you to shave," I warned. "The ferry will be leaving soon."

"I'll just neaten it up, then," she said, snipping off the first straggly piece. Matt picked it up from where it had fallen on his knee. He smoothed it between his fingers, and then he looked up at Bessie.

"When this hair started growing out of my face, your ma was still alive," he said softly. He took a deep breath. "I've been real sad, Bessie. I'm still real sad."

She stood looking at him with solemn, round eyes.

"Uncle says I'll have a girl cousin," she said, and this time he smiled, a real smile that was not quite yet the Matt I remembered, but on the way.

"Good," he said.

Chapter 22

The new Military Road across Arkansas Territory was rough, really rough, especially once we passed Little Rock. At least the weather was dry, and there was no danger we would be delayed by flooding. As always, I became almost unbearably impatient to get home to Maggie, to see how she and the young'uns had made it on the land without me. Sometimes I woke in the night with a terrible fear gripping my heart that something bad had happened or was about to happen, now that I was this close with the money we needed. I could picture the cabin burned, or Maggie dead of a snakebite and the young'uns alone, or even worse, that Thomas Mallory had ridden up with soldiers to turn them out, just as Elwin Root had done years ago. After each of those nights, I was more desperate than ever to get home, and I pushed the mules hard, trying to cover the miles quicker.

But the wagon's wheels could bump only so fast over the ruts and rocks. I had to fend off my jitters some other way, so I took to pointing out landmarks like the Mamelle mountain and telling stories about when Maggie and I first came up the Arkansas River on a keelboat. Bessie and Mary liked the stories, but I could never tell if Matt was even listening. He sat by me on the wagon seat, staring at the countryside with eyes that seemed to be looking inside himself instead of at the trees. But at least now if I spoke to him, he'd rouse himself out of his thoughts and make an effort to answer me, more like the Matt I knew and not the surly man I'd stolen from Campbell County.

Finally, by the end of June, we reached Dardanelle. I stopped the wagon in front of Brearley's store.

"I want to write to Zeke and let them know we made it home," I told them. "Why don't you all step down and walk around a little? If you go down by the river and look to the west, you should be able to see the Dardanelle Rock leaning out toward the water. I won't be long."

They took off with Mary holding to Bessie's hand. I walked into the store, and it was just like it had been the last time I was here, with Joseph Brearley dozing behind the counter in the afternoon heat.

"Hey, Joseph," I said, and he jumped so he nearly fell off his stool.

"Hey, McKellar. When did you get back in town?"

"Just now. I need to write a letter. Can I get a sheet of paper and borrow a quill?"

He gathered what I needed, and this time there was no hesitation in putting the ink to paper.

Dear Zeke,

I'm writing to let you know we have arrived at Dardanelle safely. The roads were rough but passable. We've not yet been to the farm, but I thought I should ease your minds about us before going on home, since I may not be this way again until after the corn harvest.

Does Pa still live? If he does, let him know Matt is on his way back to us, or seems to be. I think that is Mary's doing—she gave him a well-deserved tongue-lashing one night, and he was better after that. He's even let us cut his hair, though he's kept the beard. He may change his mind about it after a few days in a hot Arkansas summer.

I will close now, because I'm eager to get home and see how Maggie and the children have fared. Give my love to Ma and to Pa if he still lives, as well as to Sarah.

Respectfully yours,

John David McKellar

I folded the letter and carefully penned Zeke's name and address on the front. Brearley sealed it for me with wax, and I gave him the coin it would take to get the letter back to Campbell County.

"What's the word on the survey of the Cherokee lands?" I asked. "Will you be hired to do that survey too?"

"Naw." He shrugged. "They brought in some government surveyor—Langham, I think his name is. I reckon they contracted with him in May. I don't care, though. I wouldn't want to do it."

"So they've contracted with a surveyor," I repeated, more to myself than to him. "That's progress."

"Not much progress," he snorted. "Laying out straight townships in those mountains is going to be a hell of a job."

I laughed. "That's for sure. Well, see you later on, Brearley."

But as I turned to leave the store, something shiny caught my eye, and I turned back. Maggie's locket was dangling from a peg sticking out from the front of a shelf.

"It's still here," I said, leaning across the counter for a closer look.

Brearley snorted. "I told you it wouldn't sell. No one around here wants such as that."

I reached into my pocket for the money bag. "I know someone who does."

⁂

Though the heat of the day was past by the time we were on the path leading to the farm, the air had a heavy, still feeling. Dry flies buzzed loudly ahead of us, stopping as we drew closer, and then starting again once we had passed. Bessie was sleeping with her head in Mary's lap. Matt sat silent on the wagon seat, looking around at the woods. I considered asking what he thought about the country I'd brought him to, but suddenly I wasn't sure I wanted to know. The closer we got to home, the tighter the twist in my gut grew. I wanted to be home, to see everything the way I'd left it. But I knew once I got there, nothing in my life would be the way I'd left it, not ever again. It's for the good, I told myself, over and over. Good for Matt, good for Mary, good for Maggie and me.

The tightness inside me eased a little as we crossed the creek and I saw corn standing in the field I'd been plowing the day Thomas Mallory came by. So she had managed to plant a crop—that was good. And the cabin was still standing behind the hackberry and the oak—it hadn't burned. And the black dog was lifting his head as we pulled into the yard—they were still here, no one had run them off. The dog got to his feet and stood stiff-legged, barking. I reined in the mules and handed the lines to Matt.

"Let me break the news to Maggie alone first," I said as I jumped down from the wagon.

I ran past the growling dog like he was Penny's kitten and threw open the door. Maggie and both young'uns looked up, startled, from where they were sitting around the table, just about to have supper.

"Oh, thank God!" Maggie cried, and then she was in my arms and we were holding to each other like wild grapevines wrapped around a tree.

"I'm glad you're back," she said, once and then again, and I pulled her even closer.

"You're all right?" I asked. "You managed all right? It looks like you did."

"We're fine." She looked up into my face. "You got the money?"

"I did."

Her whole face brightened in a smile.

"Good," she said, and then her arms tightened around me. "I'm glad of it, but I'm more glad you're home. We've missed you something awful." She loosened herself from me enough that she could turn back toward the table, where Penny was bouncing on her seat. "You may leave the table, Penny."

That was enough for Penny to leap from the bench and come flying toward me. I hugged her tight while Maggie went to fetch Jake. She set him down in front of me and he stood, swaying a little, on his chubby legs.

"He can stand!" I said, and Maggie beamed.

"Hold out your arms," she said.

With Penny still hanging on my arm, I squatted and held out my hands to Jake, and after getting a reassuring nod from Maggie, he took two tottering steps toward me before falling on his rump. I scooped him up and held him against my chest.

"So that's how they got by, is it?" I said, with a laugh. "You learned to walk so you could be the man of the house while your Pa was gone?"

Maggie laughed, and then she was tugging at my arm, pulling me toward the table.

"Sit and visit with them here. It will take me a few minutes, but I'll mix up some mush for you."

I took her hand and pulled her back toward me, leading her out onto the porch.

"You'll need to mix some extra," I said. "Remember the last time I came home and you had a surprise for me? Well, I brought a surprise for you from Campbell County."

She was hardly through the door when she gasped.

"Is that Mary?" Then she was running off the porch and meeting Mary halfway across the yard. The two of them were laughing and crying at the same time as they hugged. I carried Penny and Jake over to Bessie, who stood in the wagon rubbing her eyes.

"Bessie," I said quietly, so as not to startle her. "Here's your girl cousin, Penny. And you have a boy cousin, too, little Jake here."

I set down my young'uns so I could lift Bessie out of the wagon, and the two girls stood staring at each other for a minute. Then Penny held out her hand.

"I have a kitty," she said. "Want to see her?" Bessie nodded and took Penny's hand, and the two of them started back toward the porch where the cat was sitting on the step.

"You rascal!" Maggie said, giving me a swat on the shoulder as she came to pick up Jake. "You never let on this was in your mind!"

"It wasn't in my mind when I left here," I said. "Sometimes things happen you never expect."

"Well, this was a good surprise." She looked up at Matt, who was still sitting alone on the wagon seat, and for a moment I feared she might ask about Bess. But she only smiled and held out her hand to him.

"Come in, Matt," she said. "We'll have to wait a while, but we'll have supper here in a bit."

Mary wanted to help with supper, but Maggie insisted she would be too tired from our long travels. Instead, Mary sat with the two chattering little girls and chattered with Maggie, while Jake watched them from my lap, waving his arms and jabbering desperately. Matt sat at the end of the table, so quiet I was afraid he might be turning sullen again.

"It won't be easy, Matt," I said softly, and he nodded, with the shimmer of tears in his eyes. I held Jake out toward him, and he took him. Jake babbled and pulled at Matt's beard, and we laughed.

"You see now why I don't let a beard get longer than an inch or two," I said. "He'd yank a man's chin bald."

"It's all right," Matt said. "I reckon I've got some to spare."

It was a humble supper Maggie set before us—corn mush, fried salt pork and potatoes, boiled greens. But I looked around the crowded table—two little girls who insisted on sitting together, a chubby baby boy reaching toward a plate, two sisters who kept looking at each other with such happiness, my own solemn brother at the other end of the table—and my heart swelled to take them all in with a peace I hadn't felt since our early days in Arkansas Territory. This is home, I thought. It's not the land, not the cabin, not the cornfields. This is really my home, as God meant it to be.

Maggie reached for the spoon to start dishing out the food, but I caught her hand.

"Let's pray," I said.

※ ※ ※

We stayed up late in the evening, catching up on the news. I wanted to know how Maggie and the young'uns had fared all these months without me, and Maggie, of course, was eager to hear about the folks in Campbell County. She sobered as Mary told about their pa and I told about my pa, and then as Matt told about Bess, his voice husky and quiet. She left her seat beside me to hug him tight. He sat stiffly for a moment, but then he wrapped his arms around her with a choked sob. She patted his back in that soothing way I knew so well.

"I'm glad you came to be with us," she said, and he nodded.

"The news is not all sad, though," I said quickly, for Penny was staring wide-eyed, her chin starting to quiver. "Besides Bessie here, you have some other new cousins, Penny."

Finally, we were all talked out and Mary was yawning. Maggie would have put her in our bed, but Mary wouldn't hear of it.

"We've been sleeping on the ground for weeks now," she said. "A pallet on the floor here won't bother me a bit."

So she settled on the floor, and Matt bedded down in the wagon in the yard. I was sitting on the bed undoing my shirt buttons while Maggie checked the girls one last time, when the heaviness in my pocket bumped against my chest, reminding me of unfinished business to tend to. But not in a cabin filled with people.

"Come with me," I whispered to Maggie, laying my arm across her shoulders. She looked up at me as we stepped out onto the porch.

"Where are we going?" I put my finger over her lips, looking toward the wagon, but Matt didn't stir. She followed me then without a sound as we started down the path toward the creek.

The moon was bright enough we could easily see the way. The harsh drone of the dry flies had given way to the murmur of crickets, and the air around us was still warm from the day's sunshine. I took her to the creek, where summer's puny flow made only a trickling sound as what water was left ran over and around the rocks. I put my arms around her, and she looked up at me with a smile.

"With all the folks around, I never got the chance to give you a husband's proper greeting," I said. She laughed as I bent to kiss her, and her lips were warm and soft and just as eager as my own.

"I missed you," she said. "Not just for plowing and planting corn, either."

"For pulling out weeds?" I teased. "For chopping firewood?"

She laughed again and slipped her arms around me, inside my shirt. "You're going to make me say it?" she asked, looking at me from under her eyelashes, and I knew if I didn't take care of my business right now, I would soon forget it altogether. I reached around her to get into my pocket.

"I have something for you."

She pulled away and I handed her the small package, wrapped in rumpled brown paper, just as it had been the first time I gave it to her. The moonlight glinted off the gold as she pulled away the paper, and she gasped.

"John David! How—How did you pay for this?" I had known that would be her first question, and I was ready with my answer.

"I used some of the money Pa gave me for the land." She started to protest, but I took the locket from her and slid it over her head. "It wasn't so much. I can make it up by the time the land is surveyed and ready to sell. That's still some months away. I know you don't need it, but I want you to have it, as a remembrance for all we've been through together and a pledge for the days to come. I promise now what I promised you back in Pa's attic—I'm going to make things better for you, Maggie. No more moving from one spot to another, no more wondering where we can settle. It's our permanent home, God willing, like you asked for. Like I promised for you."

She bit her lip and picked up the locket between her fingers.

"For us," she corrected me.

I laughed. "For us."

She wrapped her arms around me again as she stretched to kiss my mouth. I gave myself to her kiss, letting it carry away all my concerns like leaves on the surface of the creek water. Yes, life would be different now, plenty different, with plenty still to do before I could keep the promises I'd made. I had money now, but I'd still have to beat Mallory to filing a claim to get the land. Matt seemed better, but I wasn't fool enough to believe it would be so easy to wipe away his year's worth of deep grieving.

But that work could begin tomorrow. I was home now, and it was good.

Author's Note

Most of what happens in this novel really happened to someone in Arkansas Territory between 1824-1829. White squatters like John David and Maggie pushed in to the Territory and settled illegally on land the U.S. government had given, by treaty, to the Cherokees. The U.S. Army 7th Infantry under the leadership of Colonel Matthew Arbuckle rooted them off the land. The persistence of the white settlers led the Cherokees to send several delegations to Washington, D.C., including the one in early 1828 that eventually signed the treaty that split Arkansas Territory and created Indian Territory. That struggle for the land is the heart of this story.

The major characters are fictional—John David and Maggie, "Little" Elwin Root, and Thomas Mallory. Many of the other characters, including all the missionaries from Dwight Mission, all the Cherokee chiefs, the Brearley family, all the U.S. government staff, and even the neighbor Richard Bean, were real people who were involved in the struggle, although they are portrayed fictionally. While writing this novel, I became especially interested in Major Edward W. DuVal, the Cherokee agent. Few records of DuVal's life remain, but fortunately, his correspondence as Cherokee agent is preserved in the Territorial papers of Arkansas, and those letters were an invaluable resource for this novel.

A footnote to one of the letters actually solved a problem I faced when first writing the story. Maggie and John David are introduced in *His Promise True*, told through Maggie's voice. However, I knew I couldn't have Maggie tell the rest of their story, because that story would involve political and social happenings that a nineteenth-century woman would never be part of. This had to be John David's story, but I was stuck as to how I could give him access to Major DuVal and the negotiations that eventually led to the treaty of 1828.

One day while researching in the Territorial papers, I found the answer. Major DuVal had included a footnote at the end of a letter in which he apologized for an error by his (nameless) transcriptionist. It was a perfect opportunity! John David became that transcriptionist— my apologies to the actual man whose place in history John David usurped!

I can't end this note without saying how profoundly the process of researching and writing this novel has impacted my view of the place in the world where I live. Our farm is on land that was part of the Cherokee allotment granted in 1817 by the Turkeytown Treaty. It may not have been John David, but white settlers wrested this land away from the Cherokees, who had to, as DuVal stated in one of his letters, "leave their opened fields and improvements, which they have been making and toiling on for years...and again settle in the forest, comparatively remote from many of the conveniences which they now enjoy, and create every thing requisite to ordinary comfort anew!" Like John David, I know the tide of history can't be reversed, but knowing what happened to allow me to live here is humbling.

It is my intention to develop more fully the historical information behind *A Permanent Home* on my website, www.emzpineypublishing. com, and to perhaps someday compile the records of these five years of historical records into a documentary resource. But please be patient with me! Mary has a story she's anxious to tell....

About the Author

Greta Marlow lives with her husband and two nearly-grown children at the foot of the Ozark Mountains in Arkansas. By day, she teaches communication, speech, and public relations courses at a small, private college in Arkansas. By night, she dreams what it must have been like to live in Arkansas when it was still a Territory. (Ok, she daydreams that sometimes, too.)

Acknowledgments

Writing this second novel was distinctly different from writing the first one, since so much of the plot is built around real events in history. I'd like to thank the staff at the Pope County library in Russellville, Arkansas, first, for having all three volumes of the Territorial Papers of Arkansas, and second, for showing me numerous times how to use the microfilm reader so I could look at the early issues of the *Arkansas Gazette*. I should also thank my employer, the University of the Ozarks, for granting me a sabbatical in 2010, which is when the biggest portion of this book was written.

Thank you to my early readers—Jeff Marlow, Cara Flinn, and Charlotte Rowbotham—for their time spent with the book and their encouraging words. And finally, thank you to the friends at church who kept asking me when the next book was coming out. You don't know how encouraging it was to hear that readers were anxious to know how Maggie and John David's story would turn out!